If there was one word to ⟨ ⟩ *ambitious* **would be at the very top. She went after what she wanted, and tonight, for her twenty-first birthday, she wanted Luke O'Connor. Preferably naked.**

It was bad enough that she'd spent most of her adolescence pining over someone who only seemed to look at her like a little sister, but she also had to compete against the flock of women parading around Chicagoland hoping to catch Luke's attention. She didn't have a claim on him. Had never dated him. Yet that didn't stop her from feeling like Luke was hers, whether he realized it or not.

"Are you having fun?" her friend Cheyanne asked as she handed her a red Solo cup.

"Of course I'm having fun." Kyra glanced around the birthday party that her college friends had thrown her. "Have you seen my brothers and their friends?"

Cheyanne glanced around. "I think your brother Ajay went with Mike to get more ice. But Taheim should be here somewhere. He was with his guys. Jaleen and—"

"Luke," Kyra supplied. "Those three are inseparable sometimes."

Cheyanne wiggled her eyebrows. "Right. How could I forget about your unhealthy crush?"

"It's not unhealthy," Kyra said.

"Oh, really? You've liked the man since you were ten. Probably before that. Are you telling me you don't think it's unhealthy for your state of mind to like him and still not say anything?"

Kyra shrugged, taking a sip of her drink. "I'm just waiting for the perfect moment."

Sherelle Green is a Chicago native with a dynamic imagination and a passion for reading and writing. She enjoys composing emotionally driven stories that are steamy, edgy and touch on real-life issues. Her overall goal is to create relatable and fierce heroines who are flawed, just like the strong and sexy heroes who fight so hard to win their hearts. There's no such thing as a perfect person…but when you find that person who is perfect for you, the possibilities are endless. Nothing satisfies her more than writing stories filled with compelling love affairs, multifaceted characters and intriguing relationships.

Books by Sherelle Green

Harlequin Kimani Romance

If Only for Tonight
Red Velvet Kisses
Beautiful Surrender
Enticing Winter
Wrapped in Red (with Nana Malone)
Falling for Autumn
Waiting for Summer
Nights of Fantasy
A Miami Affair
Her Unexpected Valentine
A Los Angeles Passion
Road to Forever
Her Christmas Wish

Visit the Author Profile page
at Harlequin.com for more titles.

SHERELLE GREEN
and
SHERYL LISTER

Her Christmas Wish &
Designed by Love

HARLEQUIN® KIMANI™ ROMANCE

ISBN-13: 978-1-335-47098-0

Her Christmas Wish & Designed by Love

Copyright © 2019 by Harlequin Books S.A.

Her Christmas Wish
Copyright © 2019 by Sherelle Green

Designed by Love
Copyright © 2019 by Sheryl Lister

Recycling programs
for this product may
not exist in your area.

Printed in U.S.A.

CONTENTS

I would like to dedicate this to the Kimani readers who have given me so much book love and support over the past few years. Please accept this as a token of my gratitude and appreciation! I hope you continue to read the amazing stories myself and others are releasing and writing for your enjoyment. There are so many amazing novels out there waiting to be read by you!

Acknowledgments

To my cousin, Stefanie, who continues to inspire me every day! You've always been such a go-getter and instead of waiting for someone to do something for you, you've always tackled it yourself. Whether it be in school, sports or your career, your ambitious spirit shines. Your loyalty is something I've always admired and I know I can count on you for anything. Plus, your sarcasm and wittiness keep me laughing. It's so obvious that you enjoy life, and your spontaneity has provided you with some pretty amazing adventures. I am so proud of the woman you've become and honored to have a front-row seat to your bright future! Love you! Keep on shining, Fe!

HER CHRISTMAS WISH

Sherelle Green

Dear Reader,

Wow! It's hard to believe that this is my last installment in my Bare Sophistication series. I've been waiting to write Kyra's story since she was initially introduced in the first book in the series, *Enticing Winter*.

Kyra Reed is ambitious, feisty and a little sister to Taheim and Ajay in every way. Luke O'Connor has been trying to fight his feelings for Kyra since he was young. Luke was first introduced in book two in the series, *Falling for Autumn*, but we only got a quick glimpse of him. For anyone who has read *Single AF*, a 2019 novella in my Social Experiment series, you may have learned more about Luke.

It takes a certain kind of man to handle Kyra, and Luke is definitely that man. I hope you enjoy their story!

Much love,

Sherelle

authorsherellegreen@gmail.com

Prologue

If there was one word to describe Kyra Reed, *ambitious* would be at the very top of the list. She went after what she wanted, and tonight, for her twenty-first birthday, she wanted Luke O'Connor. Preferably, naked.

It was bad enough that she'd spent most of her adolescence pining over someone who only seemed to look at her like a little sister, but then, she also had to compete against the flock of women parading around Chicagoland hoping to catch Luke's attention. She didn't have a claim on him. Had never dated him. Yet, that didn't stop her from feeling like Luke was hers, whether he realized it or not.

"Are you having fun?" her friend Cheyanne asked as she handed her a red Solo cup.

"Of course I'm having fun." Kyra's gaze traveled around the birthday party that her college friends had thrown her. "Have you seen my brothers and their friends?"

Cheyanne glanced around. "I think your brother Ajay went with Mike to get more ice. But Taheim should be here somewhere. He was with his guys. Jaleen and…?"

"Luke," Kyra said. "Those three are inseparable sometimes."

Cheyanne wiggled her eyebrows. "Right. How could I forget about your unhealthy crush?"

"It's not unhealthy," Kyra said.

"Oh, really? You've liked the man since you were ten. Probably before that. Are you telling me you don't think it's unhealthy for your state of mind to like him and still not say anything?"

Kyra shrugged, taking a sip of her drink. "I'm just waiting for the perfect moment."

Cheyanne rolled her eyes. "Girlfriend, he's known you most your life. How much more time do you need? The Kyra I know always goes after what she wants."

Kyra cringed at her words because it was true. She did go after what she wanted. "No need for the best-friend talk because I plan on telling him how I feel tonight."

Cheyanne's eyes widened as she asked, "Are you for real? You're finally admitting your feelings?"

"I'm very serious. It's long overdue."

Cheyanne squealed. "I'm so proud of you, and for telling me this, I'll tell you where he is."

Kyra carefully slapped her on the arm. "Are you saying you weren't going to tell me where he was unless I admitted I'd tell him my feelings?"

Cheyanne nodded. "That's exactly what I was going

to do." She motioned with her head to indicate the back door. "The boys are in the backyard."

Kyra gave her friend a quick hug and wasted no time heading to the backyard. It wasn't until she was almost out the door that she heard Cheyanne ask her what she'd planned on doing to get Luke alone. Kyra hadn't made it that far, but she was good at winging it.

The moment she stepped into the backyard, it felt like no one existed at the party except for Luke. People said "happy birthday" as she walked past, but the smile she gave them had less to do with the warm wishes and more to do with the sexy twenty-six-year-old man standing a few feet away from her.

Kyra had always wondered if the reason Luke often kept his distance was because of their age difference, and for that reason, she'd been anxious to become an adult to see if he paid her more attention. Much to her dismay, when she turned eighteen, he'd seemed to treat her like the same ol' Kyra. At nineteen, not much changed. At twenty, he got a little friendlier, but for the most part, he'd kept their relationship rated G, with a couple of PG-13 episodes thrown in the mix.

At twenty-one, she was tired of waiting for him to notice her, and tonight, she was laying out all her cards whether he liked it or not.

"Hey, guys," she said as she approached. "Enjoying my celebration?"

"Your friends know how to throw a party, sis," Taheim said.

Jaleen nodded. "Yeah, they weren't doing parties like this way back when I was in college."

Kyra rolled her eyes, slightly annoyed by the way Jaleen made it seem like he was so much older than her.

"Jay, you talk like y'all are old as hell, when you're only in your upper twenties."

"Wait until you start working in the real world," he said. "You'll start to feel the same way."

Taheim pulled her in for a hug and ruffled her hair. "Can't believe my baby sis is twenty-one now."

Kyra pushed him away. "Stop, Taheim. You'd think after all this time you'd learn to treat me like an adult. Didn't Mom ever teach you not to mess with a black woman's hair?"

He smirked in that annoying big-brother sort of way. "She did, but I chose to ignore that lesson when dealing with my little sis. A girlfriend maybe, but not you."

She crossed her arms over her chest. "Just my luck." Turning to Luke, she batted her eyes and asked, "How has life been treating you?" *In other words, please tell me you're still single.*

"Life is good," Luke said with a nod. "I can't complain. What about you? Excited to graduate soon?"

"Can't wait." She adjusted the strap of her blush-colored dress, enjoying the way Luke's eyes were slyly taking her in as he sipped his drink. *Progress.* A year ago, he never would have looked at her like that. Taheim started talking to Jaleen, giving her the chance to have a slightly more private conversation with Luke.

"I'll miss living down South during the school year," she said. "The weather here is beautiful." Kyra had chosen to go to an HBCU in Georgia, but planned on moving back to Chicago after graduation.

"I'll bet," Luke said. "I went to school in New York, so the weather wasn't much different than Chicago. Have you decided what you want to do after graduation?"

She shrugged. "My degree will be in business management, but no idea what I want to do. I love being a retail-store manager, so maybe I can find something in Chicago."

Luke laughed. "You're the only person I've ever met to say they love retail."

"I do love it," she replied with a laugh. "There's so much more to it than people think. For example, in some positions, you only use certain skill sets. I, on the other hand, must have an array of knowledge to tackle what goes on day in and day out at a store. Right now, I work at a chain shoe store, but I only got the job because the previous manager went on maternity leave and never came back. So I felt like I had a lot to prove. That was a year ago. Today, the district manager loves me and said I'm the youngest to ever hold my position and do so well."

Luke smiled. "That's impressive, but you've always been impressive. Nice to hear that your district manager thinks so, too." His eyes dipped to her lips and had Kyra not been glued to his every move, she wouldn't have caught his glance.

Not wanting to lose the spark, she turned as if she was surveying the backyard to give him a view of her firm, round butt, which was just the way she wanted it thanks to Cheyanne dragging her to the gym every day for squats and those machines that made her calves ache. "Looks like the crowd is dying down out here."

She turned back to Luke in time to see him raise his head as he looked nervously from her to Taheim, who wasn't even paying attention to what he was doing.

"Sis, we're about to meet up with Ajay and Mike," Taheim said, interrupting the moment. "The game is on at one of the bars down the street. Mind if we dip early and catch you at breakfast before we fly out?"

"Of course not," she said. "If you stayed, you'd just whine about missing the game, anyway." *Plus, I want to be with Luke without your prying eyes.*

"Yeah, you already know." Taheim nodded to Luke as he and Jaleen began to walk out the back gate. "Man, you coming?"

Luke glanced from Taheim back to Kyra. "Uh, yeah, I guess I am."

"Actually," Kyra said, lightly gripping Luke's arm, "I'm having some problems with the real-estate class I'm taking and Luke offered to help me."

Taheim lifted his eyebrow at the same time Luke asked, "You're taking a real-estate class?"

"Yes," she lied. "I want to be well versed in every aspect that I can. Who knows if I'll ever want to sell real estate on the side?"

"I don't remember you mentioning that class before," Taheim said while an amused Jaleen stifled a laugh. Kyra couldn't be sure, but she got the distinct feeling Jaleen knew exactly what she was up to.

"I don't have to tell you everything about my life," Kyra snapped at Taheim. "I rattle off classes I think interest you. But for this one, I am in way over my head. I should have dropped it at the beginning of the semester, but now, I'm stuck with it. This last homework assignment is really stumping me."

"I could take a look at it," Luke suggested. He turned to Taheim and Jaleen. "How about I take a look at Kyra's homework and then walk to the bar and meet you guys there?"

It wasn't unusual for Luke to help Kyra with her homework. When they were younger, she used to ask her brothers, but they always made it seem like she was annoying them when she asked. Luke wasn't like that. He stopped what he was doing every time she needed help.

Taheim looked skeptical for a moment, then shook it off and texted Luke the address. "If we change bars before you get there, I'll let you know."

Luke nodded his head. "Bet." Once they were alone, minus all the folks still at the party, Kyra wasted no time tugging Luke toward the house and up the stairs.

"Whoa, why are you walking so fast?" Luke asked, tripping up the stairs.

"I'm just really anxious for you to help me with this homework," she lied again as they entered the house. "It's been bugging me for years."

"Years?" Luke asked as they reached her bedroom. "You just said you started taking the class this semester."

Kyra groaned. She may have a huge crush on Luke, but perceptive, he was not. "I'm not really taking a real-estate course," she said, shutting and locking her bedroom door. "I just lied to get you in my bedroom." His eyes widened in surprise, so Kyra took the opportunity to push him down onto her bed while he was still surprised. "Why do you think I wanted to get you to my bedroom, Luke?"

Luke opened his mouth, but no words came out.

"I'll make it easier for you." Kyra reached for both her dress straps and let the material fall to the floor, leaving her in just her blush-colored lingerie. "Why do you think I wanted to get you to my bedroom, Luke?"

He visibly swallowed as his eyes roamed up and down her body, taking her in. "Uh, I don't want to assume you took me up here to have sex, but the way you just removed your dress, it's looking that way."

Kyra smiled. "Good job. That's exactly why I lied to get you up here. I'm tired of denying how attracted

I am to you and I'm pretty damn sure you're attracted to me, too."

Luke looked her up and down again. "Uh, although that may be the case...we can't have sex. That can't happen."

"Why not?" she asked.

"Because you're Taheim's little sister."

She shook her head. "Try again."

"Because you're five years younger than me."

"But still an adult," she countered. "Try again."

"Because your brother Ajay would kill me."

"Nope, not the right answer." Sticking with her plan, Kyra removed her bra next and was rewarded with a slow whistle of appreciation. And if that wasn't enough to prove he was interested, she noticed him growing harder by the second.

"I have a girlfriend," he spluttered. "So it's wrong for me to even be in here."

Kyra smirked. "What's her name?"

"Whose name?" he asked, eyes glued to her nipples.

"Your girlfriend, dummy."

"Her name is, um... It's, uh... Her name is Jaime."

Kyra frowned and looked toward her desk, which had a picture of herself with her childhood dog, Jaime. Stepping closer to Luke, she straddled him on her bed so that her breasts were almost level with his eyes. "Are you making up your girlfriend, Luke?"

He nodded his head.

"Did you make her up because you want to have sex with me tonight but are worried about the consequences?"

He nodded his head again. Dropping her mouth to his right ear, she whispered, "Screw the consequences."

She wasn't sure what made him grip the back of her head and bring her in for a kiss, but his mouth was on hers before she could say any more words. Just as she'd imagined, the kiss felt amazing, his lips bringing the perfect amount of pressure.

His hands were all over her backside, roaming up and down her thighs in fluid strokes. He smelled delicious. Even better than he had a couple of minutes ago because all of her senses were heightened with him so close.

"Kyra," he whispered in between kisses. Gone was the kid-sister voice he often used when talking to her. The way he'd said her name was the way a man spoke to a woman he was interested in, and the fact that she'd even gotten Luke to loosen some of his caution-when-approaching behavior was causing her insides to do a happy dance.

Unable to help herself, Kyra began twisting her hips, relishing the fact that he was getting even harder than before. "I always imagined it like this."

"Imagined what like what?" he asked.

"Imagined what kissing you would feel like. I've waited for this for so long, I can hardly believe we're finally about to have sex."

Luke froze, his hands gripping her hips to stop her from moving. Blame it on her big mouth. Or blame it on the tequila shots she'd had earlier in the night, but somehow, she'd managed to break the trance they'd been in a few moments ago.

Without warning, Luke hopped up from the bed, nearly knocking her over in the process. He caught her right before she hit the floor and helped her stand, then thrust one of her blankets at her.

"This was a huge mistake," he said. "We can't do

this." He ran his hands over his curly hair. "In fact, this never happened."

Kyra shook her head. "Of course it happened and you can't act like it didn't. I've been waiting to be with you my entire life."

He groaned. "Kyra, you can't say shit like that. We can't get together."

"Why not?" she yelled. "Don't bother telling me you aren't attracted to me because I know that's a lie."

"You're an attractive woman," he said. "But you're also off-limits."

"Says who? My brothers? Why do you care what my brother's think?"

"They're my best friends," Luke explained. "Had I known this is what you wanted me to stay behind for, I never would have agreed. Have you even had sex before?"

Kyra shrugged. "What does that matter?"

Luke shook his head. "I should go meet the guys. We can talk about this more in the morning."

As a last-ditch effort to get him to stay, Kyra pulled Luke down for a kiss. To her surprise, he actually kissed her back, until he pulled away from her again a few seconds later. "No, we can't do this. I'm sorry I let it get this far."

"I'm not," Kyra yelled. "Not even close. You want to be with me just as much as I want to be with you. No use denying it." She stepped closer to him. "Do you honestly think I haven't seen you watching me since I was sixteen? Admiring me even more at eighteen? Checking me out downstairs now, at twenty-one? You want me, too—you just don't want to admit it to yourself."

Luke shook his head. "You make me sound like a

creep. I'm way too old for you and this can't go further for reasons you're too young to understand. Find a boy your own age."

Kyra huffed. "I can't believe you're acting like this right now. If you think I won't try this again, you've got another thing coming."

Luke's eyes darkened in frustration. "Kyra, the truth is, although you're beautiful on the inside, I could never be with a woman like you. You and I don't mix, and as far as personalities go, I could never date someone who's so surface. Besides, you need to do some more maturing and growing right now. There's a man some-where on this campus who would love a woman like you, but me? I'm looking for a woman with more sub-stance right now."

Kyra stepped back, his words shooting at her like piercing bullets. Blame it on her I-don't-care attitude, but it wasn't the first time someone had assumed she didn't have much substance. She just never expected it to come from Luke.

"Get the hell out of my room," she spat. "Right. Now."

Luke shot her a look of sympathy, as if he wanted to take back his words. Kyra wanted to tell him it was no use. She'd already heard them and although she wished they hadn't hurt, they did.

He mumbled something when he neared the door, but she couldn't make out what he'd said. The minute he shut the door, she succumbed to the tears she'd been holding. She cried over his false assumptions about her character. She cried because her decade-long crush was now over. But even more upsetting, she cried for the amazing man who'd just broken her heart in two, because there was no way Luke could take back those words. They were tattooed on her brain and after she picked herself up from this heartbreak, she'd be smart to remind herself that this situation would be the last time she let a man make her feel as though she was unworthy of love.

Chapter 1

Ten years later...

"I don't care how many winters I spend here, this will never feel like Christmas," Kyra Reed huffed as she flicked her finger at the small Santa figurine that sat next to the register at Bare Sophistication Boutique and Boudoir Studio in Hollywood.

Kyra always thought it was crazy that right after Halloween, Christmas decorations were immediately put up. That was too soon in her book. However, since she worked in retail, she had to follow the wacky tradition.

"It doesn't seem much different to me," Aaliyah Bai-Burrstone, her pregnant ex-coworker, said. "Feels more like Christmas here than when I'm back home."

"That's because our husbands are our home," Nicole explained. "Plus, we're from Miami and I'm sure Kyra was talking about the fact that in Chicago, she's used to all that snow during this time of year."

When Nicole LeBlanc-Burrstone wasn't working at the production company she owned with her husband, Kendrick, she was at the boutique doing makeup and hair for the boudoir studio. Nicole and Aaliyah had originally worked at Bare Sophistication Miami. However, when the owners of the boutique chain decided to open an office in Hollywood, both of them, along with Kyra, who was working at the shop in Chicago, had decided to move to Cali.

Nicole and Aaliyah had also both married cousins and while Aaliyah still popped in every now and then to do boudoir photoshoots, she was now pursuing her dream as a professional photographer, traveling around the world with her husband, Bryant, whenever they got the chance.

"That's exactly what I mean," Kyra said, smiling at the way Aaliyah rubbed her protruding belly. "Personally, I can't stand the snow. But back in Chicago, the first snowfall was a clear indication that Christmas was right around the corner. I mean, I've seen more Santas dressed in swim trucks than I have in fluffy red suits."

"Yeah, that part is weird," Nicole said. "Cali seems to be infatuated with Surfboard Santa. It's not like that in Miami."

Aaliyah made a strained sound, causing Kyra and Nicole to turn her way.

"Are you okay?" Kyra asked.

Aaliyah nodded her head. "I'm good. Just wishing baby Burrstone would calm down today so I can help you both pack. He or she seems to want me sitting still with little movement."

"We got this," Nicole said. "You just rest."

"And let us do all the work?" Kyra laughed. "I honestly can't believe that after only a few years, we are switching locations, but I'm excited for this change."

Nicole glanced around at a couple half-filled boxes. "Are you sure we should be packing these up? We don't even have a new location for the shop yet."

Although Kyra loved the location of the current shop, when her sisters-in-law, Winter and Autumn, had visited her in Hollywood, she'd pitched her idea of expansion and, thankfully, they'd agreed that their quaint Hollywood shop had outgrown the space it was in.

"I've checked our inventory and I don't think we need to put out these items until spring. I plan on finding the perfect location before New Year's so we can jump-start the New Year with a bang!"

"What about your apartment?" Aaliyah asked. "Isn't your lease up soon, too?"

Kyra sighed as she continued to pack the box full of lingerie. "Yeah, which sucks because I should have started looking for a new place months ago."

"You can stay with us until you find somewhere," Nicole suggested.

"I'm good, but thanks, Nic."

"Or Bryant and I," Aaliyah offered.

Kyra glanced down at her friend's belly. "Ah, no. Definitely not. I love y'all, but you and Bryant need to enjoy the time you have before that baby pops out of your belly. Plus, you will not be using me as a babysitter if it takes me too long to find a place."

"Shoot," Aaliyah muttered, snapping her fingers.

"I'm sorry we can't be more involved in the move," Nicole said. "But I know a couple good Realtors in the area, so I could reach out to them and set up some more appointments."

Kyra shrugged. "It's no big deal. You're both newly married and, Nic, you have your beautiful baby girl, who is top priority. And that's not to mention your production company. And Aaliyah, you're a soon-to-be mom and have a ton of photography gigs lined up. I'm excited for more responsibility at Bare Sophistication and Taheim already said he knew a real-estate agent here who could help me. As a matter of fact—" she stumbled, removing her phone from the back pocket of her jeans "—he asked me to call him tonight since we're closing early. Leave it to me to forget. Do y'all mind?"

Aaliyah and Nicole both nodded their heads as Kyra began to dial her brother's number. He picked up on the third ring.

"Sis, I was hoping you remembered to call me."

"I almost forgot," she said with a laugh. "How are Winter and the kids?"

"Good, good. Everyone's good. But listen, I know you're in a time crunch to find a new location for the shop and are looking to buy a condo. You're trying to do this all before the New Year, right?"

"Yes, I am. I was aiming for before Christmas, but I haven't even started looking yet with less than two months to go."

"You know, Winter and Autumn will understand if you can't find a shop before then. These things usually take at least half a year."

"I know they'd understand, but I at least want to try and find something. I promised them I would manage this expansion and I want to keep my word."

Taheim laughed. "I figured you would say that. Which is why I called in a favor to have one of the top real-estate agents in the game to help you out."

Kyra perked up. "Okay, big brother, enough with the secrecy. Who is it?"

"Luke O'Connor," Taheim said proudly. "You remember Luke, right? One of my guys. Last you saw him was probably at my wedding."

Kyra frowned. *Luke O'Connor.* Did she remember Luke? Of course she did. All sexually frustrating wish-I-could-knee-him-in-the-balls-for-rejecting-me Luke. "Uh, yeah, I remember Luke. But I thought you mentioned last year that he'd moved to London?"

"He did, but he surprised us by coming back. In fact, he just moved to LA a couple months ago."

Kyra swallowed hard. "He—he lives here? In LA?"

"He does. What are the odds you'd both end up in the same city, right?"

"Yeah," she said, her voice cracking. "What are the odds?" She glanced at Nicole and Aaliyah in time to see them share a curious look.

"Yes, he's living there and from what he's told me, he just opened the new O'Connor Realty Group office with his younger brother."

Kyra shook her head. "Wait, Luke has a younger brother?"

"Sure does. His pops never told him. He only found out he existed a couple years ago. They've been building their relationship and his brother is from LA, so moving there felt right."

"Did his girlfriend move here, too?"

"What girlfriend?" Taheim asked. "If you're talking about the one he dated a few years ago, they broke up a while back."

Broke up? I really haven't been focused on his life

like I used to be. In other words, she hadn't done any social-media stalking in a while.

Kyra pinched the bridge of her nose. "Okay, so, Luke agreed to help me find two locations. Are you sure he even has time since he just opened his office?"

"Yeah, he has time. You know how we do in Chicago. We look out for each other. Living in Cali doesn't matter."

Kyra waved her hands. "Taheim, if you haven't talked to him yet, you don't have to. Nicole actually knows a couple of great real-estate agents."

"Sis, I said I called in a favor, remember? So there's no need," Taheim said. "As a matter of fact, that's him on the other line. I'll hit you up after, sis."

"No, wait. Taheim." She called his name, but it was too late. Kyra tossed her phone to the side and dropped her head into her hands. "This cannot be happening."

"Okay, who is Luke and why is he causing you to look so distraught?" Nicole asked.

"Yeah, I can't tell if you want to cry or throw up," Aaliyah added.

Kyra lifted her head. "Definitely throw up. Y'all know me. I'd never cry over a man."

Nicole nodded her head. "True. Then what gives?"

Kyra bit her bottom lip. "Back in the day, I used to have a crush on this guy, Luke. A part of me thought he even knew it, and at one point, it seemed like maybe he felt the same way. So I asked him, point-blank. And he told me he didn't. So I guess you can say that Luke is the man I always wanted to be with, but couldn't."

Aaliyah shot her a look of sympathy. "And knowing you, there's more to the story that you aren't telling us."

Instead of responding, Kyra just looked away.

"There's always more to every sad love story, isn't there?" And unfortunately, hers wasn't the type of self-reflection she wanted to have this close to the holidays.

"I'm sorry, what was the favor you needed again?" Luke had heard loud and clear what Taheim had asked him, but he needed to hear it again. Just for clarification.

"Man, your head must be in the clouds," Taheim said with a laugh. "I was just asking if you could help out Kyra. She's looking for a new location for the boutique and a condo for herself. She's short on time because she's trying to purchase both before the New Year."

Kyra Reed needs my help. Yeah, he'd heard him right. "I don't know, man. Are you sure she needs my help? Maybe she already has a real-estate agent to help her."

"She doesn't," he said. "I told her you would be the best man for the job. I know you already got a load of clients, but are any looking for large real estate? Finding a place for the new Bare Sophistication office could be good for you, right?"

Luke frowned, rubbing his forehead. Although he'd landed some great clients since opening a couple of weeks ago, he'd given most of them to his younger brother, Nash, so he could focus on other aspects of the business.

But there wasn't anything he wouldn't do for her. Even if that meant spending time with her when he'd made a promise to avoid her as much as he could since he'd just moved to LA.

"Okay, man. I'll hit her up so we can meet. Text me her number."

"Thanks, Luke," Taheim said. "This means a lot." They chatted for a few more minutes before ending the call.

"Damn," Luke muttered, leaning back in his desk chair. He shouldn't have been at the office so late, anyway, but he didn't quite feel at home at Nash's place yet. Nash had insisted that he stay with him when he learned he was living at a hotel until he found his own place. Reluctantly, Luke had agreed, but damn, he liked having his own place and his own space. Besides, he was only going to be in LA for the next six months or so. Luke had offices in his Chicago hometown as well as New York, but until he showed Nash the ropes of running the LA office, he'd be living here.

Standing up to finally gather his belongings and leave for the day, Luke wondered if Kyra was as cool with him helping her as Taheim had made it seem. The last time they'd truly spoken was at Taheim and Winter's wedding, and Kyra had made it very clear that he was the last person on earth she wanted to see.

When he reached his car, he called the number Taheim had sent him. Surprisingly, she answered on the second ring.

"Hello?" Her sexy voice filled the line, making him lose his train of thought. *Why does she always sound like that?* It was a mixture of sultry and breathless, making his thoughts anything but PG-13.

"Hello?" she repeated.

"Kyra, hi. It's… It's Luke."

"Hi, Luke," she responded with zero emotion. *Tough crowd.*

"Taheim mentioned that you need help finding a couple locations and since I just moved to LA, I was wondering if you wanted to meet sometime this week to discuss your needs."

"My needs?" she asked.

"Yeah, I want to help you get everything you want." Luke cringed at his words. *Could you sound more like a personal ad!*

"Right, well, I can meet tomorrow."

Damn. He didn't think she would say she could meet so soon. "I can meet tomorrow as well. How about noon?"

"That would work. I'll text you the address to a café near the boutique. Thanks for calling."

"Okay, sounds—" The call was cut short before he could even finish his sentence. "That's more like the Kyra I know," he muttered to himself. In the back of his mind, he knew he deserved her anger. Back in the day, he hadn't treated her well after learning that she had a crush on him. He'd tried to say enough to get her to understand that they could never be together, but it had backfired and resulted in them not talking for years.

Feeling so distant from Kyra was something he never thought would happen. Often, he'd told his mom that even if he and Taheim weren't friends anymore, he couldn't imagine not having Kyra in his life. Although he'd had a decent childhood, it wasn't all sunshine and roses. Kyra was a beacon of light for him. A reminder that there were good people in the world who cared about you even when you didn't care about yourself.

And what did you do, idiot? He'd pushed away one of the few people who meant a lot to him. That night she'd tricked him into going to her bedroom, he hadn't just lost one of his closest friends, he'd lost the woman whom he'd promised to always be there for. He'd apologized years ago, but she hadn't been willing to hear him out. At least now, he hoped helping her find a location for the boutique and a new home would show her that deep down, he was still the same Luke he used to be.

Chapter 2

There wasn't anything more nerve-racking than waiting for a meeting to take place that you were absolutely dreading. Kyra had arrived at the café ten minutes early to snag a table and calm her nerves since meeting with Luke today was probably on her list of things she'd be okay never doing again.

In retrospect, asking him to meet today had been a bad decision, but all she'd been thinking about was getting the meeting over with so that she wouldn't dread it all week. She hadn't planned to be rude and hang up on him, but just hearing his voice, all deep and husky, made her stomach drop. She hadn't heard it in so long after dreaming about it more times than she could count. It wasn't fair for him to sound that good and her only worry was that he looked better than he sounded.

She had an idea of how fine he still was, but she was

proud of herself for not stalking his social-media pages like she used to. In fact, she had even blocked him from a few platforms so she wouldn't be tempted to look.

It's okay, girl, she thought to herself. *You're a strong-ass woman and seeing the man who broke your heart all those years ago will not shake you.*

"Kyra?"

She closed her eyes at the voice, counting to three before looking upward. The minute her eyes landed on Luke in his dark gray suit and pearly white smile, she knew she should have at least counted to ten before setting eyes on him.

"Hi, Luke."

Even though she was sitting down, his eyes slowly looked her up and down in a way that surprised the hell out of her. "I almost didn't recognize you," he said. "You look nice with the copper highlights."

Kyra ran her fingers through her shoulder-length hair. "Thanks. I just got them, actually. I'm surprised you noticed."

He smiled as he took a seat across from her. "I've always noticed you."

Always noticed me? Kyra squinted, confused by this version of Luke. Instead of letting her thoughts wander, she decided to ask him about what he'd said. "What's wrong with you?"

He squinted. "What do you mean?"

"What do you mean, 'what do I mean'?" She leaned closer so that he could hear her without her voice carrying. "You said you've always noticed me? In my mind, that's the complete opposite of how you've always treated me."

Luke dropped his head a little. "In the past, I've

called you and apologized for how I treated you on your twenty-first birthday. After that, I texted you an apology. Then, at Taheim and Winter's wedding, I—"

"Let's not talk about my brother's wedding," Kyra said, cutting him off. "And while I appreciate your apologies, you've still never openly mentioned noticing me at all."

Luke shook his head. "Why are you always so difficult?"

Kyra shrugged. "It's in my DNA, but regardless, you don't have a right to say that about me anymore. So how about we just continue on with the meeting."

"Are we not even getting anything to eat?" Luke asked, glancing around.

"There is no time to eat. I have to get back to work soon," she lied. She took out the packet of info she'd put together with what she was looking for in regard to the location for the boutique, as well as a condo. "This packet has all the information you need to get started on setting up appointments."

Luke flipped through the pages, shooting her a look of surprise. "Uh, this is very thorough, but I sort of thought we would talk about everything in person. Hence the meeting."

Kyra leaned back in her chair. "Regarding the boutique, we're looking to stay within a mile of our current location. Unlike the current building, we need a storefront and would love a storage facility or something connected to it for us to stock additional merchandise. And we don't want to be on a run-down block. The current square footage of our boutique is listed in the packet and we now want at least one thousand square feet more.

Also preferably it would be two levels or sections for the boudoir studio."

Luke nodded his head. "Of course. I've been to the boutique in Chicago and I even checked out the one in Miami. I'll have to check out this location to make sure I find some options with the same vibe and energy as the others."

"You can stop by anytime this week," she said. "I'll be there every day during store hours and after hours prepping for the move."

Luke smiled. "Wow, you're already packing up? I'm glad you're confident that I will find you some great places."

"I'm not," she stated. "But I'm confident in me finding a real-estate agent capable of finding the perfect place if you don't show me some good options within the next two weeks."

Once again, Luke shook his head. "Different hairdo, same sassy Kyra." He flipped through several more pages. "The wish list for your condo is pretty long. Are you sure you're looking for three bedrooms?"

"Of course I'm sure," she said. "My bedroom, the guest bedroom and my activity room."

"Activity room?" Luke asked. "Like the type of room parents create for their kids."

Okay, clearly, he doesn't want to get in my good graces. "No, not like the type of room parents create for their kids. Mine is an adult activity room, not that it's any of your business why I want three rooms. You're just my real-estate agent. You aren't allowed to judge."

"But I am allowed to remind you that with the budget you listed, finding three bedrooms in LA is next to impossible. Especially since you're also asking for an outdoor space, walk-in closet and an in-unit washer and dryer."

"I have expensive tastes."

"And a shoestring budget," Luke huffed.

Kyra rolled her eyes. "See, this is why I didn't want your help finding a place, but Taheim insisted. I suppose having these places purchased before the New Year is asking too much, too, right?"

"A little bit, yeah. Finding the place is one thing. Finalizing all the documents, getting the lawyer and accountant involved, and working out your loan approval are other issues entirely."

Kyra frowned. "I thought you're supposed to be one of the best real-estate agents around? Are you saying you've failed before you've even started?"

"I'm just trying to be realistic," he explained. "That's all."

Kyra glanced at her phone before looking back to Luke. "Well, keep all that realism to yourself until you've actually tried to find what's on my list. Deal?" She started gathering her stuff, not caring about the fact that Luke was looking at her as if he wanted her to stay and finish their conversation.

"Deal," he finally said.

"Great. If you have any additional questions for me that aren't answered in the packet, then text me. Other than that, I'll see you when you drop by the shop."

Luke blew out a breath. "Okay, I'll see you then." Walking out of the café, Kyra made sure she held her head high and reminded herself to stay firm on her decisions. True, she knew her list was a little unrealistic, but didn't care. Apologies or not, she wasn't ready to let him back into her life easily.

* * *

"Wait, and who is this again?" Nash asked, following Luke into their new office building.

"Kyra is one of my closest friends' sister," he explained. "She needs help finding a couple locations, but she wants to nail this down by January."

"Did you tell her finding anything that soon is damn near impossible?" Nash asked.

"Of course I did. But if you knew Kyra, you'd know it's no use. I guess you can say she lives life on her own terms, and if you try and tell her any different, she's not trying to hear you."

Nash smiled as he settled into his office right across from Luke's. "Sounds like my kind of woman. Is she cute?"

Luke froze. "Uh, yeah. I guess."

Nash shook his head. "Ah, nah, she doesn't sound like it based off that look you're giving right now."

"No, trust me, she's attractive. *Very* attractive. And she doesn't even try to be. It just naturally pours out of her, inside and out. It's that type of beauty that slaps you in the face when you aren't looking. She tries to act all tough like she doesn't let much bother her, but deep down, she's a softy. I remember when she went through her tomboy phase. Even then, she was cute."

Luke wasn't sure how long he rambled on. However, when he noticed how quiet Nash was being, he looked across the hallway to see his brother wearing an amused grin. "What's that look for?"

"Bro, you could have saved a lot of breath complaining about Kyra on the way to the office if you'd just told me up front how much you're feeling her." For more emphasis, Nash wiggled his eyebrows.

"Yeah, we used to be close when we were younger, but I'm not feeling her the way you're implying. I just know a lot about her."

Nash lifted an eyebrow. "Right. Keep telling yourself that."

"I'm serious. Didn't you hear the part where I said she's my best friend's sister?"

"Nope. I heard the part where you called Taheim a close friend. I figured it was strange considering you've told me so much about Taheim and Ajay. So I know they are a couple of your best friends. I also have eyes just like you do. Taheim's always posting pictures of his family on Instagram and I think I've seen his sister in a few. She's bad, though. Got that Zoe Saldana vibe going on. I understand why she'd get you all hot and bothered."

Luke waved off his comment. "Man, you don't know what you're talking about. Kyra doesn't make me hot or bothered. She's like a little sister to me."

"In that case, thank God we don't have a little sister. Unless we don't know she exists yet, just like we didn't know about each other. Oh, wait..." Nash snapped his fingers. "Have you had a DNA test done on Kyra to make sure she's not our sister?"

"No, fool. I didn't do that. Trust me, Kyra Reed is not related to us. I've known the Reed family most of my life. She's definitely not our sister."

"Great, then you can ask her out on a date and stop tripping."

Luke put his hands in the air. "I can't ask her out. Have you not been listening to anything I've been saying? She's Taheim and Ajay's younger sister. That's like, asking to fuck up two decades of friendship."

Nash squinted his eyes. "Taheim and Ajay don't

strike me as the type to give the you-can't-date-my-sister speech. Especially when it was Taheim's idea for you to help her out in the first place."

"Well, they did," Luke said, thinking back to the conversation he'd had with Ajay all those years ago. "Kyra had a crush on me and everybody but me knew it."

"Because you were too busy denying your own feelings for her," Nash said.

"Exactly!" Luke's face dropped. "Wait, that's not what I meant. What I meant to say is I was too busy dealing with my own shit to recognize anything else going on back then."

Nash smirked. "Right. I get it." However, his look was saying that he absolutely didn't buy it.

"I'm serious, but you look like you don't believe me."

"How long have we known each other?" Nash asked.

Luke shrugged. "About a year, I guess."

"And how long does it feel like we've known each other?"

Luke thought about the quick friendship he'd built with his brother. "Feels like we've always been in each other's lives."

"My point exactly. I may not have been in your life back then, but I know you better than you think I do. My guess is you suspected she had a crush, but you were too busy denying your own feelings for her. Don't you get it, bro? You're living in your own romance movie right now. Boy meets friend. Friend introduces boy to little sister. Boy adores little sister. Sister begins to have crush on boy. Feelings continue as boy and girl get older. Boy messes up. Girl gets pissed. Years later, boy has chance to make it up to girl. Girl makes boy pay for breaking her heart. Boy and girl have revelation. They fall in love and live happily ever after."

Luke blinked. "What makes you think I messed up with her?"

Nash snorted. "Man, please. Men always mess up. Now is the part of the movie when you try to win back her love in case you weren't following."

Luke shook his head. "Uh, you have quite the imagination."

"All I'm saying is now is your chance to finally see what could have been. And although Taheim will probably be the best man, you betta make me a groomsman."

"For my imaginary wedding?"

"Yeah, fool. Have you not been listening? We already know how this story ends. At least, that's how you want it to end. There's also the possibility that you will mess this up again and girl will run off with another guy, but I'm going to help you out so that you don't lose her before your relationship even starts."

Luke laughed. "I don't know whether to listen to your crazy advice or just forget we had this conversation."

Nash walked across the hall and leaned against the doorjamb of Luke's office. "Were you listening to anything I just said? Bruh, you were already taking my advice before I even finished giving it. Man, are you sure you're not the younger brother here?"

"I have three and a half years on you," Luke said. "So, yeah, you're the youngest."

Nash popped his collar. "But clearly, I'm the intelligent one."

"Nah, I'm just entertaining you this morning because I figured your ego needed a boost since you're talking all this romance mess."

"My ego never needs a boost," he said. "I stay ready. Don't hate because I'm spitting that knowledge."

Their banter continued for a few more minutes and Luke had to admit, he'd wished he'd had Nash in his life growing up. There wasn't a day in his adolescence when he didn't wish he had a brother, but he'd also known it wasn't going to happen. His parents were the type that never should have had kids together in the first place.

Now that he had Nash in his life, he tried not to think about all the parts of his childhood that he wished he could change, but rather, he was focused on building his relationship with his brother. Already, dude was saying things that got under his skin, but then again, what younger brother didn't say things to annoy their older brother? Regardless, Luke couldn't deny that Nash had his mind racing with how he needed to proceed with Kyra.

Chapter 3

"Um, I don't like this place, either," Kyra said for the third time that morning.

"Let me guess," Luke said. "The view from the front balcony isn't good enough?"

"No, the view is great. But this is only one and a half bedrooms and no washer and dryer in the unit."

Luke shook his head. "This is a two-bedroom unit and I already told you that it could be installed for a little extra."

"You call this closet a second bedroom?" Kyra asked, nodding her head to the bedroom on the left. "You could maybe fit a twin-size bed in there, but not much else. They should just call it a closet."

"They already have a master closet in the other bedroom," Luke reminded her. "This is definitely a second room."

Kyra shrugged. "It's still a closet."

"This is LA. Some rooms are small."

"Well, then I need you to do better and find me something that's not a closet."

Kyra wasn't really surprised that she and Luke had been disagreeing for most the morning. She was surprised when he'd called her last night and asked if she could check out three condos with him. She'd only just met with him two days ago.

Luke sighed. "Please tell me you're not going to be this difficult the entire time."

Kyra shook her head, ready to tell him that she wasn't being difficult, when a thought came to mind. Luke may have given her a half-assed apology back when he'd made her feel like she was absurd for flirting with him, but he hadn't felt her full wrath yet. She'd been too busy nursing a broken heart and avoiding him at all costs—which had been pretty difficult considering her brothers seemed so intent on inviting him to everything.

Turning on her heels, she crossed her arms over her chest and told him, "I can be difficult if I want because this is a big purchase for me. My first big purchase, in fact. Would you talk to your other clients this way?"

"When they are being unreasonably rude, yes."

"So now I'm unreasonable, too?" she huffed. "And you really think it's for no reason?" Kyra walked toward the front door. "This was the last place we had to see today, right? How about we just meet up when you find more places."

"Kyra, wait," Luke said, approaching her as she neared the door. "I think we knew early this morning that today wasn't going how either of us planned. So how about we have lunch—and I mean actually have lunch—at the café near the boutique. I really do want to find you a condo you will love and I want to have at least a couple store-fronts for you to check out this week, so I need to see the place."

Kyra bit the side of her cheek and observed Luke, taking note of the sincerity in his voice. Oh, she still wanted to make him pay for how he'd treated her, but she also wanted to hit. She'd skipped breakfast because her nerves were so bad. "Okay," she finally said, sticking out her hand. "For the sake of a tasty turkey-and-cheese sandwich, let's call a truce so we can eat lunch."

Smirking, he slipped her hand in his, the warmth immediately giving her those tingles she hadn't felt in far too long. "It's a deal."

Luckily, when they arrived at the café, the lunch crowd wasn't too bad. They both ordered sandwiches and took a seat in a booth by the front windows.

"This is my favorite place to sit," Kyra said, doing her best to refrain from soaking in how delicious Luke looked now that she'd called a truce for the next half hour. "I do the best people-watching here."

"You still people-watch, huh?"

"Always! I also still play the people-watching game I used to play when I was a kid. The one where you decide a person's occupation, age and main personality traits based off how they dress and walk."

"I remember," Luke said with a laugh. "Didn't your mom tell you to quit being so nosy when Mr. Henderson who lived next door complained about you?"

"He only complained because I caught him cheating on his wife," Kyra explained. "I may have only been eight at the time, but even then, I knew he shouldn't be kissing that woman who used to sneak into his house after his wife went to work."

Luke laughed. "Detective Kyra, blowing up marriages even at a young age."

She lifted an eyebrow. "The way you're saying it makes it seem like I've blown up other marriages."

"You have."

"Whose marriage?"

"Remember Mr. Roscoe who drove the ice-cream truck? One day, he didn't give you the ice-cream bar you wanted because he said he didn't like your attitude."

"My attitude? You know how Mr. Roscoe was. He had an attitude every day, but had the nerve to try and cheat little kids out of money by serving those off-brand Popsicles and ice-cream bars."

Luke nodded his head. "That may be true, but you didn't have to walk all the way to his house and tell his wife that he spent a little too much time with Shirley from down the street. All it took was one accusation for his wife to follow him the next day and find him at Shirley's house stepping out on his marriage."

Kyra shrugged. "Not my fault. He should never have tried me in the first place. Had he treated us kids better, I never would have said anything."

Luke laughed, the sound causing her to laugh right along with him. It was always that way with Luke. One minute he'd be saying something to annoy her, and the next they'd be laughing over something one of them said.

"I've missed this," he admitted after he took a bite of his sandwich. "I understand why we grew apart, but I've missed laughing with you over stupid stuff."

Kyra smiled. Luke's dark-honey complexion and deep brown eyes almost made her choke on her water as she watched him. Observed him. Wondered when he'd chosen to cut off his curls and trade them in for a low fade. He was the same Luke, yet he was far from the boy she used to know. However, there was a part of her that also felt like not much had changed. His core was still the same. Despite how pissed he'd made her when he'd broken her heart, he really was a good guy. Still cared about doing charity work and giving back to his community, unlike some other guys she knew. Social media couldn't tell her everything, but it told her enough to paint a picture of the type of man Luke had turned out to be.

"I know what you mean," she finally replied. Her eyes held his as she took a bite of her own sandwich. Back in the day, she felt like she always knew what Luke was thinking. However, the man sitting across from her was harder to read. His feelings were more guarded than she'd remembered.

Understanding teenage Luke and young-adult Luke was a quality she'd perfected. But grown-up Luke, who was looking at her with low-lidded eyes? Yeah, she needed more practice with this one.

"Here's the shop," Kyra announced as they walked through the door. As Luke had predicted, the shop was buzzing with customers on their lunch break. "The main level is our boutique and the top level is our boudoir studio."

Luke glanced around, admiring the shop. "I really like the decor," he said. "Seems to fit the flow of the Chicago and Miami boutiques, but it has a certain Cali flair."

Kyra smiled. "That's what we were going for." She spoke to a couple of the associates who greeted them when they walked past toward the stairs. "Follow me and I'll show you the studio."

They ascended the stairs, Luke's gaze focused on Kyra's backside even though he wasn't trying to check her out. *Damn.* Kyra still knew how to wear a pair of jeans better than any woman he'd ever met before. Even though he shouldn't have been checking for her back then, he knew from years of watching her when he thought no one was looking that she was one of those women who was just born with an extra switch in her hips and curve to her thighs.

"You better not be checking out my ass, O'Connor," Kyra said, glancing over her shoulder.

"Uh, I was just watching your feet to make sure you don't trip."

She rolled her eyes. "I'm sure you were." When they reached the top, once again Luke was caught off guard by how similar it looked to the Chicago location with regard to the decor. However, the vibe in this studio was different than any he'd felt before.

"It feels good up here," he said, walking past the grand bed in the corner covered in a plush white comforter and large beige pillows. "I'm not sure what it is that's different, but I like it."

When his eyes met Kyra's, he noted the look of surprise. "I've thought that exact same thing so many times before. Decor-wise, my sisters-in-law wanted the studio to be similar to Chicago, and although we achieved that, I remember walking into this place after the interior was finished, wondering what was different. I even told Nicole and Aaliyah, who opened this location with me, and neither one of them could put their finger on it, either."

She walked past some more furniture that Luke

assumed was staged for the next photoshoot. "Unexplained reasons like this are exactly why I like to see the current locations of businesses before finding them a new home."

"That makes you a great real-estate agent."

"Wow! Did Kyra Reed just give me a compliment?"

She smirked. "Don't let it go to your head. All I meant was that most of them wouldn't care about something as small as a feeling."

"The good ones would," he said. "Being a good real-estate agent is a lot like being a matchmaker."

"Oh, hold on," Kyra said, pulling him over to two stools. "I have to be seated to hear how you plan on justifying that a real-estate agent is anything close to a matchmaker."

"Whoa, slow down." Luke held out his arms. "I said a good real-estate agent, not all real-estate agents."

Kyra waved him off. "Some. All. You know what I meant."

He shook his head before explaining. "In real estate it's about helping a person find their next home or business. It's about showing them the different options available to them in the hopes that they will find something they love. It's about that feeling in the pit of their stomach that they get when they've found the perfect one. When they've fallen in love with the right one. Most people think being a real-estate agent is like being a salesperson, when in all honesty, it's more like being a matchmaker than anything."

Kyra observed him with an amused look on her face. "Well, well, well, O'Connor, dare I say that your words have gotten much deeper than that time you made the correlation between a garbageman and a bartender."

Luke laughed. "I was drunk when I tried to connect those two. You shouldn't hold that against me."

"Oh, I will definitely hold that against you, but seriously, I love that. The real-estate agent being the perfect matchmaker." She leaned closer to him, causing his heartbeat to quicken. "So now is the time when I ask you to use matchmaker terminology with me until you're able to find my *perfect one*."

Luke wasn't sure if it was the fact that she was leaning toward him or the way her lips curled into a mesmerizing O when she said the last word, but he wanted to kiss her. Badly. And the fact that they hadn't talked out any of their issues was only part of the reason he needed to maintain control. So it only felt fitting when he told her, "Absolutely not."

Chapter 4

"I can't believe you and Kendrick are planning another party," Kyra said to Nicole as the two of them and Aaliyah walked into Nicole and Kendrick's home. "Now you know I love me a good party, but y'all just had a ridiculously huge one a couple months ago."

The ladies had been at the shop longer than usual to finish up a boudoir photoshoot. Kyra had insisted that Nicole return home to set up for her party tonight, but she'd assured Kyra that they would arrive in plenty of time before the party. Glancing at her iPhone and noticing they had an hour before the official party kickoff, she was right.

"That party was my idea after we finished producing that romance movie in the studio. This party was Kendrick's idea because we wrapped up on that action movie he was dying to get his hands on."

Aaliyah shook her head. "Nic, you and Kendrick are the only couple I know who try to throw parties to outdo one another."

"I agree," Kyra said. "But it's so y'all."

"You're married," Aaliyah added.

"You sure are," Kyra agreed.

"So his party is your party and vice versa. It shouldn't matter which one is bigger and better."

Kyra stopped walking and turned to Aaliyah. "And that's where my agreement stops because when I get married, he better be prepared for me to outdo him in every way possible."

"That's my girl," Nicole said, slapping Kyra's hand.

Aaliyah shook her head. "Sometimes, I don't know what to do about the two of you."

Kyra and Nicole both opened their mouths to comment, but neither got a chance when Kendrick walked into the living room. "Looks like the Three Musketeers are all here."

"I hate that nickname," Kyra said, giving him a hug after Aaliyah gave hers.

"I kinda like it," Aaliyah said. "That movie was good, too."

Kendrick pointed to Aaliyah. "You see, that's why you're my favorite of Nicole's friends."

Kyra rolled her eyes, but she couldn't help but laugh at the way Aaliyah teared up at Kendrick's words. Aaliyah was already an emotional person—add pregnancy hormones to that and she was a walking cry-bomb.

"Kyra, you're just in time. I'm dying to know if anyone ever called the cops on you for people-watching?"

Kyra blinked rapidly. "Wait, what? Why would you

ask something like that? And how did you know about
my people-watching?"

Her question was answered the moment Luke slid
into the living room looking guilty. "My bad, Kyra. I
may or may not have said something to Kendrick about
it." Bryant, Aaliyah's husband, walked into the room
right after, wearing an amused look on his face.

"Why didn't you tell us you knew Luke?" Bryant
asked.

Kyra shook her head. "Better question. How do you
know Luke?"

"When we lived in Chicago, he attended the same
boys-and-girls club that we went to," Kendrick answered. "When I heard he'd moved to Cali, I knew we
had to get him to a party."

Luke took a step forward and reached out his hand
to Nicole. "You must be Kendrick's wife. It's very nice
to meet you."

"Nice to meet you, too," Nicole said, winking at Kyra
as she did so.

"And you must be Aaliyah," he said next. "Bryant
has been talking about you all night."

Aaliyah's eyes widened in surprise. "How did you
guess I was Aaliyah and not Nicole?"

Luke laughed and turned to Bryant. "You're right,
man. She is funny."

"She is," Bryant replied, a big grin on his face. "But
she's dead serious. The pregnancy has her acting a little
different." As if her husband's words made it click, she
glanced down at her belly and started laughing, finally
understanding how Luke knew she was Bryant's wife.

"When I saw you yesterday, you didn't mention you
would be here tonight," Kyra said to Luke.

"When we were together, I didn't know I was coming, either. Kendrick called me this morning."

Kyra glanced from Kendrick to Nicole. "Funny that all of a sudden, Luke was invited tonight."

"I thought the same thing," he admitted.

"Enough with the awkward introductions," Kendrick interjected. "Nicole and I still have some setting up to do before the others arrive, but why don't you all get something to eat and hang out while we finish."

"I'll help y'all," Bryant said, following Kendrick and Nicole. Aaliyah looked between Kyra and Luke before smiling and waddling out of the room behind her husband.

Great. Kyra had thought she was in for a night full of fun with her friends during which she'd be able to vent about the fact that Luke had walked back into her life. *Guess the joke is on me.* And why did he have to look so good in a pair of dark jeans and a navy polo? He was sporting that look that was a cross between bashful and sexy, his eyes darting across her face, studying her. Observing her.

"If you take a picture, it will last longer," she said with a smirk.

He smiled. "Did anyone ever tell you that your mouth may get you in trouble one day?"

"My entire life," she told him proudly. "You can give me that look all you want, but you knew I was going to call you out."

"I did," he admitted. "I guess I wanted to hear that smart mouth of yours to break the tension."

"Oh, there is a lot more where this came from."

He shook his head. "Don't I know it."

"If you know it, then I suggest you tread lightly."

Kyra glanced around the empty front room, the soft sounds of whatever holiday playlist that was coming through the Bluetooth speakers filling the silence in Nicole and Kendrick's living room.

"I love this song," Luke said as a new song started.

"Me, too. 'Santa Baby' has always been one of my favs."

"Especially Eartha Kitt's version," he added. They stood there for a few long minutes, Kyra unsure of how to fill the awkward silence.

"I'm sure you've already guessed this," she said, "but my friends wanted to give us alone time to talk. Funny thing is, I feel like this was more the guys' idea than my girls', but that doesn't make sense. Kendrick and Bryant aren't the meddling type."

"I may have had something to do with that," he admitted. "I'm not on social media much, but I remembered Kendrick and Bryant from back in the day. Also remember seeing them at a wedding I went to years ago."

"Their cousin Imani's wedding, right?" Kyra asked. "She's close with Taheim and I remember the three of you hanging out when I was little."

Luke squinted. "Sometimes your memory surprises me."

She shrugged. "My memory isn't that great." She left out the part where at one point, she thought Luke had a crush on Imani so, of course, even as a young girl, she'd paid close attention. Plus, she'd always liked Imani.

"Anyway, I reached out this morning and Kendrick hit me up, asked me what I'd been doing since I moved to LA. I mentioned you and he said you were a good friend of his and his wife and invited me to the party."

"When you mentioned me, what did you say?"

Luke's eyes widened. "Oh, you know. Just that I've known you most my life and that I'm close to your brothers. That sort of thing."

Kyra got the distinct impression that he wasn't telling her everything, but she didn't push it. "You know, we don't have to stand here and make awkward conversation. We can just join the others and help them finish setting up."

"I don't know," he said, stepping closer to her. "I kinda like making awkward conversation with you. Although if I'm being honest, it doesn't feel all that awkward. You've always been one of my favorite people to talk to."

Kyra widened her smile. "I like talking to you, too." And that meant she had a serious problem.

"So let me get this straight," Nicole said as they approached a juice bar along the beach in Santa Monica. "Your plan to deal with the feelings that you clearly still have for Luke is to drag out your attraction for as long as possible?"

Kyra nodded her head, looking from Nicole to Aaliyah. "Exactly! I can't just give in to his cuteness. I need to make him sweat a little."

"But you do expect something to happen between the two of you?" Nicole asked.

"Exactly. I see it plain as day. He's attracted to me, too."

"That doesn't sound like a good plan," Aaliyah stated. "Why would you make him sweat if you already know you like him?"

"I don't need a reason," she said as they ordered their

usual. "I just... I need to do this." There was so much that Kyra wasn't saying, but she wasn't in the mood to divulge all the details to her friends yet. Besides, she didn't expect them to understand.

"Try us," Nicole said. "We know you better than you think."

"What do you mean?"

"You just mumbled that we wouldn't understand," Aaliyah explained. "But I think we're already beginning to get it."

Crap. Luke was really messing with her state of mind if she was speaking her inside thoughts out loud. They grabbed their veggie-and-fruit juices and started walking down the path. "I won't get into all the girlie details, but I guess you can say that the crush I had on Luke growing up was the type of all-consuming crush where I didn't see anything besides him.

"Although Luke was Taheim's friend, he always took the time to ask me how I was doing or make sure I was doing my homework. It could have been my imagination, but when I turned sixteen, he started spending a little less time with me. Then at eighteen was when he really steered clear. But y'all know me. It didn't matter because I knew how I felt about him. On my twenty-first birthday, I was tired of waiting for him to notice me, so I took matters into my own hands and told him how I felt in the way I thought was best. But the night went completely wrong and ended with me in tears and him telling me all the reasons why he could never like me the way I liked him." Kyra glanced at her friends. "He made me feel like a fool. Like my feelings for him were unjustified and childish."

"Did you ever think about the alternative?" Aaliyah asked.

"What alternative?"

Aaliyah glanced at Nicole, then said, "That maybe the reason he pushed you away all those years ago was because even though you felt like your crush on him was strong, his was a lot stronger?"

"And like some men when faced with coming to terms with their feelings," Nicole continued, "when shit gets real, they run as fast as they can in the opposite direction."

"You need to figure out how you're going to deal with having Luke back in your life," Aaliyah advised.

Nicole nodded. "Because based off what we saw yesterday, he's done running. Now he's doing more of a slow jog."

Kyra sighed, wondering if they could be right. "When you two finish each other's sentences, I know I need to listen."

Aaliyah smiled. "Yep! You helped us realize how we felt about our men, so even if Luke is not the one, you owe it to yourself to figure it out."

"All he's doing is helping me find a new location for the boutique and a condo. Not exactly the type of setting for romance."

"Um, I'm sorry, but you're Kyra Reed," Nicole said. "You are never deterred from a situation. You tackle it head-on every time."

"He may not want me," Kyra said, voicing one of her fears. "He may just be trying to rebuild our friendship."

"Then rebuild with him," Aaliyah suggested. "Figure everything else out along the way. You don't always have to have the answers."

"Yes, I do," she said. "Having the answers means you're prepared. Being prepared means you won't get hurt. And if I don't get hurt, then…" Her voice trailed off, since she wasn't sure what should come after that.

"If you don't get hurt, then you aren't living," Nicole said. "And you're one of the most ambitious people I know. You always go after what you want. Don't let fear of getting your heart broken keep you rooted in place or afraid to try."

Afraid to try. Nicole's words echoed as they continued their walk. Her friends were right. There wasn't much that scared her, and if something did, she tried to face that fear as best she could.

The conversation soon changed to another topic, but Kyra's mind was still on her friends' words. She knew she didn't have to have all the answers right now, but she had some feelings she needed to sort out before she met up with Luke for more showings.

Chapter 5

Luke tried his best to conceal the smile on his face as he escorted Kyra into a space that had recently become available. "Okay, so you may not have liked the first two locations I showed you today, but I'm sure you'll love this one."

She shrugged. "We'll see. I doubt I'll find something I like for the boutique today since it's our first time looking at store locations, but I'm open to seeing everything you have on your list."

Luke smirked, thinking she was about to eat her words. "I was excited to see this space come on the market because it fits the boutique's needs if you're okay with the warehouse being in a different location."

"I love the brick exterior," she said. "But it's a little far from the area I wanted the shop to be."

"Just give it a chance. This space has been here for

decades," he said, entering a code to unlock the door. "The previous store owners decided to move locations and place this gem on the market."

The moment he opened the door, Kyra gasped. He smiled as he escorted her through the doors. "Wow," she exclaimed as they walked farther inside.

"As you can see, the main section is divided into three levels," he explained. "The second level has an open floor plan with the balcony overlooking the main floor. There are also fitting rooms on both levels."

"I love this layout," she said. "I always imagined a balcony overlooking the floor when I imagined the boutique." Kyra walked around the space, snapping pics with her iPhone. After a couple of minutes, Luke asked her to follow him.

"In addition to the rounded staircase, there's an elevator here that will take you to the third level," he said as they stepped onto the elevator. "It's divided into two parts and I think this space on the left would be perfect for the boudoir studio."

He opened the swinging doors and Kyra squealed with excitement. "This is almost better than the first two levels," she said. "And the amount of sunlight is fantastic. Our current location is great, but Aaliyah and our guest photographers are forever having to find creative ways to bring in the sunlight."

Luke smiled, loving the way Kyra walked around the empty space. His goal today had been to place a smile on her face and, luckily, he'd done just that. He gave her a few more details about the space, then told her, "And that's not it. There is one more feature to this property that I'm sure you'll love."

He nodded his head for her to follow him to the other

side of the third level. "When I saw this next section, I immediately thought about the parties you love to throw at the boutique." He motioned for her to walk in ahead of him, but instead, she just froze in the doorway and glanced around the space. Her eyes slowly took in everything.

"Luke," she huffed. "This. Is. Amazing."

"I know," he said. "Now what was that about you not expecting to fall in love with a store location today?"

She lightly hit him on the arm. "That was before you showed me a three-level space with an outdoor furnished rooftop! Are you sure you quoted me the correct price? Rooftops usually cost a fortune."

"The price is right, but I may have lied about it just coming on the market," he explained. "I know the couple selling this place and it hasn't gone on the market yet. They want to sell it by March of next year, but for now, they've just leased it out for the next three months to some art gallery who will only be in town for a short time."

Kyra walked around the deck and glanced at the bar before looking up at the lights twirled around the wooden pergola. "I could lay out in this mini courtyard all day. I wouldn't even get any work done."

Luke smiled as she fell back into a lounge chair. "Knowing you, you'd find a way to take every break up here."

"You damn right." She stood back up and walked toward Luke. "Okay, Lukey, you got me. I still want to see a few more places for the boutique that are in the area I originally wanted, but this is a real contender."

"I hate it when you call me Lukey," he said.

"Which is why I do it," she said, smirking. "So how long do I have to make a decision on this place?"

"Mr. and Mrs. Thomas aren't in the country right now, but I'd love to let them know before Christmas. Sooner would be better. I have another place to show you today, so how about we talk about it more over lunch after we visit the next location?"

Kyra laughed. "Every time we're together, you ask me to have lunch with you." She took a step toward him, but he refrained from pulling her even closer, like he wanted to do. "If I didn't know any better, I'd say you like spending time with me."

"I've always enjoyed spending time with you," he admitted. "That hasn't changed." There was so much more he wanted to say, but didn't. *In due time*, he thought. He was finally feeling like he was getting his friend back. The last thing he needed was to push her away again.

The next place Luke showed Kyra wasn't nearly as nice as the previous location. However, just like she'd asked, it was in a prime location.

"You're still thinking about the Thomas place, aren't you?" he asked as they were seated at a Thai restaurant for lunch.

"I am," she admitted, taking a sip of the water that was already at the table. "It's hard to forget a three-level place with a courtyard. I think I may call my sisters-in-law and send them the pics I took. I'm sure one of them would want to see if before we make any final decisions, but so far, that place is at the top of my list."

Luke nodded his head. "Good. Now all I need to do is help you find a condo you like just as much."

"You have your work cut out for you," she said. "I can be hard to please at times."

He smirked. "Don't I know it."

Snarky Kyra would have asked him what he meant by that comment. However, the Kyra who was now feeling slightly nervous under his gaze wouldn't dare make him explain.

"What are you doing for Thanksgiving?" he asked her after they ordered.

"Well, I thought I would be spending it with my family as usual, but my brothers and their wives are headed to France to visit Winter and Autumn's father. And my parents are on a fourteen-day cruise enjoying their retirement. So I figured I would go to Chicago and spend some time with my girl Cheyanne's family."

Luke smiled. "I remember Cheyanne. You two met in college, right?"

Kyra nodded. "Yeah, we were roommates. Been friends ever since."

"I actually ran into Cheyanne in Chicago a couple times. We also share a mutual friend."

Kyra snorted. She knew all about the mutual friend they shared and it seemed Luke had forgotten that the last time he saw her before Taheim's wedding, he'd been with that mutual friend. Instead of embarking on a topic she didn't want to discuss, she dryly said, "Nice."

For a second, she noticed the way Luke observed her and figured he noticed the change in her mood, but he must have shaken it off because he changed the topic and asked her when she was heading back home.

"I haven't decided yet, but I guess I should contact Cheyanne since Thanksgiving is next week."

Luke laughed. "Kyra Reed, never making plans too early. I guess that hasn't changed, either."

Kyra shrugged. "I make plans, I just don't believe that everything needs to be planned out. You know how we do in Chicago. There are a ton of houses I can crash at for the holiday if my nonplans fail."

"Yeah, I know. But I still couldn't do what you do. My plans have been made for months."

"What are you doing?"

"Going to St. Lucia," he said. "Did you hear that my mom moved back there?"

Kyra nodded. "Yeah, I heard that." *More like snooped on Facebook, but whatever.*

"Well, since my dad is from there, too, I wanted to take my brother, Nash, there so he could see where he's from."

"Oh, wow," she said. "That's a big deal. My brother told me you found out you had a brother not too long ago."

Luke frowned a little. "Yeah, I still haven't forgiven my dad for not telling me he had another kid out there. Nash was put into the system right after his mom gave birth to him and was adopted as a baby. He didn't even know anything about his birth parents and when he found out he was adopted a few years ago, he hired an investigator. He still doesn't know the whereabouts of his birth mother, but the investigation led him to Chicago and to me."

Kyra shook her head. "Back in the day, I remember your parents being so happy together. Never would have thought your dad had another child."

"You and me both. But my relationship with my dad has been strained for a while, so this was icing on the cake. It all took a toll on my mom. She wanted to be close to her sisters, so she moved back to her home country."

"Did you ask your dad about your brother?"

"I've been having a hard time tracking him down. I'm not even sure where he's living right now, but after talking to my mom, I figured I didn't even want his explanation. Nash and I have been getting closer and although he's nervous about going to St. Lucia, I told him my mom wants to meet him."

Kyra smiled. "Your mom always has been one of the sweetest women I've known."

"She's a godsend," Luke said with a smile. "Don't know what I'd do without that woman."

Kyra reached over the table and placed her hand over his. "I think it's awesome that you're reconnecting with your brother. Forget about your father. This is about you and Nash."

He nodded his head, placing his opposite hand over hers. "I'm trying my best to remember that." His eyes held hers, the moment making her breath catch. *This is the opposite of what you're supposed to be doing, girl!* She'd just told her friends the other day that she wanted to make him sweat a little, yet here she was, doing the opposite.

She pulled her hand away just as their food arrived. "I think you'll have a great time in St. Lucia."

"Me, too," he said, glancing at her over his fork as he took a bite. "If any of your nonplans fall through, you should think about coming with me and Nash to St. Lucia."

Kyra almost choked as she swallowed. "Uh, you can't mean that. This trip is about you and your brother getting to know each other and your mother meeting him for the first time. Pretty sure inviting your best friend's sister isn't part of that plan."

He shrugged. "I just think going to St. Lucia is better than house-hopping in Chicago. Plus, you can enjoy eighty-degree weather instead of twenty."

Oh, my God, he's serious. Kyra thought she could concoct some crazy ideas at times, but this took the cake. In fact, she could think of a couple of her friends who'd been faced with this exact decision. The men of their dreams wanted to whisk them away on a trip. In the past, she probably would've jumped at the idea, but now, she was a little baffled.

"Why are rich men always trying to fly women places in private jets and showering them with diamonds to win their hearts?"

"Private jet?" Luke blinked. "Uh, I'm not rich, but I do well for myself."

"Same difference," she said with a shrug.

He laughed. "Not really. Nash and I leave in a couple days. We'd be flying commercial, although I have first-class seats because economy seats are bad for my knees. So I'd get you one, too. And who said I'd buy you diamonds? Are you fishing for a diamond?"

Kyra's mouth dropped. "Oh, no, I mean… That's not what I meant. It came out wrong."

Luke laughed again. "For the record, I don't mind buying you jewelry if you see something you want while in St. Lucia, but let's get through our first trip together before you start getting too crazy."

Our first trip together? She wasn't sure how to handle everything he was saying, so she said the only thing she could say. "I'll think about it."

Luke nodded, pinning her with a look she couldn't

quite place. A look that seemed to hold the answers to questions she hadn't yet asked.

Despite the awkward start, the rest of lunch was enjoyable and Kyra even found herself looking forward to the possibility of vacationing with Luke, assuming she even said yes to his offer. Which she wasn't. No way.

Chapter 6

"There is no way we're letting you turn down a free trip to St. Lucia," Nicole said as she took a sip of her wine. Like most Friday nights when they were all in town, Kyra, Nicole and Aaliyah were lounging around Kyra's apartment getting caught up on missed episodes of *Grey's Anatomy.*

"Don't you think that's a bit crazy?" Kyra asked. "Who up and goes on vacation with a man when they have so much unfinished business?"

"Uh, I kinda did," Aaliyah said.

Nicole smiled. "Me, too."

"And didn't you encourage your friend Kiara to do the same when that millionaire mogul, Trey Moore, wanted to whisk her away?"

Kyra frowned. "That may have been the case with all y'all, but I fail to see the point."

"You know the point," Nicole said. "How many times do we have to tell you to quit being scared and take the opportunity to get to know the man Luke has become. Not the boy you fell for all those years ago."

Kyra sank deeper into her chair and groaned. "I swear if he wasn't still the sexiest man I'd ever seen, telling him no would be so much easier."

Aaliyah and Nicole laughed. "Said every woman who's gotten hung up on a man," Nicole said. "Sis, at least you're in good company."

"I don't want to be in good company," Kyra moaned. "I can deny it all I want, but a very large part of me wants to say yes to his offer."

"Then say yes," Aaliyah said. "Stop overanalyzing it and just say yes. It will probably be the trip of a lifetime."

"Do you think it's wrong of me to even consider it since I'll be invading on his time with his family?"

"He invited you," Aaliyah reminded her. "He wouldn't have done that if he thought you were invading his family time."

"You're right."

"Then what are you going to do?" Nicole asked.

Kyra sighed. "I'm not sure yet, but I figure I should let him know by the morning. Still more to think about."

Nicole and Aaliyah nodded and directed their attention back to *Grey's Anatomy* just as Kyra's phone rang. She glanced at the caller and told them she'd take the call in another room.

"Hey, Taheim," she said upon answering. "What's up?"

"Nothing much, sis. I told Ajay and Winter that I'd check in on you to see what plans you'd made for

Thanksgiving when a thought hit me. Why don't you come with us to France? No sense being in Chicago by yourself for the holiday."

"I already told you I'd be fine," she said. "Besides, I already tagged along with you guys on the two past trips to France. Your father-in-law is looking forward to seeing you all and his grandkids. I'll be fine."

"We just feel bad," he said. "Did you call Cheyanne to see what her family was doing?"

"Not yet. I've been distracted with work and some other stuff." Kyra cleared her throat. "I got an offer to go someplace else for Thanksgiving week, though."

"From who? Nicole and Aaliyah?"

"Not exactly." Kyra looked to the ceiling, wondering what her brother would say when she told him. "Luke invited me to St. Lucia with him."

Taheim grew quiet, then asked, "Luke invited you back to his hometown?"

"Yeah, he did."

"Are you going with him?"

"I'm not sure yet," she said. "If I say yes, would you be cool with that?"

It took a few seconds for him to respond, but Taheim finally said, "Yeah, of course, I'd be cool with it."

He didn't sound convinced, but Kyra didn't push for him to say any more. She knew her brother. Knew how he thought. He may have been clueless about her feelings toward Luke back in the day, but now he was wondering if anything was going on between them— he just wasn't outright saying it.

Truth be told, Kyra wished she had an answer to the question lingering in the air because she was clueless as well.

"Let me know what you decide," Taheim said before they ended the call.

"I'm leaning toward saying yes, but I'll text you tomorrow."

"Wow, you're really thinking about going, huh?"

Kyra took a deep breath, acknowledging for the first time that she actually was thinking about going. She hadn't said those words aloud, but by the time she hung up with her brother, she was pretty sure she was going to take up Luke on his offer to join him and Nash in St. Lucia.

"You invited her to St. Lucia with us, didn't you?" Nash asked with a smirk. Luke leaned back in his desk chair and ignored his brother as he continued to toss his mini basketball in the air.

"You can ignore me all you want, but you were the one who walked into the office this morning and said you had something important to tell me. Now all you're doing is procrastinating. I know you spent most the day with her yesterday, so you might as well just fess up."

Luke stopped tossing the ball. "Why do you think I invited her on our trip?"

"Because all you've done lately is talk about her and if I was trying to win back the heart of a beautiful woman, I'd take her on a romantic trip to the Caribbean."

"What makes you think I'm trying to win her heart?"

Nash raised an eyebrow. "Bro, I know we haven't known each other long, but we share DNA. Give me some credit, all right?"

Luke shook his head. "What was I thinking, asking her to come along? This is supposed to be a trip for you and me to get to know each other more and for me to show you St. Lucia."

"We've been catching up since we found out about each other," Nash said. "I'm looking forward to this trip, but I don't mind that you invited Kyra. Based off what you've told me, she seems cool."

"She is," he said. "She hasn't told me if she's coming or not, but I'm second-guessing why I asked her in the first place."

Nash sighed. "We've already been through this. You like her. She used to like you. Now she still holds a slight grudge that you rejected her. So you want to prove to her that you're not the same idiot you used to be."

"Something like that," Luke said with a laugh. "Are you sure you'll cool with it if she decides to come?"

"Yes, man. I'm good. I'm not some little boy wanting to spend time with his older brother when all he wants to do is lay in bed all day with his girlfriend. I'm a grown-ass man and if you want Kyra to be in your life more permanently, I want to get to know her, too."

Luke smiled. "I hope you're ready for everything St. Lucia has to offer. It's a small but mighty island. The people are great and I'm sure lots of folks want to meet you."

"I just want to learn more about my background," he said, his voice solemn. "Your dad may not have wanted to know me, but that doesn't mean I don't care to learn more about where I came from."

Luke tossed the ball to his brother and they began throwing it back and forth. "He's not the man I thought he was. Your adoptive dad is a better person than ours will ever be."

"You still haven't talked to him?"

Luke shook his head. "Nah, and I doubt I will anytime soon."

When the ball reached Nash again, he held it. "I get that, but I hope you know that if it has anything to do with me, I don't want my existence to be the reason you and your dad have a broken relationship."

"I appreciate that, bro, but it's not just you. There's other issues we have to work out."

Nash nodded. "Okay. But if you ever need to talk, just let me know."

"Thanks, man." Luke's cell phone rang, interrupting the moment. Luke answered on the fourth ring.

"Hey, Taheim, what's up, man?" At the mention of Taheim's name, Nash raised his eyebrows and walked over to Luke's desk.

"Hey, Luke, you busy?"

"Uh, not really. What's on your mind?"

Even before he asked, Luke suspected that it was about Kyra. It was confirmed when Taheim said, "Listen, man. I know I asked you to help Kyra find a condo and location for the boutique, but now she tells me that you asked her to go with you to St. Lucia?"

Nash quickly went back to his office and returned with a dry erase board. Luke mouthed, "What the hell are you doing with that?" but he had his answer when Luke wrote something down and turned the board around to show the message—*Tell him yeah and that you want to date his sister.*

Luke pushed away the board. "Yeah, I invited her to go to St. Lucia with me. You cool with that?"

"It depends," he said. "I thought you and Kyra hadn't talked in years, and now you're bringing her to your home country?"

"Well, technically, I was born here in the US."

"You know what I mean. You've never brought a woman to St. Lucia. I thought you said taking a step like that with a woman was important and you'd never do so unless you were serious about the relationship. So I'm asking you—is there more going on between you and Kyra than just friendship?"

Nash laughed and showed Luke the board again. This time it said, *Taheim is trying to figure out if you are bringing Kyra to St. Lucia to sleep with her or if you're already sleeping with her.* Then Nash erased the board and wrote another message that said, *And if you are sleeping with her, his ass will probably be on the next flight to LA.*

Luke shook his head. "We're just friends. I'm surprised you even had to ask." Nash put the board in front of Luke's face with the word *LIAR* written in all caps.

Taheim was quiet for a few seconds, then finally said, "I guess I gotta take your word for it. Something about this doesn't sit right with me."

"Man, come on. You know me. If something was going on between me and your sister, I'd tell you." Luke heard a female voice in the background, sparking another thought. "Is that Winter? Did she put you up to this?"

Taheim sighed. "She may or may not have mentioned that she suspected something was going on between y'all, so I got to thinking and figured I would call you."

Luke shook his head. *I should have known.* Taheim was great when it came to business, but when it came to treating Kyra like a woman and understanding that she wasn't a little girl anymore, he was clueless. "Listen, if anything changes in my relationship with your sister, I'll let you know out of respect." Nash shook his head and mouthed "wrong answer."

"So, Winter's not trippin'. You do think something more could happen between y'all?"

Luke pinched the bridge of his nose. "T, don't let Winter make you overthink this. I'm going to St. Lucia to introduce Nash to our family and I thought it would be nice if Kyra joined us since she mentioned not having any solid plans."

"Oh, Nash will be there, too?" Taheim asked.

"Yeah, Kyra didn't tell you?"

"Nah," he said. "She failed to mention that part."

Luke shook his head. It was just like Kyra to leave out important details. She'd rather keep folks guessing even if that meant him getting calls from Taheim about his intentions. "Well, yeah. It's a family trip that I invited her on."

"Why didn't you say that in the first place?" Taheim asked. "I mean, you my boy and all, but when it comes to relationships, you suck. The thought of you introducing my little sister to your commitment issues was messing with my head. Glad to know you were just looking out for her."

Nash shook his head and wrote *Well, damn* on the board. "He'll be looking out for her all right," he whispered.

"What was that?" Taheim asked.

"Nothing," Luke said, waving away Nash. "Nash just had a question about something. But, anyway, I got to get back to work. It seems like Kyra might be turning down my offer to vacation with us, anyway."

"Nah, man. She sounded like she was going when

I talked to her," Taheim said. "That's why I figured I should give you a call."

Luke looked to Nash, who mouthed "told you so." "Are you sure she sounded like she would be going?"

"Yeah, she definitely did. In case she forgets to text me, can you let me know if she decides to go with you? You know how she is with her secrets and shit."

"If she decides to come, I'll definitely let you know."

"Thanks, man. I knew I could count on you." They spoke for another minute before ending the call.

"Wow, I'm glad I'm not you," Nash said after they hung up. "It was hard enough watching you lie to your best friend, but listening to your voice get all high and shit was hilarious."

"Man, shut up. You were messing me up with that dry erase board."

"Bruh, that's because I was speaking the truth and you were too chicken to say what I was writing."

Luke shook his head. "All you know is what I've told you. You were just speculating."

"Whatever." Nash waved off his comment as he glanced out the window. "And you know what else I speculate?"

"I'm afraid to ask, but what?"

Nash smirked. "That you better not stumble over your words the next time you talk to Kyra like you did on the phone with her brother."

"I don't stumble," Luke said. "She's probably not going with us, so I'll do some self-reflection in St. Lucia."

Nash laughed, but just when Luke was about to ask him what was so funny, the bell at the front door chimed, indicating that someone was walking in. Just like Nash had predicted, Luke could barely form a sentence when his eyes landed on her. "Kyra. Uh, what are you doing here?"

Her long lashes batted as she looked him up and down, and as much as Luke was trying not to look at her just as hard, he couldn't help himself. She was wearing black jeans, black booties and a maroon top. Simple, yet so sexy on Kyra.

Her hair was down, flowing around her shoulders, and the colored gloss she was wearing matched her top.

"I was close by your office," she said. "So I figured I would stop by and tell you that I decided to go to St. Lucia." She glanced to Nash, then back to Luke. "If you guys will still have me."

Luke glanced to Nash, who answered, "Most definitely, we will still have you." Nash walked over to Kyra and reached out his hand. "I've heard a lot about you. I'm Luke's brother, Nash."

"Nice to meet you, Nash." Kyra looked between the two men. "Wow, I didn't think you'd look so much alike. You look just like Luke."

"Just the slightly taller, sexier version," Nash said with a wink. "And might I say that you look even more beautiful than Luke described you."

Kyra laughed. "And clearly, you're trouble. But thank you." She looked to Luke. "Is it okay with you if I still come?"

"Of course," Luke said. "I was hoping you'd come with us."

She smiled. "Great. I guess I need to pack since we leave soon."

"Yeah, I can reserve your ticket and send you over the details."

"Sounds good." She glanced down at her phone in her hand. "I should probably get back to the shop, but I appreciate you letting me tag along. I'll see you both in a couple days."

Nash didn't even wait a full minute until after she'd left before he started whistling. "Okay, bro. Now I see why you've been talking my ear off about her. You mean to tell me that she threw it at you back in the day and you threw it right back in her face? What the hell is wrong with you?"

Luke sighed. "Tell me something I don't know. That mistake has followed me around for years. I've thought about what I would do if given a second chance more times than I can count."

"Well, now is your second chance," Nash said. "She came here to talk to you in person and based off what I saw, y'all still have mad chemistry."

"You think so?" Luke asked.

"Man, get out of here with that hopeful look," Nash teased. "But, yeah, I think so. Now all you have to do is play your cards right in St. Lucia and win her over."

"I'll try," he said, finally admitting that was exactly what he wanted to do. Unfortunately, he had a feeling it was going to be easier said than done.

Chapter 7

Sitting on the plane next to Kyra had been pure torture. First, it seemed every time she adjusted herself in
her seat, her hip brushed against his. Then she'd fallen
asleep in her chair and conveniently rested her head
on his shoulder, with her hand draped over his thigh.

If that hadn't been enough, every now and then she
would softly moan in her sleep, the sound serenading
Luke in a way that made it extremely difficult to rest
with her so close. He'd been thanking God when they
finally reached their layover, so for the second part of
the flight, she was fully awake. However, that didn't
stop her from brushing past him when she had to use
the restroom even though he could have gotten up. He
wasn't sure if she was doing any of it on purpose, but
it sure as hell felt like it.

"Welcome to St. Lucia," he announced to Nash and

Kyra as he watched her get into the back of the rental car wearing her formfitting olive dress and gladiator sandals.

Nash leaned into Luke and whispered, "Bro, are you talking to me or Kyra's ass?"

Luke choked on air. "I was talking to both of you."

Nash tilted his head to the side and glanced into the car. "I don't blame you if you were talking to the booty because cutie has a nice, round one. I can see why you can't stop talking about her."

Luke shoved Nash. "Man, quiet down before she hears the crap you're talking."

"I already heard y'all," she yelled from the car. She leaned her head out the open door. "Now if both of you are done admiring my ass—which I work very hard on in the gym, mind you—can we get it moving? I'm dying to see more of St. Lucia than the airport."

Luke's mouth dropped, but Nash closed it shut. "Don't drool, brotha. You'll be with her for the next five days and no one likes a slobbery man."

"Uh, we weren't… I wasn't…" Luke stammered.

"Yes, he was," Nash said. "But she's right. We gotta go." Nash packed the last suitcase into the trunk and got into the passenger seat.

Dude, what's wrong with you? Luke had always had game and could charm the panties off any lady. Clearly, he was out of practice or out of his element because so far, he wasn't showing any of that charm to Kyra.

He got into the driver's seat and began making his way toward their destination. "I have some motion-sickness medicine in case either of you need it," he said to Nash and Kyra.

"Motion sickness. Are we getting on a cruise or something?" Kyra asked.

"No, but St. Lucia is pretty mountainous, so it has many hills, and here we usually go up and down about five to six hills a day. More if you need to get to the other side of the island."

"I usually don't get sick when driving in a car, but I'll let you know if I need any," Nash said.

Kyra nodded. "Ditto what he said."

"Sounds good." Luke turned a corner and started the ascent up the first hill. "Okay, my home is in the mountains. So, before we head there, we're going to stop by and see a few folks."

Luke glanced over at Nash, whose eyes were wide. "Relax," he told Nash. "You aren't meeting my mom today. She's visiting a friend in Barbados, so she flies in tomorrow. These are just friends."

Nash exhaled. "That's good. I really want to meet her, but I—I'm not—"

"You weren't prepared to see her right when you got off the plane," Luke said, finishing his brother's sentence. "I get it. That's why I figured I'd introduce you to a few locals first."

After twenty more minutes, they arrived at their first stop. "We're here," Luke announced.

"Ralph's Wharf," Kyra said, reading the name. "Are we eating here?"

"Not exactly," Luke explained, getting out the car. Nash and Kyra followed him to the entrance just as the door opened and a large, burly man walked out.

"Well, I'll be a monkey's uncle. If it isn't my nephew looking like he hasn't seen the sun in days."

Luke laughed. "Uncle Ralph, still cracking jokes, I see. For the record, I'm out in the sun every day."

"I doubt it, boy. Your skin too light. You need more vitamin D or a day out on my fishing boat to darken you up."

Luke heard Kyra and Nash laugh behind him. He'd really missed his uncle's island accent and the way he was always ragging on him. "Well, when you're done teasing me, I want to introduce you to my friend Kyra and my brother, Nash."

"Nice to meet you, beautiful," Ralph said, pulling Kyra in for a hug.

She smiled. "Nice to meet you, too."

"And you," Ralph said. "You look just like my nephew. I thought Luke said you grew up in California, boy. Thought you'd be darker."

Nash looked from Ralph to Luke. "Is he my uncle, too?"

Luke shook his head. "He's my mother's younger brother."

"But you're my nephew, too," Ralph said, pulling Nash in for a hug. "Here on the island, we don't do all that division crap. Family is family, so you call me Uncle Ralph."

Nash smiled. "Sounds good, Uncle Ralph."

Luke glanced at Kyra, who was watching the exchange as closely as he was.

"Well, come on inside," Ralph said. "I just got a batch of fresh fish and seafood. Y'all must be hungry after traveling."

When they stepped into the place, Luke breathed in the familiar scent. Yeah, the fishy smell may bother most, but Luke didn't mind. To him, it smelled like home.

* * *

Kyra couldn't remember the last time she'd eaten so much food. Ralph was an amazing cook and, aside from the accent, so much of him reminded her of Luke.

"This was so good, Uncle Ralph," she announced. "I wanted to eat that last crab leg, but I don't have anywhere to put it." Normally, she wasn't even a fan of seafood, but there was something about the way Ralph made it that left her craving more.

"I agree," Nash said. "I haven't eaten this good in years."

"We could tell," Kyra said.

Nash frowned. "What's that supposed to mean?"

"It means, you were smacking the entire time you ate like you hadn't had a decent meal in a while."

"Huh?"

"It's not you, Nash," Luke said. "Kyra has an issue with hearing people chew. She'll get over it."

"I don't have an issue with people chewing," she defended. "I just think that you should eat with your mouth closed. People who chew loudly are annoying because it's unnecessary. I swear, they'd enjoy their food more if they chewed properly. And don't even get me started on those who talk, then smack on food, then talk, then smack again. I could go on and on about this."

Nash blinked. "I can see that. Remind me to eat even louder next time."

Kyra threw a straw at him as all three men laughed at her expense.

Ralph smiled. "Anytime any of you want to eat well while you're here, just drop by."

"Will do," Kyra said while Nash expressed the same

sentiment. She barely knew Nash, but so far, she really enjoyed his company. He kept her laughing and, just like Uncle Ralph, parts of him reminded her of Luke. They looked so much alike.

When she'd dropped by their office a few days ago, Kyra had been taken off guard by how much the two brothers looked alike. Like replicas of each other in a way that could even pass for twins.

"What are your plans for the rest of the day?" Ralph asked.

"Since Mom gets in tomorrow, I was thinking of relaxing at the house for a bit. I had it cleaned and the fridge stocked for our arrival."

"Trista is having a party tonight at Lou's Reggae Lounge in town, so you may want to check it out."

"That sounds fun," Luke said. He turned to Kyra and Nash. "Trista is my cousin and Uncle Ralph's daughter. I guess you can call her the official island party planner."

"She's the head of St. Lucia tourism and other islands are taking notice," Ralph explained. "At a young age, my wife and I tried to control Trista, but it was no use. Better to embrace it than change her. And we were tired of cutting down bamboo trees outside her window just so she wouldn't climb out."

Kyra laughed. "Sounds like my kind of girl. My parents used to say I was the reason for all their gray hairs."

"I'm pretty sure they still say that," Luke said, smirking.

"I'm a lot better," she defended. "I tell them more information now than I ever did before."

Luke raised an eyebrow. "Not according to Taheim. Just the other day, you left out important details about this trip when you talked to him."

"Details like what?" she asked.

"Details like I was bringing Nash to St. Lucia to meet the family."

Kyra crossed one leg over the other and adjusted herself in her chair, knowing that Luke was following her every move. "I told Taheim you'd invited me to St. Lucia for the holiday. Why was it important to tell him about Nash, too?"

Luke pinned her with a look. "You know why."

"Clearly I don't," she said with amusement. "Why don't you enlighten me?"

"Kyra," he said sternly.

"Luke," she said with a smirk. "You only look at me like a sister, right? So telling him Nash would be here wasn't important, correct?"

"I'm not doing this with you," he said. "Taheim called me and didn't seem too happy that I'd asked you to come here with me."

"Taheim should have gotten a clue years ago," she said. "If he had, he never would have asked you to be my Realtor."

Luke sighed. "Just forget I said anything."

Kyra wiped her hands clean. "Already forgotten." She took a sip of her water, holding Luke's gaze. If he thought for a second she would own up to anything when he wouldn't do the same, he needed to think again.

"Oh, this trip is gonna be fun," Nash said, sharing a knowing look with Uncle Ralph. "In case you haven't guessed it, these two have some unfinished business."

"I knew they did the moment he introduced her," Uncle Ralph said to Nash. "He's been whining about this one for years."

Kyra broke Luke's gaze and looked to Uncle Ralph.

"What do you mean? Luke told you about me? What did he say?"

Uncle Ralph held up his hands. "It's not my business to repeat. But, yes, girl, I've known about you for a long time."

Kyra looked back to Luke, who had the nerve to sit there without an expression on his face. *Enough of this.* "As amusing as this conversation is, I really need to take a nap or something. Do we have many more stops or can I take a taxi to your place?"

Uncle Ralph laughed. "A feisty one you got here, nephew. You'll have your hands tied this week."

"Don't I know it," Luke said. "No need to take a taxi. We're headed to my place now." Luke looked to Nash. "Ready to hit it?"

"Yeah, let's go." As they were walking out of the restaurant after saying their goodbyes to Uncle Ralph, Nash leaned to Kyra and whispered, "Luke is always so calm, yet you rattle him unlike I've seen before. You pulling his leg or making him sweat for what he did back in the day?"

"He told you about that?" she asked in surprise.

"Not the whole story, but enough."

Kyra rolled her eyes. "Not that it's any of your business, but I'm not that petty." *Ha! Tell that lie again, sis.* She was about to repeat herself when she noticed that Nash had stopped walking beside her.

"What?" she asked. "I'm not."

"You know that saying, 'game recognizes game'?"

She shrugged. "Yeah."

"Well, I see what you're doing," Nash said. "And, yeah, you're entitled to make him sweat, but just know that

Luke isn't that great at hiding his feelings. I want to see y'all work it out. Just don't make him pay all vacation."

Kyra's face grew serious. "Although I may not care for what you're saying, I love that you care so much."

Nash smiled and glanced at Luke, who was leaning on the car looking out into the water. "We haven't been brothers long, but he's my guy."

"You've always been brothers," she said. "Just because you didn't know the other existed, doesn't make that any different."

"I guess you're right." He turned back to face Kyra. "While I have you alone, there's just one more thing I need you to keep in mind while you're here."

Of course there's more. "And what might that be?"

"If you decide to make Luke do anything stupid on this petty quest of yours, make sure I'm around to capture it on camera."

Kyra laughed so hard, she almost doubled over. "I was not expecting that," she said in between laughs.

"I wouldn't be a younger brother if I didn't capture the embarrassing stuff," he said. "Do we have a deal?"

Kyra glanced down at his outstretched hand, still laughing, and accepted his request. "Deal."

"I already don't like whatever y'all are agreeing to," Luke yelled from the car. "Now can we get out of here, or do the two of you have to conspire some more?"

"We're good," Nash announced as they reached the car. "Kyra, I want to lay down until we get there. Can you ride shotgun?"

She glanced from Nash to Luke. "Uh…"

"Great." Nash was in the backseat so fast, she didn't have a chance to really answer. Reluctantly, Kyra got in the passenger seat of the rental and they headed off.

"How far is your home?"

"Only an hour," Luke said.

"An hour? You say that like it's nothing."

Luke laughed. "On the island, it really isn't long. I live in the mountains, and with us having a huge rainforest and overall hilly terrain, an hour is typical."

Kyra sank deeper into her seat. "Would you kill me if I took a nap until we got there? The motion is getting to me a little."

"Do you want to take something?" he asked.

"No, I think I'll be good if I just rest a little."

"Okay, I'll wake you and Nash when we get there." He glanced her way before looking back to the road. "If you change your mind, let me know so I can give you something."

Kyra nodded. "Thanks, Luke. I will." The last thing she remembered seeing before she closed her eyes was Luke's smiling face.

"We're here." Kyra heard Luke's words and she gently nudged awake. She slowly opened her eyes to a beautiful glass-and-white-concrete villa surrounded by lush trees and greenery.

"Damn, bro," Nash said from the backseat. "I knew you said you had a home in the mountains, but this place is huge."

"Not huge. Just five bedrooms, four bathrooms and a pool."

Kyra glanced back at Nash, then both of them repeated Luke's words in a mocking voice.

"Stop it," Luke said with a laugh. "That came out wrong. I just meant there are much bigger mountain villas in St. Lucia than mine, but I fell in love with the place the first time I saw it."

"I can see why," Kyra said, stepping out of the car. "We haven't even walked inside and I can already tell it's going to be hard to leave."

"Then how about I give you both the tour and then we can get the luggage."

Nash nodded. "Sounds good to me."

"You've got to be kidding me," Kyra said as they followed Luke to his home. "You have a bridge over a small pool that leads to your front door?"

"That was the designer's idea," Luke admitted. "The water is only a foot deep, but she felt like the bridge would be a nice way to greet visitors."

"I fully support this designer already," Kyra said as Luke opened the front door and she stepped inside. "Although seeing this foyer and grand staircase might give the bridge a run for its money." Kyra didn't think she was impressed by many homes since she knew a lot of people with grand estates. Hell, she'd even been raised in one. However, there was something about Luke's villa that was giving her a very lush and lavish vibe that she wasn't quite sure she'd experienced before.

As Luke took them through each bedroom in his villa, her mouth dropped even more at the beauty. Nash was on such a high searching through every room, Kyra wasn't even sure when they'd lost him.

"Everything is so crisp," she said. "Was it your idea to have this white, heather gray and light blue color scheme or was that the designer?"

"The color choice was all me," Luke said with pride. "I wanted it to have that warm Caribbean vibe and

I've never been one for bold colors. This palette works for me."

"It suits you." She stepped deeper into the last bedroom and second master of the villa, her steps faltering when she noticed that the balcony doors opened into a private plunge pool separate from the main pool. "This has to be where you sleep."

Luke laughed. "Did the plunge pool give it away?"

"Heck yeah! All the bedrooms are beautiful, but who would pick any of the other rooms when they could have their own private pool."

"True," he said, stepping out onto the balcony. "That's why I want you to stay in this room while you're here."

Kyra shook her head. "Oh, no, I couldn't put you out like that. This is your home, so I'll just take one of the other beautiful bedrooms."

"I insist," he said.

Kyra shrugged. "Well, pull my arm, why don't you? I'll stay here if you insist."

He laughed. "That's the Kyra I know."

"The one and only," she said with a twirl. "But seriously, thank you for being so gracious."

"You're welcome." His eyes studied hers and she wished like hell she knew what he was searching for. "I'm just glad you were able to join us on this trip."

Kyra cleared her throat. "Me, too. So far, this definitely beats house hopping in Chicago in the cold."

"St. Lucia suits you," he said, his voice getting deeper.

Kyra's heartbeat quickened. "You can't possibly know that. We haven't even been here for a day yet."

"I know," he said with conviction. "And in case I forgot to tell you, you look beautiful today."

Kyra glanced down at her dress. "Thank you. At first, I thought it was too much for the plane, but I'm glad I wore it."

Luke looked her up and down, his eyes lingering on her legs. "I'm glad you wore it, too." At his words, Kyra's breath caught. *Okay, who are you and what have you done with the real Luke O'Connor?* The old Luke would never openly flirt with her like that, let alone check her out. If she didn't know any better, she'd say this St. Lucia heat was getting to him.

Breaking the tension, she walked away from him and past the pool so she could look out into the greenery. "At first, I couldn't even imagine living in the mountains. But now, I see what all the fuss is about."

Luke approached and leaned over the railing next to her. "Since I grew up in the States, it was an adjustment when I purchased this home. I didn't plan on getting a house that was so off-the-grid, but that's exactly what happened when I found this gem. It needed some love and care, but after the renovations, it became my dream home."

He was so close, his masculine cologne teased her nostrils. "In case you can't tell, I'm already in love with this place."

"I can tell," he said with a smile. "And if you like all this, wait 'til you see the rooftop."

"Please tell me you do not have a rooftop deck."

Luke extended his hand. "Then how about I show you rather than tell you."

Kyra glanced down at his hand, noting that she'd had more physical contact with him in the past week than she had the entire time she'd known him in her past. "Lead the way, maestro."

As she followed him through the bedroom and up a spiral staircase in the back of the home, she tried to remind herself that she wasn't the type of woman who liked to hold hands. Yet somehow, she didn't want to let go of Luke's hand.

Chapter 8

"Kyra, I swear you'll like it," Luke said, gently pulling Kyra toward a makeshift booth on the beach.

"No, I won't," she said. "I hate the water. There's nothing about it that I like. Plus, I really don't want to get my hair wet."

Nash laughed. "Said every black woman that I've ever dated."

"Shut up," she said, flicking him off. "As I recall, you didn't want to go zip-lining earlier today and Luke didn't push you on that."

"That was different," Nash said. "I'm two hundred and fifty pounds of solid muscle. Those little-ass ropes couldn't hold my weight."

"You are not two hundred and fifty pounds," Luke said with a laugh. "Since that was the weight limit, you lied to the guy so that you wouldn't have to go."

"So," Nash retorted. "Did you see the way that man looked when I told him? He knew I'd dodged a bullet. Zip-lining from tree to tree is not the black man's way."

Kyra laughed. "Oh, my God, you did not just make this a black thing."

"More of a man thing," Luke said.

Kyra rolled her eyes. "Just admit that you hate heights."

"For what," Nash said. "This is about you now. I thought you said you've ridden a Jet Ski before."

"I have," she said. "A couple times."

"So what's different between then and now?" Nash asked. "Unless you're lying."

"Lying?" Kyra exclaimed. "Dude, come on."

Luke shook his head as he listened to Kyra and Nash go back and forth as they had since they'd arrived in St. Lucia. "Y'all argue like brother and sister."

"If you weren't tryin' to get her in your bed, you'd probably be arguing with her like this, too," Nash said. "She's annoying sometimes."

"Do you think about the crap you say before you say it?" Luke asked.

Nash stuck out his arms in defense. "What? I thought that was common knowledge."

"You're an idiot," Kyra said. "And for the record, I've Jet-Skied on lakes before in a situation where I knew I wouldn't fall off."

"How could you know that?" Nash asked. "You just got lucky and didn't fall off. But I'm sure you got your hair wet."

"Why am I even arguing with you about this?" she huffed. "I'm not doing it."

"Would you do it if you were on the back of the Jet Ski with me?" Luke asked.

She frowned. "Uh, no. I don't trust either of you to not flip us over."

"I didn't volunteer," Nash said. "But if you get on with me, I'll definitely be flipping your ass off it."

Kyra whacked his arm. "Remind me to never vacation with you again."

Nash laughed. "You know you're enjoying my company."

"Nope. Negative."

Luke shook his head as they went at it again. When his mom, Athena, had called this morning and said that she wouldn't be arriving until tomorrow instead, Luke had thought he'd treat Nash and Kyra to some fun island activities. But had he known they'd be so difficult, he would have let them spend the day lounging around his place instead.

"Okay," Kyra said, interrupting his thoughts. "I'll go on the Jet Ski with you." She walked closer to Luke and poked him in the chest. "But you better not flip us over, or else I will make the rest of this trip hell for you."

Nash snorted and mumbled something under his breath. He couldn't make out his words, but he was pretty sure he shared the same sentiment.

"You've already been acting like a princess, so I'll take my chances." He led them to a guy at the booth on the beach who set them up with Jet Skis. Luke had Jet-Skied more times than he could count at a bunch of different places. However, nothing could compare to the beaches of St. Lucia.

While Nash didn't waste any time hightailing it out

into the ocean, Luke started off slow, making sure Kyra held him tight as she got used to the waves.

"I can't believe I'm doing this," she yelled as they picked up speed.

"Believe it, baby," he said with a laugh as he kicked it up a notch so he could catch up with Nash.

"Are you gonna slow down?" she yelled when he reached the speed he normally rode at.

Luke smiled slyly even though she couldn't see him. "Not a chance."

Nash was just as good on the Jet Ski as Luke was and, eventually, he heard Kyra comment on how beautiful the small islands were that they passed by. "It's really pretty," she yelled.

"I agree," Luke yelled back. "There's nothing like it." He slowed down so that she could admire one of his favorite small islands. "I took a small boat over to that island over there with my uncle a couple times when I was a teenager to do some exploring."

"You and Uncle Ralph are really close, huh?"

Luke nodded. "Yeah, he and my dad never got along, but we've always had a close relationship. Most of St. Lucia knows Uncle Ralph and whenever I visit here, he always made me feel like a son. I learned more about this island from him than my own father, who was also born here."

"You're lucky to have each other," she said. "I definitely want to get another meal or two from him before we leave."

"Oh, you'll get plenty." Luke looked to his left when he saw Nash speed past them yelling about Luke being a slow rider. "But for now, I have to show my little brother up."

"Just be careful," Kyra yelled as Luke took off. But it was no use. He was already speeding fast, passing Nash. A minute later, Nash passed him again, standing as he tackled the incoming waves. Although Luke had to remain seated because Kyra was gripping his life jacket for dear life, he managed to ride Nash's tail, almost passing him. Then without warning, his brother slowed down and began to turn, pointing ahead.

"Crap," Luke mumbled as he saw a huge incoming wave heading their way. Nash managed to turn easily, avoiding the wave, but Luke wasn't so lucky and they flipped over, both going under.

When they rose to the surface, Luke quickly flipped over the Jet Ski, but Kyra was already freaking out.

"Oh, my God, I can't believe you flipped us." She flailed her arms, glancing around the open water. "Why is the water so dark blue here? Are there big fish out here?" Her eyes widened. "Or sharks? Oh, crap, it's an ocean so there's definitely sharks, right?" In a panic, Kyra gripped the side of the Jet Ski.

"Don't do that," Luke yelled. "It will flip it back over." Unfortunately, she wasn't listening and managed to flip over again and go under. Since Luke was so close, he helped her rise back to the surface.

"Are you okay?" he asked after she stopped coughing.

"No, I'm not okay," she yelled. "We flipped over. In the ocean. Which is exactly what I was afraid of. You promised we wouldn't flip over." Kyra was talking a mile a minute, which wasn't normal for her. Luke knew she was still freaking out, but no matter what he said to try and calm her down, it wasn't working.

He wished she didn't look so sexy all heated and wet,

but she did. She always did. If asked, he'd never admit it, but he'd done his fair share of social-media stalking. He'd convinced himself he was just checking on her to make sure she was okay, and strategically hounded Taheim for details of her exes when he saw a new guy pop up on her pages. Luke always thought through his actions, but ever since he'd moved to LA, he'd done less thinking with his mind and more thinking with his heart.

"Are you going to help me back on this thing?" she asked, still in a panic. He wanted to help her. He really did. However, thanks to this whole thinking-with-his-heart thing, he couldn't help her the way she needed, but rather, in the way he'd been thinking about ever since the moment they'd shared in her bedroom back in college.

Not giving it any more thought, he gently pulled her face to his, grateful that he didn't have to tread water much thanks to the life jackets. To his surprise, Kyra melted into his kiss instantly, her hands snaking around his neck, causing him to moan as she allowed him to deepen the kiss.

There were so many times when he thought about what it would be like to kiss her again, but never had he considered it would happen in St. Lucia, floating in the Atlantic Ocean. Had the waves not continued to crash into them and the Jet Ski, he would have kept on kissing her.

Reluctantly, Luke pulled away, then gently rubbed his thumb against her wet cheek as she looked at him in surprise and arousal. *Join the club*, he thought because she'd been arousing him all freaking month. When he heard someone clear their throat, Luke finally glanced away, his eyes landing on a very amused Nash.

"Don't mind me," Nash said, leaning over the handles of his Jet Ski. "I just wanted to make sure that the dolphins didn't frighten y'all since the three of us are enjoying the show."

"What dolphins?" Kyra asked, her voice breathless from the kiss. Nash nodded to his right at two eight-foot-long mammals that Luke could barely see because they were dipping in and out of the ocean. "Oh, my God," she screamed as one of them dipped their head above the water. And just like that, Kyra flipped over the Jet Ski. Again.

"Damn, Unc wasn't kidding," Nash said. "Trista knows how to throw a party."

"She does," Luke said with a smile as they walked to the VIP section of Lou's Reggae Lounge. To be honest, he wasn't smiling because his cousin was great at planning a party. He was smiling because they'd just arrived in St. Lucia yesterday and already, Nash was calling Uncle Ralph *Unc*.

That, and the fact that he was still on cloud nine after that kiss with Kyra. A kiss he'd hadn't stopped thinking about since it happened.

"I'm surprised Kyra chose to miss out," Luke said. "She usually loves parties."

"You're joking, right?" Nash asked. "I'll admit, she was just as into that kiss as you were, but she freaked out on you after. You really need to question why she didn't come out with us?"

Luke frowned as he thought about how she'd gone from yelling at him for kissing her to being quiet during the rest of the drive home. "Yeah, I guess you're right. I didn't mean to kiss her right then. It just happened."

Nash sat down in the one of the VIP booths while

Luke took a seat beside him. "Bro, don't think about it too much. It was bound to happen sometime. You and Kyra have so much sexual chemistry, I almost thought about asking Uncle Ralph if I could crash with him so y'all could have the house to yourselves."

Luke laughed. "I think you're getting ahead of yourself, little brother."

"Yeah, okay," Nash said, raising an eyebrow.

"Oh, snap, Luke is in the building," a voice said from beside them. Luke turned and spotted his cousin Trista.

"Trista, what's good?" he asked, standing to hug her.

"Not much," she replied, giving him a hug. "Dad told me you were coming into town since it's Thanksgiving in America." She glanced over Luke's shoulder. "Then he told me you were bringing your newfound brother along with you, but I think I heard my dad wrong because he looks more like your twin."

Luke laughed. "Trista, this is Nash. Nash, Uncle Ralph's daughter, Trista."

"Hey, cousin, it's nice to meet you." Trista gave Nash a hug. "Glad you made it to St. Lucia. My dad already told me that you may look like Luke, but that y'all are opposites, which makes me glad because as much as I love my cousin, he tends to think I'm reckless."

Nash laughed. "Great to meet you, too. And, yeah, I think it's safe to say that no one is quite like Luke here."

"Agreed," someone said, clapping him on the shoulder. "Luke, my man, what is up!"

Luke turned around. "Maceo, what's up, man? Last I heard, you were married and living in Barbados."

Maceo sighed. "Yeah, I was. But that didn't work out."

"Sorry to hear that, man."

Maceo shrugged. "It was for the best. We weren't right for each other from the beginning. I think we both knew it, but we stayed together for our kid."

Luke nodded. "Trying to do the right thing. I get it." Luke waved over Nash. "This my brother, Nash. Nash, this is one of my good friends, Maceo."

"Nice to meet you, man," Nash said, dabbing his fist.

"You, too." Maceo looked from Luke to Nash. "Yo, you look just like each other."

Luke laughed. "Yeah, we've been getting that a lot."

Maceo nodded and glanced over Luke's shoulder at Trista. "Long time no see, Trista."

"Only because you stay busy," she said with a smile. "What gives? Too good for my parties?"

"Nah, just trying to get a handle on this single-dad life."

"I'm just teasing," she said. "But glad you could make it." She glanced to all three men. "In fact, I'm glad all of you could make it. But, Luke, where's this woman my dad was telling me about? Said she has your nose wide open."

Nash laughed, but Luke didn't find anything funny. "Man, Uncle Ralph needs to stop telling stories."

"It ain't a lie, bro," Nash said. "You been feelin' Kyra since you were young. It's obvious as hell."

"Bruh, why don't you share that info with a few other people in the lounge. I'm not sure they understood who you were talking about."

Nash shrugged. "Why not?" He stood on the VIP couch and yelled over the music that Luke had a crush on a girl named Kyra. A few folks standing nearby asked who Kyra was, while a few others yelled for him to get down.

"Are you happy with yourself?" Luke asked, ignoring the way Trista and Maceo were laughing.

Nash gave him a Chuck E. Cheese smile. "Very."

"Good, because you're taking a taxi home."

"Fine with me," Nash said, glancing at the front door. "I'll just take a ride back with Kyra."

"She's not here," Luke said. Instead of answering him, Nash nodded his head toward the door. Luke knew she was there before he even turned fully around, and when he did, the sexy black dress she was wearing almost made him stumble. *Damn.* True to Kyra's personality, she'd already washed and straightened her hair, but that wasn't what had Luke speechless.

Her eyes landed on them and the way her hips were swaying in that dress even under the dim lighting had him wishing they were anywhere else but in the lounge.

"Hey, guys," she said as she joined the group. "I remembered the name of the lounge and figured I'd take a taxi here. Glad I made it."

"You should have called me," Luke said. "I would have come and got you."

"I called Uncle Ralph and he called a friend to get me."

"That's my dad," Trista said with a smile. "Hey, Kyra, I'm Ralph's daughter, Trista. I've heard a lot about you. Glad to finally put a face to the name."

"Nice to meet you," Kyra said, giving her a quick hug. "I met your dad yesterday and he's already one of my favorite people."

"He has that effect on people," Trista said proudly. "And this here is Maceo, a friend of mine and Luke's."

"Nice to meet you," Maceo said, shaking her hand. "Welcome to the island."

"Glad to be here." Kyra glanced back at Luke. "Hope you didn't have too much fun without me."

"He hasn't," Nash said for him. "He talked about you the entire ride here." Luke elbowed Nash in the ribs, causing him to let out a groan. "Be a lover, Luke. Not a fighter."

"Shut up, Nash." Luke took another head-to-toe glance at Kyra. "You look beautiful."

"Thanks," she said. "You don't look too bad yourself."

"Oh, yeah," Maceo said to Trista. "Luke's in trouble with this one."

Unable to help himself, Luke asked Kyra if he could chat with her for a minute.

"Sure," she said with a nod. There weren't too many private places for them to go, so Luke pulled her deeper into the VIP area.

"Are we okay?" he asked, leaning down to whisper.

"You mean because you kissed me or the fact that we almost got attacked by dolphins?"

He laughed. "Those dolphins weren't going to attack us."

She huffed. "Yeah, okay."

"Seriously, though, are we good?"

She looked to him, studying his eyes in a way that made him feel like she was undressing him in her mind. "We're good. I know you kissed me on an impulse and didn't really mean it. Everything's cool."

"Nah, I meant that shit," Luke said. "It was impulsive, but I don't regret anything."

She smiled. "Me, neither." At her admission, his eyes dropped to her lips, eager to taste her again, but not wanting to lay it on too strong. Especially in front of a bunch of people.

"Y'all should join us tomorrow," Trista suggested, calling over to them. "Maceo and I, along with a couple other locals, are thinking about going on a hike in the rainforest."

"That sounds like fun," Kyra said, walking back over to the group. Luke followed.

"Seriously?" Nash exclaimed. "You're afraid of water, but you're down to hike?"

Kyra rolled her eyes. "How are the two of you even remotely related?"

Nash shrugged. "I just thought you were one of those women who didn't like to do anything outside. More of an air-conditioned kind of girl."

Kyra looked to Luke and pursed her lips together. "You may be down one brother after this trip."

"That's if I don't get to him first," Luke said, shaking his head as the two got into another argument. Luckily, this time, Trista and Maceo were there to run interference.

Chapter 9

"Tell me again why I agreed to go on this long-ass hike in this scorching heat," Nash yelled as they made their way up a deep incline.

"Aww, is Ashy Nashy tired when we're only twenty minutes into the hike?" Kyra teased.

"The baby talk is one thing," he said. "But you ain't gotta call me 'Ashy.' I made sure I lotioned, put on sunblock and bug spray. Ya boy is moisturized up here in these trees."

The group all laughed and Kyra took the moment to pull out her GoPro and capture a few photos and a video of Nash taking a break to fan himself with a towel. Even though she'd just met Trista and Maceo, she felt like she'd known them forever. She liked their vibe. And, yeah, Nash may annoy her, but she'd felt like she'd known him for years, too. He was like that annoying best guy friend she always wanted but never had.

"We're almost there," Trista said after another twenty minutes.

"We're almost where?" Nash asked, panting from the heat. "Luke and Kyra had agreed to go on this hike before they told me all the details."

"We're almost to Wishing Waterfall," Maceo explained. "It's a place only St. Lucians know about."

"Sounds like my kind of place," Kyra said. "I love spots that aren't overrun with tourists."

"Me, too," Luke said. "The first time Trista took me to this waterfall, I told her I didn't want to leave and could live in the trees in this rainforest."

"He really did," Trista said with a laugh. "He was only twelve then, so I believed him."

"I'd never live in the rainforest," Nash said, now using the towel to wipe the sweat off his face. "It's too damn hot. I thought it was supposed to rain a lot."

"Most of the time, it does," Maceo confirmed. "We're just lucky today, I guess."

Nash mumbled something under his breath that Kyra couldn't make out, but she was sure he was still complaining. They walked for another ten minutes until Trista announced that they'd finally made it.

"The waterfall is right over this hill," she said. "Nash, this is your chance to cool off because we're getting in."

Kyra cringed. "More water? Did Luke tell y'all that he flipped me over in the Jet Ski and we were almost attacked by dolphins?"

Maceo and Trista froze. "Dolphins bothered you?" Maceo asked. "Our dolphins are usually friendly."

Luke laughed. "They didn't attack us, but Kyra was flapping around in the ocean trying to get back on the

Jet Ski and they thought she was playing, so they were following her around."

Everyone laughed. "Okay, so maybe they didn't attack me, but those things were huge! I'm not a water person, so yesterday was a bit much." Although, had she not been locking lips with Luke, she wouldn't have been in the water at all.

She hated to admit it, but yesterday had been a great experience. However, she'd be lying to herself if she didn't acknowledge that their kiss had confused the hell out of her. Kissing Luke was everything, and even though her body was craving for more, her mind was warning her to tread lightly.

His lips had been so soft and just like the first time they'd kissed all those years ago, he'd applied the perfect amount of pressure with enough tongue to drive her insane with need, emphasis on the *insane* part. She'd put her heart out there again and kissing Luke yesterday had reminded her that if she wasn't careful, there was a possibility it would get broken again.

"You don't have to get in if you don't want to," Trista said, "but at least check it out before deciding." Kyra nodded her head and followed Trista—who was ahead of the pack—up the hill.

When they reached the top, Trista stretched out her arm. "Welcome to Wishing Waterfall, St Lucia's very own fairy godmother."

Kyra's eyes widened at the beautiful sight before her. "Wow, I'm not sure what I expected, but this is beautiful." There were only a few other people in the waterfall and when they noticed them and the others on the top of the hill, they waved.

"Do you know them?" Kyra asked.

"Yes, they are the friends that Maceo and I were meeting. If you come in, I'll introduce you."

Kyra studied the decently sized body of water. "How deep is it?"

"Hmm, no more than twenty feet in the deepest part. Only about three feet at the base."

Kyra swallowed. "Twenty feet! That's it, huh?"

Trista laughed as they made their way down the hill. "It will be fine, trust me. We brought a couple life jackets with us, so you can have one. And we have some tubes that us island folks keep stashed in an empty shed. They should already be pumped with air, so we can tie together."

Kyra watched Luke, Maceo and Nash begin removing their clothes so that they could get into the water. *Hmm...nice.* Despite her best efforts, she couldn't take her eyes off of Luke's six-pack. She'd seen it yesterday, but goodness, the man still had it.

"You guessed why we call it Wishing Waterfall, right?"

Kyra tore her eyes away from Luke and glanced at Trista. "Because you can make wishes at it?"

"Yes, that's true, but not just any wishes. There's a story St. Lucians are told in school." Trista pointed her finger to the top of the waterfall. "It's said that many years ago, right up there, there was a young woman who'd lost her fiancé at sea due to a storm that killed everyone on the fishing boat. To escape the heartache of having to face everyone in town, she had her father build her a small cabin right above the waterfall for her to live at. Every day at sunset, she'd come out of her cabin and cry up to the night sky for the love she'd lost to find his way back home her. But he never came. She waited at the top of that hill for years, crying every day for his return."

"Did he ever return?" Kyra asked.

Trista shook her head. "No, he didn't."

"What happened to her?"

"No one knows for sure," Trista said. "Yet, the way the story goes, she cried so much that, eventually, her tears turned into a stream. That stream turned into a river. And that river turned into a waterfall. When the girl's father came to the cottage to find her, he noticed this waterfall, although it wasn't originally there when he'd first built her home. He also found a note his daughter left saying that she hoped the people of St. Lucia would visit this waterfall and remember how special love can be. She hoped that their hearts would always return to their true loves because she didn't want any visitor to ever feel alone. She wanted us to be encouraged and make wishes knowing that there was someone in the world who was listening, hoping that all our dreams come true."

Kyra glanced at the waterfall. "Have love wishes ever come true as a result?"

Trista smiled. "More than I can count. Personally, I know over thirty people who have found the heart of the one they love after visiting this waterfall."

"So in a way, she scarified herself for the happiness of others," Kyra said. "That's a beautiful story."

"That's a messed-up story," Nash said, sneaking up behind them and interrupting the moment.

Kyra hit Nash on his shoulder. "Dude, I was really listening to that."

"I could tell," he said. "But why tell kids that story in school? I mean, the woman basically dies of a broken heart and we're supposed to swim in her tears and be okay with that? Nah, bruh. As a kid, that story would have done just the opposite and scared me away from a relationship." Nash looked to the whole group. "Tell you what. When I dive in, I'll make a wish, but my wish will be for all the kids who may have been deterred from love after hearing that story. May they still find their way to that one special someone."

Maceo laughed. "In a twisted way, that makes sense."

"Don't encourage him," Luke said. "Nash, you have to respect the story. It's older than you by decades."

Nash walked over to the water and waded right in. "I respect the story, bro. I'm just being realistic. I mean, was anyone concerned that this woman went missing? What father do you know that will accept a letter assumingly written by his daughter as a sign that she's okay? Especially when she's up in these hills all by herself."

Luke and Maceo went in after him. "You have a point," Maceo said. "I never thought of it that way." While the men debated the story a little more and made their way to the other people in the water, Kyra and Trista removed their clothes and began wading in slowly.

"Thank you for sharing that story," Kyra said to Trista once they'd both gotten into their tubes.

"You're welcome," she said. "I hope it helps you find the answers you're searching for. Or should I say, I hope your wish for love comes true."

"I may not make a wish."

Trista rolled her eyes. "Oh, honey, please. I see the way you look at my cousin. And I see the way he watches you. You'll make a wish before we leave today and I'd bet money that he's doing the same thing."

Kyra thought about denying it, but it was no use. She had a good poker face at times, but being in St. Lucia was making her soft. She could blame it on the heat, but there was no point doing that, either.

Maceo grabbed the rope that was keeping her tube linked to Trista's and pulled them together with the others. When Kyra's tube waded right next to Luke, she smiled, loving the smile he was giving her in return. Since they'd been with the others, they'd barely spoken to each other today, but somehow, she felt like they'd still been communicating. Whether it was the looks he was shooting her way or the private smiles he gave her when the others were occupied, their body language had been having major conversations.

When she heard Nash mention Christmas and ask the St. Lucians how their Christmas differed from the States, a thought crossed Kyra's mind. She'd been honest when she told Trista she wasn't sure if she'd be making any wishes, but now—being here with Luke—she could think of at least one wish that she wanted to make for the holiday. So without hesitation, she slowly closed her eyes and inwardly made her Christmas wish, her hands wafting over the water when she did so.

She opened her eyes, glad that the group was still engrossed in a conversation about Christmas. Only when she couldn't shake the feeling that someone was watching her did she look Luke's way and spot him—his eyes were fastened on hers.

Kyra swallowed the lump in her throat as she observed him more closely. *Crap.* She hoped he hadn't known she'd made a wish, because if he did, she didn't need him suspecting that the wish had anything to do with him. Yet, judging by the smirk on his face, he already knew it did.

Chapter 10

Luke could tell that Nash was nervous to meet his mother, but Luke wouldn't dare tell him that he was just as nervous.

"Are you okay?" Kyra asked from the passenger seat of the rental. Before Luke answered, he glanced back at Nash to make sure he still had his headphones in.

"I'm a little nervous," he admitted. "My mom is amazing, but I know this will be a lot for her. For them both."

Kyra covered Luke's hand, which was resting on his thigh, with her own. "Nash and your mom both need this and while it may be hard, you having Nash come to St. Lucia to meet her was the right thing to do."

Luke nodded. "I know you're right. For my mom, I hope this doesn't dig up memories of my father's infidelity. And for Nash, he still doesn't know his birth mother, so I hope it doesn't trigger his feelings about that, either."

"There's a good chance this will trigger emotions for both of them," Kyra said. "But that's natural given the circumstances. Until we get to your mom's house, try to think about the positive side. This trip needed to happen, and so far, it's gone well."

For the rest of the drive to his mom's house, Luke took Kyra's advice and tried not to think about everything that could go wrong with this visit, but rather, everything that could go right.

When they arrived at his mom's place, as expected, she was sitting on the porch, ready to greet them. Luke looked back to Nash as he removed his headphones.

"Is that her?" he asked. Luke nodded and all three of them exited the car. Luke was still trying to figure out if he should hug his mom first and then introduce Nash or the other way around, when Kyra made her way past both of them.

"Ms. O'Connor, it's so great to see you," Kyra said, pulling her in for a hug. "Should I still call you Ms. O'Connor?"

Athena laughed. "Yes, child, I kept my married name." Athena sat back. "Ooh, would you look at you. If you aren't just as beautiful as the day I met you."

"Thank you," Kyra said with a smile. "I've missed you."

Athena clasped a hand over hers. "I've missed you, too, sweetie."

Luke went to his mom next, hugging her tightly since he hadn't seen her in a few months. "I've missed you, Mom," he said. "But I'm glad St. Lucia is treating you well."

She leaned up and hugged him back ever so tight. "I needed this, baby. I needed my people."

Luke nodded, knowing exactly what she meant. The divorce had taken a bigger toll on her than Luke had been prepared for. "I want you to meet someone." Luke waved over Nash, who was still standing at the bottom of the stairs. "Mom, this is my brother, Nash. Nash, this is my mom, Athena."

After coming up the steps, Nash looked uneasy, like he wasn't sure what to do. Extending his hand, he told her, "Nice to meet you, Ms. O'Connor."

Instead of accepting his handshake, Athena stood from her porch chair and lightly touched his cheek. "Nash, it's very nice to meet you, too. You look so much like my boy." Athena opened the screen door. "Come. Let's go inside."

Nash smiled as he stepped into the home. "We've been getting that a lot. Guess our dad has strong genes."

Athena nodded, her eyes full of emotion. "You do look like Nick," she said. "Maybe even a little more than Luke does."

Luke took a seat next to Kyra on the couch. He wasn't sure if he should leave the room so they could get to know each other without him there, or if they should stay. When Kyra took his hand in hers, he figured that was her way of saying they should stay.

"Thank you for wanting to meet me," Nash told Athena.

"Honey, I wanted to meet you the moment Luke called and told me about you."

"So you didn't know I existed?"

Athena shook her head. "My ex-husband is a lot of things, but honest isn't one of them. Had I known you existed, I would have made Nick do right by you."

Nash visibly swallowed. "I appreciate that. I was

adopted when I was a baby and my parents are great. But I always felt a little off in my family and then they told me I was adopted."

"And you found my Luke," Athena added. "I remember how scared and excited he was to get to know you."

Nash laughed. "I was probably even worse than Luke." His face grew serious. "The investigator I hired didn't find much on my father."

Athena shook her head. "Nick has always had a wandering spirit and I didn't know until Luke was in high school just how wandering that meant. If Nick doesn't want to be found, he won't be found. That doesn't mean you should stop trying. It only means that you may not like what you find when you track him down. Luke can probably help you. Nick tends to reach out to him from time to time."

Nash frowned. "After talking it over with Luke, I'm not sure I even want to find him." Nash glanced at Luke before returning his gaze to Athena. "Do you know anything about my birth mother? Or have an idea as to who she might be?"

"I've thought about those early years with Nick many times upon finding out that you existed, but I can't recall Nick even being friends with another woman back then. I wish I knew more, but I was kept in the dark about a lot of things."

"So there was never a clue that he had another son out there?"

Athena shook her head. "Nick and I had some dark times, so I may not remember every fight we had that made him walk out, or every guy trip he went on that could have been covering for something else, but sometimes, our subconscious chooses not to see things to try and save us from the heartbreak of our situation."

Nash nodded. "I understand. Figured I had to ask."

Athena placed her hand over Nash's. "I know you already have a family, but Luke's family is your family, too. We don't do all that half this and half that around here. You are family, Nash, and when you're ready to learn more about your past, tell my Luke and he'll get you in contact with Nick. Unfortunately, he may have the answers you're looking for. But I must warn you, the years have not been kind to him. You may not like what he has to say."

"I've been preparing myself for the unexpected ever since I learned I was adopted," Nash said. "If I decide to learn more, I'll try to handle it best I can."

Athena smiled. "That's all any of us can do, Nash. And now that we've met, I hope you know that you can always come to me when you need someone in your corner."

Nash glanced over at Luke, who couldn't really read the expression on his brother's face.

"I really appreciate that," Nash told Athena.

"Good." She lightly touched his cheek once more before announcing that dinner was waiting on them all in the kitchen. "Should we eat?"

"Oh, man," Kyra said. "I'm probably going to gain ten pounds from all this good food, but I'm down to eat more." They followed Athena into the kitchen and sat around the table. It had been a while since Luke had tasted his mom's cooking, but she definitely didn't disappoint.

Conversation flowed easily as he and Kyra caught up with his mom and Nash learned about some of the antics Luke and his friends used to pull back in the day. At first, it seemed like Nash was enjoying all the stories, but as dessert neared, Luke noticed Nash seemed to be a little distant.

"Are you good?" Luke asked after dessert.

"I think so," Nash said. "But I'm overwhelmed."

"Anyone in your situation would be that way," Luke said.

"But it's not just that. It's hard, hearing stories of a life that feels like I should have been a part of, but wasn't. I mean, it's as if we've been brothers our entire lives, but we haven't."

"We'll get there," Luke said. "We can't replace the years we lost, but we can make new memories."

"I know we can and I may sound like a jealous little brother, but sometimes, it feels as if Nick already had you, so you were the son he decided to keep and I was the one he decided to throw away. And Athena can't remember some of the dark times in their relationship, but she can remember every moment of your childhood. Even the good memories with your dad."

"That's not fair," Luke said. "My mom hasn't had an easy life, either. She's still coming to grips with how her relationship with our dad went."

"Your dad," Nash said. "Not mine. I don't even know the man."

Luke nodded. "Fine. My dad." Given how quiet it was in the kitchen, Luke assumed Kyra and his mom were now listening to the conversation.

Nash pinched the bridge of his nose. "Listen, I loved meeting your mom and I thank you for bringing me to St. Lucia, but I think I need to head out." Instead of waiting to get a response from Luke, Nash said goodbye to Athena, hugged her tightly and walked out the front door.

"We can head back," Luke said, following him out the house.

Nash sighed. "I just need a minute. Some space to think. Maybe I'll get a hotel room tonight if you're cool with that."

"I don't want that, but I understand that this is hard for you," Luke said. "It's difficult getting taxis this time of night, so I'll give you a ride."

"No need," Nash said. "I texted Maceo during dessert and he'll give me a ride. He should be here any minute." Nash walked over to Luke and clasped his shoulder. "Bro, I appreciate everything you've done since we met and I love you for it. I just need some time. Seeing you and your mom… Knowing that you were able to at least grow up with Nick and get to know him… It's all harder than I thought it would be. Athena is a sweetheart just like I imagined she would be. But I need some time by myself to think about everything that's happened."

Luke clasped the back of Nash's head and brought their foreheads together as Maceo arrived. Luke was staring at the street long after they left, until he felt someone loop an arm around his. He glanced down to see Kyra, her eyes warm and comforting.

"He just needs time, son," Athena said, stepping out onto the porch. "He's a good man and his parents raised him right. But this is a lot for anyone to handle."

"I know," Luke said with a nod. "I guess I just hate feeling like I'm the reason he's overwhelmed right now. It was my idea to bring him to St. Lucia. Dad doesn't even have family here anymore, so I'm not sure why we even came."

"Because even though your dad isn't handling this situation right, you still wanted your brother to see where he came from," Kyra said. "It was the right thing to do, even if Nash is having a hard time handling it right now. He'll appreciate you later."

"How could he do this?" Luke asked, looking to Athena. "How could Dad father a son and not tell us anything about it? Even if Nash's birth mother wanted to give him up for adoption, how could he turn his back on his own flesh and blood?"

Athena walked down the stairs and met them in the street. "Who knows why your father made any of the decisions that he has. We can't spend all our time trying to figure out why he did this or that. We just have to learn to heal and accept that Nick has made mistakes that cannot be undone."

"I wish Nash could realize that," Luke muttered.

Athena glanced at her son. "Nash is a lot like you, you know."

"How so?"

"You've always needed to take a moment to process things. You've been like that since you were a boy. There are some people in this would who would have found out they had a sibling and wouldn't be doing everything in their power to incorporate them into their life. You're one of the good seeds, Luke."

Luke hugged his mom. "Thanks, Mama. Don't know what I'd do without you."

Luke glanced to Kyra. "Ready to head out?"

"Yeah, let's go home."

Luke smiled, touched that she said "home" so easily.

"Take care of him," Athena said, giving Kyra a hug. She whispered something in her ear that Luke couldn't hear, but Kyra was smiling when they broke their embrace.

The night had been more mentally exhausting than Luke would have liked, but the forty-minute drive from his mom's place with the windows rolled down and Kyra sitting beside him wasn't half-bad.

"Having you there tonight made all the difference," he told her.

"Duh," she said. "I'm kinda awesome. Shocked you never realized it before."

"Oh, I realized it," he admitted. "I've always known how great you are." He briefly glanced over at her. "Always felt how much I need you in my life."

Since he had to look back to the road, he didn't have time to see her expression, but he figured the hand that was resting on his thigh was a good sign. *I'll take it.*

Chapter 11

Kyra's heart was beating out of her chest as they walked into Luke's home after leaving his mom's place. She knew the night hadn't gone how he'd planned, but she was glad Luke had introduced Nash to his mom.

"I don't know about you," she said, walking over to his bar, "but I could use a drink or a shot."

Luke laughed, following her. "I think I need a shot. What are you in the mood for?"

Kyra scanned the liquor bottles. "Ooo, Jameson. Definitely a whiskey kinda night."

"How could I forget," Luke said, getting out two shot glasses. "You've been a whiskey girl since you were old enough to drink."

"Nope," she said with a smile. "Way before that. I was a whiskey girl since I snuck my first bottle out of my parents' liquor cabinet."

"I think I remember you getting in trouble for that," Luke said, pouring the whiskey. "Your parents found you and your friends drunk in the backyard. You were like sixteen, right?"

"I was," she said with a laugh. "Can't believe you remember that. Taheim and Ajay were pretty pissed, too. But I remember you telling me that although it seemed like the end of the world to have my entire family upset at me, it was a teenager's rite of passage to misbehave."

He nodded his head. "I did say that, but I have to admit, you scared the hell out of me, too. I'd never known someone who had to get their stomach pumped from too much alcohol."

"I didn't drink until I turned twenty after that incident," she explained. "It was really my first time having liquor, so I didn't know how my body would take to it. You would think I'd hate whiskey after that, but I like to forget that I ever had to go to the hospital."

"I could never forget," Luke said, clinking his glass to Kyra's before they both took the shot. "You looked so helpless in the hospital and your parents had told me you were asleep. I wasn't expecting that you'd wake up when I came in the room."

"I felt you there," she admitted. "I'd been out of it most the night, but something pulled my eyes open. I'd wanted it to be you and, surprisingly, it was."

"Really?" he asked, his eyes studying hers. "Pretty sure I thought you wanted it to be someone from your family instead of me."

Kyra rolled her eyes. "Luke, I had the biggest crush on you and that was the year that I finally noticed a hint of flirtation in your eyes that made me think that maybe you didn't see me as a little sister anymore."

"That hint of flirtation you saw scared the crap out of me. I'm not gonna lie—I still looked at you like a little sister back then. But it was in a rare moment when we were hanging out at one of your family's parties and I actually forgot that I shouldn't be noticing certain things about you, like how your hair fell over your shoulders or the way your eyes twinkled when you laughed." Luke poured himself another shot. "Jaleen noticed it at that same party and you called me out. Warning me that if Taheim and Ajay picked up on it, they'd kill me. Plus, I was in college and you were in high school. It just felt wrong."

Kyra played with the rim of her shot glass, nervous to ask a question she'd had for years. "I understand why you felt the way you did back then. But by my twenty-first birthday, we were both adults and our five-year age difference didn't seem that strange to me."

"It wasn't about the age thing at that point," he said, holding her gaze. "Do you remember Jessica? My ex?"

"The one you were engaged to?" Kyra asked. "Things ended right before my birthday party. I thought that may have had something to do with it, but you'd seemed fine."

"I thought I was fine, too," he agreed. "Jessica was never good for me and deep down, I knew that. She only cared about herself and what I could do for her. If it didn't revolve around making money or high social standing, she didn't want to be concerned about it. She got her hooks in me in college because she knew even before I did that I would make something of myself. I was the one who broke off the engagement after overhearing her saying to the partners at her law firm that she was only with me because it looked good and that she'd already landed more clients because they liked the person I was."

"That's messed up," Kyra said. "And you projected those feelings on me?"

"I did. And I'm so sorry because that was wrong of me. But I was in a bad place and didn't know how to get out of it. I didn't mean anything I said about you, but I knew the words would hurt and as much as I hate to admit it, I needed someone to hurt more than I was. It was an asshole move and I vowed to never make anyone feel less than after that situation. The guys had invited me down for your birthday because they knew I needed a change. Plus, I'd found out some news about my dad that had really messed up my head."

"What was it?" she asked.

Luke sighed. "Back then, I knew damn well my dad was cheating on my mom. The first time I noticed something was going on was back when I was in like the third or fourth grade. Even then, I knew Dad shouldn't have women in the house when my mom was at work. But he was my world when I was younger. I wanted to be just like my father."

"He's always been charismatic," Kyra added. "Most young boys look up to their fathers, so it's natural for you to only want to see the good."

"That may be the case, but I was an idiot. When I finally decided to take a stand against my dad, we got into a huge altercation. Punches were thrown. Words were said. Revelations surfaced. And my only regret is that it took me so long to call my father out. I didn't know Nash existed, but I shouldn't have been surprised when he found me."

"I'm so sorry, Luke," Kyra said. "I had no idea that was going on between you and your dad. But you do know that it's not your fault that Nash didn't know your father growing up, right?"

Luke shrugged. "Yeah, I know. But I still feel guilty. Every time he brings up his birth mother, I can't but wonder if she was one of those women I caught my dad with."

"You may never know, and you'll drive yourself crazy thinking about it."

"I told Jessica some of it," he said. "That mess with my dad went on for years and I confided in her only for her to tell me that I needed to get over my family issues and suck it up."

"Like you said before, Jessica wasn't good for you," Kyra said. "She didn't have a bone of empathy in her body. Besides, she never liked me, anyway."

"Most of my exes didn't like you," Luke stated. "Clearly, despite my best efforts, they saw what I'd failed to acknowledge."

Kyra swallowed. "What might that be?"

Luke held her eyes for a while, then he walked around the bar and placed his arms on either side of Kyra, pinning her still. "That I was crazy about you even when I tried convincing myself that I wasn't."

Kyra closed her eyes. "Or maybe you just think that you were because all of these stories about the past are making you nostalgic."

Luke shook his head. "Nah, I know damn well what I'm feeling. What I've always felt. I may have tried to ignore it when I didn't want to jeopardize my relationship with your brothers, but we're adults and, quite frankly, I'm tired of fighting my feelings."

Kyra opened her eyes, locking them with his. *He's dead serious.* She could tell by the way he was staring at her, observing her, waiting for her to comment on what he'd said. Usually, she could find the words, but it was hard to say something during a moment she'd waited so long for. A moment she'd craved and dreamed about in every fantasy she'd ever had.

She liked to think she was a strong woman who could make the man of her dreams sweat a little before he won her over, but sitting on that bar stool, pinned between Luke and the counter, she couldn't think of one good reason why she shouldn't be taking full advantage of this opportunity to finally get with Luke.

Pulling his head down to hers, Kyra placed her lips on his, the taste of whiskey on each of their tongues increasing her awareness of the situation. As with the kisses they'd shared before, it was as if their mouths knew what their minds were still trying to figure out.

Luke clasped her around the waist and lifted her so that she was on the counter, the move catching her off guard. She felt like she was starring in her own romantic film, but the problem was, cheesy romance movies were so not Kyra. She didn't do the pick-me-up-and-kiss-me-senseless thing. Up until college, she'd been a hard-core tomboy for goodness' sake, thanks to her brothers. Yet sitting on this counter, her long skirt pushed up as Luke's hands roamed her thighs, she couldn't even handle how hot the moment was.

"Kyra," Luke breathed between kisses. She wanted to answer him back. Had planned to say his name, too. Yet she was feeling too many emotions all at once to do anything other than soak in the moment with him.

Luke broke the kiss first and rested his forehead against hers. "Do you want this to go any further?"

She nodded. "Yes. Hell yeah."

"Then we have to go to the bedroom," he said with a laugh. "I don't have a condom down here."

"I can't wait that long." Kyra looked around the bar for her purse and spotted it. She pulled out a condom and tossed it to him. "We're good."

He looked from the condom to her. "Did you expect this would happen tonight?"

She shook her head. "No, but I figured it would happen sometime on this trip, so I wanted to be prepared. Now are you gonna keep talking or are you gonna help me off this counter and onto that soft-looking rug down there."

Luke smiled before kissing her again, his lips not leaving hers as he lifted her off the counter and gently placed her on the rug in his living room. Kyra felt like she could feel him on every part of her body as they were lying there, kissing and touching in a way they never had before.

When Luke leaned up to remove his shirt, Kyra's hands went to his pants. She unbuckled his jeans and helped him slide them down his hips, leaving him in only his boxers. She took a moment to admire his delicious-looking stomach, strong thighs and overall manly physique.

"You've always looked good," she said. "But this…" She motioned up and down. "This body is on another level."

"Thank you," he said with a laugh. "I've been working on it."

"It shows," she replied, removing her shirt without warning. Luke's eyes widened as she stood to unzip her skirt and slid it down her hips, leaving her in only her black lingerie set.

"Damn," he said, kneeling to place soft kisses on her stomach and thighs. "You look amazing." Instead of responding, she unhooked her bra and tossed it to the side with the rest of her clothes.

Luke visibly swallowed. "Was not expecting that." She slid off her panties next. "Was expecting that a little more after the bra," he said, causing her to laugh. The laugh didn't last long because Luke was pulling her down to the couch instead of the floor and widening her legs.

"What are you doing?" she asked, the question dying on her lips the moment she felt his tongue teasing her nub. She expected him to take it slow because this was their first intimate moment together, but Luke clearly hadn't gotten that memo because he was swirling his tongue and causing her to buck off the couch, showing no remorse for the way she was panting over how good it felt.

"Luke," she whispered, trying to push his head away and pull it closer all at the same time. He hadn't even been pleasing her long, and already she felt like she would burst if she didn't have an orgasm soon. "I can't take it."

"You can," he said, dipping his tongue even farther. The strokes of his tongue increased and sent her overboard as her orgasm erupted faster than she'd been prepared for. When she finally came down from the pleasure, Luke finally stood, a cocky look on his face.

"I'll never forget your orgasm face," he said.

"Ugh, please do. I'm sure it was horrible."

"It was beautiful," he said, helping her to the floor and putting on the condom. He planted her with a serious look.

"What's wrong?"

"Are you still a virgin?"

She laughed. "Hell no. I got tired of waiting for a man who was convinced we shouldn't be together, so I gave it up to the next sucka."

Luke frowned. "That was a low blow."

"And the truth," she muttered, placing a soft kiss on his neck. "Now we can reminisce more about all the ways you passed up on the best woman you've ever known, or we can participate in an activity that allows us to get naked and behave like savages. Personally, I think we've talked enough for one night."

"I've always preferred sweatier activities," he said.

She smirked. "Good choice." And just like that, he thrust inside her, causing her words to get caught in her throat. Inch by inch, he branded her, marking territory that as far as she was concerned was already his years ago. She'd compared every man she'd dated to Luke. None of her exes had measured up to the man she'd never been with, but always imagined she would.

Luke had no idea the way he'd impacted her life, but now wasn't the time for her to dwell on that. Now it was time for her to focus only on the pleasure he was bringing her way. When he was fully inside her, he stilled. Both of them breathing a sigh of relief that they were finally both in the right place at the right time of their lives.

"This means everything," Luke whispered. "Thank you."

She closed her eyes at his words. "You're welcome," she finally said as she began to move her hips. For a second, she thought Luke wasn't going to join in, preferring to stay still a bit longer. Thankfully, he put her out of her misery and began meeting her movements. Soon he was running the show and all Kyra could do was soak in every moment of it.

She wasn't sure how long she lasted, but her next orgasm snuck up on her quick and fast, her warning for Luke to get his first falling on deaf ears. She convulsed as her orgasm shook her to her core, causing her to cry out his name. She was thankful that Nash wasn't in the house to hear how unusually loud she was being. As the tremors subsided, she wasn't sure she could even take much more because every single nerve in her body felt alive. So she was thankful when Luke grunted and pulled her even closer as he welcomed his own release, the moment being much more erotic than any Kyra had ever had in her life.

Using his upper-body strength, he stayed positioned above her, careful not to crush her. "Are you okay?" he asked.

"Perfect," she replied, the sincerity in his eyes touching her heart. She pulled his head back down to hers and kissed him passionately, hoping that he understood how much this moment meant to her without her having to say the words. Judging by the way he kissed her back, he knew.

"Round two?" she asked, surprising herself. She wasn't the only one surprised as Luke looked at her, his eyes wide.

"Are you sure you don't need a break?"

She shook her head. "Nope." This time, when she kissed him, he was smiling and shaking his head at the same time.

Chapter 12

Kyra would have paid good money to see city-boy Luke out on the water fishing with Uncle Ralph, but she'd passed on the opportunity. As amazing as last night was and as much as she wanted to spend it in bed all day with Luke, she knew he needed some quality time with his uncle.

So instead, she'd decided on another mission. One that she hoped would help her traveling companions.

"What are you doing here?" Nash asked.

"I asked Maceo to give me a ride to the same hotel he'd dropped you off."

Nash stood aside and motioned for her to come inside. "How did you find my room number?"

Kyra shrugged. "A little flirting, a little French and voilà."

Nash raised an eyebrow. "Since when do you know French?"

"Since I picked up some words to help me communicate with those who may not speak English. Now are we gonna debate all day or are you going to let me be a friend and help you."

Nash took a seat on the edge of the bed while Kyra took a seat at the only chair in the room. "Help me with what?"

"Help you not spend the rest of the vacation sulking in your feelings."

"I'm entitled to some time to think," he said.

"I get that. I just want to make sure that you also realize this is the best time for you to get some of those answers you need. Ms. O'Connor may not be able to tell you exactly what you want to know, but she's a sweetheart and if you want to know more about your background, she'll be able to tell you the St. Lucian ways. Plus, this is still the country where your birth father was born and raised, meaning it's in your blood. Get to know your people."

Nash was silent for a few minutes until he finally said, "You're right. I should make the most of being here. It's just, sometimes I get frustrated when I think about how different my life could have been if I'd grown up with Luke. If his dad would have chosen to be in my life. If my birth mother would have chosen to keep me. It almost seems wrong to have had a good life but still wonder 'what if?'"

"I think that's a natural reaction," Kyra said. "We live in a society where we're always thinking about what could have happened or should have happened. When, honestly, we should be paying attention to what is, not missing moments that may otherwise seem unimportant."

Nash nodded his head. "You know, that sounds like something Luke would say."

Kyra laughed. "Yeah, well, he's a lot like my brother Taheim in that way. The two of them together probably rubbed off on me."

"Probably," he said, eyeing her with a curious look on his face.

"What?" she asked.

"Not sure," he replied. "Something seems different about you." He looked her up and down again. "I know what it is." Subconsciously, Kyra ran her fingers through her hair, thinking there was no way he would guess. "You and Luke finally had sex, didn't you?"

"What?" she gasped. "Why would you say that? And what do you mean 'finally'? I think you've been in this hotel room too long already."

Nash lifted an eyebrow. "Damn, Luke didn't waste any time putting on the charm. And when I say 'finally,' I mean the two of you are good together and I know you both have feelings for each other, so it's nice to know y'all had a good night."

Kyra shrugged. "What if the night wasn't all that great?"

"Uh, was it not great? Because I don't mind kicking my brother's ass if he did something stupid."

She smiled. "I appreciate that, but there's no point in lying. So yeah, we finally had sex and it was pretty damn amazing."

"It always is when feelings are involved," he said. "Or so I've heard."

Kyra dropped her head into her hands. "We haven't really talked about things, so I have no idea where we stand. But today isn't about me, it's about you."

"Nah, this is more interesting," he said. "I know I warned you not to hurt him, but I don't want you getting hurt, either. This is probably breaking bro-code, but he talks about you a lot and if he finally made a move, it wasn't a temporary thing. When Luke commits to something, he does so fully. When the time is right, y'all will talk it out."

Kyra lifted her head. "Thanks, Nash. I'm sure whatever it will be, it will be. In the meantime, I'm trying not to make a big deal about it."

"But it is a big deal," he said. "Luke knows that, too. I didn't know y'all back then, but something tells me that you two were going to end up together in some way eventually. If it's happening now, it's happening at the time it should."

"Wow, look at you," she teased. "Being all prophet like and whatnot."

He popped his collar. "You know me. I try my best."

"Okay, Nash, I see you."

They started talking about random topics, Kyra hopeful that the light conversation eased Nash's mind after all the deep thinking he'd been doing. She was glad when he walked her to the door and finally told her, "Thanks for this. I really needed it. And you're right, I'll call Luke later and take advantage of this chance to get to know more about our family and St. Lucia."

Kyra gave him a quick hug goodbye. "I think that's a great idea. And if at any time, you need to talk to someone who's not related or semirelated to you, just let me know."

Nash laughed. "Are you, though? Not related. Because I gotta admit, it kinda feels like you're my brother's wife giving me advice right now. I'm getting mad sister-in-law vibes."

"Wife? Ha!" *Oh, how many times I've dreamed about being that man's wife.* It was sad when she thought about it. Completely unhealthy. Out of nervousness, she started to awkwardly laugh. "Boy, please. How about you just admit that our friendship is blossoming and leave it at that."

"Deal," he said with a smirk. "But when y'all do end up together, remember this conversation because I plan to tell you I told you so."

Kyra shook her head. "I can't wait to meet someone you like so I can tease you."

"Hate to burst your bubble, but I've never been a one-woman kind of guy and I accepted that years ago."

"That doesn't mean there isn't a woman out there crushing on you," she explained.

"Nah," he said. "I'm clear up front with any woman I'm feeling, so they know the deal."

"Do you hear yourself?" she asked. "Men are so dense sometimes."

Nash stuck out his arms. "I'm just spitting facts. I even brought two girls to prom and they were cool with it."

Kyra shook her head. "And just when I thought we were getting somewhere in this friendship, you do something to remind me that you're an idiot. I'm not knocking the game because I've been known to be a bit of a playa in my day, but Nash, just because you think you're laying out the rules doesn't mean they're being followed."

Kyra spent the next hour debating with Nash the pros and cons of playing the field. And just like most topics they discussed, they couldn't agree on much. Kyra left the hotel thinking that Nash had nailed one point right on the head… This thing—whatever it was—between her and Luke had been a long time coming, and for the first time in years, everything felt perfect.

Luke glanced at his phone for the tenth time in the past hour, wondering when Kyra was going to get home. He was on one of his favorite places in his home—his rooftop. But his mind couldn't settle until he saw Kyra after the night they'd had.

He'd had a great day with his uncle and his mom and she'd picked up on his attraction to Kyra right away. In fact, she told him he'd always known, which didn't surprise him. A part of him thought a person would have had to have been blind not to catch the way he started looking at Kyra the older they got.

Except Taheim. He wasn't sure if his best friend just chose to ignore it, knowing Luke would never cross that line, or if he'd been oblivious. When they'd had the conversation about him never messing with his sister, they'd also been talking to their friend Jaleen and others. Taheim had seemed to be talking like any big brother would, but looking back, Luke wasn't sure if he'd actually had a clue. Even Kyra's brother Ajay had picked up on it once and called him out a few years back at Taheim's wedding, but Luke had denied it. Mainly because he'd been in a serious relationship at the time and thinking about Kyra would have been heading down a bad path.

He glanced at the time again, thinking she should have been home by now. Unable to help himself, he called Maceo again.

"Yes, Luke," he said dryly.

"Did you pick up Kyra yet?"

"This is crazy, you know," Maceo said. "You've been calling me most the day. The only reason I told you that I dropped her off at Nash's hotel was so that you wouldn't worry. Not so you could blow up my phone."

"Sorry, man. Just wondering where she's at."

Maceo sighed. "You know, after this trip—better yet, *on* this trip—you better tell Kyra how you feel because holding in your feelings for this long ain't healthy."

"It hasn't been that long," Luke lied.

Maceo snorted. "Brotha, who are you kidding? You think I don't remember you coming to St. Lucia and going on and on about this woman you'd known since you were younger who you compared every woman you've ever dated to? You've been in some pretty serious relationships and you've never brought any of them to St. Lucia. Yet you brought Kyra."

Luke grew quiet, then said, "I see your point. I'll talk to her before we head home."

"Thank God," he mumbled. "And by the way, I dropped her off there about twenty minutes ago."

"She's here?" Luke asked, getting up from his chair.

"Yeah, she's there. Seemed just as anxious to see you, too, if it helps."

Luke got off the roof and went into his house, finally spotting Kyra outside by the pool, sitting in one of the lounge chairs. "Found her. Thanks, man."

Maceo laughed. "Anytime, man."

Luke hung up and walked outside, noting that she seemed to be watching the sunset.

"It's beautiful, isn't it?" he asked.

She grabbed her chest. "Jesus, you scared me! I saw

the car, but couldn't find you, so I thought you went on a walk or something."

"I was on the roof," he explained. "Thinking about you and wondering when you'd get here."

She smiled. "I've been thinking about you, too. Nash says hi by the way and that he'll be here tomorrow."

Luke nodded. "I'm glad you went to talk to him. I think he needed a friend."

"He did," she said. "And he's fine. Just needed a moment to reboot."

Luke sat down on the lounger beside hers. "My mom told me to tell you hi as well and that she's glad we finally stopped ignoring our feelings toward one another."

Kyra's eyes widened. "You told your mom about last night?"

"Hell nah, but she said she could tell something was up between us when we were at her place."

"But we hadn't even had sex yet when we were over there."

"Our relationship started changing way before that," he told her, lightly running a finger up and down her arm.

She glanced down at his hand. "Yeah, that's true. But it's still crazy to me to think that last night happened after all this time. A few years ago, I'd finally accepted the fact that you and I would never be together."

"I thought you'd come to that conclusion after the night of your twenty-first birthday."

"Nope," she said. "I was hurt as hell, but I didn't finally drop it completely until Taheim and Winter's wedding."

Luke thought back to their wedding and couldn't

think of anything that happened. "Why was that the turning point?"

Kyra sighed. "Right before their wedding, I'd been hanging out with my girl Cheyanne and she'd told me that there was a friend of hers that she wanted me to meet. She'd barely had time to warn me who I was meeting before your ex-girlfriend popped up. Apparently, Cheyanne had just found out that her coworker was dating you."

"Crap," Luke said. "You must mean Meeka, right? We'd just started dating. I think we were only like a month in. I almost didn't even bring her to the wedding, but she'd been going through a lot and needed a break, so I took her as my plus-one."

"I know," Kyra said. "She told me all about you when we met and even though I admitted that I knew you through my brothers, I refrained from acting like I'd always looked to you like a friend, too."

"Cheyanne knew how you felt about me?" he asked.

Kyra nodded. "Yeah, she did. But just like any friend would, she was pissed that I still seemed hung up on you despite how you'd treated me years prior. She said she'd been talking to Meeka at work and found out she'd be at the wedding. She didn't want me to be blindsided. Plus, she didn't want me to hold out hope for a relationship that may never happen."

"I get that," he said. "But Meeka and I weren't that serious back then."

"It didn't matter," Kyra said. "Meeka was a little on the crazy side, but in a good way. She was my kinda girl and we all had fun that night. Eventually, I asked her how old she was and when I realized she wasn't that much older than me, I suddenly got very annoyed.

I mean, here I was hanging out with a pretty great woman, who even a month into her relationship seemed crazy about the same man I'd had a crush on growing up. I don't know what came over me, but at the end of the night, I told Cheyanne that I was done chasing after a dream relationship that would never happen. I needed to move on and, unfortunately, that meant letting any ideas I had about me and you die."

"That's why you were acting so nonchalant at the wedding, right?" Luke asked. "I hadn't seen you in so long and I'd been excited to finally catch up and apologize in person, but you were chumming it up with Meeka and Cheyanne most the day and it felt strange trying to steal your attention away given the circumstances and the fact that you were connecting with my current girlfriend. She was the only one you never disliked."

"She wasn't the type to get threatened," Kyra said. "Her and I clicked instantly, so, yeah, I didn't dislike her and she didn't dislike me."

Luke smiled. "Even though it was nice to see y'all getting along, I was glad when we finally did get a few minutes alone."

"When we almost kissed," Kyra stated. "I'm glad we didn't."

"Me, too," he said. "Even so, I'd wanted to. Badly."

"But you've never been that guy," she said. "You're loyal. Faithful. As much as I hate to admit this, I wasn't the one who stopped that kiss, but I was the one who started it. Yet before I even got close, you stopped me. In my mind, it was going to be a goodbye kiss, but it would have been messed up on so many levels."

"I was there, too," he said. "It took two to almost kiss."

Kyra shook her head. "Sort of. It was mainly on me. Which is why I decided to own up to my feelings, and before you left the wedding, I pulled Meeka aside and confessed to my crush on you, but told her that I wanted what was best for you and that what was best at the time was you being with her."

Luke's eyes widened. "I had no idea you told her that. She never said anything to me about that conversation."

"That's because she's cool as hell," Kyra said. "She hugged me after and said under different circumstances, she could see us being friends. She didn't give me a look of pity like I was prepared for and I respected her for that. Instead, she promised that for however long your relationship lasted, she would do what she could to make you happy, which made me happy."

Wow, I had no idea. "That explains a lot," Luke said. "Back when we were together, I was ready to propose to Meeka. She checked off every box I had. She was funny, outgoing, always the life of the party. Knew how to make me smile when I was having a bad day. Pushed my buttons in ways I desperately needed. We were complete opposites, but it just worked. The only thing that didn't work was the fact that she and I weren't meant to be each other's forever."

Kyra squinted. "What do you mean? Sounds like a match made in heaven to me."

Luke thought back to the time he was with Meeka. "I told her that I'd always imagined marrying a woman just like her and she felt what I felt. She knew I was going to propose, and in true Meeka form, she stopped it before it happened."

"Wow," Kyra said. "I didn't know that."

"Many don't," he stated. "Not even Taheim. Wasn't something I wanted to explain to folks, especially since our breakup was one of the best things that could have happened to both of us."

"How so?" she asked.

"Easy. We would have been together out of convenience and comfort, not passion and excitement. Meeka told me that the reason she checked off all the boxes on my list was because I'd grown up with a girl in my life with those same qualities. She actually brought you up and said that even though her and I shared an amazing friendship, I'd never love her as much as I'd love…" His voice trailed off as he realized what he almost said next. "Anyway, by then, you'd already moved to LA, so I told myself I had to be okay with how things were."

"I left for LA because being in Chicago was too hard," she admitted. "Cheyanne was great about not having me go out with Meeka too much because it was too weird, but suddenly, Chicago felt too small given how I felt. When Winter and Autumn told me that their sister, Summer, had two of her employees opening the office in LA, I knew it was the change I needed."

"I always wondered if I was part of the reason you left," he said.

"It wasn't just you," she confessed. "I also needed to live on my own without my parents and brothers there to help me whenever I needed it. I needed to grow up and moving to LA helped me do that."

"I'm proud of you," he told her. "You've never needed your parents and brothers to thrive, but it's amazing watching you succeed in LA without any of them there to guide you."

Kyra smiled. "Thank you. It means a lot to hear you say that." She stood from her lounge chair and straddled Luke. "What does this mean for us now?"

He placed his hands around her waist. "I know we still have more to work through, but I was hoping you'd be my girlfriend."

"Uh, aren't we skipping a few steps since we haven't even gone on a date yet?" she asked with a laugh.

"I promise to date you the way a man should, but I'm also done with us ignoring this, so I just want to put it out there that I want to date you and only you. You're too important to me for us to just casually date."

She smiled. "Okay then. In that case, I'll be your girlfriend. You just have to get both my brothers' blessing first."

Luke raised an eyebrow. "You're kidding, right? I mean, yeah, I gotta talk to Taheim and Ajay because that's what a man would do, but you want me to get their permission to date you?"

"Yes," she said. "I want you to call them right now and ask. Otherwise, this can't continue."

Luke studied her for a moment, then said, "Okay, let's get this over with." He took out his phone and went to his speed dial.

"Oh, my God, stop," she said with a laugh. "I was just kidding. Didn't think you'd really call them right now."

"I told you I'm serious about this."

"Well, serious or not, I was playing." Kyra took his phone and placed it on a table nearby. "Tell you what, my parents' anniversary party in Chicago is in two weeks. Did you plan to go?"

He nodded his head. "Of course."

"Good. Then how about we take this time to figure out how this will play out and if we see it getting more serious, we'll talk to my brothers then. Deal?"

He studied her eyes, wondering if she really thought there was any way things wouldn't get serious between them. They'd waited too long. Dated too many of the wrong people. Even with the words left unspoken, it was clear to Luke that things were already pretty serious, but he'd been the one to mess it up all those years ago, so now, he'd do things Kyra's way.

"Okay," he finally said. "It's a deal."

"Good." Her hands slipped into his basketball shorts, cupping him in a way that made him harder by the second. "Now are we done talking or is there more that you want to discuss right now?"

Luke may do some stupid stuff at times, but he wasn't a fool. So he kissed his woman the way he'd wanted to kiss her all day, and for the first time, he made love on his balcony to the woman he'd had in mind when he'd told the designer to make sure it was as private as possible.

Chapter 13

"You know, when you mentioned that we'd be having our first date right now, I didn't think it would involve you making me get in the water for the third time on this trip," Kyra said, pouting as they walked on the beach. "Did you forget what I said about not liking water?"

Luke laughed. "I didn't forget, but you came to an island. Didn't you think it would involve a lot of water?"

She shook her head. "No, because I've gone to islands before and they typically include a lot of being on land, too."

"Trust me, this is not what you think it is. I just wanted to walk to get there."

She groaned. "I know your mom is spending the day with Nash, but maybe I should have joined them because I could have sworn your mom mentioned a car—meaning, they are driving to wherever they're going."

"Be patient," he said with a laugh. "You'll like it."
Twenty minutes later, they'd arrived at their destination.

"A boat?" she asked as they approached a small yacht
that was sitting on a small dock.

"Yes, I'll be taking you on a cruise around the island to show you some of the best places you can only
see by boat."

"Well, why didn't you say so?" she said. "I love cruising on the water. It's getting in the water that I have an
issue with."

They got on the boat and Luke showed her around
the vessel. "I love it," she said. "Who's driving us?"

"I am," he stated. "I've been operating boats for longer than I've been driving."

"Wow, I had no idea."

"Not surprising," he said. "I've never driven a boat
back in Chicago. Most of my experience is on the open
waters in St. Lucia. Are you nervous?"

She smiled. "Not at all. I'm actually more excited
for it now. Feels like our first real date."

"It is our first real date, but if at any time you feel
uncomfortable out on the water, let me know and we
can do something else on land."

"I think I'll be okay?" She glanced to the side of the
boat. "Can you take a picture of me before we take off?"

"Sure." He took out his phone and swiped to the camera. "Step a little to the right so I can get the mountains
in the background."

She did as she was told. "Make sure you get that side
profile of my small waistline. I'm in a competition with
a few friends."

"Uh, do I even want to know?"

"Nothing serious," she said, waving off his comment.

"Cheyanne and a couple other single friends are trying to see who can keep their waistline close to what it was when we were in our late teens and early twenties. We started it when we turned thirty."

"Women," he said, shaking his head, snapping the first shot.

Kyra rolled her eyes. "Oh, no, don't do that. Taheim told me all about that mess y'all do with seeing who can have the most toned body and abs."

Luke shrugged. "Nothing wrong with staying fit."

"Or making a competition out of it," she added.

"Okay, I see your point." After Luke was done with Kyra's mini photoshoot, he snapped a few selfies of the two of them before starting the engine. Kyra wasn't new to dating, so she'd been on some pretty great dates; however, sightseeing St. Lucia by cruising around the island definitely took the cake.

"You can't really see it, but just over those mountains is Sulphur Springs, the Caribbean's only drive-in volcano."

"That sounds cool."

"It is," he said. "Maybe before we go I could take you and Nash there." Luke continued describing more of the island. Kyra couldn't remember the last time she was so engrossed with sightseeing. St. Lucia was a beautiful place, but she knew her enjoyment had less to do with the island and more to do with the man showing her around.

"I packed lunch for us," Luke told her. "I figured we could stop by one of the smaller beaches for a little more privacy and eat there. Are you down for that?"

"I'm down for anything," she said, wiggling her eyebrows.

Luke laughed. "You always were trouble." Five minutes later, he announced they were almost at the beach. "This is one of my favorite beaches, so we'll eat here."

Kyra nodded, noise from the beach catching her attention. "Uh, are you seeing what I'm seeing?" she asked.

Luke squinted. "If what you see are several men drinking beer on the beach while wearing Santa trunks and hats, then, yeah, I see it, too." As if they knew they'd been spotted, they started yelling for Luke and Kyra to come join them in a drunken slur.

"Nah, we're good," Luke said. "Enjoy yourselves."

"Maybe we head to that other small island instead," she suggested.

"Yep." They made it to the other island fairly quickly, and like they'd hoped, it was almost deserted. "That's much better," he said, dropping the anchor.

"How are we getting to the island?" she asked.

"With the Jet Ski I have on board," he said. "I just have to lower it into the water."

"Great, another Jet Ski," she said sarcastically. "You see, this is the whole getting-into-water part that I was afraid of."

Luke laughed. "You'll be fine. I'll station it and all you'll have to do is sit on it after I get on."

"Okay," she said hesitantly. "Are you sure it's safe to leave the boat in the middle of the water?"

"We're not that far from shore. Nothing will happen to it."

Kyra nodded and followed Luke to the back of the boat while he lowered the Jet Ski into the water and got on before she did. "Can you put that backpack on?" he asked. "Everything we need is in that bag."

She nodded and put on the backpack before accepting Luke's extended hand to help her get on the Jet Ski. "We made it," she said as they neared the beach. "We didn't fall into the ocean like last time."

Luke laughed. "I was going about ten miles per hour, but I guess you're right. Glad we made it." After they got off, he pulled the Jet Ski onto the beach and walked them over to a section with palm trees that provided good shade. Then he opened the bag, pulled out a large blanket and spread it out for both of them to sit on.

"Is there food in there, too?" she asked.

"Of course." He removed two sandwiches, chips, two bottles of water and two thermoses.

"Are these Uncle Ralph's famous sandwiches?"

"Sure are. I picked them up early this morning. And I also got some of Trista's bomb rum punch since I don't remember you trying it at the lounge the other night."

"Nice! She told me about it, but no, I didn't get to try it." She glanced around the beach at a family that was on the opposite end and the greenery behind them before digging her feet into the white sand. "It's beautiful here. You can tell this beach isn't used too much."

"St. Lucia has so many beaches to choose from, but, yes, this one is secluded and just as nice as the others. Back when I was in my early twenties, Trista and Maceo told me this beach was where most of them used to run off to and have sex. You can get here by car and it's a pretty far drive from where they grew up, but I imagine having sex here would be pretty memorable."

Kyra placed her hand over her chest. "Why, Lukey, did you just suggest sex on the first date? What kind of woman do you think I am?"

His eyes widened. "No, that's not what I meant. It's

just being here with you made me realize that I've never had sex on the beach. But it wasn't to imply anything."

She laughed. "I'm just messing with you. Did you forget that we've already had sex twice before our first date?"

"I know, but I still wasn't trying to make you uncomfortable. I want this date to go perfect."

She couldn't help the smile that crossed her lips at his words. He was nervous and it was so adorable. Didn't he know that she enjoyed anything they did together? Even the activities that she'd previously never enjoyed?

What part of "I've long had a huge crush on you" didn't he understand? In some ways, she felt like she'd waited most her life for the chance to have these moments with him, and now that they were happening, she was determined to make the most of them.

Her only hesitation so far had been yesterday, when she'd found out why Luke and Meeka had broken things off. She'd had no idea she played a part and it seemed as if Luke was close to saying some words he wouldn't have been able to take back once they were out there in the universe, but he'd caught himself and she was glad for that.

If they fell in love—and not the kind of "I got love for you" that they'd always had—she didn't want to second-guess anything. She didn't want to wonder if he meant it or if it would change next week. They'd had some pretty eye-opening conversations since arriving in St. Lucia, but Kyra was curious to know how dating Luke would be in LA without the beauty of St. Lucia serving as a backdrop to the time they spent together.

And don't forget to protect your heart. It might sound crazy considering it was just their first date, but in a way, she felt like she was moving too fast. Ten years seemed like a good amount of time to get her heart back intact, but deep down, she was nervous about the possibility of being rejected by Luke again. Still, she didn't want to ruin their date by letting her insecurities about Luke steal the show.

Luke brushed some sand off his calves and shot her a sexy smile, so, of course, the only thing she wanted to do to him was precisely what he'd accidentally suggested. Kyra glanced down at where the family was, grateful to see they were gone, leaving only her and Luke on the beach under the palm trees.

She lifted herself from the towel and straddled him, loving how his hands automatically wrapped around her waist. "What are you doing?" he asked.

"Isn't it obvious?" She placed a soft kiss on the side of his neck and tugged at his red swim trucks. "Did you bring a condom?"

He nodded and unzipped the front pocket of the bag to pull out a condom. She slightly lifted her hips so that he could slip it on, and while he did so, she untied the sides of her olive-colored swimsuit.

Luke opened his mouth to say something, but she didn't give him time as she buried him deep inside her, the sensational feeling causing both of them to moan into the sky.

"I didn't expect for this to happen," he mumbled, his eyes following her every move as Kyra slowly began to rotate her hips.

She smirked. "I did."

"You shouldn't be so sexy," he said in between the kisses he was placing down her collarbone.

"We're allowed to be freaks right now," she said breathlessly. "We've waited too long to get to where we are. So, my suggestion? We make up for lost time."

Luke laughed. "I like the way you think." A few seconds later, his laughing was cut short as she adjusted her hips and began to ride him in a way that had him gripping her just so he could hold on.

Being with Kyra was everything he ever imagined it would be. She consumed his thoughts so it made perfect sense that she'd consume his body as well. Originally, Luke had thought that they'd be taking their relationship slower, but he'd underestimated the neediness they would both feel upon waiting so long to be together.

In past relationships, his exes had accused him of never fully sharing himself with them. He was a nice guy. One of the good ones, they'd say. However, there was an emotional wall Luke had built up around his heart, and although he knew his father had a lot to do with that, so did Kyra.

She'd always been the precious fruit he shouldn't have, but craved like nobody's business. A rare rose among the thorns and even though a five-year age difference didn't seem like a lot now, back then, it hadn't always felt right to have a crush on his best friend's little sister. Especially when said little sister was probably one of the hardest people in the world to ignore.

Kyra demanded attention whenever she walked into a room and since he was constantly at the Reed house, she walked in and out of plenty of rooms while he was there. He didn't think he could ever forgive himself for making her feel like she was anything less than special to him back then; however, it was true what they said. Men took longer to mature than women.

"I'm close," she whispered, tossing her head back, her moans teasing his ears.

"Me, too." He gripped her hips even tighter and angled his so that he could sink deeper into her wetness. The move must have been just what they both needed because she cried out at the same time that he groaned.

Kyra's orgasm hit her first, her convulsions bringing him even closer to the edge. Using all the strength that he had, he reached between them and found her nub, teasing her in a way that he hoped would make her come again despite the fact that she'd just had a release.

A few minutes later, Kyra was bucking in his lap, her moans turning into screams of passion as she rode out another pleasurable wave, this one bigger than the last. Luke couldn't hold on after that and he soon followed her, releasing his own pleasure, his grunts loud and foreign to his ears.

"I think we're getting the hang of this," she said breathlessly after they both began to come down from the climax.

Luke laughed. "Pretty sure no one does it better."

She smiled, gently nudging her head underneath his neck. "Pretty sure you're right."

There was so much more that Luke wanted to say. Like the fact that the reason it felt so freaking good was because when it was right, it was right. Kyra was the woman he was always meant to be with—it just took him a while to get on board. Now all he had to do was convince her it wasn't too late for them, but rather, they were right on time.

Chapter 14

"I don't like it," Kyra said for the third time that day.

Luke rubbed his forehead. "I'm starting to think there isn't anything you will like." It was the third condo he'd shown Kyra that morning and just like the others he'd shown her earlier, and the day before, she didn't care for it.

They'd gotten back from St. Lucia four days ago and even though their dating life had been great so far, their Realtor-and-client life was anything but.

"What's wrong with this place?" he asked.

Kyra glanced to the ceiling. "Do you hear that noise?"

"What noise?"

"Those heavy-footed neighbors."

Luke stopped talking and listened, barely hearing a footstep. "They aren't that loud."

"To me they are," she said. "Nope, this won't do. What's next?"

Luke glanced at the time. "Kendrick mentioned watching tonight's football game at his place. Not sure what the women are doing, but I'm bringing Nash so he can meet them. Did Nicole mention anything to you?"

Kyra nodded. "Yeah, we're supposed to hang out at her place, too, but while y'all are in the basement, we'll be catching up on *Grey's Anatomy.* It's kinda our thing."

Luke laughed, pulling her toward him. "I'm glad we'll be in the same vicinity tonight. Is it cool if I stay at your place again tonight, or do you want some time to yourself?"

She looped her arms over his shoulders, her lips close to his. "I'm not tired of you yet, Mr. O'Connor, so you should plan on spending tonight and tomorrow morning in bed with me."

There was a smile on his lips as he kissed her the way he'd been doing since they finally started dating. And as much as he hated to admit it, she was right about the condo. Luke would never let anyone interrupt him kissing his girl, but even consumed in Kyra's bliss, he could hear the neighbors upstairs walking around.

When it got even louder, he broke the kiss. "What the hell are they doing? Jumping around?"

"I told you," she said. "It sounds like a stampede up there."

"Let's get out of here," he suggested. "I have a feeling the fellas want to ask me about you and I'm sure Nicole and Aaliyah want to do the same."

"You really think Kendrick and Bryant are going to ask if we're together?"

"Yeah, because Kendrick was already asking me a million questions when he called about the game."

"Do you think they'd tell my brothers?" she asked warily.

"I doubt it since they don't talk that much, but I'll mention it just in case."

She nodded her head. "Thank you." She placed another kiss on his lips, but it was cut short when they heard the footsteps start back again. Kyra rolled her eyes. "You're right, let's go."

"I knew St. Lucia was going to be amazing," Nicole said. "And your first date on the beach sounds really romantic."

"You can tell he's so into you," Aaliyah added. "His face was glowing when the two of you walked in."

She'd only been at Nicole's place for the past half hour, but it seemed *Grey's Anatomy* was the last thing on their minds. They'd begun questioning her and Luke the moment they walked into the house.

Nash hadn't helped them out at all and had even decided to introduce himself to the group so that they wouldn't have to divert their attention away from grilling her and Luke. It had worked for a couple of minutes, but then, the group became engrossed with getting to know Nash and, not surprisingly, he fit in perfectly.

"I can also tell how close you and Nash are," Nicole said. "I know you just met, but I would have believed you if you'd told me y'all had been friends for years."

Aaliyah nodded. "I agree. He treats you like a sister already."

"He's a pain in my side," Kyra corrected. "Like the

brother I never wanted because I already have two of those."

Nicole adjusted herself in her chair. "Speaking of brothers, when do you plan on telling yours that you're dating one of their friends?"

Kyra sighed. "Honestly, I doubt Ajay will care. Sometimes he treats me more like an adult than Taheim does. However, I'm dreading Taheim finding out. I haven't told Luke this because I don't want him to freak out any more than he already is, but I'm really nervous about this coming between them. Taheim was clueless about my feelings for Luke growing up and he treats me like a little girl sometimes."

"Luke doesn't seem like he's freaking out to me," Aaliyah said.

"He doesn't, but I know him. Taheim is his best friend. And the last thing he'd want to tell his best friend is that he's sleeping with his sister."

"Well, yeah, if Luke says it like that, it won't be good," Nicole stated. "But anyone around the two of you can tell it's more than that, so if he handles it the correct way, Taheim will understand."

Kyra sighed. "He has to understand because it has taken me way too long to get to this point with Luke for Taheim to mess it all up."

"I'm loving this new you," Aaliyah said, waving her hand up and down at Kyra. "Before you left for St. Lucia, you were so confused about you and Luke. And now you're ready to defend your relationship with your mind to anyone who comes between the two of you, whether it's your family or not. It's so Romeo and Juliet."

Kyra leaned to Nicole and whispered, "Uh, has she been watching more classic romance movies lately?"

"It's the worst," Nicole confirmed. "She was bad enough before she was pregnant, but Bryant said all she wants to do is watch sappy films and cry about you. And we both know Bryant is not the type to watch that cheesy mess."

Aaliyah waved a hand. "Hey, I'm right here. I can hear you both, you know."

"We know," Nicole replied, deadpan.

"For the record, Bryant can be a sap sometimes, too, so he happily watches those movies with me."

"No, he doesn't," Kyra said with a laugh. "But he loves you and your sappy romantic pregnant self, so your husband is willing to do whatever he can to make you happy."

"And I make him happy in other ways, too." She grinned and shook her feet like a little kid. "You know, pregnant sex is the best sex."

Nicole shook her head. "Kendrick and I tried that and it didn't go too well once I got to be six months pregnant."

Aaliyah perched up in her chair. "There's a trick to it that helps him get deep without your stomach being in the way. As soon as Bryant and I figured it out, we've been making love that way ever since."

As Aaliyah and Nicole dived into a conversation about pregnant sex and post-baby sex, Kyra took the time to let her thoughts breathe for a moment. She hadn't had a chance to really think about everything that transpired in St. Lucia since they'd returned, but her gut was telling her she needed to have a plan of action for when she and Luke went to Chicago next week.

Their relationship was really beginning to take shape and, yeah, she wanted to act like a big girl in front of her friends, but deep down, she was also coming to terms with the fact that she'd been running from serious relationships since Luke's rejection.

Now that he was texting throughout the day and randomly dropping off lunch to the shop, or letting her talk to his mom via FaceTime when she called and they were together, everything was beginning to feel *very* real.

Tread carefully, girl. She'd spent years giving her friends advice and convincing them to follow their hearts, so it was time for her to do the same. If only she could stop her inner thoughts from creeping in just when things were starting to get good.

"Yeah!" the men yelled when the team they were rooting for made a touchdown. Since he'd arrived, they'd been engrossed in the game, which Luke appreciated since he hadn't expected to walk right through the door and be questioned about his relationship with Kyra.

However, now that it was halftime, he noticed Kendrick and Bryant exchanging looks and Nash smirking like he knew what was coming.

"I'm guessing St. Lucia was really good for you and Kyra," Kendrick said.

Luke nodded. "Yes, it was pretty good. No complaints."

"So y'all are together, right?" Bryant asked. "Dating and all?"

Luke laughed. "Yeah, man, we're together. It's been a long time coming if you ask me."

"He's downplaying it," Nash said. "At first, this dude was stumbling over his words when we picked up Kyra for the airport and the awkwardness continued until the two of them finally acknowledged that what they had was more than friendship. I'm telling you, fellas, I felt like cupid out there."

"Bro, you didn't do anything," Luke said. "Except annoy Kyra."

Nash shook his head. "Not true. I gave her some good advice on this trip. I was something like a counselor." Kendrick and Bryant laughed.

"We should have left you back in St. Lucia."

"You already know I loved it there, so that would have been fine."

Luke smiled at Nash's statement since he had wanted so badly for his brother to enjoy St. Lucia and, luckily, everything had worked out. His mom had even told Nash that he felt like a son to her since the two of them bonded after spending the day together. Uncle Ralph and Trista had expressed the same sentiments. St. Lucians had welcomed Nash with open arms and even though he didn't get some of the answers he'd wanted, Luke saw a sense of acceptance and appreciation from Nash that he hadn't seen before. *Which is why you need to be honest about everything.* Luke knew he needed to circle back to Nash about their father, but things had been going so good, he'd been putting it off. But seeing Nash fit in so well with everything in his life, Luke knew the longer he waited, the harder it would be to talk to Nash.

"Have you told her brothers yet?" Kendrick asked.

"Nah, I haven't. Kyra and I are going to tell them next weekend after her parents' anniversary party."

"I heard about that," Bryant said. "My dad and Aaliyah's aunt are going."

"I'm not surprised," Luke said. "Folks tend to move out of Chicago, but y'all know how it is. We tend to stick together regardless." Luke cleared his throat. "Which brings up the fact that I hope you fellas can keep my relationship with Kyra under wraps until we can tell her family?"

"Say no more," Bryant said. "We've all been there. That's your business to tell, not ours." Kendrick agreed and Luke thanked them both.

"Seriously, though, I'm proud of you for making things right between you and Kyra," Nash said. "I may tease you both, but it's nice to see you together. Don't worry about what her family will say because anyone can tell you two are good together."

Luke smiled. "Thanks, man. I'm still surprised we're together after all this time. This feels differently than my other relationships. It feels like I'm finally with the woman I'm supposed to be with."

"I know the feeling," Kendrick said. "It was like that with me and Nicole, too. I fought my feelings for her for a while, but when I finally accepted them, there was no turning back."

"Aaliyah and I were a little different," Bryant stated. "I knew she was it for me a while before she even decided if she liked my ass or not. I still fought it when my feelings slapped me in the face, but I'm so glad she's mine."

The room got quiet, each man thinking about the woman who'd stolen their heart, until Nash broke the moment when he said, "Damn, y'all could be the poster men for dudes like me who don't want to settle down for fear of becoming soft. These women have y'all in here talking about feelings and emotions during halftime instead of drinking beer and catching up on sports news."

Kendrick looked to Bryant, who shrugged. "You're right, man," Bryant said, taking a swig of his forgotten beer. "Aaliyah is hormonal right now and I swear,

I found myself changing as a result of all the things she's been experiencing. I even caught her crying in the bathroom the other day because she had to kill an ant, and after she gave a moving speech about why the ant should have lived, I found myself damn near in tears." All the men laughed.

"Nicole was like that when she was pregnant, too," Kendrick said.

"Where is your daughter, anyway?" Luke asked.

"My mom took her to Europe for some work she's doing," Kendrick said.

"I swear, that little girl travels more than I ever did," Bryant added.

All the men nodded their heads in agreement as Kendrick explained, "Nicole has been giving me the hint that she's ready for more kids. She's also been making me take all these love-language quizzes," Kendrick admitted. "She said it will make us feel more connected to one another. I knew it was bad when I almost texted you guys to ask you what your love language was."

Luke laughed. "Kyra and I are just starting out, so I haven't been faced with any of that stuff yet."

"Beware, my brother," Kendrick said. "It's coming."

The game continued and Luke appreciated having men he could talk to about Kyra, considering he couldn't talk to some of the other men in his life. Soon, the doorbell rang and Kendrick stood to get it, but he stopped when he reached the stairs.

"I got it," Kyra yelled down to the basement. A couple of minutes later, she came downstairs with a carton of drinks in tow.

"Who was at the door?" Kendrick asked.

"I had some veggie juices delivered for the ladies.

We love this stuff and can't watch *Grey's Anatomy* without it." She took a sip of her drink and walked over to Luke. "Here, try some."

Luke eyed the green concoction and shook his head. "No thanks. I think I'm good with beer."

"I get it," she said. "I used to hate it at first, but it's good for you. Much more nutritious than beer." She leaned down to whisper in his ear so that the others wouldn't hear. "And word has it, this juice increases your stamina in the bedroom."

Luke lifted an eyebrow and took the cup, taking a large sip. "Hmm, that's actually better than I thought it would be."

"Good," she said with a smirk. "Because I brought four. That one is for you." She took another cup out of the carton and took a sip as she winked at him and went back up the stairs.

"This really is good," he said to himself. He turned his head back to the game and sipped the juice. When he noticed the room was rather quiet, he turned to see three sets of eyes staring at him curiously.

"Told you it would happen sooner than you think," Kendrick said.

"And Kyra can't whisper at all," Nash added.

"Is it really good?" Bryant asked. "Aaliyah has been trying to get me to try that for months."

"You should try it," Luke said. "It takes a couple sips to get used to it." The conversation once again turned to a topic that made Nash groan in frustration.

Chapter 15

"How in the world is it time for Chicago already," Kyra said as they made their way to the restaurant her parents owned where they were meeting the family for the anniversary dinner. They'd closed the entire place for the occasion and although, normally, Kyra would have come into town early to hang out with her family, she hadn't been ready for all the questions she was sure she'd get about Luke.

The past few weeks with him had meant more than she'd ever imagined, and now they were in the city they both grew up in and all Kyra could think about was trying to keep her distance from Luke so that her family wouldn't pick up on anything.

"It will be fine," Luke said, placing a soft kiss on her lips. "It's your parents' fortieth anniversary. Everyone in attendance will be busy congratulating them and celebrating. They won't have time to think about us."

"I hope you're right," she muttered as they arrived at the restaurant and parked. Walking around the corner, Luke continued to say encouraging words, but it wasn't working. She'd feel better once they got through the dinner and told her close family that they were dating.

They opened the door to the restaurant and were welcomed by her parents and some family friends, who were all eating, drinking and celebrating.

"Sweetie, you made it," her mom said, pulling her in for a hug.

"Hey, Mom. Happy anniversary!"

"Is that my sweet pea?" her dad asked, pulling her toward him. "I've missed seeing you around here. Are you sure you aren't ready to move back home?"

"Not yet, Dad," she said with a laugh. "But I'm sure you already knew that."

He shrugged. "It was worth a try."

"Your brothers are on the second level," her mom said, looking from her to Luke. "Luke, honey. Glad you could make it."

Luke leaned down to hug Mrs. Reed. "I'm happy to be here. You know, you and Mr. Reed have always been like second parents to me."

"And you're like a son to us," she said, beaming just as Kyra's dad pulled Luke into a conversation about real estate.

"So you and Luke, huh?" her mom asked once her dad was distracted.

"We traveled here together if that's what you mean."

"That's not what I meant and you know it." Mrs. Reed leaned closer to Kyra. "You both seem happier than I've ever seen you. Took him long enough to notice how special my baby girl is."

Kyra's eyes widened. "You mean, you suspected something was going on in LA?"

"Child, please. I'm your mother. You've had a crush on that boy since you were a little girl and I suspected the reason you stopped coming around whenever you heard he was at the house visiting was because he didn't know how to accept his feelings."

"I guess it was something like that," she said. "I don't think he liked me like that back then, though. His feelings seem more recent."

"Sweetie, please tell me you're not that blind. That man has liked you for far too long and dated many women who weren't right for him to try and fill the void of the one who was. And I wasn't the only one who noticed. Your dad and Ajay brought it up to me years ago, especially after Taheim's wedding, when things seemed awkward between you. We could all tell how you two felt about each other, but it wasn't our place. Y'all had to get there on your own and judging by the way he keeps smiling over here at you while he talks to your father proves that you both have come a long way."

Kyra smiled. "Yeah, things have been pretty great in LA. We're officially boyfriend and girlfriend now."

"Aww, thanks for telling me that, baby," her mom said, giving her a hug. "Athena called me while you were in St. Lucia and gave me an update, but I told her I'd hoped you would tell me yourself when you're ready."

Kyra rolled her eyes. "I should have known you and Mrs. O'Connor were talking about us. She kept giving me this look while I was there and it made me feel like I was missing something."

"You're our kids. Of course we were talking about you. We knew the two of you would end up together eventually, we just didn't know it would take so long. Athena is ready for some grandbabies and I'm ready to see my daughter become a mom."

Kyra blinked. "Uh, moving a little fast, don't you think?"

"Absolutely not. You've known each other most your lives. In some situations, I agree, a couple should date first for a good amount of time before moving to the next step. However, in this case, sweetie, you both aren't getting any younger. You've never felt about any man the way you seem to feel about Luke."

Kyra sighed. "Yeah, you're right. He's always had my heart."

"And you've always had his. I liked that loud-talking girl he dated—um, what was her name?"

"Meeka," Kyra informed her.

"Right, Meeka. They were good together, but not the way you and Luke are together. I always thought that if they'd ended up together, he always would have wondered 'what if?'"

"He said something similar," Kyra confessed. "Do you think Taheim ever picked up on our feelings for one another?"

Mrs. Reed waved off her question. "That son of mine was too busy chasing around anything in a skirt to notice that his best friend had feelings for his sister. But now, I think he may suspect something thanks to Winter planting the seed."

"Guess that means we should talk to him."

"You should," Mrs. Reed said. "The others are waiting upstairs for the conversation."

"Dang," Kyra gasped. "They couldn't even wait until after your party."

"No, they couldn't. You know your brothers. Besides, your father and I are ready for you to talk to them so that the party can continue without any awkwardness. Your brothers are reasonable. Just talk to them."

"Okay," she said with a sigh. "I'll tell Luke we have to talk to them now."

"Good. And word of advice, please let Luke do most of the talking. Your brothers will want to hear from you, too, but they need to hear from Luke more than they need to hear from you."

Kyra nodded. "Understandable. I will."

"Is it just me or does it feel like we're walking before a jury ready to defend our relationship?" Luke asked.

"It does," Kyra said with a laugh. "But we have to get this over with and my mom told me now was the time."

Luke nodded. "I still can't believe my mom told your mom before we got a chance to."

"I'm relieved," she said. "Your mom told my mom and my mom told my dad, so they were already used to the idea before we got here.

"Is Nash going to make it to the party?"

"Not sure," Luke said. "The plan was for him to come, but we had a big corporate office stop by looking for a property ASAP. So we have a lot of work ahead of us and Nash is leading that charge. He said if he can get away, he may stop by tomorrow for the brunch."

Kyra nodded. "Sounds good. I just thought he'd make a good buffer."

Luke stopped once they were around the corner from where her brothers were at and pulled her to him. "Maybe this will help ease your tension." He dropped his lips down to hers, kissing her in a way that he hoped would distract her. He knew she'd rather be doing anything other than talking to her brothers right now, but Luke hoped she knew he would be by her side every step of the way.

Once he felt some of the tension leave her shoulders, they both took a deep breath and rounded the corner. Luke had figured that his friends would be engrossed in conversation or something, but to his surprise, when he and Kyra walked in on them, everyone glanced at them as if the topic of the hour had finally arrived.

Luke had expected Taheim, Winter, Ajay and Autumn to be there, but he hadn't expected to see his other best friend, Jaleen, his wife, Danni, and Winter and Autumn's sister, Summer, along with her husband, Aiden.

"Uh, hey, everyone," Kyra said, seemingly as surprised as Luke was.

"Hey, sis," Taheim said, standing from his seat. "Hey, Luke."

"Hey, man," Luke said, prepared for what would come next, but dreading it nonetheless.

"Care to tell me why you waited so long to tell me you were sleeping with my sister?"

Winter hit Taheim on the arm. "I told you to ask him if they were dating, not imply they're sleeping together."

Taheim shrugged. "Figured I would skip the obvious since we already know they are dating."

"How would you know that?" Kyra asked.

"Mrs. O'Connor posted a picture of y'all on her Facebook page. Anyone with a set of eyes could tell."

Luke shook his head. *Note to self: tell my mom she doesn't need to post everything on Facebook.* "I think that's a private question, but we've been officially dating for a couple weeks now. Had I not had my head up my ass, we would have started dating years ago."

"Way to tell him, Luke," Jaleen said with a laugh. In turn, Danni hit his arm as well. "What did I say?"

"Let them talk this out," Danni said. "They don't need any feedback from the peanut gallery."

"Then why are we all in this small-ass room looking like this is a scene from *The Godfather*?" Jaleen said. "Besides, Luke has had a crush on Kyra for years. I'm shocked he waited this long to get her in his bed." Danni slapped his arm again and Taheim pinned him with a hard stare.

"You're not helping, Jay," Luke said.

He shrugged. "My bad, dog. I'll take my wife's advice and shut up."

"Good idea," Ajay said, standing from his chair and walking over to them. "Unlike Taheim, I've always known how you guys felt about each other, but I think we should talk about this more privately." Ajay glanced to the group. "Do you all mind if Taheim and I talk to Luke?"

"Can I stay?" Kyra asked.

Ajay shook his head. "Nah, sis. We need to talk without. But give us ten minutes and everyone can come back in so we can enjoy the rest of the night."

Everyone began filing out of the room. "You got us kicked out," Aiden whispered to Jaleen on the way out. "This was the most entertainment I've had in months."

Once the room emptied, Luke remained standing and faced Taheim and Ajay. "It was never my intention to keep you both in the dark for long," he said. "Kyra and I just needed to do this without the input of the people who mean the most to us."

Ajay nodded. "You and I have had this conversation before. I've always known how you felt about her, so I get it."

Taheim looked to Ajay. "I didn't have a clue. Why didn't you tell me?"

"Because you still look at Kyra like she's a little girl instead of a thirty-one-year-old woman," Ajay answered. "When I talked to Luke, he was still in denial about how he really felt, so I didn't think I needed to tell you anything."

"I was in denial for years," Luke said. "At first, I blamed it on my relationship with the both of you. Then I convinced myself our age difference had more to do with it. But to be honest, I never thought I was good enough for Kyra. Not after I found out how much my dad was cheating on my mom and how much his dad had cheated on my grandmother. He said it was in our blood to suck at marriage and somewhere along the line, I started believing him."

"You were always a better man than your father was," Taheim said. "And any man who will walk out of his son's life after breaking apart his family isn't a man at all. I agree, you're not good enough for Kyra, but that's only because I feel like no man is good enough for my sister."

Luke nodded. "Fair enough. I'd be the same way if I had a sister."

"You're a good guy," Ajay added. "But I'm sure you already know how much Kyra means to us. We'd kill for her and hurt anyone who would dare hurt her. You may be fam by choice, but we wouldn't hesitate to put you in your place if you ever did anything to hurt her."

"I understand," Luke said. "I wouldn't expect anything less and I'd never do anything to purposely hurt her."

"So it is serious then?" Taheim asked. "You aren't just dating her just because?"

"It's very serious," Luke exclaimed. "She's it for me, fellas. I know it's too soon to start talking to her about marriage, but I'm dating her now with the goal of marriage in mind. I think it's never worked out with those other women because I was always meant to be with Kyra. She makes me want to be a better man and my only regret is that it took me so long to get to where I'm at with her today."

Taheim looked at Ajay, the two of them sharing a smile. "In that case, we give you our blessing to date our sister."

Luke nodded his head. "I appreciate it, man, and I'm sure Kyra will, too."

"She never needed our blessing, but we figured you would want it," Ajay said. "Kyra's gonna do what Kyra's gonna do despite how we may feel about it."

Luke laughed, his heart full now that he'd spoken with his friends. "Ain't that the truth." The three of them caught up some more before the others began coming back into the room. Luke was glad the conversation had taken place when they arrived because now he could focus on having fun and enjoying himself. However, while he enjoyed catching up on everyone's lives, he was even more grateful that he'd kept his downtown condo because he'd always imagined having Kyra up there with him, seeing the sunrise over the lake from his bedroom balcony. There was nothing like a St. Lucia sunrise and sunset, but he'd like to think his little Chicago haven was a close second.

Chapter 16

"Okay, sis, spill the details," Winter said, taking a sip of her mimosa. "We wanted to ask last night, but the group never parted long enough for us to get the inside scoop."

Kyra laughed as she looked at Winter, Autumn, Summer and Danni, who were all looking at her expectantly. Unfortunately, Nash hadn't been able to fly to Chicago, so Kyra and Luke still had no one they could redirect the attention to.

At the start of brunch, Kyra had assumed everyone would be talking about her parents' party last night, but instead, everyone was spread out at different tables and her sisters-in-law and friends had managed to corner her in a separate section.

"We've heard some of the story from Nicole and Aaliyah," Danni said. "They called to check on us and couldn't stop gushing about how cute you and Luke were."

"She's right," Summer confirmed. "Then we got here and realized that Winter and Autumn hadn't gotten to talk to you yet."

Kyra shook her head. It seemed even if she and Luke had thought they could still keep their relationship a secret, it wouldn't have worked. They were the talk of their group. "Well, since it seems to be common knowledge, I've had a crush on Luke for years. But on my twenty-first birthday, when I'd finally gotten enough courage to tell him how I feel, he rejected me in the worst way he could have." She shivered even still thinking about it.

"Men are dense sometimes," Winter said. "It's obvious that he felt the same way and couldn't handle it."

"It's obvious now," Kyra stated. "Back then, it really wasn't."

"He's clearly trying to make up for lost time," Autumn said. "He hasn't stopped looking this way since we all sat down."

Kyra glanced toward Luke, who smiled back at her. Not that she could have stopped it, but her heartbeat quickened at the sight of him.

"Y'all are too cute," Summer said. "I understand what it's like to have feelings for someone and it feel like it takes you forever to get to where you are today. It was like that with me and Aiden, too. My advice is to make the most of it now. Don't focus on the time lost, but rather, the time you have now. Together."

Kyra swallowed back some emotion. "I've been telling myself that every day, but it helps to hear a reminder. I guess a part of me is also nervous because the man I'm started to get real feelings for is the same man who broke my heart all those years ago." Kyra looked back to the women. "I won't drag out the details, but he said words to me that night that I have never forgotten. In a way, those words molded how I handled the men that came after him."

"That's a tough pill to swallow," Winter said. "Have you told Luke how much he hurt you?"

"Sort of, but I'm not sure. I wanted to spend time making him pay for what he did while he helped me find a condo and a space for the new shop. I wanted him to feel that pain I'd felt back then."

"Guess that didn't work out," Autumn said. "Or did it?"

Kyra shook her head. "I failed miserably because instead of spending time with him to make him sweat it out, it just reminded me of all the reasons I fell for him in the first place."

"Ain't that how it always goes," Danni said with a sigh. "Men walk out of our lives, drive us crazy in the process, then walk back in and all you're thinking about is how much you will make him pay, but instead, you end up falling further in love."

"Cupid is cruel," Summer added. "But now is the time for you and Luke to work through all those feelings you have. Men think that they can just proclaim their love while all we're doing is waiting for them to do so when that's not the case at all. Just like he needed time to figure out how he felt about you, you should be given that same courtesy to work through your feelings about him now."

"We all know Luke's a good man," Winter said. "But, sis, he's talking to the guys about spending forever with you. To him, he's acknowledged how he feels and he's ready to go out and buy a ring. And as sweet as that is that he finally caught a clue, you have to be okay with knowing that you are allowed to take the time you need to figure things out."

"You don't work on his time schedule," Autumn stated. "You work on yours and you don't want to go into a marriage with resentment for things that happened a decade ago, when maybe all it takes is a conversation to work it out."

"But what if he thinks we've already worked through it?" Kyra asked. "In St. Lucia, we had a conversation about that and he apologized. Honestly, ladies, he's apologized for it so many times throughout the years, that I'm starting to wonder if something is wrong with me because I can't seem to shake how I feel. I accept his apology, but a part of me is still upset for what he did and I know it makes me so spoiled for saying that."

"It doesn't make you spoiled," Summer said. "You are allowed to still be upset over something that changed who you are as a person. You don't have to apologize for needing time to figure *you* out. Too many times, women apologize for having too many emotions about a situation when we are rightfully allowed to feel whatever we want, whenever we want."

"What if what I need is to take a step back from dating?" she said, her voice cracking. "Am I completely insane for finally getting the man I've always wanted, but taking time to process everything that has happened?"

"You're not insane," Danni said. "And if Luke truly loves you, he'll understand that you need time."

Autumn placed a hand over Kyra's. "It's understandable that you need to process the fact that you and Luke have finally gotten together because you've spent the better part of your life thinking it would never happen."

Kyra took a sip of her mimosa. "We haven't said 'I love you' yet."

"That man loves you," Winter said. "And you love him. We all see it whether you've said the words or not."

"I stopped believing in fairy tales the day he rejected me," Kyra confessed. "And then up he pops into LA, making me remember all the reasons why I feel for him in the first place."

"Ugh, men," Danni said. "With their goofy grins and sexy smiles and masculine swag. I swear, if I didn't love Jaleen, I'd be ready to kill him with the mess he's always putting me through."

Autumn sighed. "Then, when life knocks you down and reminds you that you don't have everything under control, there they go, saving the day by helping you remember that you are a strong black female and were made to overcome obstacles and rise above all adversity."

"Amen," Winter said, nodding her head.

"Ditto," Summer said. "Then they make sweet love to you, making you feel more beautiful than you ever have in your life, and next thing you know, you're pregnant and pushing a small human out of your tiny hole."

Kyra was glad she'd finished her drink because she would have spit it across the table. "Uh, not there yet, guys, and based off how you described that, I think I'm good for now."

"We always think we're good," Autumn stated. "Until that test shows up positive. I love our kids, but my hips haven't been the same since I pushed those rascals out."

"But the sex is worth it, though," Winter said, a dreamy look on her face.

"Ugh, I'm trying to forget that two of you are married to my brothers."

Winter's eyes widened. "Oh, right. Glad you reminded me before I started describing what Taheim did to me last night."

"Oh, my God, I can't with you," Kyra said with a laugh. She'd been trying to get Winter to filter her sexcapade conversations since she started dating her brother.

"I can share instead," Summer offered. "Since no one is related to my husband."

Kyra nodded. "Please do!"

"Then Kyra can tell us how good Luke is in the bedroom," Winter suggested, wagging her eyebrows.

"Now that, I can talk about," she said with a smile. "Let me just say, it was well worth the wait to finally get to sample some of Luke O'Connor."

"I knew it," Autumn said with a smirk. "I bet y'all had sex first, talked after, right? Too much sexual tension to hold off on that convo."

"Wait, don't answer that," Danni said. "This calls for more drinking. Where is the waiter?" Danni glanced around. When she finally spotted him, she lifted her empty glass in the air. "Buddy, we need another round of mimosas." Kyra wasn't sure if it was because the waiter could tell that Danni meant business or if he was just a fast server, but three minutes later, they had a fresh round of mimosas and the stories started flowing.

Kyra had really needed to talk to her girls, but now that she'd gotten advice and decided to be honest, she didn't know how to act toward Luke. A part of her wanted to save the conversation for when they got back to LA tomorrow, but he'd been sweet all day, placing soft kisses on her cheek even when her family was around. And he'd made sure she'd stayed hydrated despite the fact that she'd only been drinking mimosas.

He'd even been fielding questions from her relatives all day, playing the role of perfect boyfriend, and it seemed everyone in her family had agreed. They were great together. And her sisters-in-law and friends were Team Luke, even though they also encouraged her to be honest with him about what she was feeling.

"Is everything okay?" he asked, after he'd given her a tour of his condo.

"Everything is fine," she said, taking a seat beside him on the couch. He looked like he didn't quite believe her, but he didn't push her.

"Do you want to watch a movie? I think one of the *Avengers* movies is on HBO right now."

"That would be great," she said while he flipped to the channel. They'd watched movies together while they were in LA, so she curled up into his side just like she did when they were back home. The only problem was she still couldn't ignore what was going on in her mind.

"Actually, I lied before," she said, sitting upright. "Everything isn't fine."

Luke muted the television. "What's wrong?"

Kyra sighed, trying to find her words. "How do you feel about me?" she asked.

He smiled. "I care about you more than I've ever cared about anyone in my life. Even more than that, but I'm not sure you're ready to hear the words."

"I'm not," she said. "Because my gut is telling me

that you're in love with me and the problem is, I'm in love with you, too."

"How is that a problem?" he asked hopefully. "We haven't said the words, but we know we're in love with each other. Have been for years."

"That's just it," she said. "I haven't known you felt that way for years. You only just told me how you felt about me recently. I've spent so much time convincing myself that my feelings for you were only one-sided and now, you come back into my life telling me that was never the case."

"It wasn't," he stated, taking her hands in his. "I just wasn't ready to accept my feelings."

She nodded. "I understand, but regardless, our past changed me in a lot of ways. And now that we are together, I'm just so unsure about things."

"Unsure in what way?" he asked.

She closed her eyes, then opened them to find a pair of sympathetic ones staring back at her. "This is so hard for me," she said, her voice slightly breaking. "To finally be with the man who broke my heart and changed the way I viewed every relationship after that moment is more difficult than I ever imagined it would be. How do you put your feelings aside after all this time?" she asked.

Luke studied her eyes. "I don't know. I knew I'd hurt you that night, but I guess I never knew I'd caused you so much pain."

"You did," she said, unshed tears drifting to her eyelids. But she refused to cry. She'd never been a crier and she wasn't going to start now. "You've finally realized that I'm the woman you've always been meant to be with and as much as I've waited most my life to hear that, a part of me still sees you as the man who walked out on me after I bared my soul. The man who rejected my love in a way that hit me harder than I ever could have imagined."

Luke leaned back on the couch, surprise evident in his features. "I am so sorry that I put you through that, Kyra. If I could take it back, I would."

"I know. But you can't, and honestly, I'm not sure I would even want you to. I became a woman that night. Up until then, my life had been going how I'd expected with not many twists and turns, yet you came and turned my world upside down whether you meant to or not. It's not fair of me to still be harboring these feelings toward you when you've apologized to me time and time again. But they are there, lingering beneath the surface, and I'm worried that if I don't address them, this won't go any further."

"What are you saying?" he asked, looking defeated.

"I'm saying that I need time to think," she said. "I'm not saying we have to break up, but I do need a break to figure out how to get over this."

"That's the same as breaking up," he said. "Can't we work through it together?"

She shook her head. "I need to work through this on my own. But I don't expect you to wait around for me. So date, go out, do whatever you want to do."

Luke frowned. "I don't want anyone but you, so I'll wait for you. Take all the time you need."

Kyra released Luke's hand and stood. "I'll stay at Autumn and Ajay's tonight, but I'll see you at the airport in the morning."

"So you're really leaving right now?" Luke said. "You can't just stay here tonight?"

She shook her head. "I could, but I don't think that would be good for either one of us. Just like I need time to process things, you do, too. Having me here would just be a distraction."

"It wouldn't be," he said, shaking his head. "We've spent every night sleeping beside each other since we started dating. I don't think I'll be able to sleep well ever again if you leave."

"You'll be fine," she said as she grabbed her purse and walked over to her traveling duffel, which was still by the front door. "This is hard for me, too, Luke, but I hope you'll respect my wishes. I'll text you when I get to Autumn's."

Without giving it another thought, she shut the door and began walking toward the elevator. Halfway there, she almost thought about turning back, but she reminded herself that she needed this. She owed it to herself to figure out why, after finally landing the man she'd always wanted, she was feeling a little overwhelmed by everything.

Chapter 17

"Enough of this," Nash said, cutting off the television.

"I was watching that," Luke said, reaching for the remote.

"Not anymore. You've spent the week going to work, then the gym, then sitting here watching all these horror movies every day."

"That's because horror movies have little romance," Luke said. "And when they do, one of them usually dies."

Nash shook his head. "How many times do I have to tell you that Kyra telling you she has to do some thinking is temporary. Anyone who knows the two of you knows that you will be back together in no time. You know what's not fair? Subjecting me to having to watch you pout every day."

"I don't pout," he said. "Men don't pout."

"Oh, but you do, brother, and trust me, it ain't cute."

"You don't know for sure that we'll get back together. She could decide she's done for good."

"Luke, she was hurt for years over how you rejected her, so do you both a favor and let her take all the time she needs. She's allowed to, bruh."

"I know and I told her I was cool with it, but I'm not," he said. "I don't want to get her only to lose her again. It took us too long to get to this point. And I refuse to let that man be right."

"What man?" Nash asked. "Kyra is dating someone else?"

"What? No, she isn't." Luke grew quiet, choosing his next words carefully. "Back in the day, my dad— our dad—was the first one to pick up on my feelings for Kyra. Said he noticed how I was always watching her, enjoying her company. I told him that we were just friends, which back then, we were. I mean, I was young and at one point in time, I really tried to treat Kyra as if she were a sister. Hell, for many years, she *was* like a sister to me." Luke sighed. He needed to own up to some stuff because how he treated Kyra on her twenty-first birthday wasn't the only thing weighing heavy on his heart. "I guess now is a good time to tell you that I lied before when you asked me if I'd ever suspected that he was cheating on my mom, because the truth is, I did suspect it. I even caught him a few times."

For a split second, Nash looked surprised. Then, he shrugged and said, "I figured. Had this gut feeling."

"You did?"

"Yeah, I can tell when you're lying. I figured you had your reasons for not telling me."

Luke frowned. "When your investigator found me, I was mad at myself for not questioning my dad more.

For not telling my mom what he was up to earlier. For not being the type of brother you needed me to be."

"Luke, I don't blame you for that man disowning me," Nash said. "You were a kid. He was an adult. I asked you if you suspected he'd stepped out on Athena, but I feel like I knew the answer before I even asked."

"I shouldn't have lied about it," Luke admitted.

"Nah, you shouldn't have. But we still have a lot to work on to build that trust with each other. I mean, I trust you, but I know you have your secrets just like I have mine."

"You're right," Luke said. "And I know you always say you wish you knew him, but be glad you don't. He wasn't a good man. He pretended to be and I let my friends think he was, but he wasn't."

"When I spent the day with your mom, she pretty much said the same thing."

"It's the truth," Luke continued. "He was the type of man who made you believe that if he wasn't worth anything, then you wouldn't be worth anything, either. He cheated on my mom, said my grandfather cheated on my grandmother. He made certain things seem like they were just the way of life and I knew better, but he was my dad and I wanted to keep my relationship with him intact."

"I'd probably felt the same way," Nash admitted. "Even knowing the type of man he is, I still want to meet him even though I try to convince myself I don't have to."

Luke nodded his head. "That's understandable. And even though I've mentioned it before, if you really want to track him down, I think I can. There's a few States he seems to frequent, depending on the time of year."

"I appreciate it," Nash said. "And when I'm ready, I'll let you know. In the meantime, you got to figure out a way to not let him take more from you."

Luke squinted. "What do you mean?"

"Well, you waited a while before you told your mom that your dad was cheating on her. You waited over a year to tell me that you knew our father had been cheating. You waited over a decade before you admitted to yourself and Kyra how you feel about her. Bruh, you pull the trigger fast when it comes to other aspects in your life, but the more serious the issue, the more you hold back information."

Luke sunk deeper into the couch—Nash's words were really getting to him. "You're right," he admitted. "I guess in a way, I've never wanted to see someone hurt or, better yet, I didn't want to be the bearer of bad news."

"That's not healthy, man," Nash said. "You can't go through life keeping so many secrets and carrying around so much baggage. Especially when that baggage isn't only yours to carry."

Call it brother's intuition, but as Luke looked to Nash, it was almost as if he could tell Nash knew what Luke needed to say. Like he had a feeling that the last secret Luke was keeping was important.

"I promise you, I did not think about this until a couple days ago," Luke said honestly. "But I know— I may know—" *Crap.* He couldn't even get the words out.

"You think you know who my birth mother is, don't you?" Nash asked.

Luke sighed, partially in relief and partially in guilt for not realizing it sooner. "Yeah, I think I do. That day our father had the conversation with me about Kyra, he mentioned something about wishing she was at least eighteen. It had thrown me off, but I knew what he was fishing at. She was, like, thirteen at the time, and like I said before, I really did look at her like a sister at one point. But the anger I felt when her and Taheim stopped by the house one day and I caught our father looking at her in a way he shouldn't have, it disgusted me. I never invited them over again after that."

"Understandable," Nash said, clenching his jaw. "And I feel like I'm really not prepared for what you're gonna say next."

"Want to shelve the conversation for another time?"

Nash shook his head. "Nah, keep going. I can handle it."

Luke took a deep breath. "Not only was that the day he stopped being my father, but something in me snapped. I was graduating soon, anyway, and I remember distancing myself from Taheim and Jaleen because I couldn't cope with anything." Luke cleared his throat. "When I was visiting home that summer after college, there was a woman waiting outside the house when I got there. Right away, I noticed that she was that same young woman I'd caught in the house. She seemed out of it and I didn't know if it was drugs or what, but she was rattling on about our father making her life a living hell and that she gave away the most important thing in her life because of him.

"When I asked her to explain, her eyes widened and she recognized who I was, too. Even though I wasn't trying to run her off since all I wanted was answers to my questions, she made up some lie about being a Jehovah's Witness and left. I never saw her again and I put the entire incident behind me. I truthfully have not thought about that in a while."

For a few minutes, neither brother said anything and Luke wondered if he'd laid too much on Nash too soon. However, he was grateful when Nash said, "It's because of Kyra. That's why you didn't remember."

"Huh?" Luke asked.

"Since you're five years older than Kyra, I assume growing up, liking her felt wrong, correct?"

Luke nodded. "It did."

"And knowing you, you didn't want any sign of thinking you were like our father, so you pushed that shit far from your mind."

Luke swallowed, unsure of how he should feel since he'd never heard anyone voice his biggest fear out loud before. "Yes, that's right."

Nash shook his head. "Luke, from what I've heard, you sound nothing like our father and all that asshole did was put you in a position to have to lie to those close to you. I appreciate you telling me about that woman you caught outside your house and, yeah, she could be my mother. But while I was listening to you, all I was thinking about was how unimportant both of my birth parents are right now."

Luke's eyes widened, as he was surprised by Nash's admission. "You're not upset with me for not remembering?"

Nash shook his head. "Nah, bro. I'm tired of getting upset with the wrong people. My parents are amazing and I've had a good life. The best thing to come out of learning I was adopted was meeting you and Athena. I'm not saying I'll never want to meet our father or find my birth mother, but I'm good right now with the blessings I've been given."

Nash leaned to hug Luke and he accepted the hug.

He was surprised by how mature Nash was handling everything and made a mental note to take some cues from his brother...even though he'd never tell him that.

"We can talk more about all this deep shit later, but now, you need to come up with a plan of action for how you're going to get Kyra back," Nash announced.

Luke laughed. "I thought you told me to give her the space she needs?"

"I did. But if she decides to drag this out too long, you have to win back the woman you love and convince her that you're not the same man you were years ago. Let her know that her heart is safe when it's in your hands."

Luke nodded. "Thanks, bro. I needed that wake-up call and to get that stuff off my chest."

"You're welcome. Just remember to name your first son after me. Nash is a pretty dope name."

"What if Kyra and I have a girl?" Luke asked, entertaining his brother's idea.

"Nashena after me and your mom."

Luke frowned. "Ugh, that's a horrible name for a girl. Kyra would never go for it."

"I happen to think it's a great name for a female."

Luke shook his head. "Nah, that was pretty bad."

"Okay, name her Nashay then. Or Nashika."

"Do you ever want her to get a job?"

"Low blow, bro," Nash said. "I happen to think those names are pretty damn good."

"Tell you what," Luke said. "How about I thank you by making you my best man instead because Kyra may need some convincing, but I plan on marrying that woman."

"Best man," Nash said in surprise. "But what about your friends, like Taheim?"

"Taheim is my best friend, but you're my blood. My brother. The only I got."

Nash smiled. "Thanks, man, I'd be honored." They hugged it out until Nash got a thought. "You don't think we have any more siblings running around, do you?"

Luke's eyes widened. "Damn, you never know. We could."

"Hmm. Maybe I'll get my private investigator on it when we're ready to tackle that."

Luke nodded. "Sounds like a plan."

"We close in ten minutes," Kyra yelled when she heard the front door of the boutique open.

"Kyra, is that any way to greet your mother?"

Kyra looked up from the register. "Mom, what are you doing here?" She walk-ran to the front door and gave her a hug.

"I know I just saw my baby girl, but when Winter and Autumn got back to Chicago and told me that you and Luke were taking a break, I knew I had to come out here and talk to you."

Kyra frowned. Her sisters-in-law had only been in LA for a few hours to view the new location, and not surprisingly, they loved it just as much as Kyra did.

"I know you're probably disappointed in me because we were finally together and I went ahead and ruined it."

"Sweetie, you have it all wrong. I'm not disappointed in you. I'm proud of you for realizing that you needed some time to figure out what it is that you want. If Luke isn't it, then you owe it to yourself and him to put that information out there."

"That's the problem," Kyra exclaimed. "Luke is everything I want and more, yet for some reason, I can't shake this feeling I have in the pit of my stomach, re-playing how he rejected me back when I was in college."

"I think I know why," her mom said, motioning for Kyra to join her on the bench by the fitting room. "Kyra, you've always gone after what you wanted no matter whether it be in school, or sports, or your career. Your father and I have always admired your tenacity to take life by the horns and make the most of your opportunities. When it came to Luke, you didn't tackle your feelings for him any differently than you have everything else in your life.

"You knew you wanted him as soon as you hit adolescence. Maybe even before then. Your father and I began to notice little things, like the way you'd ask him to help you with your homework. Or the way you would play in the yard with your brothers all night when Luke was with them rather than going to bed, something you never did when Luke wasn't around. And you know what else your father and I noticed?"

"What?" she asked.

"We noticed how much Luke cared for you right back. We noticed that even if he wasn't good at a subject, he would study up on it just to help you out. We noticed that when you all played in the backyard and you got so tired that you'd fall asleep in the grass, he was picking you up and bringing you inside. From what we saw, Luke never looked at you inappropriately when you were growing up, but it became harder and harder for him to ignore as you got older. By your eighteenth birthday, the boy was doing everything he could to ignore your flirting. By nineteen, he was downright rushing out the room when you were visiting from college and he was in town from grad school. At twenty, there was one time we couldn't even get him to come by the house at all. And at twenty-one, I wasn't sure what happened around that time, but I could tell something shifted between you two because that's when you started avoiding him at all costs."

"Why didn't you ever say anything?" Kyra asked.

"I figured you would talk to me if you needed to. Besides, I wanted you to distance yourself from Luke because you needed to grow on your own without chasing after that boy."

Kyra frowned. "Maybe I should have run a little faster when he popped up in LA."

"It wouldn't have worked," her mother said. "Once Luke decided to chase after you this time, you didn't stand a chance. No woman does when it comes to loving the right man."

"You think he's right for me?" she asked.

"Of course I do. You've always been right for one another. You were just in different places in your life. But now, you're at the right place at the right time."

Kyra sighed. "I thought so, too, but I can't seem to shake this eerie feeling."

"You're worried the other shoe will drop," her mom explained. "You're worried that now that you finally have him, something will happen and you'll lose him again. It's a natural reaction, but based off what I saw, you don't have to worry about that with Luke."

"How can you be so sure?" Kyra asked. "How can I know if I won't get my heart broken again?"

Her mother gently cupped her cheek. "No one can know that for sure, baby girl. Love is all about taking risks and hoping that it works out for the best. What I do know is that Luke didn't just up and decide he loves you. That boy has loved you since the day he met you. And at Taheim and Winter's wedding, even though he was dating someone, he only had eyes for you. He couldn't help it. He's always watched you. Observed you. Checked to see if you were okay. Randomly asked me and your dad how you were doing when he didn't want to ask your brothers. I'm not saying you shouldn't take the time you need to work through your feelings, but you shouldn't pass up on a great love because you're scared to put yourself out there again."

Kyra took a deep breath, letting her mom's words soak in. "I hear you, Mom. I'll definitely keep all of that in mind."

She smiled. "Good. Now that that's settled," her mother said, clapping her hands, "it's time for you to put me to work. Winter mentioned that you may be placing an offer on a new boutique soon, which means, you need help packing."

Kyra reached over and pulled her mom in for a hug. "I love you, Mom. More than anything."

Her mom patted her and ran her fingers through her hair, just as she'd done since Kyra was little. "I love you, sweetie."

Chapter 18

Luke was a nervous wreck as he waited near Santa Monica Pier for Kyra to show up. When she'd called and asked him to meet her there, he'd said yes almost immediately. Back in Chicago, he'd had no idea that taking time to think meant he wouldn't be communicating with Kyra for two weeks. Two excruciating long weeks in which he drove Nash crazy.

His phone rang, interrupting his thoughts. He'd hoped it was Kyra, but was disappointed to see it was Taheim. "Hey, T, what's good?"

"Hey, Luke, at least you sound better than you did a few days ago."

"Your sister asked to talk today, so I'm hoping it's good news."

"I think it will be," he said. "But that's actually not what I called for. Winter is pregnant again and though it's too early to tell if it's a girl or a boy, I was hoping you could be my child's godfather."

Luke stopped pacing. "Me? Are you sure?"

"Of course I'm sure. You're one of my best friends and my child would be lucky to have you as a godfather. And I guess I should let you know that we plan on asking Kyra to be the godmother."

Luke smiled. "This truly means a lot to me, man. Yes, I will be your child's godfather and I promise to take the responsibility seriously." Luke knew how careful Taheim and Winter had been in choosing godparents for their other two kids, so he could only imagine that they had chosen him and Kyra just as carefully.

"I needed this news," Luke said. "You called at the right time."

"I had a feeling," Taheim stated. "Just remember, Kyra loves you. Before you ask, no, she hasn't told me anything, but I know my sister. You two are going to end up together. Just keep your head up."

"I will, man," Luke said. "I just miss her so much. As soon as I see her, I'll feel better."

Taheim laughed. "Man, it's still hard hearing you talk about her like this. I made myself sick the other day thinking about everything I know you've done with other women, realizing that now, that woman is my sister."

"What do you want to know?" Luke teased.

"Not a damn thing," Taheim said, practically yelling into the phone. "In fact, I'm mad I even started the conversation down this road. How about you just give me a call later after you see Kyra."

"Okay," Luke said with a laugh. "Thanks again for this great honor."

"You're welcome, Luke. Thank you for accepting the responsibility." Luke said his goodbye and hung up the phone, then resumed his pacing. Five minutes later, he was still too anxious to stand still.

"I can't wait much longer," he said to himself as he glanced at his phone.

"You got here too early," a voice said from behind him. He turned to find Kyra wearing a white crop top and long black maxi skirt. She was looking so delicious, he wished they could skip the talking part and go straight to the kissing part. "Do you want to take a walk?" she asked.

He nodded. "Sure." Luke felt nervous, as if he wasn't meeting with someone he'd known most of his life. Awkward or not, he was happy to see her. "I've really missed you," he confessed.

She smiled. "I've missed you, too."

Okay, that's a good sign. Luke felt himself stand a little taller with her admission. They walked in comfortable silence for a few minutes before Kyra broke it.

"Do you remember about a year before Taheim met Winter, it was around Christmastime and you stopped by my parents' house to drop off a bottle of rum?"

Luke thought back to that day. "I remember. I'd gone to Puerto Rico for business and brought back a really nice bottle of rum for your parents that I got from the Bacardi factory."

"They were excited to see you since it had been almost a year since you'd dropped by," she said. "I remember the surprised looks on their faces when you called."

"You were there?" he asked in surprise. "I don't remember you being home when I was there."

"I'd been visiting that day, too, but I told them I was

leaving before you got there. I was still really hurt back then and it was pretty raw. I didn't think I could face you without getting pissed off all over again, so I dipped off. Or at least tried to."

"You stayed?" he asked.

"More like watched you from the backyard window," Kyra said with a laugh. "Looking back, it seemed pretty creepy to watch you from afar, but I'd missed you and needed to see you even if you didn't see me."

Luke nodded. "I know the feeling. I hate to say it, but I'd only visited your parents because I'd missed you and you still weren't talking to me."

"Really?" she asked. "You'd missed me?"

Luke sighed. "Kyra, when I'm not with you, I always miss you. That's never changed no matter what state we live in. I love your parents, but I was missing you like crazy and I didn't want to keep asking your brothers about you because I figured they would catch on to how I felt. So I'd ask your parents and they were so proud, they always kept me updated. For a while, I wondered if they'd picked up on anything, but I'd stopped myself from asking."

"They did," she said. "They picked up on our attraction, but my parents weren't the type to make things awkward so they left it alone."

"I was really glad when we ran into each other downtown," he said. "It felt like fate had been on my side."

"I'd felt the same way," she admitted. "I remember stumbling over my words because I didn't know what to say to you. I'd heard that you and your dad had grown distant, so it seemed like a safe topic to bring up, but I regretted it the minute I said anything."

"You shouldn't," he told her. "That day, I'd needed to

vent about him. To say how I really felt without having to explain too much. When you hugged me that day, I couldn't remember ever needing a hug that badly before. I knew you were still upset at me, but you put your feelings aside to offer me comfort."

"I did, but I was thinking back to that moment earlier today and I realized that there were so many moments in our lives where we were there for each other in ways we never really paid attention to." She cleared her throat. "Luke, I said I needed some time to think and to gather my thoughts and I appreciate you for giving me the space to do so."

Oh, no, he thought. *This is it. She's either willing to make it work, or she wants to end it for good.* Luke couldn't imagine it being the latter. He felt like they were just getting started. There was so much more life to live together and he'd never forgive himself if he didn't tell her that.

"I love you," he blurted out. "And not just in the we've-known-each-other-most-our-lives kind of way, but I'm in love with you and I have been for longer than I can remember." He stopped walking and stood in front of her. "Kyra, these past couple weeks have been some of the toughest weeks I've ever had because all I wanted to do was spend that time with you. There aren't enough apologies in the world for letting you chase me for all those years without me chasing you back because, baby, I wanted to chase you more than you realize. You deserve to be chased every damn day because you're special and loved. More important to me than anyone in my life."

Her eyes watered, which Luke hoped was still a good

sign. "That was beautiful," she said breathlessly. "And much better than the speech I was going to give."

He studied her eyes. "Give it, anyway."

"Okay," she said. "Luke O'Connor, I want to thank you for being patient with me, but I don't need any more time apart because all I've learned in these past couple weeks is how much I love you and want to spend as much time with you as I possibly can."

He grinned, finally feeling the tension leave his shoulders. "Why didn't you start with the I-love-you part?"

She shrugged. "I don't know. It just came out that way. Do you want me to take it back? Because I can arrange that, too."

Luke laughed. "There's my sarcastic girl. I almost had you in tears. Wasn't sure who I was dealing with for a minute."

She punched him in the shoulder. "Keep teasing me and I won't give you the surprise I had for you today."

He raised an eyebrow. "Is this a surprise I can watch? A surprise I can eat? Or a surprise I can touch?"

"All three depending on how you look at it," she replied, waggling her eyebrows.

"Damn, what are we still doing walking around this pier then?"

She laughed. "Actually, I really wanted to ride the Ferris wheel. Don't ask me why, but I was thinking about how this conversation would go and thought ending it on the Ferris wheel would be nice. Especially since the entire thing is decorated in Christmas lights! I mean, who gets to ride a Ferris wheel decorated in holiday lights?"

"Random, but I'm down for it," he said, pulling her to him. "As long as I get to spend the rest of the night kissing you senseless to make up for all the time we missed."

"How many kisses would you say we missed in a day?"

"Um, at least one hundred a day," he said.

"Guess that's a whole lot of making up," she stated. "Tell me, do these kisses all have to be on my face? Or are there some other places you can kiss to make up for lost time?"

"Oh, there are definitely some other places in need of my intimate attention." His eyes dropped down to her lips. "But for now, I'm going to kiss the pair I've been looking at since you got here." With that, he dipped his mouth to hers, capturing her lips in a hungry kiss that had him groaning aloud.

He heard a few people clap and a few others tell them to get a room, but Luke didn't pay them any mind. He was too busy kissing the woman who owned his heart. The woman who'd helped him realize what it meant to not just have love for someone, but to truly love someone.

It almost seemed like they'd had to go through every obstacle they'd faced in order to ensure that they'd end up in this exact moment at this exact time.

"Mmm, that was nice," Kyra whispered against his lips. "Maybe we should skip the Ferris wheel and head back to my apartment to pack?"

"Pack? Where are you going?" he asked.

"Did you forget my lease to my apartment was up last week? You didn't finish your job, Mr. Real Estate Matchmaker."

Luke's eyes widened. "Damn, can't believe I forgot about that."

She playfully swatted him on the shoulder. "It's about to be Christmas soon and I'm going to be homeless! The only good thing about being homeless in LA around a holiday is that hopefully, I can put one of those red tin cans right next to a tent in Hollywood and collect money. Folks are more giving at Christmas."

"You are so dramatic," Luke said with a laugh. "Why aren't you staying with Nicole or Aaliyah?"

"I didn't want to impose on them. I figured maybe I need to just do a month-to-month lease until I find the perfect place."

"You can stay with me and Nash," Luke said without giving it a second thought.

"Uh, I appreciate the offer, but you both are still bonding. I'd just be in the way."

Luke took out his phone and called Nash. He answered on the second ring. "Hey, Nash, I have a favor to ask you?"

"Hey, Luke. Need me to help you serenade Kyra or something? You can pick any song, but I draw the line at Christmas music."

Luke laughed. "Nah, bro. We're back together. No serenading needed."

"Congrats."

"Thanks," he said. "Kyra's lease is up and she's living in a hotel. Would you mind if she stayed with us until we find her a place?"

"Put me on speakerphone," Nash said. Luke eyed his phone curiously, but he did as Nash asked. "Hey, Kyra, can you hear me?"

"Hey, Nash! Yeah, I hear you."

"Okay, so now that you're both listening, yes, I'm cool if Kyra stays with us for a while," Nash said. "But did either of y'all think that the reason she never found the perfect condo is because you both were supposed to find a condo together?"

Luke raised an eyebrow. "Uh, my stay in LA was supposed to be temporary, though."

"Is that still the case now that you and Kyra are together?" Nash asked.

Luke gave a goofy smile that matched Kyra's. "Nope. I guess not."

"Exactly. I love you and everything, bro, but I need my own space. I haven't had a roommate since college. And I think it's pointless for you to look for a condo and Kyra to look for a separate condo when y'all are gonna be together all the time, anyway. Save money and save yourselves the headache of packing a bag every night."

"You know what, Nash," Luke said. "I like the way you think, brother."

"That's probably one of the best ideas you've ever had," Kyra added.

"That's what I've been saying all along," Nash said. "I'm pretty amazing. And that's why you'll name your first daughter Nashonda after me."

Kyra gasped. "Nashonda? That's a hideous name."

"It's better than some of the others he came up with," Luke said.

"I find that hard to believe," Kyra said with a laugh. That laugh died on her lips as Nash started going through his list of baby names. To Luke's surprise, the names actually got worse as time went on.

Epilogue

Three months later...

Kyra couldn't believe everything they'd accomplished in three months. Not only had they closed on the Thomas property, but the Bare Sophistication ladies in Chicago and Miami had also come together to make sure the LA boutique was ready for the grand reopening.

On top of that, Kyra and Luke had finally found a condo that they both could agree on, and so far, living with Luke was even better than she ever imagined it would be. They'd needed to get out of Nash's place because they were driving him crazy. They hadn't been fighting or anything, but Nash had said it was too lovey-dovey in his bachelor pad and that hanging out with Luke's friends was making him question his bachelorhood.

Luke and Nash still hadn't heard much from their father, but Kyra felt like their relationship was better without him in it. Plus, Luke's mom and Nash were also getting closer. Already, they were planning another visit and Kyra couldn't wait because as crazy as it sounded, she was missing those beautiful St. Lucia beaches.

"It's almost time," Nicole said, speaking to all the ladies who were gathered inside the boutique while their families, friends and others in the public and media waited outside the shop.

"I can't believe it," Winter said. "This may just be my favorite location out of all the boutiques."

"It's definitely my favorite," Summer said. "Danni and I are already talking about searching for a new storefront for Miami."

"I think we'll look at upgrading in Chicago, too," Autumn said. "Can't let LA get all the fun."

"I just love this sisterhood," Aaliyah said, clasping her hands together. She had given birth to a healthy baby girl two and a half months earlier, but Aaliyah was still hormonal and emotional. Kyra and Nicole had both told her it was possible she'd turned around and got pregnant again, but she refused to believe them.

"I agree," Nicole said. "I can't imagine what my life would have been like had I not joined the Bare Sophistication team."

Kyra looked to Winter, Autumn, Summer and Danni knowing that they felt the same way, especially since three of them had founded the boutique chain. "I love y'all," she said to everyone in the room.

"Can we have a *Baby-Sitters Club* moment?" Aaliyah asked.

Autumn glanced around the room. "What's that?"

"It's when we all stand in a circle and hug each other," Kyra explained. "She's been making us do this for a year now."

Summer laughed. "I'm all for hugging it out. Let's do this." All seven women hugged, each grateful in their own way for their Bare Sophistication journey. A knock on the window made them break their embrace.

"It's showtime," Kyra announced. "Ladies, you ready?" They all nodded their heads and filed out of the boutique, where they were welcomed by a huge crowd of people who were clapping and screaming for them.

"Thank you all for coming to the grand reopening of Bare Sophistication Boutique and Boudoir Studio in Hollywood," Kyra announced. "We are so appreciative of all the amazing people who have helped make the Bare Sophistication brand a success. When Winter, Autumn and Summer initially created this idea, they had no idea it would be so well received. Not only am I so proud of my sisters-in-law, but I'm equally proud of these strong black women standing beside me who have poured their blood, sweat and tears into this business." Kyra turned to the women. "Ladies, I am a better woman because of each of you." They each blew her kisses and Aaliyah, who was standing beside her, gave her a tight hug.

"To our parents, spouses and partners, we couldn't do this without you. To our friends and loyal customers, thank you for supporting the brand and help making Bare Sophistication shine." She made sure the red ribbon was in place and Nicole was nearby with the big scissors.

"And without further ado, we'd like to—"

"Hold on," a voice said, cutting her off. *Why does*

that sound like Luke? she thought. When he made his way through the crowd, she saw that it was Luke.

"Uh, baby, I'm kinda in the middle of something."

"I know," he said, taking the mic. "But considering we've had a pretty busy few months, I couldn't think of a better time to do this." He cleared his throat and everything around them quieted as Kyra realized what was going on.

"Oh, my God," she said, her hand flying to her mouth.

"Kyra Monica Reed, I am so in love with you and have been for most of my life. You amaze me in so many ways and because of you, I'm a better man. I know that I still owe you so many dates, but I honestly can't imagine going on another date with you as just boyfriend and girlfriend." Luke got down on one knee and opened a ring box that revealed a huge princess-cut diamond.

"It's beautiful," Kyra whispered.

"Not as beautiful as you," he said. "Kyra, would you do me the honor of making this official and becoming my wife?"

She nodded her head. "Absolutely!" He slipped the ring on her finger and stood to give her a kiss. Kyra could hear the crowd cheering in the background, but she couldn't bring herself to break apart from him. Grownup Kyra was ecstatic and ready to spend the rest of her life with this man, but little-girl Kyra was running around outside in circles and screaming, "He finally did it, y'all!" She'd wished she could tell her young self that the patience paid off because she landed the man. Better yet, he landed her because she was a catch and she knew it.

The ribbon cutting went on without them, but she didn't care. In fact, she would have stood outside the shop and continued kissing Luke if she hadn't remembered something.

"What are you doing?" Luke asked when she took out her phone.

"I have to text your cousin Trista," Kyra said.

Luke raised an eyebrow. "Now? Why?"

"Because the rest of my wish came true," Kyra said, shooting a message over to Trista. "I thought that story was so fake, but the wish I made at Wishing Waterfall came true."

Luke smiled. "Did you wish for us to be together?"

"Technically, I wished for us to be together by Christmas, which we totally were," she said. "Then, I wished for us to engaged before Easter, which we are."

Luke shook his head. "Of course, you made two wishes."

"Three, actually," she said, holding up three fingers. "I may or may not have also wished for our wedding to be in Alaska."

He frowned. "You can stop texting her because that part hasn't come true yet. And by hasn't, I mean, it will never come true. I don't want to get married in Alaska."

"Baby, we gotta be different," Kyra said. "Most the folks we know have already gotten married and done so extravagantly. Do you know what that means? Means Alaska is the only thing that will top it."

"But you don't even like the cold," he said.

She rolled her eyes. "We have to work on this husband-and-wife thing before we say our vows," she said. "Basically, whatever I say goes and whatever you say, doesn't. Got it?"

He opened his mouth to argue with her, but Kyra beat him to it by shutting him up with a kiss. Granted,

Alaska may not be the best place to get married, but wherever they chose, she was fine with it. A wedding was just semantics, anyway. She was already the happiest she'd ever been having landed a great career, amazing friends, a supportive family and a life partner who did crazy romantic things like propose in front of a huge audience. He made life more interesting and, more importantly, he loved her for her.

* * * * *

"I don't know what impresses me more, beauty or your brains."

She whirled around at the sound of the deep, seductive voice. Mr. Athletic had a hip propped on the table a few feet away, his arms folded and a twinkle in his eye. He straightened and sauntered toward her with one of the sexiest walks she'd seen in a while.

"It's the brains, I'm thinking." He stuck out his hand. "I'm Jeremy Hunter."

"Serita Edwards, but then you already knew that." His large hand engulfed her small one.

Jeremy smiled and a dimple appeared in his right cheek. "That introduction was for the workshop. This one is personal. I really enjoyed your presentation."

"Thank you." Serita belatedly realized he hadn't let go of her hand and she gently pulled back. He towered over her five-foot-three-inch frame by a good foot or more and looked even better close up. He stared at her with such intensity, Serita felt her cheeks warm. To distract herself, she glanced around to make sure she had everything. "How long have you been in the field?"

"Sixteen years. And you?"

She tried to do a mental calculation. If he'd been in robotics that long, it would put him closer to forty, and he didn't look anywhere near that age. "Just over eight years."

"Are you in a rush?"

"I... No." She really should have said she had evening plans, especially since she sensed his interest. She didn't do long-distance relationships—okay, she didn't do them at all right now—but couldn't resist the opportunity to talk shop for a few extra minutes.

Sheryl Lister is a multi-award-winning author and has enjoyed reading and writing for as long as she can remember. She is a former pediatric occupational therapist with over twenty years of experience, and resides in California. Sheryl is a wife, mother of three daughters and a son-in-love, and grandmother to two special little boys. When she's not writing, Sheryl can be found on a date with her husband or in the kitchen creating appetizers. For more information, visit her website at www.sheryllister.com.

Books by Sheryl Lister

Harlequin Kimani Romance

It's Only You
Tender Kisses
Places in My Heart
Giving My All to You
A Touch of Love
Still Loving You
Sweet Love
Spark of Desire
Designed by Love

Visit the Author Profile page
at Harlequin.com for more titles.

DESIGNED BY LOVE

Sheryl Lister

For all of you who believe in love at first sight.

Acknowledgments

My Heavenly Father, thank you for my life
and for loving me better than I can love myself.

To my husband, Lance, you continue to show me why
you'll always be my number one hero! I couldn't do
this without you. Twenty-five years and counting…

To my children, family and friends, thank you for
your continued support. I appreciate and love you!

A very special thank-you to Nanette Kelly.
I'll never see the game the same again. Love you!

Thank you to all the book clubs who have hosted
and supported me. Y'all rock!

They always say to find your tribe and I've found
mine. They know who they are. I love y'all
and can't imagine being on this journey without you.
Thank you for keeping me sane!

A very special thank-you to my agent,
Sarah E. Younger. I can't tell you how much
I appreciate having you in my corner.

Dear Reader,

Do you believe in love at first sight? Every now and again a hero comes along who is all in when it comes to love, and Jeremy Hunter is one of them. Serita Edwards isn't ready for a man who pursues her with a passion unlike anything she's ever known. I hope you enjoy the ride as the final member of the Hunter family claims his forever love.

This is a bittersweet ending, as not only does the series end, but this is also my last Kimani Romance. I've enjoyed bringing you stories of African American love and will continue to do so. I so appreciate all your love and support and I thank you for taking this journey with me. Without you, I couldn't do this. I love hearing from you, so be sure to email and let me know your thoughts. Stay tuned for what's next!

Much love,

Sheryl

www.SherylLister.com

sheryllister@gmail.com

www.Facebook.com/SherylListerAuthor

Twitter.com/1Slynne

Instagram: SherylLister

Chapter 1

"We miss you, Jeremy!"

Jeremy Hunter smiled at his family. They were huddled around his brother Cedric's iPad screen while Jeremy sat in his hotel room Sunday night. They were celebrating his cousin Alisha's three-month-old baby daughter's christening. "I miss you guys, too."

"How's Madrid?" his mother asked.

"So far, so good. The time difference is still giving me fits, but I slept a lot today." He had chosen to fly in two days early for the weeklong engineering conference that would start tomorrow.

"Don't forget to take a lot of pictures."

He chuckled. "I won't." His mother had only reminded him twenty times in the last week—in person, by phone and by text.

Cedric took the iPad back. "What day are you speaking?"

"Wednesday. I'm glad it's not tomorrow and that it's earlier in the week. It'll give me more time to relax, explore and not be worried about the presentation." He would be conducting a session on medical robotics.

"Hey, brother-in-law." Cedric's wife, Randi, waved into the screen. She sat next to Cedric and laid her head on his shoulder, and Cedric kissed her forehead.

Jeremy shook his head at his brother's expression. His diehard bachelor brother had fallen for the feisty fire investigator in less than three months, and Jeremy had lost a two-hundred-dollar bet because of it. "Hey, Randi. How are you feeling?"

She smiled and rubbed a hand over her belly. "Growing," she said with a laugh. "Eight weeks and four days to go, but who's counting?"

"I can't wait to be an uncle." He could hear the animated chatter in the background. His aunt, uncle and cousins from LA had made the trip to Sacramento, and Jeremy wished he was there. He laughed at the irony that in the past few years, along with his brother and three female cousins, all of his male cousins had married. Each of them had been adamant about keeping his bachelorhood intact, and each had met a special woman who'd made him change his perspective. Jeremy had always been the only one who believed in love and wanted to find Mrs. Right, and he'd told them he would know her on sight. He had endured years of teasing when they were younger, and yet he was the only one still single.

"Does that mean you'll be available for babysitting whenever we need you, Dr. Hunter?"

"Ced, with the way you hardly let Randi out of your sight, I'll be lucky to see my new niece or nephew before she or he is five."

Randi laughed. "You've got a point."

Cedric divided a glance between his brother and wife. "Isn't it past your bedtime, baby brother?"

Jeremy chuckled. "That worked when I was five, but I can do whatever I want now. You'll have to save that for your kids." He'd teased his brother about settling down before he got too old to have kids, but at age thirty-six, he had started to wonder the same thing concerning himself.

"I can't wait." He placed another quick kiss on Randi's lips. "Speaking of kids, you might want to hurry up and find that Mrs. Right you've always talked about, otherwise *you'll* be the one pushing a stroller in one hand and balancing a cane in the other."

"Whatever."

"Any prospects?"

"Not yet." The last woman Jeremy had dated complained that he didn't wine and dine her often enough. She had been upset when he'd suggested they have an evening in and acted almost offended by his offer to cook dinner. That had been right around Valentine's Day and Jeremy decided he needed a break. "It is almost midnight, though, and there are a couple of morning sessions I want to attend, so I need to call it a night."

"Okay. Email and let me know how your presentation went. If you can find someone, have them record it."

"Will do."

"I'm proud of you, Doc."

Smiling, he said, "Thanks." It meant everything to have his big brother's support. Initially, he had thought about going the same route as Cedric and working for their family's construction company, but, after being introduced to robotics, had changed direction. "Tell

Alisha I'll bring Kali's gift over when I get back." They spoke a few minutes longer, then ended the call.

Jeremy went to stand on the balcony and stared up at the dark sky. The daytime temperatures had reached eighty, but the nights dropped down into the fifties and reminded him of home. He stood there awhile, thinking about how fortunate he'd been in his career. He'd started his own medical robotics company three years ago after the notoriety he gained when he won an award for his contributions to robotics and automation. Since then, he'd secured a couple of grants and three contracts for building surgery robots. They'd afforded him the ability to hire three other engineers, along with his best friend and business manager, Christian Hill, and a reception-ist. He did have some concerns about completing the latest contract, as one of his engineers had given notice last week. Jeremy had left Chris in charge of advertising and hiring for the position, and hoped there'd be some good news by the time Jeremy made it home next week.

His thoughts shifted to his presentation. He would spend a little time on it tomorrow, but he was as ready as he could be. He'd presented at a few smaller con-ferences, but not on the international stage. Recording the session would not only give his family an oppor-tunity to see it, but also allow Jeremy to make adjust-ments. After a few more minutes, he went back inside and closed the door. He had already showered, so he set the alarm on his phone, turned off the lamp and slid beneath the covers.

Jeremy woke up Monday morning feeling refreshed. His body had finally adjusted to the time change. He ordered room service and, while eating, went over the conference schedule. This morning, he planned to attend workshops on soft robotics and autonomous robot design. The session that most excited him wouldn't be until Tuesday afternoon with a Dr. S. Edwards, who would discuss tactile sensors. It was of particular interest to him because he'd started a personal project to develop an artificial hand that closely mimicked human function.

On the way to his first session, he nodded greetings to a few people he'd met at other conferences. The long hall leading to the various meeting rooms had tables lined against either side of the walls with all manner of promotional brochures. Jeremy's steps slowed. A beautiful brown-skinned beauty sat in a chair next to an information table scribbling furiously on a notepad. She wore a pair of stylish rose-gold-rimmed glasses with some kind of bling bordering them and had a mass of curls sitting on top of her head. She lifted her head and their eyes connected briefly. He felt a jolt of awareness and his lips tilted in a smile. Her eyes widened and she looked away hastily before continuing to write. He noticed she wore the same badge identifying all the attendees but couldn't read her name from where he stood. Jeremy toyed with stopping to ask, but his session would be starting in five minutes and he still had to find the room. With any luck, their paths would cross later in the week. There were few women in the field of robotics and even fewer women of color, which aroused his curiosity further.

Jeremy found the room just as the speaker started and slid into a chair near the back. Fifteen minutes in, he could barely keep his eyes open. While the information presented was interesting, he couldn't say the same about the man talking. The monotone sound of the man's voice had several other people's eyes closing, as well. Jeremy sincerely hoped the rest of the day didn't go the same way. His mind drifted to the woman in the hall—beauty and brains, a lethal combination in his book, and he wouldn't mind getting to know her. As soon as he found her again.

"Excuse me, Miss. I seem to have gotten myself turned around. Can you tell me how to get to this room?"

Serita Edwards stared up at the man pointing to a room on the conference brochure and mentally counted to ten. He was the fourth person to ask her for directions in the past half hour. "I have no idea. I'm—"

He let out an impatient sigh. "What is it with you hotel staff?"

She lifted a brow. "*I beg your pardon.* I am not part of this hotel's staff. I paid my money just like you did to attend this conference, which is why I'm wearing the exact same badge as you."

The man had the decency to look embarrassed. "Oh, I just assumed since you were sitting here…"

Granted, she was sitting next to the information table, but not behind it. "There are two other people sitting on the other side of this table, yet you didn't ask one of them. Now, if you'll excuse me." Serita snatched up her belongings and with a parting glare stalked off down the hallway. She went to one of the cafés and ordered a cup of café con leche. She had never been a coffee drinker, but Caroline, a woman she'd met at a previous conference, urged her to try it yesterday when they'd had breakfast together. Serita had been immediately hooked. She would definitely be finding a good recipe for this once she returned home.

As she sipped the warm drink, she thought about all she needed to do when she returned to the States. As an adjunct professor, her appointment had been a temporary one and, after not having her contract renewed for the semester at the college where she taught in Nevada, she'd decided to move back home to Sacramento, California, at the end of October. That gave her a month to get her condo sold and all her belongings boxed up. Serita had already started sorting through everything and put the condo on the market, but finding a job topped her priority list. She'd been an adjunct professor for three years, but found she missed the excitement of working in the field. Glancing down at her watch, she realized she only had an hour before her session, and the butterflies began dancing in her belly. Her best friend, Gabriella Lewis, couldn't understand why Serita would be nervous, since she made a living talking in front of a class. In Serita's mind, talking to students was far less intimidating than speaking in a room full of peers, some who had much more experience and knowledge than she did. She was tempted to go over her notes again but resisted the urge. She knew the presentation by heart.

Serita closed her eyes and drew in a deep, calming breath. *You can do this*, she repeated to herself over and over. She relaxed, opened her eyes and met the amused stare of the gorgeous giant of a man she'd seen yesterday. Even though he stood behind a small group of people, his towering height gave her a clear view of his face. She wondered if there was some sports thing happening in the area because he certainly had the look and body of an athlete. She gave him an imperceptible nod and went back to her coffee. When she finished, she went up to her room for a moment to freshen up, then headed downstairs for her session.

Thankfully, her assigned room didn't have a session that hour, which gave her ample time to set up her materials and have the staff ensure the microphone worked. People started trickling in as she finished and Serita went back to the podium, clipped the microphone to her top and the battery on her pants waistband. She believed in starting on time and, at precisely two, began her presentation.

"What if we could create a tactile sensor that had the ability to measure touch and vibration, both in the air and under water?" She waited a moment and saw several people in the audience lean forward. She smiled inwardly, then continued her discussion of the uses and benefits of the device. She scanned the room and went still, promptly losing her train of thought for a brief moment. Sitting in the far corner of the room was Mr. Athletic. This time, unlike the previous times she'd seen him, she had a clear view of his badge. Shaking herself mentally, Serita refocused on her talk, grateful that she knew the information like the back of her hand. Two hours later, she ended with, "These sensors offer an alternative route to imitating the functions of human skin and are suitable for use with artificial skin applications, smart gloves for robotics, as well as surgery tools. They're cost-effective, and have a wide range of sensitivities and are able to operate wirelessly."

Afterward, Serita took as many questions as time allowed. Because there were no other sessions after hers, many people stayed around to ask more questions.

She collected business cards from those who wanted more information on the research and handed out the brochure she'd created. When the last person left, she gathered up the remaining materials and placed them in her tote bag.

"I don't know what impresses me more, beauty or your brains."

She whirled around at the sound of the deep, seductive voice. Mr. Athletic had a hip propped on the table a few feet away, his arms folded and a twinkle in his eye. He straightened and sauntered toward her with one of the sexiest walks she'd seen in a while.

"It's the brains, I'm thinking." He stuck out his hand. "I'm Jeremy Hunter."

"Serita Edwards, but then you already knew that." His large hand engulfed her small one.

Jeremy smiled and a dimple appeared in his right cheek. "That introduction was for the workshop, this one is personal. I really enjoyed your presentation."

"Thank you." Serita realized belatedly he hadn't let go of her hand and she gently pulled back. He towered over her five-foot-three-inch frame by a good foot or more and looked even better close up. He stared at her with such intensity that Serita felt her cheeks warm. To distract herself, she glanced around to make sure she had everything. "How long have you been in the field?"

"Sixteen years. And you?"

She tried to do a mental calculation. If he'd been in robotics that long, it would put him closer to forty and he didn't look anywhere near that age. "Just over eight years."

"Are you in a rush?"

"I… No." She really should have said she had evening plans, especially since she sensed his interest. She didn't do long-distance relationships—okay, she didn't do them at all right now—but couldn't resist the opportunity to talk shop for a few extra minutes.

"Great. Would you like to have dinner?"

"Dinner?"

He chuckled. "Yes, dinner. I thought we could continue our conversation over a good meal."

"Oh." Of course, he only wanted to discuss robotics. That seemed to be the story of her life. Either men only wanted to talk about work or thought she was too nerdy and wanted to change her.

"So what do you say? We can eat here, but I'd rather explore the city. Maybe we can check out Plaza de España. I'm sure we can find something in that area."

The Plaza de España had been one of the places Serita planned to visit and figured she'd be on her own, but it might be nice for them to go together. At least she'd have someone to take her picture, instead of trying to manage selfies that never turned out. "Actually, that's one of the spots on my bucket list. I'll accept your invitation."

Jeremy grinned, then checked his watch. "It's almost five now. What time would you like to leave?"

"The earlier we leave, the longer we can hang out. I can meet you near the registration desk in thirty minutes."

"Thirty minutes it is, Ms. Edwards."

"Please call me Serita."

"Only if you call me Jeremy." He angled his head thoughtfully. "Serita. I like that name." He paused. "It fits you."

She waited for him to say something else, but he continued smiling and gestured her forward. They made small talk on the way to the elevator and every time she answered him, she had to crane her neck. "How tall are you?"

"Six-four, why?"

"Because I feel like I need a ladder to see your face."

Jeremy laughed.

"I think our conversations are going to have to be conducted while we're sitting. Otherwise, I'm going to need some serious therapy on my neck."

An elevator arrived as they approached and he stepped back to let her enter. He selected his floor and stared down at her. "I'd be happy to help you out." He lifted his hands and wiggled his fingers. "These babies right here can give you a massage you'll never forget." He tossed her a bold wink.

No way am I touching that comment. Serita didn't have to touch it. Her mind visualized his big hands massaging and stroking her body just fine. Warmth crept up her spine. She hit the button and clamped her jaws shut.

They got to her floor first and he held the door open. "I'll see you in a few minutes."

He was staring at her again in that penetrating way, as if he'd seen inside her mind and knew her thoughts. "Okay." She forced her feet to move and hurried down the hallway without looking back.

In her room, Serita changed into black jeans and a gray short-sleeved top. The temperatures had reached eighty that day, but she knew it would cool off in the evening, so she took down her black jacket and laid it over the back of the chair. She applied lip gloss, then stood in the bathroom trying to decide whether to leave her hair up or let it down. After a minute, she went with the latter. It had taken her a while to get her natural curls to behave, but she loved the style.

Since she still had some extra time, she powered up her laptop and checked her email to see if she'd gotten any responses from her job applications. Serita sighed. Not one had replied, as yet. Just as she closed the browser, her FaceTime popped up. She opened the application and smiled when she saw Gabriella calling.

"Hey, Serita. How did the session go?"

"It went well and I had a lot of questions at the end."

"I knew you'd be fine. I can't believe how worried you were." Gabriella rolled her eyes.

Serita had expressed her fears to her friend more than once. "This was presenting on an entirely different scale. I've seen people with far more experience tank in front of an audience, and I worked extra hard to make sure my name didn't get added to the list. Initially, I wasn't too happy about having my presentation on the second day, but now I'm kind of glad. I can relax and enjoy the rest of the week."

She smiled. "Be sure to take lots of pictures."

"I plan to."

"Any news on the job front?"

Serita blew out a long breath. "Not yet." She had hoped to find a job before her scheduled move back to Sacramento at the end of October. Although she missed her parents, she didn't want to have to move in with them.

"Well, I'm confident you'll find one soon. You know I've got you covered, girl. You can stay with me until something comes up."

She frowned. "What happened to Jodi?"

"Not paying her half of the rent on time for the past

three months is what happened," Gabriella said. She had allowed Jodi, another one of their college friends, to move into her two-bedroom condo six months ago, and lately the woman had one excuse after another as to why she never had her share of the cost.

"I thought she had a good job."

"She does, but her priorities tend to be on finding the latest and cutest outfit rather than her bills. So, I told her she had thirty days to find another place. That was two weeks ago. She keeps asking me about extending the deadline and, in the same breath, saying she needs more time to come up with the money. I'm *done*."

Serita didn't know what to say. Jodi had seemed so focused and together in college. Serita guessed she hadn't known her friend well at all. "Wow. I'm sorry." Gabby had always been a good friend, and people tended to take her kindness for granted until they found out Gabby didn't allow anyone to walk all over her.

"Me, too. Something told me it would be a bad idea to let her move in." Gabriella shook her head. "I should've listened. Anyway, it's just about dinnertime there. Are you going to try out one of those restaurants in the city?"

She gasped and glanced at the time. "Oh, shoot! I have to go. I'm supposed to be meeting Jeremy in five minutes."

Gabriella's eyes widened and a smile curved her lips. "*Jeremy?* I see you didn't waste any time. You go, girl."

She waved her friend off. "It's not like that. He attended my session and said he wanted to continue the conversation. It'll be just talking shop, nothing more." And it still bothered her for some reason.

"What does he look like?"

"About six-four, athletic build, bronze-like skin and fine with a capital *F*." An image of his smile floated through her mind, along with that sexy dimple. "I'll talk to you later in the week."

"Preferably tomorrow, so you can fill me in on *all* the juicy details of this date."

Serita chuckled. "I'll try." She ended the call, shut down the computer, and grabbed her jacket and purse. As she made her way to the lobby, she shook her head. It was just her luck to meet a sexy-as-sin man, and the most interesting thing she had to offer him was her expertise in robotics.

Chapter 2

Jeremy stood in the lobby waiting for Serita. The impulse to invite her to dinner had come out of nowhere. He hadn't been exactly forthcoming with her, however. Yes, he'd been captivated by the knowledge, but even more so by the woman. When he'd seen her in the hallway earlier, he had sensed something and wanted to know what it was. He straightened from the wall when he saw her exit the elevator. She scanned the area and, spotting him, hurried over.

"I'm so sorry I'm late. My friend called and I lost track of time," Serita said in a rush.

"Yeah, you're really late by like…" He glanced down at his watch. "A whole thirty seconds." He chuckled. "You're fine. Ready?"

She visibly relaxed. "Yes."

"Did you come up with any dinner suggestions?"

Serita stared up at him. "No. I had planned to Google some places, but didn't get a chance."

A group of people passed, forcing her to move closer to him. Whatever fragrance she was wearing played havoc on his senses. The mixture of sweet and sexy had him tempted to bury his face in her neck and trail kisses there. His gaze dropped to her gloss-slicked lips and he fantasized about tasting them. The urge to kiss her rose up so strong inside Jeremy it shocked him. "There are some restaurants within walking distance, so I'm sure we'll find something."

She nodded.

Jeremy gestured her forward and tried to understand why he felt so drawn to Serita. Outside, several other people seemed to have the same idea. They strolled leisurely down the street, stopping more than once to take in the sights.

"Have you been here before?"

He looked down at her. "No, it's my first time. What about you?"

"It's my first time, too."

"Then we should make each moment count." Their eyes held for a lengthy moment before she turned away and continued walking. The attraction between them seemed to be rising by the second. He knew they were both there for the conference, but outside of that, he wanted to spend as much time with her as possible. The tree-lined street had several storefront shops with second-story wrought-iron balconies. He wondered if the shop owners lived above their businesses.

"This is so nice." Serita pulled out her phone and snapped a couple of pictures. "Can you take one of me? I suck at selfies."

Laughing, he reached for her phone. "Sure." He got a number of shots with her in front of the different stores. She had the most beautiful smile, and Jeremy couldn't resist capturing it on his own phone before turning the camera toward the street. He held it up for a selfie, then bent close to Serita and took one of the two of them. He had no idea if he'd ever see her again and wanted a memory of their evening.

She peered at his phone. "Can I see?"

He showed her the photo.

"Mine never come out like that," she said with a pout. "They're either blurry, too close, or I cut off half my face."

Jeremy smiled inwardly. She had just given him his opening to spend more time together. "I tell you what— if you agree to be my tourist partner for the week, I'll teach you how to take selfies like a pro."

"I…um…" Serita folded her arms and studied him. "Exactly what does that entail?" she asked, still sounding a little unsure.

He shrugged. "Exploring the city and whatever else you want to do."

She didn't say anything at first. Finally she said, "Okay."

A grin spread across his face. Her agreeing to his proposal gave him a week to figure out whether the pull he felt was a pure case of lust or more. Jeremy needed to know if she was the woman he'd been waiting for. His Mrs. Right. He extended his arm. "Then let's get this party started."

She gave him a bright smile and hooked her arm in his. "Sounds like a plan."

They walked another few steps and came to a painted-brick-and-concrete storefront restaurant.

"What about here?"

He studied the menu mounted on the wall for a couple of minutes. "What do you think?"

"I think we have a winner."

Jeremy held the door open for her.

"Wow, it's a lot bigger than I thought."

The Dantxari had a cozy feel, wooden tables covered in red tablecloths with matching napkins, antique clocks and stained-glass windows. "I agree." They had a short wait before being led to one of the tables near the back. He went to pull out Serita's chair and she jumped. "Sorry, didn't mean to startle you. I just want to help you with your chair."

"Thank you."

Once she was seated, he rounded the table and took the chair across from her. "Does this mean you've never had a man pull a chair out for you?"

Serita picked up her menu. "I haven't."

He took quiet satisfaction in being the first. "No? Well, this week, you can expect your doors to be opened, your chair pulled out and me standing when you enter a room. Oh, and I'll be paying for dinner." Along with every other expense during their time together in Madrid.

She jerked her head up. "Wait. What? Why would you do all those things? And I was going to... You can't pay for my dinner."

He smiled inwardly at her flustered state. "To answer your first question, I'll do all those things because it's how I was raised to treat a woman. And second, why can't I pay for your dinner? I invited you."

"Because you can't. I mean, we aren't dating or seeing each other or anything. I just met you a couple of hours ago."

Jeremy laughed softly. She mentioned them not dating or seeing each other, but he wondered what she would say if he told her he wanted to do just that. "I realize this is the twenty-first century and some men choose not to maintain the chivalrous behavior of their fathers and grandfathers, but, again, that's not how I was raised. Whether we met two years ago or two hours ago won't change my perspective." She eyed him for a moment and he winked. He picked up his menu. "So, what looks good?"

Serita lowered her head. After a couple of minutes, she said, "I'm not sure."

A server came to the table and explained several of the dishes. They both decided on cod croquettes, white asparagus in butter sauce and beef steak for two. While waiting for their food, Jeremy got up and came around to her side of the table.

"What are you doing?"

"We're going to have your first selfie lesson?"

"Here?"

"Yes. I'm sure you want to show your family and friends the highlights of your trip. Restaurants top the list of photos."

She groaned. "Are you serious? I figured you'd just take one of me at the table and we'd start tomorrow or something."

He shook his head and smiled. "Come on, it's not hard."

She rolled her eyes and took out her phone. "I'd better come away with at least one good picture," she said, holding up one finger for emphasis. But she was smiling.

"I promise." He moved one of the chairs and sat next to her and explained the best angles to take the selfie.

Serita held the phone up and snapped one, looked at it and let out a sigh. "See, I knew it wasn't going to come out right. Every time I think I have it in the right spot, the camera moves when I push the button. Your hands are bigger than mine, so I need two hands."

"Actually, you can use the volume down button."

She stared. "Are you serious?"

"Yep. Try it."

She tried again. "Finally, a decent picture. All this time I could've been using that button, instead of trying to hold it in one hand and hit the button on the other." She shook her head. "It's still a little dark, but at least I didn't cut off any body parts this time." She smiled at him, then seemed to realize how close they were and backed away.

Once again, Jeremy had an overwhelming desire to kiss her. Instead, he went back to his seat. "That'll be lesson number two." The server returned with their food.

"This looks really good."

"It does. Great restaurant choice."

Serita snapped a picture of her plate, then turned the phone toward him. "Now, this one I can do."

He laughed and, after reciting a silent blessing, dug in. Jeremy found himself enjoying her more and more.

Serita sat across from her dining partner waiting for him to bring up the subject of robotics. They were almost finished eating and he had yet to ask one question. They'd talked about everything from the weather and jet lag to some of the sessions they had attended earlier. All except hers. She set down her fork. "I thought you wanted to talk to me about robotics."

Jeremy grinned sheepishly. "Actually, I just wanted to ask you out to dinner to get to know you. I wasn't sure you'd agree, so I said the first thing that came to mind. You aren't mad, are you?"

She stared. How could she be mad at a man who wanted to spend time with her for something other than work? "No. Truthfully, I'm a little flattered, and I probably would have said yes anyway."

A slow smile spread across his lips. "Good to know. So, next time, I'll just tell you up front that it's a date. But since you brought it up, how did you get into robotics?"

Next time? A date? He'd slid that first comment in so smoothly she almost missed it. "You think there's going to be a next time?"

"I most certainly do. Did you forget that you said you'd hang out with me this week in exchange for selfie lessons?"

Yeah, she'd forgotten that quickly. "Of course I remember." The smile on his face said he didn't believe her for a second. The heated intensity in his dark brown eyes said a whole lot more, and she resisted the urge to fan herself. She'd never had a man look at her the way Jeremy did and, although they'd just met, for a brief moment she fantasized about how it would feel to spend time with him past the week. A soft touch on her hand drew Serita out of her reverie.

"Hey, where did you go?"

"Oh, sorry. Just thinking about how we're going to manage the selfie lessons with the conference and all."

Serita applauded herself for being able to tell that lie with a straight face. She thought it time to change the subject. "You asked how I got into robotics. Initially, I'd planned to go to med school, but in tenth grade, my friend's father lost his arm in a factory accident, and I was fascinated by the prosthetic arm he had. Granted, they were nowhere near as functional as they are now, but I was intrigued nonetheless. I started researching and changed my direction. My high school had a pre-biomedical track and that helped. How about you?" Before he could answer, the server came back to clear their plates and take their dessert order. They both opted for the lemon sherbet with champagne and vodka.

Jeremy leaned back in his chair and continued the conversation. "I've always liked building things. My family owns a construction company and I figured I'd follow in my dad and older brother's footsteps, but I also enjoyed science. My parents sent me to one of those science camps when I was about eleven or twelve, and one of the options was robotics. I chose that one, since it included building a robot. It was the best time of my life, and by the time I left that camp I knew what I wanted to do with my life. Before I got to high school, I'd found the college I wanted to attend and did everything I could to make sure I got into that program."

The server returned with the desserts. After thanking her, Serita asked Jeremy, "Where did you go?"

"UC Davis for undergrad. I didn't want to be far away from my family in Sacramento, so I could easily drive to Davis and back daily. But I ended up at University of Michigan, Ann Arbor, for my doctorate."

Serita almost dropped her spoon. *Sacramento?* But since he'd been in the field so long, chances were that he still lived in Michigan. Even if he had moved back home, Sacramento was a big city. She doubted they'd run into each other. She tried to concentrate on the sweet, tart taste of the sherbet mixed with the crisp champagne.

"Where did you go to school?"

"University of Nevada at Reno."

"Is that where you live?"

"Yes." *For now.*

His smile widened. "That's only a couple of hours from Sac and an easy drive. We'll have to exchange contact information before the week is up. I'd like to keep in touch, so we can hang out together sometimes."

"Um…okay." He'd given her the perfect opening to mention her move back to their hometown, but she didn't want him to get any ideas. Professionally, it couldn't hurt to keep in contact, but that was as far as she wanted to go. She didn't have a good track record with men. While finishing dessert, the topics went from their respective careers to hobbies. She realized they had a lot in common.

"Do you want anything else?"

"No, thank you." She wanted to try to make him see reason about paying for her dinner but imagined it wouldn't do any good, so she kept her mouth closed.

Jeremy settled the bill, then came around to her side to help her up. "It's still pretty early and not quite dark yet. How about we walk off some of this food?"

"Sounds good." Their walk took them to the Plaza de España. The temperatures had dropped some and Serita shrugged into her jacket. She jumped slightly when she felt Jeremy's hands brush her nape as he helped her. The only other man she'd seen do these kinds of things was her father. "Thank you." With towers in the center and at either end, the semicircular brick building had a stunning architecture. Along the wall sat a number of alcoves with benches to represent each of Spain's provinces. In the front, a canal followed the curve of the building. She braced her hands on the railing. "This is amazing."

"And it's a good place for photos," he said with a wink.

She shook her head but couldn't stop the smile that peeked out. "You would say that."

His laughter rang out in the square. "Hey, I'm just trying to keep up my end of the agreement. I'm looking forward to the rest of the week."

"If you conduct all the lessons today, you won't have anything to do the rest of the week."

His hand came up and pushed a lock of hair off her face. "Oh, I'm sure I can come up with a few things."

The intimate gesture and the accompanying look made her pulse skip and nearly melted her in a heap. For a long moment, neither of them moved and she could feel her attraction rising. Serita reminded herself that she didn't do well in relationships and that she should put a halt to whatever seemed to be brewing between them. She took a step back. "I'm going to take a few shots of the building, then see if I can get a selfie without any help."

Jeremy gave her a soft smile. "I'll wait right here."

Serita nodded, her heart still racing. It took several seconds, but she finally tore away her gaze and went to take her pictures. Though the sun had started its descent, a fair number of people still remained. Many couples strolled hand-in-hand, cuddling on benches and stealing kisses near the water. It made for a romantic scene. On her way back, she saw Jeremy leaning with his forearms braced on the railing, his face turned slightly in her direction. In his short-sleeved pullover, the position put his muscled biceps on full display. With his good looks and toned body, he could have graced the cover of every model magazine. Instinctively, she held up her phone and hit the button. She wanted something to remember him by.

"Let's see what you've got," he said when she approached.

Smiling, she held out her phone, and he angled his head close to see.

"Look at you. You'll be a pro by tomorrow at this rate."

She glanced down at the photo of herself with the building behind her and smiled. "You think so?"

"I do."

"I have to admit it's the best one I've ever taken. I might have to blow it up, frame it and hang it on my wall, just in case I never get it right again." She faced him. "I had a great teacher."

"You think so?"

"Yep." The air between them shifted suddenly, and before she could blink Jeremy brushed his lips across hers in a soft, sweet kiss. They both gasped and Serita couldn't tell who was more shocked.

"I'm sorry. I—"

"It's okay," she added with a nervous chuckle,. "It's kind of hard not to get caught up with all this beauty." And she was definitely *caught up.*

"Are you ready to head back?"

"Don't you want to take some pictures?"

"I already did." As if it were the most natural thing, he reached down and entwined their fingers. He smiled at her once more and they headed back to the hotel in companionable silence.

Serita was glad for the reprieve because she needed to think. She wanted to blame the crazy feelings swirling around in her belly on the romantic surroundings, but she'd had the same ones earlier while standing in an empty conference room, so it had to be something else. *What is going on?* Okay, the man gave new meaning to good-looking, was a total gentleman and intelligent. And the kiss. It had only lasted a short moment, but even now the remnants of his warm, soft lips against hers lingered. With all of that, she would challenge any woman to remain unmoved.

When they arrived at the hotel, Jeremy walked Serita to her room. Standing outside the door, he said, "Thank you for your company this evening. I really enjoyed myself."

"So did I."

He seemed to be weighing his next words. "About the kiss…"

"You don't need to apologize again, Jeremy."

"I appreciate that, but since we agreed to spend time together this week, I don't want you to be uncomfortable around me." He stared at a spot above her head briefly, then back down at her. "I've never done anything like that before, and I can't explain why I did it tonight. There is something about you, Ms. Edwards, that has me acting out of character. I have the utmost respect for you, and I don't want you to think otherwise."

Serita remembered him talking about his upbringing and imagined it played a part in his thinking. She was admittedly flattered and, at the same time, wondered how she'd get him to do it again. "You're not the only one acting out of character, because I think I'd like you to kiss me again." She had never done something so bold in her life, and as the words tumbled out her heart rate kicked up once more.

He studied her. "Are you sure?"

Keeping her eyes on his, she said, "Positive."

"Then, we should step inside your room. We don't want to give anyone walking down the hallway a show."

Exactly what kind of show could a simple kiss cause? Surely it wouldn't be much more than what they'd shared at the plaza. Then again, she didn't want anyone from the conference to know her business, so he might be right. She used the keycard to open the door and was thankful that she'd left the room in reasonable order. Contrary to her daring request, as soon as the door closed, butterflies began doing a salsa in her belly. She placed her purse on the desk and turned to find him standing with his back against the door. He straightened and came to where she stood. He tilted her chin, bent and covered her mouth with his. The kiss went from sweet to hot in a millisecond. His tongue swirled slowly around hers and a soft moan escaped her. Without breaking the seal of their mouths, Jeremy turned. He sat on the bed, pulled her down onto his lap and deepened the kiss. His hand caressed her back, hip and thigh. She was completely unprepared for the whirlwind of sensations that gripped her, and she grabbed the back of his head to keep him in place. He left her mouth and trailed kisses along her jaw and throat. Serita's head fell back and her eyes closed. The way he touched and kissed her made her feel like... She didn't know how to describe it.

"Serita," he murmured between kisses. "We should—"

"Don't stop." She had no idea where the words had come from and she might be crazy, but she didn't want it to end. Any of it.

"If we don't stop now, we may end up taking this further than either of us anticipated."

"I'm counting on it."

His head came up sharply and he searched her face, as if wanting to be certain she meant what she had said.

"Yes, I'm sure. You said we could do whatever I wanted to do this week. Tonight, I want you." She would deal with the rest tomorrow.

Chapter 3

"I need you to know that I don't take this lightly, Serita." Jeremy had never been one to indulge in meaningless flings and preferred long-term relationships. Serita had drawn his attention from the first moment he had seen her and his attraction had risen steadily. And knowing she lived close enough to visit made him even more confident that their paths had crossed for a reason, the least being their love of robotics.

Serita stared up at him. "I thought this was just—"

He cut her off with a gentle kiss. "This is not *just* anything." He wanted to say more but held back. For now he would concentrate on giving them both pleasure. The rest could wait until he knew for sure what he was feeling. He slanted his mouth over hers once more, tasting, teasing. She met him stroke for stroke, making his arousal climb another notch. Jeremy took his time touching every part of her body, lingering on her toned thighs, the sweet curve of her hips and her round breasts.

"Jeremy," she whispered.

He loved hearing her soft sounds of pleasure and the way she called his name. "What, baby?"

"I need you inside me."

"I'll give you everything you need, everything you want, but I can't rush this." He kissed his way down the front of her body, pushed her shirt up and placed fleeting kisses around her smooth belly and up to the valley between her breasts. Jeremy slowly, methodically stripped away her clothes, leaving her clad in nothing but a black lace bra and matching bikini panties. With her hair spread all over the pillow, she made for an erotic picture and he felt himself growing harder. "Do you know how sexy you are?"

Serita laughed softly. "I don't think that's the case, but it's a nice thing to say." She reached up to take off her glasses.

Jeremy gently grasped her hand and placed a kiss in the center of her palm. "Leave them on."

"You want me to leave them on?" she asked, her brow knitted in confusion. "Why?"

"They make you look even sexier, and I can't tell you how much they turn me on. If it makes you feel better, next time I'll wear mine, too."

"Next time?"

"Mmm-hmm, but we can talk about that later. Right now, I want to kiss you again." He traced her lips with his tongue before reclaiming her mouth. Their tongues danced and curled around each other, and he groaned.

She grabbed the hem of his shirt, pulled it up and

over his head, then tossed it aside. Giving him a sultry smile, she skated her tongue across his chest.

He sucked in a sharp breath. After leaving the bed, he removed the rest of his clothes, dug in his wallet for a condom and donned it. He climbed back onto the bed and lowered his body on top of her hers, being careful not to place all his weight on her. His hand traveled down her left leg and back up her right to her center, where she was already wet. Her legs parted to give him access, and he used a finger to circle her clit. Her legs trembled and she opened wider. Jeremy slid one finger in, followed by another, moving them in a steady rhythm. She cried out and arched against his hand. A moment later, she screamed his name as she came. Jeremy withdrew his fingers, shifted his body and guided his erection inside her. Her tight walls tightened around him and he shuddered.

Serita moaned softly and wrapped her legs around his back.

"You feel so good."

"Mmm, so do you."

He smiled and started moving, teasing with short strokes, then long, deep ones. He rotated his hips and ground against her in slow insistent circles while lowering his head to take one dark nipple between his teeth. As he sucked gently, he kept up the languid pace and closed his eyes as the pleasure increased.

"Ohh..." Serita lifted her hips and gripped his shoulders.

Their breathing grew louder as Jeremy pumped faster and harder, rocking the bed. He crushed his mouth against hers and changed the rhythm again.

Serita wrenched her mouth away and screamed his name again as she convulsed all around him.

A heartbeat later, a raw expletive tore from his throat as the most intense orgasm he'd ever experienced shot through him with a force that stole his breath and left his entire body shaking. He held her tightly as they both trembled with the aftershocks. He held himself above her for several seconds before collapsing on the bed, rolling to his side and taking her with him. His heart still thumped erratically in his chest, and his breathing was harsh and uneven.

She stroked his cheek. "That was incredible."

"Yes, it was." He sensed something different, an emotional connection unlike anything he had ever felt with a woman. They shared another passionate kiss, then lay quietly in each other's arms. At length, Jeremy glanced over at the nightstand clock. It was just after ten. As much as he wanted to hold her all night, he had to make sure his presentation was perfect. "I need to go. I'm presenting tomorrow and I want to run through everything."

Serita lifted her head. "I didn't know you were one of the presenters. What time?"

"One."

"I'll be there."

"Thanks. Can you do me a favor and record it?"

"Sure. I'll get there a few minutes early so I can get a good seat in the front."

"I don't know about you sitting in the front. You're pretty distracting."

She smiled. "You're good for a girl's ego."

"Just speaking the truth." He captured her mouth in a long, drugging kiss. Reluctantly he rose from the bed and began to dress.

Serita pulled on a robe and followed him to the door.

"Are you attending a session in the morning?"

"Yes, why?"

"I was hoping we could have breakfast."

"We could always do dinner in one of the hotel's restaurants."

"I'll go with that." Unable to resist, Jeremy leaned down to kiss her. His hand slid inside her robe and she clamped down on it.

"Your presentation comes first. I'll see you tomorrow."

Their eyes held. Never in his wildest dreams could he have imagined what it would be like to touch and kiss her the way he had, to make love to her hours after they'd met. And he couldn't wait to do it again.

Wednesday afternoon, Serita sat in front of the room recording Jeremy's presentation. She had to give it to him—the man was a gifted presenter and knew how to keep the room interested. He spoke with a relaxed demeanor and it made her suspect he did this kind of thing regularly. She had a hard time focusing on his words, however, because the sight of him reminded her of what they had shared last night. Serita didn't make a practice of sleeping with men she'd just met. The only ones lucky enough to get that far—and it usually didn't happen until weeks or even months into the relationship—were men she dated exclusively. She didn't know what had possessed her to break her rules for Jeremy and thought she might have some regrets later. At this point, though, her only regret was that the evening had ended so early.

Serita got so lost in her thoughts, staring at Jeremy,

that she instinctively lowered the phone. She jerked it back up and met his amused gaze. She hoped whoever he'd planned to let see the video wasn't his boss or someone tied to his job. She refocused her attention on the presentation.

"One of the biggest factors for using robots in surgery is minimizing invasive procedures. Previously, surgeons had to make large incisions to access a site, but, with these machines, patients can look forward to smaller incisions and scars, reduced risk of infection, shorter recovery times and, most importantly, less pain and discomfort. If you've ever had surgery, you'll be cheering."

Chuckles and nods of agreement greeted his statement. As he continued to discuss the advancements and growing popularity, Serita could only marvel at his knowledge. She could see him commanding a college classroom easily. When it ended, more than half the audience surrounded Jeremy, asking questions, telling him how much they enjoyed his session and shaking his hand. Serita sat off to the side and waited until everyone left.

"How did I do?" Jeremy asked.

"You were fabulous."

"Are you sure? I didn't think you were paying attention. I saw you drifting off into space the whole time," he teased.

Her mouth fell open. "I was not."

"What were you thinking about?"

She couldn't very well tell him that she'd been thinking about how it felt to have his hands touching her, his naked body against hers as he thrust deeply inside her.

"I wasn't thinking about anything except how knowledgeable you are on the subject of medical robotics. And what makes you think I wasn't paying attention? You weren't looking at me."

"Baby, I never lost sight of you. Even when I wasn't looking directly at you, I could still see you."

She didn't know what to say. How could he have been paying that much attention to her and still give a perfect talk? And he'd called her baby. The possessive way he'd said it almost made her think she *was* his baby. Not knowing how to answer, she changed the subject. "Here's your phone. I recorded the whole thing. Is this for your job?"

"No, my family. My brother wanted to see it, and I'm sure my mom will ask, so I'll have it when she does." He propped a hip on the table, stroked a finger down her cheek and brushed a soft kiss over her lips. "Thanks for coming. It was nice to have a familiar face in the audience...made it much easier."

Still reeling from the gesture, she managed to say, "You're welcome, but you didn't have anything to worry about. You're a natural and should think about teaching."

"Nah, I like being hands-on. I can't see myself standing behind a podium every day. It's only four. Do you want to get dinner now or wait until later? If we eat now, we'll have a little time to explore."

Serita stood. "Then I say we eat now." She waited for him to gather his belongings, then they dined in one of the hotel's restaurants. Because it was later in the day, they opted for another walk where she could practice taking selfies.

"You're getting better," Jeremy said, checking out the

last one." He handed the phone back. "I have a proposition for you."

"What is it?"

"How about we skip tomorrow's presentations and take the high-speed train ride to Seville? It's about two and a half hours."

She thought for a moment. She hadn't expected to meet someone like him and their time together would be over in a couple of days. "Let's do it." She wanted to store up as many memories as she could.

The next morning, they boarded the AVE train for the journey to Seville. Afterward he arranged for a taxi.

"Where are we going?" she asked a few minutes after the driver pulled off.

"I figured we could take a short city tour without having to walk." Jeremy pointed to a spot. "A horse-drawn carriage ride. What do you say?"

She had a lot of things to say and ask. Foremost in her mind was why he kept choosing all these romantic activities, as if they were a couple.

"Serita? If you'd rather do something else, that's fine."

"No, that's not it. I'd love to do the ride."

He paid the driver and helped her out of the car. "What is it?"

She tried to choose her words carefully. "The intimate dinners, a carriage ride, the kisses and the… you know…last night. All this stuff gives the impression that we're dating or something, and we both know that's not the case."

He smiled. "No, we aren't dating at this moment, but as I told you before, I want us to keep in contact. I like you and, hey, you never know what might happen in the future." He gathered her in his embrace. "How about we just enjoy this beautiful city and let the rest take care of itself."

Once again he'd slid in a comment that alluded to them seeing each other beyond the week. As much as she enjoyed his company, Serita's last couple of failed relationships had left her gun-shy, and she didn't know if she wanted to put herself through the hassle of getting her heart broken again. "Yes, let's just focus on now." Minutes later, she found out that Jeremy had actually made a reservation. The hour-long ride took them past several of Seville's city landmarks, including the Golden Tower built by moors to control navigation of the Guadalquivir River, a former tobacco factory from XVIII and the Plaza de Americana, a square inside a park containing two museums. During the tour, they enjoyed Spanish champagne, fruit and sweet treats.

Jeremy draped an arm around Serita's shoulder. "Serita, I want to thank you for agreeing to be my tourist partner this week. I don't think I would've enjoyed Madrid as much had we not met."

His serious expression had her heart thumping in her chest. "I'm having a good time, too, so thank you for asking." The tender kiss that followed sent a flurry of sensations flowing through her.

The corners of his mouth tilted in a slight smile and he pulled her closer.

For the remainder of the ride, Jeremy continued with subtle touches and caresses, each one drawing Serita further into his sensual aura. By the time they made it back to the hotel, her mind and body were in such turmoil it took only one kiss for her to go up in flames. She took his hand and pulled him into her room. The fiery kisses began again and Serita closed her eyes. If she wasn't careful, she could easily fall for him.

Chapter 4

Friday afternoon, Serita sat in her room thinking about Jeremy. She hadn't seen him today because they attended different sessions. She had made plans to have dinner tonight with Caroline when they'd had breakfast on Monday and now wished she could cancel. Tomorrow would be her last full day in Madrid, and she wanted to spend as much of her time left with Jeremy. She still hadn't told him about her potential move back to Sacramento. Things were good right now and they had both gotten caught up in the magic of being abroad, but she couldn't see it lasting. It never did.

Most of the men she'd dated had taken exception to her being somewhat of a nerd and suggested she get contacts and change her style. She had no intention of allowing a man to dictate how she should look or dress, as if her glasses, conservative dress style and love of science didn't make her an ideal candidate for romance. After one too many heartbreaks, she had decided to keep her focus where it belonged—on her career. She'd been fine doing that until now. Jeremy didn't seem to mind any of those things that defined her. In fact, he said they turned him on. The man had made love to her with her glasses on both times and told her how sexy they made her look. Her body heated up just thinking about all the ways he'd cherished her.

Serita glanced at the time. She still had half an hour before dinner, so she spent some time checking her emails and doing a job search. She clicked on one from Gabby and laughed. Her friend had sent a message in all caps letting Serita know that she was still waiting on information about the date with Jeremy. Because of the time difference, Serita hadn't had a chance to call, but she would tonight after dinner before hanging out later with Jeremy. She sent a quick email back to Gabby saying just that. The pediatric doctor's office where Gabby worked closed at noon on Fridays, which would give them time to talk before it got too late. Then she scanned the job-listing site and saw a couple of promising opportunities. Although one in a small company indicated there would be a thirty-day trial period before deciding on a candidate, she applied for it anyway— along with another one—knowing she had the skills to handle anything they threw her way. Not seeing any other jobs she liked, Serita shut down the laptop and left for dinner.

She saw Caroline waiting by the entrance of the restaurant.

"Hi, Serita. I already checked in, so it should only be a few minutes."

"Okay. Did you enjoy the conference?"

"I did. I learned so much and I'm kind of sad it's over. But I won't be leaving until Monday and can't wait to tour the city without having to worry about hurrying back. When are you flying out?" Before Serita could answer, the hostess showed them to their table.

Once they were seated, she picked up the conversation. "I'm leaving Sunday morning. That gives me one more day to see the sights."

Caroline's eyes lit up. "We should do one of the bus tours tomorrow."

"I already have plans, sorry."

"Oh, that's too bad." She smiled and waved. "I hope you don't mind, but I invited a couple of the guys I met at the afternoon session to join us."

Yeah, Serita did mind, especially when both men looked as if they'd come straight from the bar. But she nodded politely when Caroline made the introductions. The server came to take their drink orders and Serita ordered a glass of chardonnay.

"Forget the wine," one of the men said. "We need a bottle of your best champagne to celebrate the ending of another great conference."

"Ooh, that sounds fabulous," Caroline said.

Serita forced a smile. "No, thank you. You all are welcome to enjoy your champagne. I'll just stick with my wine." They proceeded to order a bottle of the most expensive sparking drink on the menu and she sincerely hoped they didn't expect her to chip in to pay for it.

After the server departed, the other man, whose name had escaped Serita, said, "I attended your session. It was really good. You seem to have a lot of knowledge for someone so young."

She wondered if he always handed out insults along with his compliments. "Thank you." She picked up her menu. *This dinner can't end soon enough.* Her dining companions launched into a discussion of the field and what they would like to see. Serita followed along but didn't comment. The server returned with drinks and took the food order. Once again, the trio ordered several appetizers and expensive entrées. When the appetizers came out, she declined, citing wanting to save her appetite. Over the course of dinner, they ordered more champagne and Serita shook her head. They laughed loudly at bad jokes, drawing stares from diners at nearby tables and, more than once, Serita was tempted to toss her napkin down and leave.

Caroline took a sip from her glass. "Ron, this is the best champagne. Great choice."

He toasted her with his glass and inclined his head.

"Serita and I were talking about taking a tour tomorrow. What do you guys say?"

"I'm in," Ron said. "What about you, Evan?"

"Definitely count me in."

Serita mentally counted to ten. She'd specifically told Caroline she had other plans. "You guys enjoy yourselves. As I told Caroline earlier, I won't be available." The chicken dish she had ordered was good, but her appetite had waned considerably. When it came time for dessert, she declined but had to endure until the bill came.

Evan picked up the bill. "Whoa. It's a good thing we're sharing the costs."

Serita had always been considered sweet and demure, but when they suggested splitting the bill four ways, her inner Cali girl made an appearance. "I beg your pardon. I will *not* be paying for any part of your meals or the multitude of drinks and appetizers you all ordered. I didn't even invite you," she added, glaring at Caroline. She looked up at the stunned server. "Please separate my portion of the bill."

The young man nodded and hurried away.

She sat there seething until he returned and placed the bill holder in front of her. She retrieved the money from her purse and included a tip. "Have a good evening." She rose from her chair and stalked out of the restaurant without a backward glance. Serita didn't stop walking until she got to the elevator. She jabbed the button and paced angrily. Of all the nerve! Did they really think she would contribute to the several-hundred-dollar cost of their meals? The elevator arrived and she moved aside to let the other people off before stepping inside and riding the car to her floor.

Inside her room, she took a couple of deep, calming breaths. Seeing that it was just after nine, she powered up her laptop and FaceTimed Gabby.

"Hey, girl. How's it going?"

"It was fine until dinner tonight." She related the incident. "They actually looked offended when I said I wasn't going in on the bill."

"It's a good thing it was you instead of me. I probably would've told girlfriend she could have dinner with those guys by herself and gotten my own table. People have a lot of gall." Gabby shook her head.

"I know. It takes a lot to get me upset, but I wanted to smack her. Then she told them we were hanging out tomorrow, when I had specifically said I had other plans."

"Plans that, no doubt, include the mysterious Jeremy."

"Yes."

"Obviously, you two hit it off, since I haven't gotten one call."

Serita didn't know how to explain how Jeremy made her feel. "He's incredible. Almost too good to be true. We've been exploring the city together and he won't let me pay for anything. On Thursday, he took me on a horse-drawn carriage ride, and it was the most romantic thing ever."

She released a dreamy sigh. "Aww, it sounds incredibly wonderful. How does he kiss?"

"Who said he's kissed me?"

Gabby gave her an incredulous look. "Girl, quit playing and answer the question."

"Like he created the art." A vision of his seductive kisses floated through her mind.

She laughed. "And memorable by the look on your face."

"Very. He makes me feel so… I don't know. Sexy, desirable."

"Sexy? Hold up. I know you didn't do the wild thing with a brother you just met." Serita's expression told all. "Okay, having dinner and exploring a city is one thing, but sleeping with him is something altogether different." She blew out a long breath. "Sis, what do you really know about this guy?"

Serita understood Gabby's point because she'd said the same thing to herself more than once. "He's intelligent, makes me laugh and treats me like a queen, despite just meeting me."

She nodded. "I can get with that. Maybe he has potential."

"And he lives in Sacramento."

Gabby's eyebrows shot up. "Seriously? That's fantastic—it'll make it easier for you guys to see each other."

"He doesn't know I'm moving back," Serita said guiltily.

"What? Why not? You just said the man was fabulous."

She scrubbed a hand across her forehead. "You know how my relationships end up."

Gabby waved a hand and wrinkled her nose. "Those guys were idiots. Jeremy sounds like he's the total opposite."

"He is." From what she'd seen so far, he impressed her as being a genuinely good guy, but she couldn't help but wonder what would happen once they returned to reality.

"Has he said anything about wanting you guys to keep seeing each other?"

"He's hinted around the possibility, but hasn't come right out and said it. He knows I live in Reno and seems to be willing to make that drive, so…" She shrugged.

"You should tell him about the move. Who knows? He might be able to give you some information about jobs in the area."

"True." Serita hadn't thought of that. "Maybe I'll ask him tonight."

Gabby grinned. "If you remember."

She lifted a brow. "Why wouldn't I remember?"

"If a man kisses like you say he does, I doubt you'll be able to remember anything, including your name."

Her friend had a point. Not only did Jeremy kiss like he'd invented it, he made love the same way. Yeah, she was in trouble. Big trouble.

Jeremy sat in his room, eating dinner and working on the design for a prosthetic hand that would closely imitate natural function. He wanted it to have a more natural feel and look, which was why he'd been so excited about Serita's presentation. This was a personal project of his and he wondered briefly if she would consider working with him on it. He sat back in the chair. She elicited a spark in him he hadn't felt in a long time, if ever. He still hadn't asked her about them continuing what they'd begun, but he had one more day to do it. He hoped she would be receptive. Just thinking about her petite sexy self made him hard. With the prim and proper way she carried herself, he never would have expected her to be so uninhibited in bed. He suspected not many people saw that side of her, but he had enjoyed every moment. In and out of bed.

He finished his meal, set the plate aside and made a few more changes to his drawing. Just as he started, Christian called. He activated the FaceTime. "What's up, Chris?"

"Hey. Just checking in with you about Nelson."

"What about him?" Nelson Atkins had given his notice the day before Jeremy left for Madrid.

"Instead of leaving in three weeks, he came in this morning and said today is his last day."

Jeremy muttered a curse. "Did he at least finish his part of the motion-control system like he promised?"

"Ah, that would be a no. Which is why I'm calling. I uploaded the open position to all the job sites we use and made sure to note it was a thirty-day trial to determine the best fit."

"Thanks. I'm probably going to have to do some overtime to pick up the slack until we fill the position." He had figured they would be able to hire a replacement before Nelson left to avoid disruption in their schedule.

"Hopefully, we'll be able to find someone soon. I already have three applications. Also, I'm putting together a bid on another project."

"It sounds good, but will it be feasible with the limited staff? I don't want to put us in the position of having to work overtime to meet any deadlines."

"Which brings me to my next topic."

"What?" Jeremy asked warily. Chris had always been a go-getter, which was how he'd made his first million dollars at age twenty-two. He applied the same work ethic to their company.

"I'm thinking we should hire four for the trial and keep the two best. It would give us an extra person, so we could take on one or two more projects."

He mulled it over. "Okay, but can we afford it?"

"I ran the numbers and we'd be good financially. And if we get this next contract, it would give us a fair amount of breathing room."

"Alright. Let's go with it."

"How's Madrid?"

He smiled. "It's great. I met an incredible woman."

Chris laughed and shook his head. "Are you still talking about being able to know on sight if the woman is for you?"

"Yes, and I think it's her."

His laughter faded. "*What?* Jeremy, you can't be serious. I know you don't believe that kind of thing really exists."

"Of course I believe it. Why wouldn't I?"

"Because…because… This is reality and not some fantasy romance that you read in books."

"You don't think you could meet a woman and feel

like she's the one you've been waiting for?" As crazy as it might have sounded, that was how he felt.

"No," Chris said emphatically. "I think you've got a serious case of sexual attraction going on, nothing more."

Jeremy laughed. "Yeah, that, too."

"Oh, hell. You slept with her already?" He dragged a hand down his face. "Jeremy, this isn't like you."

"You're right, which is why I know she's special." She stimulated his mind just as much as his body.

"If you say so. What's going to happen once you come back home? I assume she's not local."

"She lives in Reno and I'm more than willing to keep getting to know her, but I won't know how she feels about it until I ask tonight."

"Well, I hope it works out. With the way things are today, you might want to proceed with caution. People aren't always who they say they are. You almost need to do a full background check."

Smiling, he shook his head. "I'll take my chances." He heard a knock. "Someone's at my door."

"Probably your mystery woman."

"Yep."

"I'll talk to you later. Hit me up when you get back on Sunday."

Jeremy nodded. "Later." He cut the connection and went to open the door. His smile widened when he saw Serita standing there. "Come in, baby." He bent to kiss her. "How was dinner?"

Serita rolled her eyes. "Ugh. I should've canceled. Caroline took it upon herself to invite these two guys to join us. They ran the bill up to several hundreds of dollars and had the nerve to suggest we split the bill."

He smiled at her annoyed expression. "I take it you weren't too happy about that."

"You take it right. I wasn't paying one dime more than what I ate."

Chuckling, he pulled her into his arms. "See, if you'd accepted my dinner invite, you wouldn't have had to deal with that kind of foolishness," he teased.

"Tell me about it. Anyway, enough of that." She backed out of his arms. "Are you working?" She pointed to his laptop, which still had mechanical parts displayed.

"A little bit." He gestured to the chair. "Have a seat."

She sat and picked up the mystery thriller on the desk. "I have this book, but haven't had a chance to read it yet."

He sat on the edge of the bed. "I just started it. How about we discuss it once you're done? We can do it over a dinner *date*."

Serita laughed softly. "So is that your way of letting me know up front?"

"Yep." Jeremy figured this would be a good time to bring up his proposal. "I've really enjoyed spending time with you this week and I'm hoping we can continue once get home. I have no problem driving to Reno to see you." He had his place in Tahoe, as well, and could see them spending a weekend there. However, he would rather do it before it got too cold and the snow started.

"I appreciate what you're saying, but how do you know it'll be the same or whether things will work out?"

"I don't know, but I'm willing to find out." What he did know was that this woman moved him like no other and he would do whatever it took to find out whether she was *the one*. "What do you say?"

"I would like to say yes, but you need to know that relationships don't seem to work out for me."

The tone of her voice gave him pause. Had she been hurt…and how many times? Jeremy left the bed, hunkered down in front of her and grasped her hands. "We've all had relationships that didn't work out, but we won't ever find the right one if we don't keep trying."

"True." She appeared to be weighing his words. Finally she said, "Okay."

Jeremy leaned up and kissed her, wanting to assure her that he would do everything in his power not to hurt her. He reached behind her, picked up his phone and opened the contacts. "Can you put your info in?"

Serita took the phone and started typing. As she handed it back, the cell rang.

He frowned. He rarely used his phone when he traveled out of the country to minimize costs and fees. Seeing his cousin Lorenzo's name on the display made his frown deepen. "Can you excuse me a moment—it's my cousin." He hit the button. "Hey, Zo."

"I know this is long-distance, so I'll keep it short. Randi went into labor an hour ago and is in the hospital."

Jeremy slowly rose to his feet, his heart pounding. "What do you mean she's in labor? She's not due for almost two months. What happened?"

"We don't know. She called Ced from her office and told him she'd been having contractions and he took off. He just called to tell me they're keeping her. He's not taking it well."

"How're my parents?"

"Worried, but they seem to be holding up okay. My parents are here at the hospital, too."

"I'm going to take the first flight out." He could only imagine the fear Ced and Randi were experiencing. He had to get home.

"Email me your flight info and I'll pick you up."

"Thanks. Keep me posted." He disconnected and closed his eyes briefly. Then he turned to Serita. "I have to go home. My sister-in-law went into premature labor. She's not due for another two months."

Serita stood and wrapped her arms around his waist. "I hope they can stop the contractions."

"I know we were supposed to spend the day together tomorrow. I'm sorry."

"No apology is necessary, Jeremy. You need to be there for your family."

"I promise to make it up to you. Let me give you my number." He had hoped to have that last day with her, and had planned for them to rent a boat and take a ride on the lake, then have a picnic. She handed him her phone and he inputted the information.

She took the phone back and dropped it into her purse. "I'll get out of your way. I know you need to make your flight arrangements."

Jeremy placed a staying hand on her arm. "No, don't leave. At this hour, I probably won't be able to get a flight out until morning, and I want to spend as much time with you as possible."

She nodded.

He smiled faintly. "Thanks." He used the hotel phone to call the airline and it took more than fifteen minutes to find a flight. Thankfully, he didn't have to pay an additional fee due to his A-list rating. He hung up. "My flight leaves at six in the morning."

"That means you're going to need to be at the airport at O-dark-hundred. It's after ten. You need to be going to bed."

He laughed. "Yeah, *early*. How about we go get your café con leche and talk for a little while? I'll be okay." And he could sleep on the long flight.

Chapter 5

Jeremy grabbed his luggage off the carousel and made his way through the airport terminal. On the way, he called Lorenzo, then exited to the pickup area. Obviously, several planes had landed around the same time because the he could barely find a spot to wait in the crowd. Luckily, his height gave him an advantage, and less than four minutes later he saw Lorenzo's Lexus SUV and waved him down. His cousin popped the trunk, and Jeremy tossed the bags in, then got in on the passenger side.

"How was the flight?" Lorenzo asked as he merged into the traffic.

"Long." He laid his head against the seat and closed his eyes. He had not been able to sleep on the plane as planned and was beyond tired. "How's Randi?"

"They have her on some meds that'll, hopefully,

stop the contractions. They've slowed, so that's a good thing."

"It is."

"You want to stop by the house first or go straight to the hospital?"

"Hospital." He could imagine the fear she and Cedric were experiencing and Jeremy needed to see with his own eyes how they were doing. Besides, if he went home, he might not make it back today. His thoughts shifted to Serita. Strange as it seemed, he missed her already. While waiting for his luggage, he had sent her an email like she'd asked to let her know he'd made it home. However, he didn't expect a reply. With the nine-hour time difference, it was already after midnight there. She'd be flying home tomorrow and chances were they wouldn't connect until sometime during the week. Jeremy didn't realize he had drifted off until he felt the tap on his shoulder. He opened his eyes and sat up slowly.

"Maybe you should've gone home to take a nap," Lorenzo said with a chuckle as he got out of the car.

Jeremy followed suit and stretched. "I'm not staying long and, yeah, I need some sleep." Inside the hospital, they took the elevator to Randi's floor. Cedric was standing in the hallway talking with their mother. Both looked up with surprise.

"Oh, my goodness! You're home early." His mother rushed over and engulfed him in a crushing hug. "I didn't expect you until tomorrow night."

He kissed her cheek. "Zo called about Randi and I took the first flight out. You know I had to come." Family meant everything to him, and he couldn't *not* be there during a crisis.

She nodded in understanding and patted his cheek.

"I'm so glad to see you. You can tell me all about your trip sometime later in the week. I'm going to go in and see if Randi is awake."

Jeremy embraced his brother. "How're you holding up?"

Cedric dragged a hand down his face and blew out a long breath. "I've been better. Hey, Zo."

Lorenzo clapped Cedric on the shoulder. "Hang in there. I know she's going to be fine." He turned to Jeremy. "I'm going to chill in the waiting room down the hall. When you're ready to go, come get me."

"Okay." Jeremy studied his brother and could see the lines of tension and fatigue lining his features. "How is Randi doing now? Zo said the contractions are slowing."

"They are, but not enough right now. She's worried. I put up a good front with her, but I'm scared to death something's going to go wrong. The doctors were talking about lung and brain development and a whole lot of other stuff that freaked me out." He let the wall take his weight. "I don't know what I'll do if anything happens to either of them," he said in an anguished whisper. "I feel so damn helpless."

"We've got to pray and believe that everything is going to be okay. You said the contractions are slowing. Let's take that as a sign things are moving in the right direction."

"Believe me, I'm trying."

"Do you need me to do anything?"

"No, we're good. You look dead on your feet."

Jeremy smiled. "So do you. I know the hospital is probably limiting her visitors, but I want to poke my head in for a minute."

Cedric waved him off. "You're fine. You should've

been here last night when the entire family showed up. We almost got put out. Mom and Aunt LaVerne scared those nurses so bad they just let us all in."

"I can imagine." When it came to their children—regardless of the fact that all were adults now—both women were very protective. As soon as Randi married Cedric, she became one of them and they guarded her as if she had been born into the family. "What about her parents?"

"They're flying in tomorrow." He pushed the door open and held it for Jeremy.

"Hey, sis," Jeremy said, approaching the bed.

"Hey, Doc," Randi said softly. "Aren't you supposed to be in Madrid wooing all the senoritas?" Even though she looked as if she had been through the ringer, she still had her wit.

He smiled. "I had to come and check on you and there's only one senorita I'm interested in wooing."

"What?" his mother and brother said at the same time. Randi stared at him.

He gave her a wink. "I'll tell you all about her when you get home. Right now, I need you to concentrate on resting." He placed a gentle hand on her belly. "Hey, little one, I know you're anxious to meet your family, but we need you to hang out awhile longer. I promise we'll all be here to greet you when it's time." He bent and placed a kiss on Randi's forehead. "Rest up, sis, and I'll check on you tomorrow."

She grasped his hand. "Thank you, and I'm sorry you had to shorten your trip."

"No apologies necessary." Saying those words reminded him of Serita saying the same thing to him. He hoped things would work out between them so he could introduce her to his family. He knew they'd love her.

His mother eyed him. "You get a good night's sleep because I will be calling you tomorrow."

Cedric laughed.

Jeremy had no doubt that she would call him by nine, generously allowing him that extra hour. He gave her another hug and kiss. "I'll be expecting it."

Cedric caressed Randi's cheek and kissed her. "I'll be right back, baby. I'm going to walk Jeremy out." As soon as the door closed, he said to Jeremy. "What do you mean wooing a senorita? Did you meet someone there?"

"I did."

"Look, bro, I know you're all into finding Mrs. Right, but Spain is a long way from Cali."

He grinned. "She doesn't live in Madrid. She's a lot closer—Reno."

Cedric's eyes widened. "Still long-distance, and how do you know she's going to go for that?"

"We already talked about it. Serita is a beautiful woman—about five-two or three, brains, sweet curves, all this curly hair and a pair of sexy glasses."

He shook his head. "Only you. So she's got some sexy nerd-girl thing going on?"

"Exactly. We spent a lot of time together this week and I really like her."

"Be careful that you don't get all caught up so soon."

Jeremy let out a short bark of laughter. "I know you're not talking to me, Mr. Slept-With-Randi-On-The-First-Date."

"Yeah, whatever. That wasn't unusual for me. You,

on the other hand, have always waited until you had some kind of commitment first."

"True…usually."

Cedric held up a hand. "Wait. Are you telling me you slept with this woman already?"

"I'm not telling you anything. I'll talk to you later. Call me if you need me. Later, big brother." He laughed at Cedric's shocked expression and left him standing there. As he made his way to the waiting room, he thought about the look of adoration Cedric and Randi shared. The love between them was palpable and it made Jeremy even more sure that he wanted the same thing in his life. He just needed to know if Serita was the one for him.

Sunday evening, Serita dropped down on Gabby's sofa, closed her eyes and groaned. "Girl, I don't ever want to move again." It was a fantasy because she only planned to stay with her friend temporarily, until she found her own place. Instead of moving in a month, she'd had to put her condo on the market and pack up to move in less than two weeks after returning from Madrid in order to start her new job.

"You're more than welcome to stay forever," Gabby said with a laugh, collapsing on the other side of the sofa. "Well, if you had taken Jeremy up on his offer to help you move, you wouldn't be so tired."

She cracked open an eye. "Shut up." When Jeremy found out she had decided to relocate back to Sacramento, he had immediately offered to help with the move and finding her a place. But she was used to doing things on her own and didn't want to start depending on any man, especially one she had known for only a short time.

Granted, she'd come to feel closer to him in that short period than she had with all the guys she'd dated combined. "He doesn't actually know I moved this weekend. I haven't talked to him since last week. He mentioned having to work overtime because someone at the company quit. And then there are the concerns with his sister-in-law's pregnancy. Thankfully, her contractions stopped, but from what he told me, the doctor's put her on bed rest for the duration of her pregnancy. We've been playing phone tag and exchanging texts here and there, but that's about all."

"How do you feel about seeing him again? I mean, it's easy to get wrapped up in the beauty of a foreign country and with all the romantic things you guys did, but do you think it'll be the same now?"

"I honestly don't know and that's part of the reason I didn't mention the move." She also didn't want it to turn into just a physical relationship. She wanted more and, at age thirty-two, didn't plan to settle for being anyone's plaything. She didn't sense that to be the case with Jeremy and, if so, he put up a good front.

"You're going to have to tell him eventually because I'm sure he'll ask. And I'm really curious about him. If he turns out to be the real deal, I need to know if he has any available brothers."

Serita chuckled tiredly. "He has just the one brother, who's married."

"Damn. Why are all the good ones taken?" Gabby asked with a mock pout.

"I don't know about you. Maybe he has a friend."

She perked up. "Ooh, yeah. I need you to get me the hookup. Just make sure the friend isn't one of those crazy men who has some whack belief system about women being barefoot, pregnant and in the kitchen."

"I thought you wanted kids."

"I do, but I don't want to have to quit my job to do it. I've got no issues cutting my hours, but I'm not the Suzie Homemaker type."

"Hey, you never know. You'll see those babies and end up being one of those women who attend every PTA meeting, coordinate all the bake sales and play chaperone on field trips."

Gabby shot Serita a look. "Bite your tongue. I. Don't. Think. So. Not in this lifetime or the next one." She shuddered.

She laughed and pointed. "I wish you could see your face."

"I don't need to see it to know what it looks like. I bet you'd say the same thing."

Serita nodded. "Yeah, no. Not quitting. I worked too hard to get where I am to just let it all go. I'd like to own a small company one day, and I won't be able to do that if I'm sitting on the sofa all day eating bonbons."

She lifted her hand and gave Serita a high five. "Amen, my sister!"

The two women fell out laughing. When they finally calmed, Serita said, "I've missed hanging out with you." There was never a dull moment with her friend around.

"Same here." Gabby yawned. "It's getting late and I need to be in the office at seven in the morning. Did you find out any more information on the company where you'll be working?"

"The website was down the other night when I checked and, with everything going on, I forgot about it. I guess I'll just wait and see in the morning. If it turns out to be a mess, I'll do that thirty-day trial and be out the door. I'm still applying at other places, just in case."

"I hope it works out."

"So do I." From the job description, it appeared to be exactly what she was looking for—challenging and cutting-edge—and it would give her a chance to sharpen her skills. She'd had little time to work in the field over the past seven years and this new opportunity gave her the same excitement she had felt when she started at her first robotics company right out of college. After working for four years, she'd gone back for her doctorate and had accepted the job in academia at the suggestion of one of her professors. "Thanks again for letting me crash here until I find a place."

Gabby stood. "Oh, girl. I'm glad I could help. I'll see you in the morning."

"Good night." She sat there a moment longer, then went to prepare for bed. After a long, hot shower, Serita felt a little better, but she hadn't used many of those muscles in a while and knew she'd probably be sore in the morning. She went through the closet, trying to decide what to wear, and settled on a pair of gray slacks and a short-sleeved black blouse. Even though the calendar read mid-October, the weather still remained near eighty degrees.

She fell asleep as soon as her head hit the pillow, and when her alarm went off at six thirty the next morning she swore she had just lain down. Serita dragged herself out of bed and got dressed. Gabby had already gone by the time Serita emerged and had left coffee. Since she didn't particularly care for it, she opted for a cup of hot peppermint tea. She had yet to find a recipe for the café con leche she liked, but vowed to search one out as soon as she had a moment. After a quick breakfast of fruit and a boiled egg, she Googled directions to the Roseville office and set off. Fortunately, Gabby's Antelope condo was less than twenty minutes away.

She arrived fifteen minutes before the scheduled eight-o'clock time and, taking a deep breath, entered the one-story building located in an office park off Douglas Boulevard. In the small lobby, a trio of chairs surrounded a coffee table filled with magazines, and photos of various types of robots hung on the walls. A young woman sat at the desk. "Good morning. I'm Serita Edwards and have an appointment with Christian Hill."

The woman smiled. "Good morning." She clicked a few keys on the computer, then said, "Have a seat and I'll let him know you're here."

"Thank you." Serita sat in one of the chairs and speculated what her job would entail. The company focused on medical robotics, and that could mean anything— surgery robots and instruments or prosthetics. A couple of minutes later, a man who looked to be around her age or a couple of years older rushed through the door. He smoothed his blond hair back and went over to the receptionist, then joined Serita in the waiting area.

"Are you starting today, too?" he asked.

"Yes."

"You must be a new grad." Smiling, he stuck out his hand. "I'm Wade."

She shook his hand briefly. "Serita." She purposely didn't respond to his assumption.

"Sorry to keep you waiting."

Serita turned at the sound of a deep voice. A tall, mahogany-skinned brother stood there with a warm smile. She stood.

"I'm Chris." He stuck out his hand.

"Wade Brewer."

Serita stifled an eye roll. The man jumped in front of her and nearly knocked her down.

Chris raised an eyebrow, then shifted his gaze to Serita. "And you are?"

"Serita Edwards."

"Nice to meet you. If you'll follow me, I'll get you all set up with the paperwork. Hopefully, the other two new hires will be here shortly and I can give the information once."

They went down a long hallway to a conference room holding a table that seated eight. She waited until Wade sat before taking a seat at the opposite end.

Chris handed them each a stack of papers.

"Chris, your other two candidates are here."

He turned. "Thanks, Nicole." He made introductions, then gestured the two men to the table and gave them the forms. "After you fill these out, I'll tell you a little about our company, and then we'll discuss the parameters of the position and the projects that you'll be working on."

"Will we be working under you?" Wade asked.

"No. I just handle the business. I leave the other stuff to the engineers." Everyone chuckled. "I'll be back in a few minutes."

Serita turned her attention to the paperwork. That was one thing she hated about starting a new job. It seemed as if employers wanted to know everything except the color of someone's underwear. *With all these papers, I wouldn't be surprised if they did ask.*

"Okay, everybody. If you're done, you can pass your papers to the end of the table. I want to introduce you to Jeremy Hunter."

Her head snapped up and she gasped. Jeremy seemed to notice her at the same time and his eyes widened for a brief moment before he schooled his features.

"How about you go around the table and introduce yourselves."

As usual, Wade jumped in first. Not only did he provide his name, he launched into a brag session of all the places he'd worked.

Jeremy cut him off. "We've gone through the résumés, so just a name will suffice for now." He reached out and shook Wade's hand.

The two other men introduced themselves as Darryl Ross and Scott Aldridge, and Jeremy repeated the gesture.

When it came to her turn, he came and stood so close to her she could feel the heat from his body mingling with her own, bringing with it memories of their week in Madrid. "Serita Edwards."

"Ms. Edwards."

Instead of the quick shake he'd done with the others, Jeremy held her hand a little longer and circled his thumb over the back of her hand. To keep from grabbing him down for the kiss she wanted to give him, she pulled back and folded her hands in her lap.

A slight smile curved his lips, as if he knew the effect his touch had on her. "Chris will start, then I'll give you a general overview of our projects. Afterward, I'll meet with you individually to determine where you'll best fit. You will only be working on existing projects, so please note that there is a form that you'll need to sign stating you understand our policy on design changes."

He spoke that last sentence while looking directly at Serita. Her pulse skipped. How was she going to get through the next thirty days working with him without wanting to be in his arms? How was she going to get through this first meeting with him?

Chapter 6

Jeremy could hardly contain his excitement, knowing that Serita would be working with him. He didn't need a month to know she would fit in with his company. He spent about half an hour detailing the various projects before talking with each person individually. He got good vibes from everyone except Wade. The man acted like he was the only one in the room with an engineering degree. Jeremy could tell right off that Mr. Brewer would be looking for employment elsewhere. Chris had also mentioned that Wade had jumped in front of Serita to introduce himself out in the lobby. Any man who disrespected a woman had no place in Jeremy's business. Typically, he would have had Serita introduce herself first, with her being the only woman in the room. However, saving her for last had been selfish in nature and given him time to linger over her nearness.

When she walked into his office, it took every ounce

of control to stand there, when all he wanted to do was hold her in his arms and show her just how much he had missed her. "How are you, baby?"

"A little shocked to be honest." Serita sat in one of the chairs opposite his desk and perched on the edge.

"Join the club," Jeremy said with a laugh. "I thought you were moving back at the end of the month. You should've called me, so I could help you."

"Things went kind of fast and I know you were busy. I had planned to call you tonight and let you know, but I guess the cat's out of the bag now."

"I guess so." He waged an inner battle with himself for several seconds. Unable to take it any longer, he rounded the desk and gently pulled Serita to her feet. "I know this is work and I'm going do my best to be professional around you, but I have to kiss you right now."

She studied him, then held up a finger. "One kiss, Jeremy. One time and that's it."

It was all he needed to hear. He traced a finger down her cheek and over her mouth. It had taken her just four days to get under his skin. Jeremy lowered his head and brushed his lips over hers once, twice. Her lips parted on a breathless sigh and he captured her mouth in an intoxicating kiss, feeding from the sweetness inside. He sat on the desk and pulled her to stand between his legs. He deepened the kiss while his hands roamed down her spine and over the roundness of her backside. It took a minute, but he finally ended the kiss. He rested his forehead against hers and their ragged breathing echoed in the office.

"We can't do this," she whispered.

"Maybe not here, but as soon as the workday ends, you're mine."

Serita's gaze flew to his.

The panicked look in her eyes gave him pause. "You didn't change your mind about us seeing each other, did you?"

"No. I just don't want to mess up this job opportunity."

"You won't."

"How long have you worked here?"

Jeremy debated whether to tell her the truth. She might change her mind about them. In the end he decided to be honest. "Since the day the doors opened three years ago."

"You know the owner well, then?"

He smiled. "From the day I was born."

She stared at him in confusion.

"HJ Robotics is my baby."

"You *own* this company?" Serita shook her head. "*Nooo*. I can't work here."

He frowned. "Why not? You're qualified."

She placed a hand on her hip and lifted a brow. "You're going to be the person deciding which of us stays after thirty days, right?"

"Yes," he answered slowly.

"Exactly my point."

It dawned on him what she meant. "You think I'll give you special preference because of our relationship."

"Yes."

"Serita, this is my business, my livelihood. I worked my butt off to get to this point. Don't think for one minute I'd do anything to jeopardize that. Now, I will admit I'd like to have you working with me because I believe you would be a great asset to the company, but I promise to judge you on your work only." At her skeptical look, he added, "I'll even put it in writing, if you want."

"I don't know."

"Come on, baby." He nuzzled her neck.

"See, this right here will have me walking out the door now."

Jeremy set her away from him and placed his hands behind his back. "Then I'll keep my hands to myself."

"And your lips."

He opened his mouth to say something, but her look made it clear there was no point arguing. "Fine. And I'll keep my lips to myself...between eight and five."

A smile spread across her lips. "I don't know what I'm going to do with you."

He wiggled his eyebrows. "I'm sure I can come up with a few ideas."

She pointed to his chair. "The only idea you're going to be coming up with right now is telling me which project you're assigning me to. You're on the clock, Mr. Hunter, so let's get to work."

He couldn't do anything but smile and do as she asked. Once seated behind his desk, he told her about the three project areas—a surgical arm, a console that incorporated the robots, instrumentation and other technologies, and a surgical system that would be used for eye surgery. "The latter has the closest deadline, so I'd like you to work on that one."

"Who else is working on the project?"

He chuckled inwardly, knowing what she was getting at. "What you really want to know is if I'm working on the project, right?"

Serita dropped her gaze briefly. "Yes."

"You don't think we can work together?" Jeremy

stood, came around the desk and took the chair next to her. "I happen to believe we'll work very well together. And I already promised you I'll be good while we're on the clock." They shut down at five and his staff was usually out the door right at that time. He, on the other hand, often stayed late. Maybe he could interest Serita in a little overtime—work *and* play. He rose to his feet and extended his hand. "Come on. Let me introduce you to Elena, and she'll put you to work."

She placed her hand in his and he helped her to her feet. "Thank you. I'm still not sure how I feel about this whole thing, but I will do my best to help you get your robot done on time."

"I have no doubt about that." He lifted his hand to touch her cheek, then remembered the agreement and let it drop to his side. He crossed the room, opened the door and gestured her forward. On the way to her assigned project, he pointed out the different work areas, bathrooms and break room. He stopped at a door at the end of the hall. "This is where you'll work." He led her over to the worktable where his two engineers stood. Both looked up at Jeremy's entrance. "Elena Arevalo and Shane Meyers, this is Serita Edwards. She'll be working with us, hopefully for a long time to come."

"Hallelujah! Finally, you hired somebody with a brain," Elena said in her Spanish-accented English. "Welcome, Serita."

Shane snorted. "Hey, I'm the only one in here with one. Glad to have you, Serita."

Jeremy met Serita's wary gaze and shook his head. "Serita, don't pay them any attention. It's never a dull moment with these two around." He told them, "Try not to scare Serita off before lunch, please."

Elena waved him off. "Oh, we'll be fine." She beckoned Serita over and said in a loud whisper, "The only one who's scary is that big man behind you."

"Sabes que puedo oírte, Elena?"

"Of course I know you can hear me." She snorted. "I don't want you to think I talk about you behind your back."

Serita laughed. "I think I'm going to enjoy working here."

He stared down at her. "I hope so." Because he was looking forward to working with her and more.

Serita enjoyed working with Elena and Shane. Contrary to Elena's teasing, Shane did have a brain, a highly intelligent one. He reminded her a little of Chris Hemsworth—minus the Thor muscles. Both had a wealth of knowledge, and she could see why Jeremy had hired them. It took Serita a short time to get her bearings, but by late afternoon, she was up to speed. The high-precision hybrid design would provide exceptional steadiness of the instrument while allowing surgeons to maintain close contact with a patient. She got so engrossed in her task that she had to suppress her disappointment when the day ended. She hadn't been this excited since her first job.

"If I get a vote, I say Jeremy needs to keep you forever," Shane said as they locked up. "I know you mentioned being out of the field for a few years, but you could never tell."

She smiled. "Thanks."

Elena patted Serita's arm. "You'll definitely get my vote. We need another woman around here to keep these men in line. Have a nice evening."

"You do the same. See you guys in the morning." She smiled. *Not bad for a first day.* Over lunch, Serita had learned that the fortysomething-year-old Elena had gone back to school and got her engineering degree a decade ago, after her youngest child turned three. It made Serita think about the conversation she and Gabby had had the night before. If Elena could juggle marriage, children and an intensive degree program, surely Serita could do it. If it ever happened. Automatically her thoughts shifted to Jeremy. Where would they end up? She didn't even want to contemplate how awkward it would be if he hired her permanently, then sometime down the road their relationship fizzled out. She'd be back at square one because no way would she be able to see him every day and remember how it had felt to be with him. As it stood now, she was going to have a hard time keeping her hands to herself. Serita had extracted a promise from Jeremy and she needed to be sure to abide by her own rules, no matter how tempting it was to touch or kiss him.

Instead of heading to her car, she went back down the hall to see if Jeremy was still there. She poked her head in the open door and saw him seated behind his desk and working on his computer. She knocked. "Are you busy?"

Jeremy grinned. "Nope. Just playing an online *Jeopardy!* game while I wait for you."

"Are you any good?"

"Of course I'm good. I can wipe the floor with you anytime." He spread his arms. "We can do it right now."

Serita chuckled. "Hmm, tempting, but maybe some other time."

"What? You scared?" he teased.

She rolled her eyes. "Please." She found herself enjoyed the silly bantering between them.

"So how was the first day?"

"It went pretty well. I think I'm going to like working with Elena and Shane."

"They're cool peeps. That's why I hired them. I had a few classes with Shane back in undergrad and we kept in touch over the years. He had gotten downsized from the other company where he worked just as I was launching mine, so I took that as a sign."

"What about Elena?"

"I met her when I went back for my doctorate. She was just returning after having her kids and I tutored her for a couple of classes. My love of Mexican food is because of her. I wouldn't take any money from her, so she repaid me by fixing some of the best enchiladas, tamales and tacos I've ever eaten." He smiled as if remembering. "She told me I was too old to be her son, so she'd think of me as a younger brother."

Serita laughed softly. "I like her."

"She's special. At one point, she had been discouraged about her ability to get through the program."

"I can understand. It's no joke." She had spent her fair share of nights, fussing, cussing and crying. But she had made it through near the top of her class.

"I told her she could do it and promised her that whenever I started my company I would hire her."

"And you made good on that promise." She was liking this man more and more. He appeared to be almost perfect, but no one could hold that title. He must have some faults.

"What are you thinking?"

"Just that you seem to be too good to be true. You're

generous, a gentleman, you tutor people for free... Everybody has at least one blemish."

Jeremy burst out laughing. "Oh, I have a few. I can be pretty anal at times, especially when it comes to my business. I've been known to stick my foot in my mouth a time or two. I work toward perfection and I expect everyone around me to do the same."

"Nobody's perfect, Jeremy."

"You're right, and I remind myself of that daily so I don't walk in one morning and find that everybody's quit." He pushed back from the desk. "Come here, for a minute."

The look in his eyes left no doubt in her mind what he wanted. She told herself they were still at the job, but somehow her feet missed the memo and she ended up right where he wanted her—on his lap. "Jeremy—"

"It's five twenty, baby, well past professional hours," he murmured as he trailed kisses along her jaw and throat. "I know it might sound crazy, but you have no idea how much I've missed you."

She wanted to tell him that yes, it sounded crazy, but she had missed him, too. But the sensations evoked by the heated kisses and slow pass of his hands down her body stacked up like lightning and made speech impossible. The best she could manage was a soft moan. She slid her hand up his magnificent chest and over his strong arms and heard his own groan of pleasure.

"I guess this is one way to ensure you get past the thirty-day trial period."

Serita's eyes snapped open and she tried to jump off Jeremy's lap. "Let me up," she whispered through clenched teeth. This was exactly what she wanted to avoid.

"You're fine right here, sweetheart. Chris already knows about you."

Her gaze flew to his, then Chris's.

Chris angled his head and lifted a brow. "Ah, no, I don't think I do."

"My mystery woman from Madrid," Jeremy said.

Chris's mouth fell open. "Oh, damn, you hired your… I mean, did you know she was one of the candidates?"

"No, and remember you did the ranking." To Serita, he said, "We rank each person by education, experience, leadership skills without knowing who they are. I have Nicole remove the name and gender before giving it to us."

She felt a measure of relief knowing that he hadn't tried to manipulate the situation. She'd had enough of that from a previous relationship.

"Well, you can thank me for your good fortune by giving me a raise," Chris said with a wide grin, leaning against the door frame with his arms folded.

Jeremy shot him a glare. "Get out of my office."

"See how bossy he is, Serita?"

Serita just smiled. "I'm not in this. In fact, I have to go."

"You don't have to leave. I was—" Jeremy glanced over at Chris. "Do you mind?"

"Oh, my bad. See you in the morning, Serita." He tossed her a bold wink and departed.

"This is why you never hire your best friends."

"How long have you been friends?" she asked.

"Middle school. Sometimes I think we've been friends too long," he said, shaking his head. "Do you want to have dinner?"

"I already made plans with my friend Gabby. She's

letting me stay with her until I find a place. Can we do it another time?"

"Sure. Do you want to go out or eat in?"

"Whichever you prefer." She knew he wouldn't consider letting her pay, so she left the choice up to him. Serita didn't want him to think she was one of those women who liked to spend a man's money.

"Eat in. I'll cook for you. Just let me know when you're available."

She leaned back and studied him. "You can cook?"

"Of course I can cook. How do you think I've been eating for the past fourteen years—going over to my parents' house every night or existing on takeout?"

Serita elbowed him playfully. "That's not what I meant and you know it. I mean do you cook well?"

"That's the same question in my book," he said with amusement. "I offer to cook for you and this is what I get. Fine, I'll just order some takeout."

"Oh, no, you don't. I want a five-star meal." The last word was said on a squeal because he started tickling her. She slapped at his hands as she laughed hysterically, but his grip was too strong. "Okay, okay, I won't dis your cooking." Finally he released her and she hopped off his lap, still trying to catch her breath. "And I'm available on Saturday."

"Saturday, it is." Jeremy shut down his computer, stuffed the laptop and some folders into his bag and stood. "I'll walk you out." He reached for her hand. "I can hold your hand, right? Or is that against the rules, too?"

She glanced up at him. "Whatever." But she couldn't stop smiling.

Chapter 7

"You look like you made it through the first day just fine," Gabby said as soon as Serita entered the condo.

"I did. Well, after I got over a major shocker about the owner this morning."

"Oh, no. Is it something bad and will it impact your ability to do the job?"

"It's not bad, per se, and it could have an impact." Although Jeremy had promised her he would judge fairly.

"Girl, if you don't just spit it out."

"Jeremy."

Gabby's hand flew to her mouth. "He works there?"

"He owns it."

"Well, damn. I wasn't expecting that."

"Yeah, neither was I. By the look on his face this morning, he wasn't, either."

A slow grin spread across her lips. "And I don't see one thing bad about it. All I see is *job security.*"

"That wouldn't be fair."

"It's not like you're unqualified for the job, Serita. You got the position on your own and you already like your boss, so it's a win-win situation for both of you."

"We'll see. Let me change into something comfortable and we can go."

"I'm thinking Arden Fair Mall because I've been craving those catfish nuggets from Delta Soul in there."

"Sounds good to me," she called over her shoulder while heading down the hall.

Thirty minutes later, Gabby circled the parking lot at the mall searching for parking. "I can't believe all these people are here. It's Monday at seven."

"Maybe they all had the same idea as you. I think someone's coming out a few spaces up," Serita said. They ended up parking near the JCPenney entrance, which was in the center of the mall. "There are a lot more restaurants than what I recall." She saw a BJ's Brewhouse and Seasons 52. "And new stores."

"The latest one is Alex and Ani, and I really don't need one of those here. Hmm, we might have to stop in, so I can see what new bracelets are in."

"Are we shopping or eating first?"

"We should probably eat first and then walk off some of the food, but tonight I want my meal to settle in real good."

They burst out laughing. "Shopping it is." They started at the jewelry store, since it was on the first floor and Gabby ended up purchasing two more bracelets to add to her collection and talked Serita into getting the rose-gold Path Of Life two-bracelet set. "This is exactly why I don't shop with you."

"You have to admit they're pretty."

"I'm not admitting anything." She pivoted on her heel and strode out the store with Gabby's laughter trailing. Serita hadn't bought herself anything in a while. Her mother and Gabby always said Serita needed to spoil herself every now and again, but Serita's practical self rarely did. "Where to next?" she asked when Gabby caught up.

"I want to go upstairs to Bath & Body Works to get another lemon mint leaf candle. I love the clean scent and it does wonders for eliminating that stale smell."

They took the escalator up to the store and ended up staying for a good twenty minutes smelling candles and lotions, spraying body mists and trying out the different types of hand soaps from exfoliating to nourishing. She bought a few soaps for the bathroom she'd be using, as well as two of the smaller candles for her room. Once they had accomplished that, the two of them walked farther down the mall to the food court and ordered the catfish nugget meal and lemonade.

Gabby opened her container when the food came. "Look at all this. And they cook them the old-fashioned Southern way with cornmeal, instead of that batter." She immediately opened some packages of tartar and hot sauces, mixed them together and dipped in a piece of fish. She popped it into her mouth, closed her eyes and moaned. "So good."

Serita chuckled and tasted a piece. "Oh, my good-ness. It *is* good."

"You have to mix the sauces together and try it."

She made a face. "I don't think so." The combina-tion looked like a pink mess.

"Don't knock it until you try it."

"I'll just stick with the hot sauce." They ate in silence for a few minutes. "Have you heard from Jodi and where she's staying?"

"That girl. She said something about staying with another friend. The thing is she was supposed to be saving up her money to get her own place. That's why I didn't charge her much. If she couldn't handle the four hundred dollars at my place, I don't how she thinks she can make it on her own."

She shook her head. "That's a bargain."

"I know. I was trying to help her, and she had the nerve to tell me she didn't understand why I was getting so upset about her not paying, since I'd been paying the full mortgage before she came."

"That's not the point."

"I said exactly that and told her she wasn't going to use extra water, gas, electricity and everything else for free. This ain't her mama's house." She rolled her eyes and ate a french fry.

Serita laughed. She couldn't believe Jodi. "I promise you won't have to worry about that with me." She had already paid her for three months, the amount of time Serita figured it would take her to find a place. She hoped to move by the start of the year.

Gabby patted Serita's hand. "You can stay for free. I haven't forgotten the semester you let me stay in your dorm room when my dad got laid off and I couldn't afford housing. If it wasn't for you, I would've had to drop out."

She dropped her head and shrugged. "It was nothing." Silence rose between them and they continued to eat.

"How do you think things are going to go with Jeremy?"

"I don't know." She sipped her lemonade. "I really like him so far. When I'm with him I feel like... I don't know. Somebody different." Thinking back, she realized her past relationships had centered around dinner or theater dates where they dressed up. Nothing as simple as taking a walk or talking for hours about everything and nothing. She had never teased with those other guys, or been so open and playful as she was with Jeremy.

Gabby angled her head thoughtfully. "I think there's something about him that makes you feel free to be the real you, and that's a good thing."

"Maybe."

"You'll know one way or another because I don't see him walking away from you so easily. He sounds like he might be a keeper."

Serita's mind went back to the moments in his office earlier when they had been interrupted by Chris. Jeremy had made his intentions quite clear and she agreed with Gabby's assessment. Each thing she learned about him only added to her attraction, and she didn't think it would be easy to walk away from him, either.

"I've been so busy with work and making sure Randi is comfortable that we haven't had a chance to talk about the woman you met in Madrid," Cedric said, handing Jeremy a box containing metal scraps, nails and bolts. "How's the long-distance thing working out?"

"Thanks for this." Three times a year, Jeremy conducted a six-week robotics camp on Saturday mornings for middle school students to get them interested in pursuing the sciences. He set the box on the floor in front of where he sat. "It's working out just fine because she's not long-distance anymore. She's closer than I ever hoped."

"Are you telling me this woman just up and moved to Sacramento so you two could be together?"

Laughing, he said, "No. She actually grew up here and was planning to move back after her teaching contract didn't get renewed. I got the surprise of my life Monday morning when she showed up as one of the four people I hired."

Cedric shook his head. "I'm sure you both were happy about that."

"Actually, she wasn't. You know I told you that they'll all be under a thirty-day trial and I'd keep the two best candidates. Serita is concerned about me giving her preference and wants her work to stand on its own."

"And are you planning to give her preference?"

"I don't have to because the woman is phenomenal. After the first day, Elena and Shane were singing her praises and all but told me I'd better hire her. But it's going to be tricky. One guy I know will be out at the end. He's been a pain in the ass from the moment he walked through the door." Shane also worked on the surgery arm project and had complained about Wade trying to take over and make changes on parts that had already been completed. Wade had told Shane he needed to think outside the box. If it kept up, Jeremy would let Wade go well before the month was up.

"I know you'll come up with a way to get it done. Do you think she's the one?"

"I do. I just need to convince her."

Cedric stared. "All these years, I figured all this talk about knowing your Mrs. Right when you saw her and falling in love at first sight was just that—talk. But you're serious, aren't you?"

"I'm very serious." He had always held out hope that he would find the woman who was perfect for him, but was realistic enough to know that he might not find her all wrapped up neatly with a bow. Now, however, reality seemed to be lining up with his dreams. He picked up the box and stood. "I need to get going. Class starts in an hour."

"You owe me for getting up at eight o'clock on a Saturday morning."

Jeremy grinned. "Just helping you be prepared for what's going to happen when the baby comes."

"I just hope this baby gives us another couple weeks at least. By then, she'll be thirty-six weeks and if she goes into labor, it should be okay."

"I'm glad to hear it."

"You can swing back by after class if you want. She should be up by then."

His class ran from ten until one in the afternoon. "I'll try to stop by tomorrow. I'm cooking dinner for Serita tonight and I have a few things to do before I pick her up. You know she was hassling me about not letting her drive over to the house, talking about it being a waste of gas."

"Randi did the same thing when we started dating, but I didn't care."

"True that." They did a fist bump. "See you later."

The classes were held in the multipurpose room of one of the Roseville middle schools. Jeremy had gone to school in the district and when he approached his old principal—she had been a teacher then—about his idea two years ago, it had been met with enthusiasm.

With her support, it didn't take long for the program to take flight. The first several classes had been comprised solely of male students. Only in the last summer session did he have one female.

Today, as the twelve students filed in, he was delighted to see the same young lady, as well as three more. His thoughts shifted to Serita and he made a mental note to ask her to join him for one of the sessions. It was important to him that students of color see themselves represented in careers other than sports and entertainment—not that there was anything wrong with those careers. He just wanted the students to know they had other options, or could do both, if they chose. He knew seeing another woman in the field of robotics would go a long way in boosting their self-confidence.

"Hi, Mr. Hunter. Did you go on your trip to Spain?"

Jeremy smiled. Davon was one of his repeat students and always eager to learn. "I sure did. After class, I'll show you a few pictures."

"Cool."

"Alright, everybody. Take your seats and let's get started. We have a lot to cover." He waited a moment for the students to get settled, then began with the introduction and the learning objectives. "Understand that this is not a time for goofing around. We're going to have a lot of fun, but be prepared to work hard." He met each student's gaze before continuing. "There are some safety rules that are very important for you to abide by. I'm passing out a sheet for you to read and sign that says you understand and will follow. Anyone who does not follow these rules will be asked to leave the class." Jeremy saw surprise on some of their young faces. He gave them a few minutes to complete the form, then started the class. He ended it with a demonstration of a few types of simple robots and a question-and-answer period. The class ended up running over by twenty minutes because of all the questions, but that didn't bother him. Their bright eyes and excitement always made him glad that he'd chosen to do the class, despite the amount of work it took.

Jeremy took a few minutes to share some of his photos from Madrid and a couple of minutes from his presentation. "This is going to be you all one day and I'll be in the audience to cheer you on."

"Do girls get to teach at the conferences, too?" Briana had a sharp mind, but tended to be very shy.

"They absolutely do." He scrolled through his photos and found Serita's presentation. He had been so enamored by her voice that he'd recorded it. He held the phone out to Briana.

Her face lit up. "Wow!"

Yeah, wow. That was Jeremy's first impression of Serita, too. A vision of them teaching together surfaced in his mind. He definitely had to get her to come to the class. "You can do the same thing. Just keep working hard and doing well in school."

"I will." She hurried off.

"Okay, let's wrap it up. I know your parents have been waiting. I'll see you all next Saturday."

Once everyone had gone, he packed up and went grocery shopping. Serita had mentioned wanting a five-star meal, so he planned to give her one. He stopped at a local florist and picked out a bouquet with half a dozen pink roses and drove home to shower.

The drive to Antelope from his Roseville house took only twenty minutes and, by traveling the back roads, he didn't have to bother with the freeway. When Serita opened the door to Jeremy, his heart started pounding. She looked gorgeous in a pair of tight jeans and a tan short-sleeved top that dipped low and emphasized the seductive swell of her breasts. Her natural curls hung loose and framed her face. "Hey, beautiful." He placed a kiss on her lips and handed her the flowers. "These are for you."

"Hi, and thank you. They're lovely. Come in." Serita stepped back for him to enter.

He followed her through the short entryway to the living room.

She placed the vase on the coffee table. "I need to grab my jacket and purse. Have a seat."

Jeremy sat and watched her hips disappear down the hall. She came back a minute later with a curvy golden-skinned woman and he stood.

"Jeremy, this is my friend Gabriella. Gabby, Jeremy."

"It's nice to meet you, Gabriella," he said.

Gabriella smiled. "Same here. You wouldn't happen to have any other single brothers or cousins hanging around, by any chance?"

He laughed. "Unfortunately, I don't. I'm actually the last one."

"Pity."

Serita shook her head. "She's outrageous."

"I'm not mad at her. You won't know until you ask," he said.

Gabriella gestured his way. "See, that's what I'm saying. Thank you, Jeremy."

Serita hooked her arm in Jeremy's. "Let's go. Bye, crazy woman."

Smiling, she said, "You two have fun."

Once in the car, Jeremy said, "I like her. Where did you meet?"

"We grew up together and ended up at the same college. I'm an only child and she's like the sister I never had."

"That had to be lonely sometimes." Despite their two-year age difference, he and Cedric were close, and he couldn't imagine not having the friendship that came along with being siblings.

"It was, but you deal with it." She fell silent for a few minutes. "I thought you said we were having dinner. Four o'clock is kind of early to eat."

"We aren't eating until later. I just wanted to spend more time with you. The earlier we start, the longer I get to enjoy your company. Do you mind if we stop at the bookstore on the way? I ordered a book and it's in. The bookstore is on the other side of town in Oak Park."

"No, though I always get into trouble when I go into bookstores."

"Same. We're all readers in my family, but my library is probably three times that of everybody else's."

"I'd like to see that," she said, facing him.

His gaze left the road briefly. "I'll be happy to show it to you, once we get to my house." They shared a smile and rode the rest of the way in companionable silence interspersed with conversation.

He parked in the lot adjacent to the building housing Underground Books and they went inside. He spoke to Mother Rose, the manager and store operator, and waited while she retrieved his book. She, as well as the Black-owned bookstore, was a fixture in the Oak Park neighborhood. Jeremy watched as Serita wandered around the store, stopping here and there to pick up a book. He walked over to where she stood. "Find anything?"

"More like what haven't I found," she said with a chuckle. "Are you in a hurry? I want to sit for a few minutes and check these out." She held up the four books.

"Nope. Take your time." He loved the bookstore's comfortable and homey feeling. R & B and jazz flowed through hidden speakers, and a sofa, matching chair and coffee table sat on the far side of the store, beckoning one to stay and relax. They sat reading and talking about the different books for a good half hour. In Jeremy's mind, it added to his growing list of evidence that she was indeed the one for him.

Chapter 8

Serita strolled through Jeremy's two-story home as he gave her a tour. "This is gorgeous." Every room in the four-bedroom four-and-a-half-bath home, with the shiny wood floors, elegant furnishings and spacious size, attested to his success. But his extensive library set in an alcove on the second floor left her breathless. "How long have you lived here? It's rather large for one person, unless you just like having lots of space."

"Almost five years. And I figured once I got married and started a family, I wouldn't have to move."

She whirled around and narrowed her eyes. She ignored that last sentence, not wanting to read anything into it. "Exactly how old are you?"

Jeremy chuckled. "Thirty-six, and you?"

"Thirty-two." That would somewhat explain his reference to being in the field for so long. She had thought about purchasing a house when she lived in Reno, but didn't want to have to worry about the upkeep or paying someone to do it. Her condo had suited her fine. But, glancing around the room now, she thought she might change her mind when she started looking this time. Of course, she didn't think she'd need such a big house, especially since she'd have to clean it. She scanned the many bookshelves and saw genres ranging from robotics and thrillers to biographies and cookbooks, and even a romance title or two. "Romance?"

"What? Men can't read romance?"

"Yes, but I just didn't expect…um…think you read that sort of thing."

He wrapped his arm around her shoulder and dropped a kiss on her hair. "Well, now you know I read romance. You never know when some of those things heroes do for their women might come in handy."

In her estimation, he did just fine in that department. Actually, from what he'd shown her already, he could have written the manual. "Like maybe you don't already do some of those things."

"I had good examples to follow."

Serita recalled Jeremy mentioning his father's role in his upbringing and wondered if his parents' marriage factored into the way he approached his own relationships. Watching the way her father had treated her mother had certainly influenced Serita's thinking, and that was why she had decided to let men take a back seat in her life. She hadn't found one that measured up. Until now. She followed Jeremy back downstairs to the kitchen. "What's for dinner?"

"I'm making that five-star meal you requested— seared sea scallops in a wine-and-herb-butter sauce, sautéed broccoli and mushrooms, roasted honey gold potatoes and homemade French bread."

Her mouth dropped. "I don't know what to say, other than *wow*. Five-star, indeed. You're going to make the French bread, too?"

"Yep." Jeremy walked over to the refrigerator, retrieved a pan and peeled back a towel covering a rising loaf of bread. "All I have to do is pop it in the oven."

"Where did you learn to make bread?"

"My mom. Before I went to science camp, I had planned to grow up and own a bakery."

She smiled. "One out of two ain't bad. You own your business."

"True. Would you like something to drink. Since we're having seafood, I opted for chardonnay or champagne."

"Either is fine." He opened the champagne, poured them both glasses and held his aloft.

"To the beginning of something beautiful."

She touched her glass against his. Their eyes held as they sipped. Yep, this man was setting the bar pretty high. She watched him pull several things from the refrigerator. "Do you need my help with anything?" she asked, taking a seat on a stool on the other side of the island.

He glanced at her over his shoulder. "Not this time. First visit gets a guest pass, but next time, we'll do it together."

"There's going to be a next time?"

Jeremy placed the ingredients on the counter and came to where she sat. He tilted her chin and placed a sweet, lingering kiss on her lips. "There are going to be many next times." Straightening, he went over and started the dinner preparations.

Serita wasn't aware she had been holding her breath until she felt the pressure in her chest. The kiss and his words had shaken her. She was falling for him, and fast. The realization scared her on one level because her feelings for Jeremy had taken on a life of their own. Despite her best efforts to slow this headlong rush down a path that could lead to heartbreak, the emotions kept gaining speed and she felt like a car careening out of control. She took a long drink with trembling hands and prayed things didn't end as they always had for her. Soon, the combined smells of bread baking and the food cooking filled the kitchen. The wonderful aroma made her stomach growl. "It smells so good in here."

"Thanks. Hopefully, it'll taste even better." Jeremy slid the pan with the quartered potatoes into a second oven and wiped his hands on a towel. He picked up a remote and held it out. The smooth sound of Maxwell singing about a little "Sumthin' Sumthin'" flowed from hidden speakers. This one happened to be the remixed slower version that had been featured on the *Love Jones* movie soundtrack. "Come dance with me."

She met him halfway, and he pulled her into his arms and started a slow sway. With their height difference, her head came to the middle of his chest and she could hear the strong, steady beat of his heart beneath her ear. The scent of whatever bodywash or cologne he wore floated into her nostrils and she moved closer to inhale the potent, warm fragrance.

"From the moment I saw you sitting in the hallway in that hotel, I imagined us here just like this, me holding you in my arms. It's as if you were made to fit right here," he whispered as his hands made a slow path up and down her back. "Your soft curves pressed against my body... Can you feel what you do to me?"

Have mercy! His words sent a jolt of electricity through her strong enough to power a room full of robots. And, yeah, she felt *exactly* what she did to him. The hard ridge of his erection sitting at her belly left no doubt.

"This thing between us was meant to be, specifically designed for the two of us."

Serita's pulse skipped. What did he mean? She lifted her head and searched his face. She read naked desire in his eyes—and something else she couldn't define. Jeremy's movements slowed until they stopped. He framed her face between his big hands and kissed her until the room spun. Her knees went weak and only his strong arm kept her from sliding to the floor.

"I need to check the bread and potatoes, and start on the rest of the meal." He kissed her again, then went over to the oven.

She stood in the middle of the kitchen, her heart racing and her body trembling. She sucked in several gulps of air, trying to get her breathing back to somewhere near normal, but it took a while. Finally she trusted her feet enough to move. He was waging an all-out assault on her senses and she was losing. By the time they sat down to dinner, she had managed to regain some measure of control.

Jeremy placed the serving dishes on the table he had set on his enclosed patio, topped off their champagne and sat opposite Serita. "You go first."

"Everything looks so good. Thank you." She filled her plate, got a piece of the still-warm bread and added butter. She moaned with the first bite. The scallops were tender and flavorful, as were the vegetables and potatoes. If she could get food like this every day, she might seriously consider never eating out at a restaurant again. "You wouldn't happen to be looking for a job as a personal chef?"

He laughed. "No, and you wouldn't be able to afford my rates," he added with a wink. "You don't cook?"

"Sure, I cook. But not like this." Cooking had never been high on her list of things to learn, much to her mother's chagrin. Serita tended to spend her time in the garage working on her latest robotic invention instead of being in the kitchen. As a result, her skills were sorely lacking. And she didn't even think about baking beyond what it took to follow directions to make a boxed dessert. "What other secret talents do you have—famous musician, world-renowned artist, sports star?"

Jeremy laughed so hard he choked on his champagne. He coughed and coughed. "You're going to make me hurt myself," he croaked. He cleared his throat and took a small sip of the drink. "None of those, although I did play saxophone in the middle school band and basketball in high school. Did you do any sports or band?"

Serita shook her head. "I led a pretty boring high school existence." She'd had friends, but not many dates. The boys had always considered her too nerdy for their tastes. She had pretended that it never bothered her, but in reality every time one of her girlfriends mentioned some great date or how well some boy kissed, it did. She didn't get her first kiss until senior prom, and it had been an awkward experience, one she'd buried and tried to forget.

"It doesn't seem boring now. Where do you see yourself in the next five years?"

She ate another bite of the melt-in-your-mouth scallops before answering. "Eventually, I'd like to do what you did and start my own company. In a perfect world, I'd teach part-time for the next two or three years while working somewhere else, then stop teaching to start my business. The field is growing and I want to capitalize on it before the market gets saturated. I still haven't decided whether that'll be here or back in Reno."

Jeremy frowned. "I thought you'd moved back permanently."

"It could be. I just don't know for sure right now."

He nodded. "About starting your own company, you should do it. I won't lie… Running a business is tough, but the ability to be your own boss makes all the hard work worth it. I'd be more than happy to help you when you're ready."

"I'd appreciate that. You really should think about teaching. You'd be great."

"I already do. I run a six-week robotics camp for middle schoolers three times a year. If you're not busy next Saturday, I'd love for you to come. There are four young ladies in the class and seeing you would be a huge boost to their confidence."

"I would absolutely love to come. Just let me know the time and place." Gabby had said Jeremy might be a keeper. Serita was beginning to think her friend was right.

Sunday afternoon, Jeremy sat in Cedric's enclosed patio with Randi and her sister Iyana eating dinner. They had taken advantage of the midseventies temperatures and cooked a tri-tip and some corn on the grill. Iyana had made the potato salad and baked beans.

"How was your date with Serita last night?" Randi asked.

"Great. I cooked dinner for her."

"Aww, that's so sweet. Your brother cooked for me, too, when we started dating."

Cedric placed a bottle of water in front of his wife. "And he cooks far better than I do."

"Really?" Iyana divided a glance between the brothers. "Randi told me that Cedric can throw down in the kitchen. See, this just ain't right." She pointed her fork Jeremy's way. "It's too bad I think of you as a brother. Otherwise, I'd be figuring out how to build one of those robots you work with to carry her off to another planet." They all fell out laughing. "I'm serious. I need y'all to hook me up with a friend, distant cousin or whatever."

Jeremy couldn't stop laughing. He had found out that Iyana was the total opposite of Randi. Where Randi had some introverted tendencies, her sister gave outgoing a new meaning. She would probably do well acting in some movie instead of being one of the makeup artists. "I'll see what I can do."

"When are you going to introduce her to the family?" Cedric asked. "Mom stopped by yesterday afternoon and asked the same thing."

"I don't know, and I told her that I'd come this evening after I leave here." Though he and Serita had been intimate and were dating, he still sensed some hesitancy on her part. She had also mentioned the possibility of moving back to Reno, and he realized he needed to slow down. He would probably scare her to death if he told her what he was feeling. Last night, as they danced in his kitchen, he'd had to catch himself after telling her they were meant to be. He saw the fear. "Hopefully, soon. I'm trying to take my time with her."

"Yeah, I don't think telling her 'I know we just met, but you're the woman I've been waiting for' is a good idea. It'll probably send her running for the hills."

"Thanks for the confidence," he said sarcastically. "That's just what I want to hear from my big brother."

Cedric shrugged. "I'm just sayin'."

"I know I would have," Randi said. "I'd met so many frogs, I didn't think there was a prince out there. Maybe Serita has experienced the same thing. If that's the case, then slow is better. But if you ever need to heat things up, you should visit Desiree's shop," she added with a grin.

Cedric skewered her with a look. "Please don't bring that up. Do you know how long it's been since—"

"Cedric!"

"What? They know what we're doing...or *not* doing," he grumbled.

Jeremy and Iyana laughed. Iyana said, "Wasn't it that massage oil from Desiree's shop that got you two in your current predicament?"

"Yes, yes, it was." The satisfied look he sent his wife this time gave the impression that he couldn't wait to do it all again.

Jeremy made a mental note to pay a visit to the shop at his earliest convenience. He'd heard a lot about that oil—warming, edible, flavored—yeah, he was all for that. An image of him licking the oil off Serita's skin surfaced in his mind and his body reacted in kind. He hopped up. "I'm going to get another bottle of tea. Anybody else want one?" They all declined. "Be right back."

In the kitchen, he took several deep breaths. He'd never had a woman who invaded his thoughts the way Serita did or aroused him with just a mention. He reached into the fridge for the tea, opened it and drank deeply, hoping it would calm his body.

"You're going to need a little more than that to help you out."

He spun around and met Cedric's amused gaze. "What are you talking about?"

"You know exactly what I'm talking about. I've never seen you this obsessed with a woman. If I didn't know better, I'd swear you were falling in love with her."

He didn't respond. He'd wondered that himself several times. The logical part of him said it couldn't be possible this soon in the game, but his heart told him something entirely different. Jeremy had always jumped into his relationships with both feet, only to come away unfulfilled. But not this time. This time everything felt right. The notion didn't scare him—he'd been looking for love—but he didn't want to make one misstep that would cause him to lose Serita.

"I take it by your silence that I'm right. I can't say I'm surprised, and I really hope it turns out the way you want. I never thought I wanted to settle down with one woman, but you were right about finding that one special woman. I'm happier than I've ever been in my life."

"I know you are and I'm glad. You know, it's pretty ironic that you and our cousins were all against falling in love and every one of you has taken the plunge into matrimony."

"You were the only one who thought differently. Your time is coming, Jeremy, and we'll all be there to celebrate with you."

He smiled faintly. "I hope so." They went back out to the patio and finished dinner. Afterward he helped Cedric clean up and left to visit his parents.

Jeremy's father answered the door. "Hey, son. Come on in."

"Hey, Dad." They shared a hug and Jeremy followed him back to the family room. His mother was seated in her favorite recliner doing one of her word search puzzles. "How are you, Mom?" He placed a kiss on her upturned cheek.

"I'm doing alright." She put the pen in the book to hold her place and set it, along with her reading glasses, on the small table next to her. "How are things at work? I remember you mentioning needing to hire another engineer."

"It's going pretty good." He told them about his and Chris's idea about the trial period. "We're only planning to hire two of them permanently and, so far, three out of the four are working out well."

"Well, there's always that one who can't seem to get it together. How's Serita, and when are you going to bring her down to visit?"

Leave it to his mother to cut right to the chase. "I'm not sure. She doesn't live in Reno anymore."

"Oh, honey, I'm sorry. I'd hoped you would have some good news."

Jeremy smiled. "I never said I didn't. She lives here now and just happened to be one of our new hires."

"What?" His dad's eyebrows shot up. Then he laughed. "Talk about bringing fate to your door."

His mother beamed. "That's wonderful, sweetheart. Then it shouldn't take long for you to bring her around."

"Mom, you do realize Serita and I only met a about a month ago?"

"I know. But at the hospital, you made it sound like she's the special woman you've been trying to find."

"I still believe that she is, but that doesn't mean she shares the same feelings. As soon as I know where this is going, I'll be happy to introduce her because I know you'll like her."

"Just don't take forever. You young people today like to drag out relationships. Either you want to be together or you don't. I'm the only one left with an unmarried child. LaVerne brags about Desiree and Jabari all the time." Desiree was Lorenzo's wife and Jabari was married to Lorenzo's sister, Alisha. "And I'm not even going to start on Nolan and Dee."

He shook his head. Even if he got married today, he wouldn't be able to catch up with his LA aunt and uncle. All five of their children were married and, between them, they had seven grandchildren. And from what Lorenzo had told him on the way from the airport three weeks ago, two of his cousins might be expecting again.

"Theresa, it's not a competition," his father said. "He'll bring his young lady over when it's time."

"I know, I know. I just want Jeremy to experience the same kind of joy we have."

Jeremy had grown up hearing all about how his father had predicted his mother would be his wife before they had even been introduced. He had fallen in love with his mother a week after meeting her and their love continued to grow and deepen, even after all these years. That's what Jeremy wanted for himself. And he wanted it with Serita.

Chapter 9

"We're so happy to have you back home, sweetheart."

Serita hugged her mother. "I'm glad to be back." Even though she had only been two hours away, she'd missed being able to drive over whenever she wanted. She'd left for college at eighteen and, aside from summer visits, remained in Reno until now. She had especially missed Sunday dinners.

"Your dad is outside by the grill."

A wide grin spread across her face. "He's making ribs?" she asked excitedly.

"Yes."

She rubbed her hands together with glee. Nobody could make ribs like her daddy.

"Is that my baby girl I hear?"

"Dad!" She launched herself into his strong arms and tears misted in her eyes. "I missed you." She had always been a daddy's girl.

"I missed you, too, baby."

Serita glanced between the two people she loved the most. David and Gayle Edwards had nurtured her, loved her and encouraged her to reach for her dreams, even when others didn't believe in them. She couldn't have asked for better parents.

"Your mama tell you I've got ribs in the kitchen?"

"Yes, she did, and I'm going to hurt myself."

His booming laughter filled the air. "Well, come on and get it."

"You don't have to tell me twice." She led the way to the kitchen and piled her plate high with the ribs, sautéed corn, macaroni and cheese, green beans and her mother's homemade yeast rolls. After they were seated at the table, her father blessed the food and Serita immediately bit into a tender rib covered in a thick, sweet barbecue sauce. "Dad, you outdid yourself. These ribs are to die for."

"Mmm-hmm, I'm going to have to agree with you, baby girl. I stuck my foot in these."

The rest of the food tasted just as good. Growing up, she had been known to eat four or five of those rolls at one time. However, her thirty-two-year-old metabolism couldn't handle that now, so she settled for eating just one. "I haven't had food that tasted this good in so long." As soon as the words were off her tongue, she wanted to call them back. She *had* eaten some great food last night prepared by a man who seemed to be working his way deeper into her psyche as the days passed.

"Tell us about your new job," her mother said.

She finished chewing before answering. "It's temporary right now, but depending on how I perform over the thirty-day trial, I could be one of two the company hires permanently." She still didn't know how she felt about dating the man who had a say in her employment, but he had promised to be fair and she had to take him at his word.

"Do you think you have a good chance?"

"Yes. The two engineers I'm working with mentioned that they believed I'd be a good fit."

"And your boss?" her father asked over his glass of iced tea.

Complicated...really complicated. "It's only been a week and he hasn't said much." It wasn't exactly a lie.

Her mother patted her hand. "I'm not worried. With your background and personality, you'll get the permanent spot. Mark my words."

"Thanks, Mom."

"I have to say we were a little disappointed when you decided not to stay here. It would've been cheaper and you could save that money for something else."

"I know, but I wanted to do this on my own. Even though the cost of living is higher here, I got a good price for my condo, so I should be okay. I'll probably start looking for my own place in a week or two."

"How's Gabriella doing? I hope she's not still dating that man we saw her with last year. Something about him made me uncomfortable. I wanted to tell her so, but your father made me stay out of it."

Serita chuckled. "No, she's not. I think she dumped him not long after that." Her mother treated Gabby as if she were another daughter and that included getting into Gabby's business.

"What about you? Have you met any nice guys that have potential?"

She had hoped to avoid this conversation but should

have known better. Her mom knew about all the heart-breaks Serita had suffered and always said that in life, one had to wade through the bad ones to get to the right one. "I did meet a guy at the conference in Madrid and he's very nice."

Her mother narrowed her eyes. "We had a long chat about that trip. Not once did you mention a man. Where is he from?"

"Here."

"I see. You'll have to bring him over so we can meet him."

Serita's father had always been her ally, so she looked to him for some sort of reprieve but found none.

"Don't look at me. I'm with your mother on this one."

Of course, when it came to men, he'd side with her mother. "I think it might be a little too soon for that. It's only been a month or so." And she'd done more with him in that time than she had with her ex, whom she had dated for eight months.

"What's his name? I assume, since he was at the con-ference, that he's in the same field."

"His name is Jeremy Hunter and, yes, he's an en-gineer."

"At least you know he has a good job," her father said, saluting her with his fork.

"He does. He owns his own company." *Just tell them*, her inner voice chimed. "The same one I happen to work at," she mumbled. Two pairs of eyes bored into her. "Neither of us knew until I walked into the office, so…" She had no idea what to say after that. She forked up some macaroni and cheese, feeling all of twelve years old.

"Sometimes things happen for a reason," her mother

said. "That job brought you back home, so I can't be too mad, but I'm really curious about this Jeremy now. I do hope that means you'll be back for good."

"I won't know until I find something permanent, whether that's with this company or another one."

"With him owning the business, I suspect he's much older than you. I'm not sure how I feel about that."

"Mom, you do realize that I'm thirty-two, not twenty-two and Jeremy is only four years older. If things start to get serious between us, I promise you'll be the first to know and I will definitely bring him over."

Her mother nodded as if satisfied.

Serita sighed in relief. *So, having sex twice, spending an entire evening at his house and hearing the man tell you the two of you were meant to be isn't serious?* She wished that annoying voice in her head would just shut up. It didn't matter that it was the truth.

Jeremy had tried diplomacy when dealing with Wade, but by Wednesday morning, he'd reached his limit. Wade seemed to forget that it was Jeremy's name on the deed to the building and not his. He had a habit of talking down to the other new hires and taking extended breaks, which, in Jeremy's mind, meant that Wade would not be a good fit for the company.

"Jeremy, I think you need to come see this."

He glanced at the terse set of Shane's jaw and knew the day was about to get worse. *It is only nine.* He just hoped nothing had gone wrong with one of the designs in progress. Pushing to his feet, he followed Shane out and down the hall to one of the work areas. Nothing could have prepared him for the sight before him. On the table lay one of the sensor components, detached from the robot console. The same one that had taken him two weeks to perfect. He'd worked late nights and weekends to get the precise specifications of the foot pedal that would be used by his client during surgery and now... It took Jeremy several seconds to find his voice. "What the hell happened in here?"

Shane nodded toward Wade.

"Wade?"

"What happened was innovation. This simple sensor would do nothing more than flip a switch when someone put their foot on it. I took the liberty of drawing up something with a little more pizzazz." Wade held out a notebook opened to a page with a sketch.

Ignoring it, Jeremy said through clenched teeth, "My office. *Now!*" He strode out of the room. When Wade got to the office, Jeremy slammed the door. "Your job was to work on designing the console from the existing schematics, not create your own."

"Robotics is about being innovative and thinking outside the box."

"You can be innovative and think outside the box on your own damn time, not mine. As of this moment, you're done here. Collect your belongings and get out."

Wade's face contorted in anger. "You can't fire me. My contract says thirty days."

Jeremy opened a file, took out a sheet of paper and slid it across the desk in front of Wade. "Actually, I can. If you hadn't been so focused on one-upping everybody in the room last week, you would have heard me mention the procedures for design change. Do you see your signature on the bottom of that page?"

He snatched the sheet up and read, then tossed it aside.

"Now, we're done here."

Wade stormed out of the office.

Jeremy paced for a good two minutes, trying to calm himself, then went out to make sure the man had left.

Serita passed and placed a hand on his arm. "Hey, everything okay?"

"Fine," he said tersely, and kept walking. He stopped. He hadn't meant to snap at her. "Serita?" He reached for her.

She held up a hand. "Obviously, you have a lot on your mind right now. It's okay." She left him standing there.

Jeremy cursed under his breath and ran a hand over his head. He wanted to follow her but remembered the parameters they'd put in place for their relationship while on the job. However, he did owe her a big apology and would take care of it as soon as possible. For now, he continued to Chris's office.

"That bad of a morning?" Chris asked, glancing up from the papers on his desk.

"Worse. Wade decided to dismantle a part of the console and tried to call it *innovation*."

Chris's eyes widened. "I hope you fired his ass on the spot. We should've done it last week."

"Agreed. Now, I'm going to have to spend many hours redoing something that shouldn't need to be done." In order to keep his bottom line down, Jeremy, most likely, would be working overtime for the next couple of weeks to get back on schedule. He hoped that the reassembly wouldn't take as long as the original assembly had.

"Well, we'll be taking it out of his check and if he complains, I'll tell him it's either that or we can sue him for destruction of property." Chris stood. "You go back to your office, and I'll make sure that idiot is gone."

"Thanks." He started toward his office, then changed direction and headed for the room where Serita worked. He poked his head in the door. "Serita, can I see you in my office for a minute, please?" He could tell she wanted to say no but, with Shane and Elena looking on, didn't.

"Sure." Serita crossed the room and sailed past him without a backward glance. She didn't say a word until they'd reached his office and Jeremy closed the door. "Yes?" She folded her arms and glared at him.

He sighed. She'd asked him if he had any faults, and he'd told her about being anal and a perfectionist. What he hadn't revealed was that until the age of ten he'd had an explosive temper. He'd had to sit out more Little League games than he could count because of it. Jeremy didn't like losing and whenever his team lost, he'd thrown bats, balls, torn down backstops and more. Of course, his mother's shoe landed on his backside as a result, but it didn't help. He didn't know how it happened, but by the time he reached age twelve, the behavior had all but vanished. In its place was the relaxed, laid-back man everyone knew. For the first time in his adult life, that old anger had risen up in him with such force that he'd almost lost it. It had been stirred to a level where he wanted to tear something apart, preferably Wade Brewer. "I want to apologize for my behavior in the hall earlier. My anger wasn't directed at you, but I was still wrong and I'm sorry." She didn't say anything, and it was killing Jeremy. Even though they were still on the clock, he had to hold her in his arms. Pulling her into his embrace, he kissed the top of her head. "Please forgive me, baby. I'm sorry."

Finally she looked up at him. "This time, but don't make it a habit."

He smiled for the first time that day. Unable to resist, he placed a sweet kiss on her lips. "I promise."

She backed away. "What are you doing? No kisses during the workday."

"That wasn't a regular kiss. It was an apology kiss."

Serita shook her head, but a smile peeked out. "I need to get back to work. What had you so upset anyway?"

"Wade."

"Ugh, that man is a pain in the butt."

"Well, he's going to be someone else's pain in the butt because I fired him. He dismantled one of the foot pedals on the console and I'm going to have to put in extra hours to redo it."

"Oh, no. I'm so sorry. Let me know if you need some help. I don't mind staying longer." She reached up to touch his face and then, seemingly remembering where they were, snatched her hand down.

"Thanks. I might just take you up on the offer. What are you doing for lunch?"

"I have to make a quick run to Target, why?"

"I thought we could have lunch, but we can do it another day."

"Okay. Do you need me to bring you anything back?"

"Nah, I'm good." He reached around her and opened the door.

"See you later."

Jeremy stared after her with his smile still in place.

"Should I be dusting off my tux?" Chris asked, coming from the other hall.

"Maybe." Jeremy laughed at the shocked expression on his friend's face.

"Hold up. I was just kidding."

"I'm not." Just like his father, Jeremy knew who he wanted and didn't plan to mess around and let her get away.

Chapter 10

Serita parked in the lot in front of Target and got out. In reality, she could have made the pit stop on her way home, but she wanted to get out of the office. While she enjoyed the job and working with Elena and Shane, they kept up a constant stream of conversation during the day. Being a relative introvert, Serita needed a break. Inside the store, she pulled out her list, grabbed a basket and started up the aisle. It took only a few minutes to get what she needed, then she made her way to the line. While standing there, she spotted a package of Skittles—one of her favorite childhood candies—and tossed them in the basket.

A few minutes later, she was in the car and on her way back, leaving her a good thirty minutes to eat a quick lunch. She had only gone a block when she felt her steering wheel pulling to the right and the unmistakable sound of a flat tire. Sighing, she flipped on her hazard lights and slowly pulled into a nearby parking lot. Serita got out. Just as she'd suspected, her right rear tire was flat. For the life of her, she couldn't recall running over anything on the road. Going back to the car, she searched for her auto insurance card to call for road assistance. Then she decided to call Jeremy first to let him know she would be late getting back.

"Hey, baby," Jeremy said when he answered.

"Hey. I have a flat tire, so I'll be late getting back. I'm not sure how long road assistance will take to get here."

"Where are you?"

"In the Rocky Ridge Town Center."

"I'll be there in five minutes."

She opened her mouth to tell him she could just wait, but the line went dead. She should have expected that would be his response. The late-October temperatures had started to drop into the low seventies, but the slight breeze made it feel cooler. Serita got her jacket out of the car and put it on. A few minutes later, her phone buzzed in her hand. She saw Jeremy's name on the display. "Hey."

"Where are you parked?"

"Near the front, by Macaroni Grill." She searched and saw his silver Audi. She threw up a wave and waited for him to park next to her Elantra. Unlike her, he had on a short-sleeved button-down shirt and no jacket. "You're not cold?"

He grinned. "Nope. Pop the trunk."

She did as he asked, then stood off to the side. While waiting, she checked her emails. It would have been the ideal time to eat her lunch, but it was at the office in the refrigerator. By the time they made it back, her lunch would be over. She'd probably have to eat on her afternoon break. Serita turned around to ask Jeremy something and froze. He had taken off his shirt. Her gaze traveled down his body from his wide, muscular chest and defined abs to the low-hung jeans riding his trim waist and his black boots. A pulsing began in her core. She was about two seconds from jumping him right then and there. She closed her eyes to bring her rampant desire under control and opened them to find him standing in front of her, concern lining his features.

"You okay?"

She nodded quickly. "Why did you take off your shirt?"

"Didn't want to get it dirty."

It made sense, but still… Serita shoved her hands in her jacket pockets to keep from running them all over him. He needed to hurry up, fix that tire and put his shirt back on. To keep herself from doing something crazy like straddling him while he was on the ground, she went around to the other side of the car. Far away from temptation. It didn't help because her mind conjured up every possible scenario of her riding him—in the car, on the hood. Beads of perspiration popped out on her forehead and she removed her jacket. That old song by Nelly played in her head. It was definitely getting hot. Unable to resist, she poked her head around to the side of the car where he worked and snapped a picture. Glancing down at the photo, she smiled. Her selfie game might still need some work, but everything else was on point. Twenty minutes later, he stored the tire in her trunk and they drove back to the office.

"I can take you to get a new tire tonight, if you want," Jeremy said.

"Don't worry about it. I can take care of it on the weekend."

He grasped her hand. "Serita, I know you can take care of it, but it's alright to let a man who cares about you do something for you every now and again. It doesn't make you any less independent."

How he'd read her mind she'd never know, but he was dead-on. She appreciated his willingness to do things for her but didn't want to become dependent on him, or any man, for that matter. However, the sincerity in his voice made her relent. "Okay. Thank you."

"I know you didn't get to eat, so go ahead and take an extra thirty minutes."

Serita nodded a smile of appreciation and headed for the break room to warm up her lunch. She took the bowl holding the last of her leftovers from Sunday's dinner, the bag of Skittles and the mystery novel she had yet to start and walked into the small office she'd been given. The ribs and macaroni and cheese tasted as good as they had the first day. After opening the book, she started reading. Three pages in, she knew it was going to be good and wished she had held off beginning until she got home. Thirty minutes wouldn't be nearly enough time. She had just put the first Skittle in her mouth when Jeremy stuck his head in the door.

"Can I come in?"

"Sure." He entered and stared down at the desk curiously. "What?"

"Why do you have your Skittles all separated and lined up like that?"

She grinned sheepishly. "I like to eat them by color, starting with my least favorite." It was a quirk of hers, just like eating Craisins and almonds. She organized them on a plate or napkin to have one of each together, so she could taste the sweet and nutty flavors at the same time. Sure, she'd been teased about it, but she didn't care.

Jeremy laughed softly. "Hey, whatever turns you on."

"This does." Just like watching him change a tire while shirtless, but she kept that to herself. "Did you want anything in particular?"

"Yes. To see if you were serious about your offer to help me with the console."

"I was." Serita popped a green one into her mouth and frowned. *What the...?* She picked up the wrapper and checked the back.

"Problems?"

"They changed the green from lime to green apple. Didn't nobody ask me." It had to have been at least ten years since she'd purchased the candy. When did that happen? She met his amused gaze. "I'm serious. This throws off the whole taste of the pack." She moved them to the side and picked up a yellow one, then glanced up at him, waiting for him to continue.

"If you have about half an hour this evening, I'd like to go over the what needs to be done, then we can make a schedule. I'll probably have Shane help out, too, since he's familiar with the project."

"I have some time."

"Enjoy your candy." He gestured toward the book. "I see you started. When you're ready, we can have our own private book club to discuss it. We'll have food and everything."

"Sounds like a plan." She was still smiling when he left. She checked the time. Not wanting to take advantage of Jeremy's generosity, she put the rest of the candy back into the package—minus the green ones. Those she threw away. Then she cleaned up and got back to work.

At the end of the day, she went in search of Jeremy and found him talking to Chris.

"How's it going, Serita?" Chris asked. "The boss isn't working you too hard, is he?"

"It's going fine and no, he isn't." She tried to keep her smile hidden.

He shook his head. "You two are a pair. I'm going home. See you guys in the morning."

"Later." Jeremy shifted his gaze to Serita. "Let's get moving, so we're not here all night."

She led the way to the design room and stood engrossed as he explained the task. She studied the 3D image on the computer, rotating it one way, then another. "So the console will have foot pedals that control the different tasks. That means each sensor needs to provide specific feedback to make it easier for the surgeons."

"Exactly." He pointed out some of the parts both on the screen and on the actual console.

She adjusted her glasses and inspected the partially completed pedal. They went back and forth for a few minutes, discussing the best way to proceed. She had gotten so engrossed that it took her a moment to realize that Jeremy had moved and now stood behind her. He slid one hand around her waist and used the other one to push her hair aside before trailing kisses along her neck. "We're supposed to be working."

"I am working."

"No, you're not," she murmured, getting lost in the pleasure his warm lips against her skin evoked.

"Yeah, baby, I am." His hands came up to caress her breasts. "I'm working hard to please you."

His words almost melted her in a heap. He continued *working* until her body caught fire. He swept her into his arms and carried her to his office. Kicking the door closed, he placed her on the small conference table.

Jeremy locked the door. "No one is here, but I don't want to take any chances. Now, where was I?" He slanted his mouth over hers in a deep, passionate kiss. "I think I was here." He dropped his head down to the part of her chest visible above her blouse. He opened the buttons, one at a time, kissing each newly bared portion. He released the clasp on her bra and cupped her breasts in his hands, kneading and massaging them.

Serita's head fell back and she braced her forearms on the table. The heat of his tongue licking and sucking her nipples sent a flurry of sensations whipping through her. But he didn't stop there. He unfastened her pants, then tugged them and her panties off. At the first swipe of his tongue against her clit, her hips flew off the table and she let out a loud moan.

"Does this please you?" He continued the sweet torture, swirling his tongue deeper and deeper inside her. "What about this?" He slid two fingers inside of her.

Serita didn't think she could take much more.

"Tell me, baby. Am I pleasing you?"

He sped up the motion and the dual sensations were too much. *"Yes!"* she screamed as she came in a rush of ecstasy that snatched her breath and left her weak. Her body continued to pulse and she gasped for air.

"I think I like having you in my office."

She liked having him anywhere.

Saturday afternoon, Jeremy went with Serita to get a new tire. He had them check the other three and found out that the tread on the front two were worn and would need to be replaced pretty soon. He didn't see the point in buying three tires and told the man to replace all four.

"Jeremy, I don't need to get all four right now," Serita whispered. "He said I still have a month or two, depending on how much I drive."

"There's no sense in coming back three or four weeks from now when we're here now. The weather is changing and it's going to start raining soon. I don't want you driving on bald tires and risking an accident." He would never forgive himself if they waited to change the tires and something happened. His heart couldn't take it. "Baby, you're one millimeter off the recommended change time. I need you to be safe," he said.

"I want to be safe, too. Okay, go ahead." She hugged him. "I really appreciate you helping me out."

"I'll always be here to help you." They made their way to the waiting area. If he had his way, he'd be there for her forever.

"We should be done with the pedal by the end of next week if we keep up the schedule," she said.

"We could, but I don't want to have you and Shane working overtime that many days in a row."

"Darryl has been a great help. He doesn't say much, but he gets the job done."

He thought the same thing. Darryl had recently moved to Sacramento to be closer to his aging mother. He had more than twenty years of experience and it showed. When the time came to choose the two best candidates, it would be a tough decision. Scott seemed to be just as dedicated. He had only been out of school a couple of years, but Jeremy expected the young man to do great things in the future. "We'll see how it goes next week. After we're done here, do you want to grab a bite to eat?"

"That works. There are a few places not too far from here."

For the next several minutes, they continued discussing the different projects and what he hoped to accomplish. Then he turned the conversation to her. "I've been meaning to ask whether you've been checking out the colleges to see if they have any openings."

"Not much. I logged onto Sac State's website a couple of times, but didn't see anything. But that was a month ago. I should probably look at the page again."

"And if I see something, I'll let you know."

The mechanic came in and called them over. "We're all done. I just need your signature here." He rattled off the total.

Serita signed the form and placed her credit card on the counter.

He took it, handed it back and put his own up there. "I've got it." She looked like she wanted to argue, but Jeremy counted on her not wanting to make a scene to work in his favor. It did. But her beautiful brown eyes flashed with irritation behind the glasses. He expected her to let him have it as soon as they exited the building, and she didn't disappoint.

She threw up her hands. "You know, I do have my own money."

"I do know that, and you can pay for whatever you want when I'm not around."

"Jeremy—"

He cut her off with a kiss. "You're special to me, and this is one of the ways I choose to show it. Can you humor me, please?"

She didn't say anything for a moment. "Only because you said please." She strutted off.

Jeremy roared with laughter and caught up in time to open the car door for her. She tossed him the keys and he got in on the driver's side. Still chuckling, he leaned over and kissed her temple.

Serita eyed him. "I guess Chris was right about you being bossy."

"Just when necessary. Any particular place you want to eat?"

"I want a big, juicy hamburger."

"Mel's is right up the street. We can go there, if you like." His phone rang before he could say anything else. He saw Cedric's name on the display. "This is my brother. Let me see what he wants." He connected. "Hey, Ced."

"It's showtime."

Showtime? Then it dawned on him. "The baby?"

"Yes. We're at the hospital."

"It's still a month early, though. Are they going to try and stop the contractions again?" Even though it was closer to the due date, he still worried about all the issues that went along with a premature birth.

"With Randi being thirty-six weeks, the doctors are going to let nature take its course."

"Do Mom and Dad know?"

"No. I called you first. Can you call them? I'm going to call Iyana so she can let Randi's parents' know."

"Yeah. I'll be there soon. I'm about ten minutes away. Good luck, Dad."

"Thanks. I need to get back in there. Text me when you get here."

"Okay." He disconnected and turned to Serita. "The

baby's coming and I need to go to the hospital. Do you mind if we go straight there? If it looks like it's going to be a while, we can go back to your house and pick up my car."

"Of course. I hope everything goes well. It's still a little early, right?"

"About four weeks. I need to let the family know first. Ced knows my mom will most likely ask a hundred questions, so I'm sure that's why he called me first."

"My mom is the same way. She wants all the details even though she'll be walking out the door before I'm done talking."

"Exactly," he said with a laugh. Shaking his head, Jeremy called his parents and relayed the message. Just as he suspected she wanted to know everything about how long Randi had been in labor and what the doctors were saying. He told her he didn't have any information and that she'd be able to find out once she got there. He heard her telling his father they needed to leave, and Jeremy wouldn't be surprised if they made it to the hospital before he did, even though he was closer. Next he sent a text to Lorenzo and Alisha. He started the car and drove off. "I have to warn you that my entire family will probably be there."

She gave him a nervous smile. "I figured as much."

This wasn't the way Jeremy had planned to introduce her to his family, but it worked just as well, because he wanted them to meet the woman who had captured his heart.

Chapter 11

Serita observed the tense set of Jeremy's jaw as he drove and sensed his turmoil. A lot could go wrong, so she understood his apprehension. She didn't know how she felt about meeting his family at this stage in the relationship, though. She was honest enough to admit that her feelings for Jeremy were growing at a pace she had never experienced, and she couldn't help but wonder where it would all lead. The way he treated her and the things he did gave the impression that he might be far more serious about them. No man was going to foot the bill for a set of tires in a casual relationship. She enjoyed being with him no matter what they were doing—talking, working, making love—because he made her feel as if she were precious and a priority.

"You look deep in thought. Is everything okay?"

She glanced his way. "I'm fine."

Jeremy placed a hand over hers. "I hope you're not concerned about my family and whether they'll like you. If so, you have nothing to worry about."

"Maybe a little. We haven't known each other every long and it's kind of early for the whole meet-the-parents thing."

"That's true, but it doesn't change what I feel for you, Serita."

Serita contemplated asking him exactly what that mean, but she wasn't sure she was ready for the answer, or to answer the question herself. Fortunately, their arrival at the hospital gave her a reprieve. Taking a deep breath, she placed her hand in Jeremy's and they headed for the entrance. Inside, he took a moment to text his brother, then followed the directions Cedric supplied. They took the elevator to the maternity floor, and she saw a man coming toward them that had to be Cedric. The brothers favored each other more than a little bit. He was a couple of inches shorter than Jeremy, but shared the same muscular body structure and was just as handsome.

"How are you guys holding up?" Jeremy asked as he hugged Cedric.

"My baby's a trouper. It's been six hours and I know she's tired, but she's hanging in there. The baby's fine, so far."

"That's good to hear. Ced, this is Serita. Serita, Cedric."

"Serita, it's a pleasure to finally meet you. I've heard a lot about you." Cedric smiled. "And don't worry, it was all good."

What had Jeremy told his brother? "It's nice to meet you, too."

"I'm sure I'll be seeing you around a lot and we'll

have a chance to talk, but I need to go check on my wife and baby."

"I'll be praying everything goes well."

"Thanks." To Jeremy he said, "Iyana is on her way and I gave her your number. Let me know when Mom and Dad get here. I know Mom is going to want to come and check on Randi." He gave them Randi's room number.

Jeremy chuckled. "You got that right. She asked me a ton of questions." He clapped Cedric on the shoulder. "I'll handle the family, you just take care of Randi. You can text me with updates and I'll relay the info."

"Thanks, bro. See you in a bit." He smiled Serita's way and hurried back down the hallway.

"This is the same floor she was on last time and the waiting room is this way." He pointed and led the way. They joined three other people already there.

They hadn't been seated more than five minutes when an older couple entered. The woman's frantic gaze scanned the room and Jeremy stood to meet them. Serita guessed they were his parents. The nervousness she'd felt in the car returned in full force.

"Did you talk to Cedric? How's Randi?" the woman asked.

"I saw him briefly and he said Randi is tired, but doing well. And the baby is fine, too."

She sagged against the older man in relief. "Thank God."

Jeremy reached for Serita and draped an arm around her shoulder. "Dad, Mom, I want you to meet Serita."

"It's very nice to meet you, Mr. and Mrs. Hunter," Serita said.

His father smiled. "Nice to meet you, Serita."

Mrs. Hunter's eyes widened and she threw her arms

around Serita. "Oh, my goodness. I've been waiting to meet you, Serita."

She didn't know what she had expected—a handshake or polite nod maybe—but not the crushing, albeit warm, embrace. Again she pondered what Jeremy had told his family about her, about them.

"Jeremy will have to bring you over for dinner, so we can get to know you." She turned to Jeremy. "I'm so happy for you."

Jeremy chuckled. "Me, too, Mom." He gave Serita's shoulder a gentle squeeze.

On the heels of the introduction more people entered the room and another round of greetings ensued. Serita met his cousin Lorenzo, Lorenzo's sister, Alisha, along with her husband, Jabari, and three children.

"Uncle Jeremy!"

Jeremy reached down and swung the little girl, who looked to be about five years old, up into his arms and kissed her cheek. "Hi, Lia. How's my big girl?"

"I'm good."

He ruffled the head of an older boy. "Hey, Corey. I think you've gotten taller since I saw you last month. How's school?"

"It's fine. I have to do a paper on what I want to be when I grow up. I think I want to build robots like you or go into the Air Force like my dad."

"Those are some great choices. You can do both."

Corey's eyes lit up. "I can?"

"Absolutely."

"Cool!"

Serita watched Jeremy interact with the children. He was a natural. Someday he would make a great father.

"Uncle Jeremy, is Miss Serita your girlfriend?" Lia asked.

Every eye turned Serita's way and she felt her cheeks warm.

Jeremy didn't hesitate. "She sure is."

Lia giggled. "She's pretty."

"That she is." The way he stared at Serita made her heart skip a beat.

"I like your glasses, Miss Serita."

"Thank you, Lia."

Alisha came over and took Lia from Jeremy's arms. "Serita, I apologize for my nosy daughter." She tickled the little girl and Lia doubled over in a fit of giggles.

"She got it honest," Lorenzo said with a chuckle.

"Mom, Ced said you can pop in." Jeremy told her where to go and she rushed off.

Everyone took seats and soon the room was filled with lively conversation. Serita contributed when someone asked her a question, but was content to sit back and listen. They seemed to be nice and she could tell they were a close-knit family, as evidenced by them all showing up at the hospital. However, being an only child, it was a tad bit overwhelming. Her reserved personality didn't help.

Jeremy went over to the baby carrier, picked up Alisha's baby daughter and brought her back to where he'd been sitting next to Serita. "This little beauty is Kali and my goddaughter."

She touched the baby's hand. "Hi, Kali." The pride in his voice was evident, as was the love and adoration in his eyes. A vision of him holding their baby popped into her head. She had no idea where it had come from and immediately dismissed it. She needed some space. Now. "I'm going to find the bathroom. I'll be right back." Serita hopped up and made a hasty exit. After searching for a couple of minutes and not finding one, she asked one of the nurses.

Serita poked her head inside and, thankfully, it was empty. She leaned against the wall, took a few deep breaths and let them out slowly. Feeling her control return, she chalked up the wayward thought to the impending birth and being surrounded by the children. Serita allowed herself another moment of silence, then headed back. Jeremy was waiting when she opened the door. "Did something happen?"

"No. I came to see about you." He gave her a gentle kiss. "Are you alright?"

"Yes. Just needed a minute. You have a big family."

"I keep forgetting you're an only child and it can get kind of loud when we're together. My mom came back and said Randi is at seven centimeters dilated, and that it could be a few more hours or a few minutes. But we can go pick up my car and I'll come back."

She could see that he was torn between leaving and staying. "You don't have to do that. Besides, you told Cedric that you would be the point of contact for your family, and you can't do that if you're gone."

"You sure? I don't mind, and Lorenzo can do it."

"I'm positive."

Jeremy kissed her again. "Thanks. I can't tell you how much it means to have you here with me."

"By the way, what did you tell your family about me?"

"Just that I enjoy being with you and how much you're coming to mean to me. That I'm—"

He had such a serious look on his face. When he didn't continue, she asked, "You're what?"

"I'll tell you later. Come on. Jabari is going to pick up some food and you can tell him what you want."

She didn't want food. She wanted him to tell her what he planned to say...*now*. That was the second time he'd alluded to his feelings. Did she dare hope that this time would turn out different than her past relationships?

Between all the overtime hours to get the console back on schedule and Jeremy visiting with his new niece—who had finally come home after having to remain in the hospital an extra three days, until her temperature regulated—Serita hadn't seen much of him outside of work. She was looking forward to spending the entire Saturday with him. They hadn't made any concrete plans outside of her accompanying him to his science class. He'd mentioned some of the lesson might take place outdoors and that she might want to pack an extra set of casual clothes just in case. She took a bag and placed it on the living room sofa, then went into the kitchen to fix a light breakfast of a boiled egg and a bowl of fruit. "Morning, Gabby."

Gabby was seated at the table reading a magazine, eating a bagel and drinking coffee. "Morning. I guess things are really heating up between you and Jeremy. You've met his family and now you're helping teach his class. Next, you'll be moving in with him."

"First, I'm not helping teach his class. He has a few female students, and he thought it might boost their self-confidence to see someone who looks like them. Second, I will not be moving in with anyone, unless there's an 'I do' beforehand."

"I can see that happening." She took a sip of her coffee and started humming the "Wedding March."

Deciding to ignore her friend, Serita brought her food to the table, then went back for a glass of orange juice. "So when are you going to take that stroll down the aisle, Miss Gabriella?"

"As soon as I find someone worthy of my heart."

She conceded her that point and agreed wholeheartedly. They both had kissed enough frogs to last two lifetimes. Halfway through her meal, her phone buzzed. She dug it out of the back pocket of her jeans and read the text from Jeremy: Bring your book so we can discuss. Oh, and I have a few other things up my sleeve. Smiling, she let him know she would. She had only gotten halfway through the book, so she wasn't sure how much they'd be able to discuss. And she was very curious about what other things he had in store.

Gabby toasted her with her bagel. "Yeah, you're going down, sis. Goofy smile all the time, drifting off into space, giggling at those texts."

"I am not," she said with mock outrage. Yet, she couldn't stop the grin spreading across her face.

"Mmm-hmm. Whatever, girl."

Serita finished her breakfast, rinsed the dishes and stacked them in the dishwasher. She went to get the book and stuck it in her tote. "What are you doing today?" she asked Gabby when she came back to the kitchen.

"I told my mom I'd stop by and go with her to pick out some new bedding, towels and other stuff for the master bedroom and bathroom. Apparently, they painted and nothing matches now. It's going to be hard getting her to spend more than twenty dollars. She is the discount queen, but I'm not letting her get anything that'll unravel before they wake up the next morning."

She laughed. "Good luck with that."

"I'm going to need more than luck—more like divine intervention."

The buzzer let them know someone was at the front gate. Still chuckling, Serita said, "I'll get it." It was Jeremy, and she hit the button to let him in. Minutes later, he appeared at the front door.

Jeremy gave her his full, dimpled smile. "Morning, beautiful."

"Good morning." She came up on tiptoe to kiss him. "I'm ready."

"Hey, Jeremy," Gabby called, passing by the living room on her way down the hall. "Y'all have fun and don't get into too much trouble."

"Morning, Gabby. No promises on staying out of trouble."

She paused, divided a glance between Jeremy and Serita. "Yeah, probably not. Well, if you're gonna do it, make it count."

Staring into Serita's eyes, he said, "I plan to do just that."

Serita's pulse skipped. "Um, we should get going." She picked up her bag from the sofa and Jeremy eased it from her hand.

"After you."

She led the way to his car. En route to the school, she shifted in her seat to face him. "So, what kind of surprises do you have up your sleeve?"

He slanted her an amused glance. "If I tell you, they won't be surprises. However, I'll make sure each one is worth every second."

She had never encountered a man like him, someone who could seduce her with a simple sentence. *I'm working hard to please you.* Every time she thought about that evening in his office, how he had pleased her, she knew he would make good on his promise and each second would be more than worth it. When they arrived at the school, she helped him carry in the supplies that the students would use to start building their robots.

"This session, we'll be building a robotic arm, and the students can choose which function they want it to perform—drawing or picking up items."

"Sounds like it's going to be a lot of fun…and hard work."

"It is, but most of the students are really plugged in and come in ready. I've only had two students in the two years that I've been doing this that I had to put out of the class." Jeremy shook his head as he positioned the parts on the long table. "Both were very bright, but saw this as a way to blow off time and I wasn't having it. I don't think they believed I was serious when I warned them what would happen. But after two weeks of them goofing off and using some of the parts for everything but the intended purpose, when their parents came to pick them up I told them they were no longer welcome."

"What did the parents say?"

"They tried to tell me that I couldn't kick their kids out of the class because they'd paid their money. I calmly reminded them of the guidelines that they signed, which stated specifically what would happ̶e̶n̶ if the rules were broken. And they forfeited the f̶e̶e̶.̶"̶

His tone had hardened and Serita didn't know w̶h̶a̶t̶ to say. He seemed so easygoing most of the time, she totally understood his viewpoint. The memor̶y̶ him snapping at her that morning Wade screwed rose in her mind. No, Jeremy did not play. The stude̶n̶t̶ drifted in one by one and Jeremy started the class p̶r̶e̶-

He watched her posture change from defensive to resolute.

"She's your daughter. Our daughter."

He stared at her in silence, but a cacophony of questions was ricocheting inside his head.

Not the how or the when or the where, but the why. Why had he not been more careful? Why had he allowed the heat of their encounter to blot out his normally ice-cold logic?

But the answers to those questions would have to wait.

"Okay…"

Shifting in her seat, she frowned. "'Okay'?" she repeated. "Do you understand what I just said?"

"Yes." He nodded. "You're saying I got you pregnant."

"You don't seem surprised," she said slowly.

He shrugged. "These things happen."

To his siblings and half siblings, even to his mother. But not to him. Never to him.

Until now.

"And you believe me?" She seemed confused, disappointed?

Tilting his head, he held her gaze. "Honest answer?"

He was going to ask her what she would gain by lying. But before he could open his mouth, her lip curled.

"On past performance, I'm not sure I can expect that. I mean, you lied about your name. And the hotel you were staying at. And you lied about wanting to spend the day with me."

"I didn't plan on lying to you," he said quietly.

Her mouth thinned. "No, I'm sure it comes very naturally to you."

"You're twisting my words."

She shook her head. "You mean like saying Steinn instead of Stone?"

Pressing his spine into the wall behind him, he felt a tick of anger begin to pulse beneath his skin.

"Okay, I was wrong to lie to you—but if you care about the truth so much, then why have you waited so long to tell me that I have a daughter? I mean, she must be what…?" He did a quick mental calculation. "Ten, eleven months?"

Don't miss
Proof of Their One-Night Passion
*available December 2019 wherever
Harlequin Presents® books and ebooks are sold.*

www.Harlequin.com

HPEXP1119

The coffee shop was still busy enough that they had to queue for their drinks, but they managed to find a table.

"Thank you." He gestured toward his espresso.

His wallet had been in his hand, but she had sidestepped neatly in front of him, her soft brown eyes defying him to argue with her. Now, though, those same brown eyes were busily avoiding his, and for the first time since she'd called out his name, he wondered why she had tracked him down.

He drank his coffee, relishing the heat and the way the caffeine started to block the tension in his back.

"So, I'm all yours," he said quietly.

She stiffened. "Hardly."

He sighed. "Is that what this is about? Me giving you the wrong name."

Her eyes narrowed. "No, of course not. I'm not—" She stopped, frowning. "Actually, I wasn't just passing, and I'm not here for myself." She took a breath. "I'm here for Sóley."

Her face softened into a smile and he felt a sudden urge to reach out and caress the curve of her lip, to trigger such a smile for himself.

"It's a pretty name."

She nodded, her smile freezing.

It was a pretty name—one he'd always liked. One you didn't hear much outside of Iceland. Only what had it got to do with him?

Watching her fingers tremble against her cup, he felt his ribs tighten. "Who's Sóley?"

She was quiet for less than a minute, only it felt much longer—long enough for his brain to click through all the possible answers to the impossible one. The one he already knew.

Her words—those three little words—made a full-blown attack on his senses. He drew in a shaky breath, then touched her chin. She blinked, as if startled by his touch. "How about 'do show,' Myra?"

Pete watched the way the lump formed in her throat and detected her shift in breathing. He could even hear the pounding of her heart. Damn, she smelled good, and she looked good, too. Always did.

"I'm not sure what 'do show' means," she said in a voice that was as shaky as his had been.

He tilted her chin up to gaze into her eyes, as well as to study the shape of her exquisite lips. "Then let me demonstrate, Ms. Hollister," he said, lowering his mouth to hers.

The moment he swept his tongue inside her mouth and tasted her, he was a goner. It took every ounce of strength he had to keep the kiss gentle when he wanted to devour her mouth with a hunger he felt all the way in his bones. A part of him wanted to take the kiss deeper, but then another part wanted to savor her taste. Honestly, either worked for him as long as she felt the passion between them.

He had wanted her from the moment he'd set eyes on her, but he'd fought the desire. He could no longer do that. He was a man known to forego his own needs and desires, but tonight he couldn't.

Whispering close to her ear, he said, "Peach cobbler isn't the only thing I could become addicted to, Myra."

Will their first kiss distract him from his duty?

Find out in
Duty or Desire
by New York Times *bestselling author Brenda Jackson.*

Available December 2019 wherever
Harlequin® Desire books and ebooks are sold.

Harlequin.com

*Becoming guardian of his young niece is tough
for Westmoreland neighbor Pete Higgins.
But Myra Hollister, the irresistible new nanny with a
dangerous past, pushes him to the brink. Will desire for
the nanny distract him from duty to his niece?*

Read on for a sneak peek at
Duty or Desire
by New York Times *bestselling author Brenda Jackson!*

"That's it, Peterson Higgins, no more. You've had three servings already," Myra said, laughing, as she guarded the pan of peach cobbler on the counter.

He stood in front of her, grinning from ear to ear. "You should not have baked it so well. It was delicious."

"Thanks, but flattery won't get you any more peach cobbler tonight. You've had your limit."

He crossed his arms over his chest. "I could have you arrested, you know."

Crossing her arms over her own chest, she tilted her chin and couldn't stop grinning. "On what charge?"

The charge that immediately came to Pete's mind was that she was so darn beautiful. Irresistible. But he figured that was something he could not say.

She snapped her fingers in front of his face to reclaim his attention. "If you have to think that hard about a charge, then that means there isn't one."

"Oh, you'll be surprised what all I can do, Myra."

She tilted her head to the side as if to look at him better. "Do tell, Pete."

We hope you enjoyed these soulful,
sensual reads.

Kimani Romance is coming to an end, but
there are still ways to satisfy your craving
for juicy drama and passion.

Starting December 2019, find great new reads
from some of your favorite authors in:

Drama. Scandal. Passionate romance.

**New titles available every month,
wherever books are sold!**

Harlequin.com

cisely at ten. She marveled at his patience and willingness to answer each and every question, and just like with his nieces and nephews, he had a great rapport with the students.

"Okay, everyone. I'd like to introduce Dr. Edwards. She's a robotics engineer and will be hanging out with us today. Let's welcome her."

More than a few eyes widened at his pronouncement, but they all greeted Serita with enthusiasm and her heart swelled. She told them a little about herself, her teaching at a college and some of the projects she'd worked on. "Does anyone know what a prosthetic arm is?" Only two hands went up. She pointed to a young man sitting in the back.

"It's something they use when a person's arm gets cut off."

"Right. Years ago, the hands and arms didn't do much, but now we're able to build them so a person can do some of the things they used to, like bending each finger, picking up objects and tying shoes. And they feel almost like real skin." Several hands shot up. She smiled over at Jeremy and he returned one of his own. "I don't have time to answer questions right now because you have a lot of work to do, but you can talk to me afterward. How does that sound?" The students nodded in affirmation and Serita turned the class back over to Jeremy. She thoroughly enjoyed herself and had no problems sitting on the floor of the multipurpose room to assist the students. More than once, she glanced up to find Jeremy watching her with an expression that made her heart race. Serita was falling and couldn't do a thing about it. She wasn't sure if she even wanted to.

Chapter 12

Jeremy placed the bag holding their lunch from a nearby deli on his kitchen counter. He still couldn't get over the way Serita had interacted with the students. He wanted her as his partner in this and everything else, but he still sensed that she was a little skittish. They hadn't talked about it, but last week at the hospital when she'd bolted, he knew it had to do with more than his large family. Even though the way they all embraced her as if she was already part of the family might have been scary enough. Every one of them could tell how he felt about her—he didn't try to hide it. And something told him that Serita knew, as well, and it scared her. More than once, he wondered about the men in her past. Had someone hurt her and made her wary of relationships? He suspected that might be the case, but he planned to do everything in his power to let her know not all men were that way. *He* wasn't that way.

"Do you want to eat in here or out in the sunroom?" He preferred his deck, but with the considerable temperature drop, the season had definitely changed from summer to fall.

"The sunroom."

"Okay. It's a little chilly, so I'll turn on the fireplace."

"That would be great. I forgot how fast the weather changes here. Last week, it was almost eighty. Now, it's barely reaching the seventies and they're talking rain."

He carried the bag outside and set it down, then turned on the gas fireplace. "Isn't it colder this time of year in Reno?"

Serita followed with their drinks, took the food out of the bag and placed it on the table, along with the napkins. She sat. "Yes, but it's not the drastic ten-degree change like here."

Jeremy took the chair across from her. He unwrapped his turkey sandwich and took a bite.

"You're really great with those kids, Jeremy."

"So are you. Would you consider teaching with me? At least for the rest of this session. They were blown away by you, especially Briana. She's a little shy." He angled his head thoughtfully. "Actually, she reminds me a lot of you. Brilliant, yet reserved."

She dropped her head and stuffed the lettuce back into the sandwich. "I don't know about brilliant, but I will confess to being somewhat of an introvert."

"I can tell. Especially last week at the hospital. But I hope you'll think about what I said."

"I'll think about it."

As they ate, he continued to study her and toyed with telling her that he was falling in love with her—more accurately *in love* with her—but decided to hold

off awhile longer. "Do you see yourself settling down and maybe having kids?"

Serita took a sip of her soda before answering. "Sometimes, but only if I find a guy who likes me the way I am. I don't like a lot of hoopla, I'm not into partying all the time and I like my glasses."

Her defensive stance confirmed that she had been hurt before. "There are men who appreciate all of that." He covered her hand with his. "I'm one of them. I like everything about you, Serita, and I think you already know what those glasses do to me. There isn't one thing I want you to change." *Except maybe your last name.*

"That means a lot, Jeremy, and maybe that's why I enjoy being with you so much. Most people think that I'm teetering on the brink of boring, but you let me be me."

He raised an eyebrow. "Boring? I don't think you're boring at all. You're pretty exciting in my book."

"Obviously, you don't get out much."

Laughter spilled from Jeremy's lips. "I get out plenty. Baby, you're a woman after my own heart."

She gasped slightly.

Their eyes locked. Yes, he had meant that literally, and she would find out soon enough. Smiling, he went back to his food. When they finished, he cleaned up, took everything inside and dumped the remnants into the trash. "Grab your book and we can get comfortable in the library."

"Okay, but I'm not done reading it yet."

"I'm not, either. So we can either talk about the first part or just read for a while."

"How about we do a little of both?" Serita said, taking her book out of her tote.

"Works for me." Jeremy led the way upstairs. "Have

a seat and I'll be right back." He went to his bedroom, took out his contacts and put on his glasses. Then he removed his shoes. Grabbing his book off the nightstand, he went to the library. He found her stretched out on the oversize chaise lounge with her shoes off.

"You wear glasses?"

"Yep. They're not as sexy as yours, but they've got a little style." The titanium rimless frame curved at the top, leaving the outer edges of the lens free. It twisted at the joint and reminded him of a robot arm.

Serita patted the space next to her. "I beg to differ. They're *very* sexy. And so are you," she added softly.

He sat next to her, covered their legs with the blanket that was draped over the back and slung an arm around her shoulder. They chatted for a few minutes about their favorite parts so far and who they thought the killer might be, then read silently. Serita rested her head against his shoulder, filling Jeremy with a contentment he had never experienced with any other woman. He had to have this woman in his life. No other one would do.

"This is getting good," she said after a long while, closing the book.

"Then why are you closing the book?"

"You said you had some surprises up your sleeve and you've got me curious."

Chuckling, he closed his book, sat up and swung his long legs over the side. "We're going to play a little *Jeopardy!* game so I can see if you're as good as you claim."

Serita snorted. "Claim? I'm going to wipe the floor with you, Jeremy Hunter."

"Let's go, Miss Thang." She preceded him down the stairs to the family room, where he already had the stack of questions waiting, along with another surprise

she'd find out about later. Jeremy turned on the fireplace and cranked up the heat a couple of notches.

"Why are you turning up the heat if you have the fireplace going?" she asked, dropping down on the sofa.

"Because we're playing strip *Jeopardy!*, sweet baby girl, and I don't want you to be cold when I take all your clothes." He wiggled his eyebrows.

She held up a hand. "Wait a minute. You didn't say anything about that."

"Surprise." The look on her face was priceless.

"What happened to playing for pennies or something like that?" she asked, waving her hands around.

Her flustered state made him smile inwardly. He shrugged. "If you're as good as you say you are, it won't matter because you'll be fully clothed, but if you're scared…" He took a seat on the floor.

Determination lined her features and she joined him. "Bring it on."

"I'll even let you go first." He gestured to the waiting cards with a flourish.

Serita pulled a card and read the question. "'This man wrote *Jurassic Park*.' Who is Michael Crichton? Easy."

Jeremy grinned and took his turn. "'This word means to dislike strongly.' What is abhor?" They went back and forth for another three rounds and neither of them missed. It came back around to him. "'The elements on the periodic table are ordered by this characteristic.' What are atomic numbers?"

"Yeah, yeah. Of course, you'd know that." She snatched up the next card. "'Elements on the periodic table in Group 18 are often referred to by this name.' Noble gases."

"Wrong."

"What are you talking about? You know that's the correct answer."

"Maybe so, but you didn't phrase it in the form of a question."

She hit her palm against her forehead and groaned.

He rubbed his hands together. "Hmm, what do I want first? I think I'll take these." His hands went to the waistband of her jeans.

Serita hesitated briefly, then lifted her hands to the button.

Jeremy shook his head slowly. "Did I mention that the other person gets to remove the article of clothing?"

"No, you did not," she said with a soft gasp.

"My bad." He rose to his knees in one fluid motion. "Lie back, baby." He kissed her until she lay flat on her back, then teased her with caresses and kisses as he eased her pants down and off. His hands and his mouth made a slow path up her legs to her thighs and inner legs before grazing her core.

She moaned and her legs trembled. "We're supposed to be playing."

"We are." He helped her back to a sitting position. He was so aroused he promptly missed the next question.

"Well, now. Looks like Dr. Hunter is going to be without his pants, too. Your turn. Lie back."

He readily complied. Instead of immediately taking off his pants, Serita straddled him and ground her body against his, forcing a low groan from his throat. He gripped her hips and arched up to meet her.

She reached for his hands and removed them. "No, baby. You don't get to touch me. It's not your turn."

Jeremy went still. She had never called him *baby*

before, or used any other type of endearment for that matter. The implications made his heart pound in his chest. Gyrating in slow, erotic circles, she slid her way down his body, then ran her hands over his erection. His breath hissed out. "If you don't stop, we're going to be playing a different game called How Many Ways Can I Make You Come."

Serita smiled serenely. She undid his belt and pants, and he lifted his hips to facilitate their removal. The faster she got them off, the easier he'd be able to breathe. When she went back to her spot on the floor, he threw his arm over his face and lay there panting as if he'd run the anchor leg of a four-by-four relay. Finally he was calm enough to sit up. He met her gaze and wondered if they were actually going to be able to finish the game. The rise of her breasts let him know she'd been just as affected. "I believe it's your turn."

"'Traditionally made vodka is done by distilling this root vegetable.' *What is* a potato?" She made sure her answer had the correct form.

Two hands later, she lost her shirt, and right after that her bra. Jeremy took sweet revenge. She got a little payback of her own when she won his shirt, which made them even—both only had their underwear left— and tormented him until he thought he would explode. Breathing harshly, he drew the next card. "'This island country's landscapes represented Middle Earth in the *Lord of the Rings* movie trilogy.'" His brain was in such a sensual haze he couldn't think.

"Five seconds."

At the last moment, he said, "What is New Zealand?"

"Lucky."

"Just take your turn," he said with a smile.

"Okay. 'The general term for beverages which mix neutral grain spirits with sugar, glycerin and flavorings.' What is schnapps?" she said smugly.

After she'd answered her fourth question about alcoholic beverages correctly, Jeremy said, "Is there something you want to tell me? Either you're an undercover bartender or you've been doing some serious testing."

Serita threw her card at him in mock outrage. "I beg your pardon. Neither. I just read a lot. Take your turn." She rolled her eyes playfully.

They continued battling back and forth for several minutes. He had never played *Jeopardy!* or any other form of recreation quite like this. But he knew from now on it would be their special game. In the end, Serita lost her last piece of clothing. "I guess that means I'm the champion." Jeremy reached up and got the blanket off the sofa and spread it on the floor.

"What's that for?"

"It's easier to wash a blanket than clean the carpet." He saw the moment it registered in her eyes. "As the winner, I get the grand prize."

"Which is?"

"You." He picked her up and placed her on the blanket. Then he stood, quickly shed his briefs and donned the condom he had placed beneath one of the throw pillows. "Remember that other game I mentioned earlier? I'm going to see how many times and how many ways I can make you come *and* make you scream." His tongue teased the corners of her mouth before slipping inside. He took his time tasting and swirling his tongue around hers, then he transferred his kisses to her throat and her breasts.

"Ohh..."

He retrieved the bottle of strawberry massage oil

he'd purchased from Desiree's shop and drizzled some over her breasts. He blew on it lightly and watched Serita's reaction.

"Oh, my goodness! It's…getting hot."

"That's exactly how I want you," he murmured, latching on to a nipple and sucking it clean.

Serita cried out. "Jeremy!"

He made a path with the oil from the center of her breasts down the front of her body and the valley between her thighs, and followed with his tongue, savoring the sweetness of the oil and her skin. Jeremy gently pushed her legs apart, added some oil to her inner thighs and kissed his way to her center. He took his time, using slow, long licks to increase her pleasure. The sounds of ecstasy spilling from her mouth sent his desire soaring straight through the roof.

She gripped the blanket, writhing beneath his mouth, her vocalizations rising. A moment later, she screamed, calling his name over and over.

Jeremy slid two fingers inside her, taking up a lazy rhythm and rebuilding her passions. She came again, gasping and arching. He needed to be inside her. *Now.* And he knew just how he wanted her. He lifted her to straddle him and lay back on the blanket. "I liked it when you were here earlier. Ride me, baby."

"With pleasure," Serita said, lowering herself onto his rigid erection.

She started the same erotic swirl of her hips and he didn't think he was going to last a minute. His hands played over the curve of her hips, up her spine and around to her breasts. He cupped both in his hands, kneading and massaging as she moved up and down on him. His hands slid back down to her hips and he plunged deeper.

He leaned up and fused his mouth against hers. No other woman had come close to arousing the emotions in him Serita did. Resuming his position, he closed his eyes and let those emotions take over. He increased the pace, and her feminine muscles clenched him tight. He trembled slightly as the sensations intensified.

"I'm going to come," she panted.

"Let go, sweetheart." Jeremy whispered erotic endearments from a place he never knew existed.

Her nails dug into his shoulders and her body tensed all around him. She let out another scream as she shuddered with her release.

He tightened his hold on her hips, setting a rhythm with deep, powerful thrusts, and came right behind her, growling hoarsely as an orgasm ripped through him. Before he could recover, a second one overtook him, snatching his breath and making him yell her name loud enough to be heard throughout the neighborhood. It took every ounce of control he possessed not to blurt out that he loved her. She collapsed on top of him and he could feel her rapidly beating heart against his. The only sounds in the room were their ragged breathing. Jeremy wrapped his arms around her and kissed the top of her hair. *I love her.* He had to do everything in his power to keep her in Sacramento.

Chapter 13

Serita lay pulsing in Jeremy's bed Sunday morning after another round of lovemaking. She hadn't planned to spend the night, but it seemed that neither of them could get enough. And she would never, *ever* be able to watch or play *Jeopardy!* without remembering what had happened last night. They had fallen asleep on the floor, awakened two hours later and gone up to shower, which ended with him taking her from behind in the oversize shower stall. Both were too exhausted to move and she didn't protest when he suggested she stay the night. Part of her felt weird waking up in a man's bed—she had never done it before—but the part of her that was falling in love with him thought it the most natural ending to a perfect night.

"As soon as I catch my breath, we'll shower, get some breakfast, then I'll take you home."

"This time, I'm showering alone," she said with a tired chuckle.

Jeremy leaned up on an elbow and ran a hand over her hip. "You don't trust me?"

She stilled his hand. "I know you're not asking me that."

He nuzzled her neck and pulled her closer. "You can't blame a brother for trying. I find myself addicted to you in every way and I may not ever let you go."

She froze. "What did you say?"

Running a finger down her cheek, he said, "Meeting you has been the best thing that has happened to me and I don't want to ever let you go. If I could keep you here with me forever, I would do it in a heartbeat. I'm going to do whatever it takes to make that happen."

He stared at her with such a look of tenderness that myriad emotions surged through her, bringing tears to her eyes. The gentle kiss that followed made her fall a little harder. She was in deep and it frightened her. Not wanting him to see it, she schooled her features and pasted a bright smile on her face. "We should probably get moving. I have a few things to do today to prepare for the week."

Jeremy sighed heavily. "So do I."

They left the bed reluctantly and showered separately, then he took her home. She declined the late breakfast he had offered to prepare.

Inside the door, he held her tightly. "I'll see you in the morning. I decided to cancel overtime for tomorrow. We can pick it up on Tuesday."

"Okay." She leaned up to kiss him. He stood there a few seconds longer, as if he wanted to say something

else. Instead, he kissed her once more and left. Serita rested her head against the closed door.

"That must have been some night."

She jumped and spun around, clutching her chest. "Gabby, girl, you almost gave me a heart attack."

Gabby scrutinized Serita for a lengthy moment. "Come on over here and spill it. I can see something's wrong."

She didn't bother to ask how Gabby knew. Gabby had always been good at reading people, especially Serita. She followed her friend to the living room and lowered herself to the sofa.

Gabby sat next to Serita. "Did something happen?"

"Yes. I'm falling in love with him."

She stared. "*O-kay*, so tell me how that's a bad thing. I mean, unless he doesn't feel the same way, which, for the record, I know he does. I can see it on his face every time he looks at you." She paused. "By your expression, I'm guessing you realize it, too, right?"

Serita nodded. "What if he's wrong and he just thinks he's falling in love. It's happened before." Her ex had confessed his love, then a month later said he'd made a mistake. It wasn't love he felt, just a strong case of lust and he didn't think they should waste their time continuing the relationship because they were too different. He had wanted her to change her look—straighten her hair, get contacts and wear clothes that *he* thought were sexier. He always wanted to manipulate her life, make it into something more in line with what *he* liked. She'd found out later that he'd been dating someone else at the same time. A woman who possessed all the traits Serita didn't, or one who could be influenced.

Gabby grasped Serita's hand. "Honey, I know where

this is coming from. I don't want to say I told you so, but the signs were there with Tate. He was a selfish bastard, and you can't punish Jeremy or yourself. I truly believe Jeremy cares for you a lot and you owe it to yourself to grab all the happiness he has to offer."

Jeremy had made her happier than she could have ever imagined when he'd waltzed up to her after her session in Madrid and asked her out. But relationships never ended in her favor and she was already in too deep.

"Did he say anything to make you think he's pulling away?"

"No, just the opposite. He keeps saying…*stuff.*" Serita waved a hand. "Things like wanting to please me and never letting me go. He even paid for my tires last week." She buried her head in her hands. "I'm so confused," she said with a groan. "He's everything a woman could want, but there's this part of me that's afraid it's all going to go away." The emotions she had for him were stronger than all her relationships put together and she didn't think she would survive that kind of heartbreak.

Gabby let out a short bark of laughter. "If the brother is saying he's never going to let you go, you can bet he's in it for the duration. In case you didn't know, *never* is a long time. Like somewhere in the vicinity of forever."

Serita shot her friend a glare.

"Don't shoot those daggers at me. You know I'm right. Get yourself together, girlfriend, and let that man love you the way you should be loved." She stood. "Now I'm going to fix me some lunch. You're welcome to join me, if you haven't already eaten."

"I haven't."

"Ooh-wee! Any man who can make you forget about food is a keeper."

She shook her head and gave in to Gabby's whack sense of humor. The woman always knew how to make Serita smile. She stood and hugged her. "Thanks for being my friend."

"You're welcome. If you really want to thank me, make sure I'm your maid of honor at the wedding. And FYI, Gabriella is a great name for a girl."

Serita latched on to Gabby's arm. "Okay, you're getting out of control. We're done with this conversation." They broke out in a fit of laughter.

Hours later, as she folded the last of her laundry, Jeremy called.

"Did I catch you at a bad time?"

"No. I'm just finishing up laundry. What's up?"

"Nothing much. I wanted to hear your voice."

She laughed softly. "You just saw me less than eight hours ago." It had been just after noon when he'd dropped her off.

"And it feels like eight hours too long." Jeremy fell silent for a few seconds. "Do you think this is crazy?"

"Some parts of me do and I wonder if it's all still some fantasy left over from Madrid."

"And the other parts?"

"The other parts want it to be real," she answered softly.

"It is real, Serita. Very real. I'm far past the age of playing games, though I never have. I know what I want, and it's you. *All* of you. I want everything that makes you uniquely you—glasses and all. I realize this seems to be happening fast and I know you're afraid. I sense it every time I hint at my feelings for you. We

can take this as slowly as you need, but understand that I'm not going anywhere. Rest well, sweetheart, and I'll see you tomorrow."

"You, too." She disconnected and held the phone against her heart. *Just maybe.*

Jeremy hit the ground running on Monday with two meetings from prospective clients in the morning and an afternoon visit to a manufacturing company looking to build industrial robots. Until now, he had dealt primarily with medical robotics, but industrial robots would expand his business into a new territory. When he got back to the office, he and Chris would have to hammer out the details and determine the feasibility of such a project. Before driving off, he took a moment to text his friend and ask him to leave an hour for them to chat.

As he drove, his mind drifted to his favorite subject of late—Serita. He'd caught a glimpse of her on his way out that morning, but hadn't gotten a chance to say anything to her. He was still blown away by their weekend, but he couldn't rid himself of the sensation that she was still holding back. Each and every time he came close to revealing the depths of his emotions, he sensed her retreat and didn't know what to do to convince her that what they had was the real thing. What she said about wanting to find someone who accepted her as is still resonated with him. He got the feeling that one or more of the men in her past had tried to change her instead of respecting the incredible woman she was. But she didn't have to worry about that with him. As Jeremy had told her, her uniqueness was what drew him. Cookie-cutter women were a dime a dozen, but find-

ing Serita had been like discovering a blue diamond, a rare and precious jewel.

Jeremy arrived at the office and went straight to the work area where he knew he'd find Serita. He knew he couldn't kiss her like he wanted, but he had to see her and talk to her for a minute to see how she was doing after their phone call last night. Without saying as much, he'd pretty much told her that he loved her. He still didn't think she was ready to hear the words outright, but he wasn't sure how much longer he would be able to hold out. "How's it going, ladies?" he asked when he opened the door.

Serita and Elena glanced up, and Elena said, "Making good progress. Did I already say that you should hire Serita permanently?"

He smiled. "Yes, you did, Elena." Serita's face was unreadable.

"And since I know you were raised to honor your elders, I have no doubt you'll follow through."

"I'll take your suggestion under advisement."

Elena eyed him over the glasses she had recently begun wearing. "You'll do more than that. Serita, go ahead and take your break," she added with a knowing smile. "That's why Jeremy is here in the first place."

Serita's eyes widened. "I don't think… I'm sure he's just making sure we're progressing on schedule," she stammered.

She patted Serita's hand. "I may be a few years older than you, *chica*, but I'm not blind. You could do worse. He's a good man." She gestured to the door. "Go. We'll continue when you get back. And you can tell me the story of how you two met. I know it's going to be a good one," Elena said with a little laugh.

Jeremy couldn't do anything but smile. Leave it to Elena to figure it out. He had been very careful in his dealings with Serita, so he had no idea how Elena knew, but he planned to question her as soon as he got the opportunity. "I'll have her back in a few minutes." He didn't say anything until they were safely behind the closed door of his office. She seemed more beautiful each time he saw her. Today she wore her hair piled on top of her head, and a few errant curls had come down. "How are you, baby?"

"I'm okay. Did you mean what you said last night?"

"Every word, sweetheart. I'm not asking for details because they don't matter, but just know whatever he or they told you about who you are is wrong. You've enriched my life in ways I can't begin to describe."

Silence stretched between them. Finally Serita said, "I feel the same, but…" She ran a hand over her forehead and paced.

"But what?"

She stopped and held his gaze intently. "It never works out in the end. At least not for me. I'm not sure I want to put myself through that again."

Jeremy blew out a long breath. Seeing her so vulnerable made his heart ache. He wanted to hold her so badly it hurt. But he'd made a promise, and he would keep it even if it killed him. And at this rate, it just might. "What can I do to help you with this? I don't want to lose you, Serita."

"Don't change."

"I won't." He stood there warring with himself whether or not to go to her. In the end, he lost the battle and gathered her into his embrace. Neither of them spoke. After several seconds, he released her and went

around to his desk. "I'm plugged in to several job sites and I received an announcement from Sac State that might interest you. I'll email it to you."

She perked up. "For an adjunct professor?"

"Yes. I wish I had seen it earlier, though. It closes tomorrow."

"No, no, that's okay. I'll get it done. Thanks for looking out."

"Hopefully, you'll get the position. It'll be a win-win situation for both of us. You get to work on that perfect world you mentioned and I'll be able to do the same."

"And your perfect world would be?"

"Doing everything I can to convince you to stay here with me." He rapped his knuckles on the desk. "I know you need to get back to work. We can talk later."

Serita shook her head. "Yeah, I don't want to give Elena anything else to talk about."

Jeremy chuckled and held up his hands in mock surrender. "For the record, I didn't say a word. I have no idea how she found out about us. I've been very careful. And I know Chris wouldn't say anything."

"She's a mother, so that probably explains it," she said, opening the door. "They always know everything."

"Right. See you later."

Smiling, she gave him a tiny wave and exited.

He stood there a few seconds longer, then went to check on his other two hires. He had only a couple more weeks before making a decision. He started with Darryl. "I just wanted to check in with you and see how you're doing."

"Good, good. This is one of the better companies I've worked for. I mean, I'm not saying that because I

want any special favors or anything," he said. "But everyone here is nice."

"I'm glad to hear it."

"And I'm glad Wade isn't here anymore. He was pretty rude to Scott. I tried sticking up for him, but…" He shrugged.

"I appreciate that because we're like family here. Speaking of family, how's your mother doing?"

Darryl seemed surprised by the question. "She's okay and is glad to have me back home. I'm looking into getting her some in-home help because she can't do as much on her own."

Which meant he would definitely need a permanent job. He knew in-home care was expensive and insurance didn't always cover everything. "I hope you can find what she needs."

"Thank you, Jeremy. And thank you for giving me an opportunity."

Jeremy asked a few more questions before ending the conversation. He met with Scott next and the young man related the same incident regarding Wade. It made Jeremy even more glad that he had booted the man out.

"I really like working here. I'm learning a lot, especially from Shane."

Scott was only two years out of school, but Shane had mentioned that the young man was a quick study and showed great potential. "That's good to know." He glanced up at the wall clock. "It's almost five, so we can call it a day." His father had drilled into Cedric's and Jeremy's heads the notion of having a balanced work life and, as soon as Jeremy's business was on solid footing, he had cut back on his working hours. He still had to put in extra hours sometimes, but he tried to make

sure his employees didn't stay beyond regular working hours unless absolutely necessary.

"Thanks. See you in the morning."

After Scott left, Jeremy rotated his chair toward the window and stared out onto the tree-lined street. It would be difficult to choose which two candidates to hire because they all possessed the skills he wanted and needed to grow his company. Serita was a forgone conclusion, even if he didn't factor in his emotions. But the other two men would be valuable assets, as well. Laughter in the hallway interrupted his thoughts. Through his open door he saw everyone leaving for the day. It pleased him to see Scott, Darryl and Serita blending so well with Shane and Elena. He stood and went to the door. "Elena, got a minute?"

"Sure." She said her goodbyes and walked over to Jeremy's office. "What's up, boss?"

"Just want to know why you think something is going on between me and Serita."

Elena reached up and patted his cheek. "I'm not blind, *mi amigo.* It's not anything you've said, but your eyes tell all. You love her, no?"

He dropped his head. "I do. Did Serita say anything?"

"Not one word," she said with a laugh. "She's a shy one. Smart as a whip, though."

"That she is."

"She's good for you."

He agreed wholeheartedly. "Thanks. See you later. Tell Eduardo and the girls I said hello."

"I will."

Jeremy watched her disappear down the hall and round the corner, then made his way to Chris's office. "Hey."

Chris leaned back in his chair. "What's going on?"

"I wanted to talk to you about the meeting I had with Archibald Manufacturing. They're looking to build a dozen dual-arm robots."

"Isn't that out of the scope of what we typically do?"

"Yes, but it'll give us the opportunity to expand into the industrial arena."

He scrubbed a hand down his face. "I don't know, Jeremy. Right now, we're pretty maxed out, timewise, on staff. Taking this on will mean increasing staff and pay, and I thought you wanted to keep the company relatively small."

"That hasn't changed." Unlike his LA cousins who owned a large in-home safety company and employed almost a hundred workers, he didn't want the increased responsibility that came along with that size business. Neither did he want a board of directors that would have input and make the decisions on the way he ran *his* company. "What if we kept Serita, Darryl and Scott?"

"Offhand, I don't know if we could offer full-time employment to all three right off the bat, especially when you factor in the benefits package."

He thought for a minute. "If we took this contract and sealed the deal for the exoskeleton, it would be doable."

"True," Chris said slowly, as if mulling it over in his mind. "If you're serious about hiring all three, I'd feel better if we offered a part-time position to the third one, with the possibility of increasing the hours. That way, we don't overextend ourselves at the outset. At the same time, we keep them away from the competitors."

"I like the way you think." They did a fist bump.

"That's why you pay me the big bucks." He made a show of thinking. "Wait. No, you don't, and I'm

still waiting on that raise for reuniting you with your woman."

"Shut the hell up."

"Speaking of Serita, are you any closer to getting to your goal?"

Jeremy sighed. "Sometimes I think yes, then other times I'm not so sure. The more we get to know each other, the more I realize how her past failed relationships are affecting what we've got going on." He still couldn't believe what she'd told him about guys wanting her to look different, and he shared some of the details with Chris.

"Some men are asses. You know, when you first talked about the whole love-at-first-sight thing, I really thought you were crazy. But I've been watching you with Serita, and I have to admit I might be wrong in this instance."

He smiled. "You doubted me? As long as we've been friends, you should've known better. It's not like I've said anything different in all that time."

"True. I'm just amazed, I guess."

Jeremy stood and stretched. "Well, while you're being amazed, I'm going home. I'm serious about Serita being my one and only, and I'm going to do everything and *anything* I can to keep her in my life." *Whatever it takes.*

Chapter 14

Serita sat at her desk Friday afternoon eating her lunch and checking her emails and messages. She saw that she had missed a call from her mother and decided to return her call first, then listen to her other messages.

"Hi, honey," her mother said when she answered.

"Hey, Mom. I'm returning your call. Is everything okay?" Her mother typically didn't call during Serita's workday. She took a sip of her water.

"Yes. Nothing's wrong. I wanted to catch you before you left work to invite you and Jeremy to dinner tomorrow."

Dinner? She choked on the drink.

"Are you okay, Serita?"

"Yes," she croaked, coughing and trying to clear her throat. "Water went down the wrong way." It took a second for it to settle. "Dinner tomorrow?"

"We've been waiting to meet him, so I thought this would be a nice way to do that. And don't give me that tired excuse about you two just meeting and it's too soon. I'd venture to say you're a lot more serious about him than you've let on, and your father and I need to check him out."

Her mother knew her well. There was nothing to do but surrender. Besides, she'd met not only his parents but just about everybody in his family. She thought it only fair that he got a turn in the hot seat. "I'll see if he's free."

Her mother's soft laughter came through the line. "Oh, I'm certain he'll be free and, more than likely, already spending the day with you. I gotta run. Call me later to confirm. Dinner will be at six. Love you, sweetheart."

"Love you, too, Mom." Serita tossed the phone onto the desk and fell back against the chair. Why was she so reluctant to introduce Jeremy to her parents? He was a man any woman would be glad to bring home. She acknowledged that she continued to have doubts about whether she had another heartbreak in store, yet she'd made no attempts to end the relationship. She couldn't. She had to keep taking it day by day and praying that her fears would subside under the growing love she felt for him.

Picking up the phone again, she listened to her missed messages. Her heart rate kicked up when she heard the one from Sac State letting her know she'd made it to the interview step. She wanted to turn a cartwheel. After writing down the contact information, she called right then to schedule. Afterward she was so excited, she packed up the remainder of her food and went to Jeremy's office.

She poked her head inside his partially open door and knocked.

"Come in."

"Are you busy?"

Jeremy shifted his attention from the computer to her. "Never too busy for you. What's up?"

"I have an interview for the position next Tuesday," she said with a grin.

He stood and hugged her. "That's great. Congratulations."

"Don't congratulate me yet. I haven't gotten the job."

"But you will. They'd be foolish not to hire you."

She came up on tiptoe and kissed him. "Thanks for the vote of confidence." Belatedly she remembered they weren't supposed to be doing this during work hours, and she nearly jumped away from him. She hadn't closed the door when she came in.

He chuckled. "No one's watching, sweetheart. You're good. And you don't hear me complaining."

Serita swatted him on the arm. "You're supposed to remind me."

"Please. I haven't held you in my arms in almost a week and as far as kisses go, I'm way overdue." Jeremy moved closer to her. "So, what do you think I should do about that?"

Truth be told, she'd missed his kisses, too. However, with them working overtime, they hadn't been able to schedule any private time since last weekend. She still had some apprehensions but had resolved to work through them. She wanted to be with him and he hadn't given her any reason to think he would change. He'd promised he wouldn't. "Nothing right now." He

gave her the smile that made her lose all reason and she knew she needed to leave. "I have to go."

"You don't like my kisses?" he asked with a sly grin, closing the distance between them.

She backed up and he kept coming. "What are you doing?"

Jeremy reached behind her and closed the door softly. "I'm going to kiss you." He slid an arm around her waist and dipped his head. "Any objections?"

Yes, yes, yes! She dismissed that voice of reason. "No."

He stared intently at her, then traced his finger down her cheek and across her lips. "Do you know how much you mean to me?"

Her pulse skipped. "Jeremy," she whispered. He touched his mouth to hers once, twice, then his tongue slipped between her parted lips, curling around hers in a long, drugging kiss. He drew her closer and deepened the kiss. After a tantalizing moment, sanity returned and Serita tore her mouth away. "I need to get out of here before you get me into trouble."

He took her hand and placed it over the solid length of his erection. "I'm already in trouble."

Serita snatched her hand away. "Yeah, well, you won't be getting into any more." She opened the door, then remembered the other reason she had come to talk to him. "I almost forgot. My parents want to meet you and invited us to dinner tomorrow evening, but if you're busy, that's okay."

"I'm not busy and I'm looking forward to meeting them. Just let me know what time to pick you up. Afterward, maybe I can interest you in another game of *Jeopardy!*"

His reference conjured up every erotic moment of that night and the space between her legs began to throb as if he were touching her. "Dinner is at six. Bye." She spun on her heel and strode down the hall, his laughter trailing. One more minute and she would have given in to everything he offered. *That man is too tempting for his own good.*

Saturday after his class, Jeremy drove over to see his new niece. He hadn't seen her in a week and wanted to check on her. So far, she was progressing well. He smiled thinking about how disappointed his students had been when he had told them Serita wouldn't be there. He didn't blame them because he had missed having her with him, as well.

Cedric answered the door. "Hey. Come on in. I figured you'd be spending the day with Serita, since you guys have been putting in all the extra hours at work."

He and Cedric went to the family room. "I'll see her later. Her parents invited us to dinner."

"More like they want to check you out over dinner." They shared a grin. "I remember meeting Randi's parents for the first time. She dropped the bomb on me on our way back from Tahoe and I had about an hour to prepare myself."

"I'm not really worried about it, but I can see why you were, since your hookups never lasted more than a month or two, *maybe*."

Cedric nodded. "For real. But I knew what I was feeling for Randi by that point and just told them the truth."

"And that's what I plan to do. Except I haven't told Serita how I feel about her. Well, not in so many words. I've hinted around but haven't come right out and told

her that I'm in love with her." Jeremy filled his brother in on what he'd learned about Serita's past relationships. "She's still a little hesitant about us."

"It was the same with Randi and it didn't help that I had been adamant about it being a no-strings-attached affair. You situation is different and, hopefully, it'll make things easier. Tell Serita how you feel, Jeremy. That'll go a long way in showing her that you're sincere. And she definitely needs to hear it from you before you tell her parents."

He thought about the advice. Serita did deserve to hear it first, and he'd do it when he picked her up. "You're right."

"That's why I'm the big brother," Cedric said.

"You're the *older* brother. I've been bigger than you since high school." Jeremy flexed his biceps.

"But I can still kick your—"

"I thought I heard voices down here," Randi said, coming into the room holding the baby.

Jeremy and Cedric stood.

She laughed. "I still can't get over this whole standing-when-I-come-into-the-room thing."

Jeremy smiled. "Hey, what can I say." He kissed Randi's cheek. "How are you feeling?"

"Tired, of course, but I'm enjoying motherhood. I assume you came to see your niece." She transferred the baby to him.

"Yes, ma'am." Looking down at the small bundle in his arms filled him with all kinds of emotions. He placed a soft kiss on her forehead and reclaimed his seat. "Hey, Aniyah. She's so tiny." With her head in the palm of his hand, the length of her body on his forearm barely reached his elbow. She stared at him curiously.

"Ced, I hope you've got your shotgun ready because the boys are going to be beating down the doors to get to this little beauty."

"Hell, I'm going to have my shotgun, do a background check and a few other things."

"And I'll run their fingerprints," Randi added.

Jeremy chuckled and stared down at Aniyah. "Looks like you're going to be well protected. Uncle Jeremy is going to keep all the knuckleheads away."

"You look like a natural holding her."

He glanced over at Randi. "And I'm looking forward to holding my own little girl."

Randi's eyes widened. "Okay, back up. I know I've been busy for the past few weeks, but did I miss something?"

"You didn't miss a thing, baby," Cedric said. "Baby brother is in love and says that Serita is his Mrs. Right. He's going to meet her parents tonight."

"Wow. Things are moving pretty fast, aren't they? Are you sure about this, Jeremy?"

"Surer than I've been about anything in my life. Yeah, it does seem fast, but I know what I feel."

Randi stared at him with concern. "And her?"

"I think she's on the same page, but she has some past hurts that are holding her back." She might not have said the words, but he could see what seemed like love whenever she looked at him, feel it when she touched and kissed him.

She placed a hand on his arm. "I hope it turns out the way you want."

"So do I." His cell rang and he shifted Aniyah so he could pull it out of his pocket. He checked the dis-

play and held up the phone. "It's Mom." He connected. "Hey, Mom."

"Hi, honey. Are you busy?"

Jeremy's senses went on alert. Whenever she asked that question, she wasn't calling for idle chitchat. "I'm over at Ced and Randi's right now and will be going over to Serita's parents' house for dinner later." The moment the words left his mouth he wanted to call them back. It was the absolute wrong thing to say.

"Humph. I've been asking you to bring her over for dinner, yet you're going to visit *her* parents."

"Mom, you've met Serita, but I've never met her parents. So, technically, you were first." He met Cedric's and Randi's smiling faces and shook his head.

"As if that makes a difference. That thing at the hospital was *not* an introduction." She fussed for a good minute.

"Mom," Jeremy cut in. "How about I see what Serita is doing tomorrow and, if she's free, we come over for dinner?"

"That's fine. Tell Cedric and Randi your dad and I will be by later this afternoon."

"I'll pass the message along."

"Make sure you call me back tonight so I have time to prepare."

"I will. Talk to you later."

"Bye, son."

Jeremy tossed the cell onto the sofa next to him. "You'd think I'd never even mentioned Serita's name with the way she was fussing."

Cedric grinned. "Glad it's not me."

He scowled at his brother. "I'd better get going. She said she and Dad will be by later. Randi, when are your

parents coming?" He kissed Aniyah, then stood and passed her to Cedric.

"They're coming back on Wednesday and staying through the weekend. I wanted us to have a couple of weeks to bond before everybody started camping out."

"If you need me to help with something while they're here, let me know."

"We will. She's already hinting at having a little family get-together, since everyone will be here," Randi said.

"Whatever they decide, you won't be doing anything," Cedric said pointedly. "Jeremy, you should plan to bring Serita. She might as well get used to being with the family."

He thought about her reaction at the hospital and her admission that she was an introvert. If she came, he would have to make sure she had some quiet moments. "Keep me posted and I'll see." When Randi stood, he said, "You don't have to walk me out. I'll lock up." He kissed her cheek. "Take it easy." He and Cedric did a fist bump. "Later, big bro."

When he arrived home, Jeremy ate lunch and went through his mail. Afterward he went upstairs to shower and change. The dinner would be a casual one. Even so, he chose to wear a pair of slacks and a button-down shirt. He planned to make a good impression because he didn't want them to have one reason to doubt that he would be good for their daughter. While dressing, he thought about how to tell Serita he loved her. Should he make some eloquent speech first or just say what lay in his heart? After a couple of minutes going back and forth in his mind, Jeremy settled on the latter.

He left a little early to stop at the florist. The last

time he'd purchased Serita flowers, he'd chosen pink roses. This time he went for red and had them placed in a crystal vase, leaving no question about his intentions. He also picked out a mixed bouquet for her mother. Initially, he had experienced a small amount of anxiety at the prospect of meeting her parents, but by the time he made it to Serita's place, it had all but vanished. He didn't have any reason to be nervous and, if need be, he could pass any background check.

Once he had gained entry to the complex, Jeremy parked and went to ring the doorbell. Gabriella answered the door. "Hey, Gabriella."

"Hi, Jeremy. Don't you look nice. Come on in. Serita should be just about ready."

"Thanks." Serita made it into the living room as he entered. Gabriella smiled and disappeared down the hall.

"Hey, baby," he said, greeting her with a kiss and handing her the vase. "You look beautiful." She had on a pair of black pants, a black-and-white-patterned cold shoulder top and wedge-heeled sandals. She'd pinned her hair up and left a few loose curls to frame her face. The bronze color on her lips perfectly complemented her dark caramel skin.

"Hi and thank you. These are gorgeous." Serita gave him a bright smile. "I'll leave them right here for now, but when I get back, they're going in my bedroom." She placed them on the coffee table. "Ready?"

"Absolutely."

When they got into the car, she said, "I should probably warn you that my mom will probably ask you a million questions and my dad will most likely sit there with his arms folded while she conducts the interrogation."

Jeremy laughed. "I'm not worried."

"You're not?"

"Not at all." He took her hand in his and brought it to his lips. "I'm not worried because when they ask me what my intentions are toward you or how I feel about you, I'll already have the answer."

"Um…you do?"

"Yes. And I want you to hear it before they do. I love you, Serita, and probably have since I saw you sitting in the hallway of that Madrid hotel. You took my breath away then and have ever since."

Serita gasped softly. "I wasn't expecting you to say that. I…I don't know what to say."

"You can tell me what you feel. But if you're not ready, that's okay. I can wait." He hoped she would tell him that she loved him, too. However, the brief flashes of fear he'd seen since they'd been together let him know she might not be prepared to say it yet.

She glanced out the window then back at him. "I'm getting there, okay?"

He smiled. "Yeah, it's okay." Placing a gentle kiss on her lips, he got them under way. She didn't talk much on the drive and he didn't push the conversation. He sensed that she needed some time to digest what he'd said.

"You can just pull into the driveway," Serita said, when they got to the house. She blew out a long breath and fiddled with her hands in her lap.

Jeremy parked and helped her out of the car. "You seem nervous."

"A little."

"Hey, you already know them and they love you. I'm the one who'll be in the hot seat."

"Yeah, you've got a point."

"I'll be fine. I don't scare easily."

She looked him up and down. "No, I guess not with your height and size."

He chuckled and got the flowers from the back seat.

"And you brought flowers? That'll earn you some brownie points."

"I'm counting on it." He tossed her a bold wink, took her hand and started up the walk. They were laughing and talking when her father opened the door. The man stood a good half foot shorter than Jeremy, had the same coloring as Serita and a sprinkling of gray around his temples.

"Hi, Dad."

"Hey, baby girl." He kissed Serita's cheek.

"Dad, this is Jeremy Hunter. Jeremy, my dad, David Edwards."

Jeremy extended his hand and looked the man straight in the eye. "Mr. Edwards, it's a pleasure to meet you."

Mr. Edwards shook Jeremy's hand. "Nice to meet you, Jeremy. You two come on in."

Jeremy stepped back for Serita to enter first, then followed them inside to a home that was simply but elegantly decorated. Mr. Edwards led them to the family room. Jeremy studied all the photos lining the walls and smiled at a young Serita. Just like him, she'd started wearing glasses in elementary school. He wondered if she'd had to endure the teasing like he had. In his case, it had taken one bloody nose to his classmate in a blow delivered by Jeremy and a threat from Cedric and Lorenzo for the teasing to stop. Had there been anyone who had stepped in to help Serita? His gaze went to the large bookcase on the other side of the room and he spotted a couple titles he owned. Just as they sat, a

petite older woman entered from the kitchen. Serita looked exactly like her mother. He stood.

"You must be Jeremy," she said, approaching with a wide smile.

"Yes, ma'am. It's a pleasure to meet you, Mrs. Edwards. These are for you."

Mrs. Edwards's eyes lit up in surprise as she accepted the flowers. "Why, thank you. That was nice of you. Serita, he's a charmer, and tall, too."

Serita glanced up at Jeremy. "Yes, he is."

"I'm going to put these in water, then we can sit down to eat. Serita, show Jeremy where he can wash up."

She led Jeremy to a half bathroom off the family room. "My mother likes you already."

"How do you know?" he asked, washing his hands.

"Usually, she's five questions in before you have a chance to sit, and she hasn't asked you one." She took her turn at the sink.

"I'm going for the gold medal."

Serita elbowed him but was smiling. "Whatever."

They joined her parents at the dining room table and Jeremy seated Serita before taking the chair across from her. "Mrs. Edwards, everything looks and smells delicious." She'd made roast chicken, green beans, mashed potatoes and corn bread. A pitcher of iced tea sat in the middle of the table.

"Thank you."

He met Serita's gaze and she did a mini eye roll. He chuckled inwardly. After her father recited a blessing, everyone filled their plates.

"Serita told us you have your own business," her father said, cutting into his chicken.

"Yes, sir, I do. I started it three years ago and it's

challenging and I have to work extra hours sometimes, but I have a great team and the company wouldn't be where it is today without them. Serita's been a great asset and I'm hoping she'll consider staying on permanently." He spoke that last sentence staring directly into her eyes.

Mrs. Edwards divided a glance between Jeremy and Serita. "Serita, how do you like working with Jeremy?"

He could tell by Serita's expression that she'd rather not answer the question.

"It's fine, but I thought this was supposed to be about you grilling Jeremy, not me."

Her parents laughed and her father said, "It is, but you're part of the equation, too."

They ate in silence for a while. The flavorful food reminded Jeremy of his mother's cooking, and the corn bread almost melted in his mouth.

Serita's mother sipped her tea. "Jeremy, you mentioned having to work hard. What do you do when you're not working?"

"I hit the gym, play basketball with my brother and cousin and read. You have a few of the same titles I have on my shelves. It's something Serita and I enjoy doing together." He didn't mind answering questions. He wanted them to get to know him because he planned to be around long term.

Chapter 15

Serita couldn't believe how easily Jeremy was charming her parents. The first and only guy she'd previously brought home had gotten nothing but glares and grunts from her father and a meal her mother made sure ended as soon as the last bite was eaten. She hadn't even served the dessert she'd prepared.

"Serita's been an avid reader all her life. She always had her nose in a book, and I'd sometimes have to pry her out of that room just to eat."

Jeremy laughed. "Same. It was either that or me building the next greatest invention to help me get out of my chores."

"I don't know why I didn't think of that," Serita said. As she listened to them talk, she learned more about the man who had openly admitted to being in love with her. She couldn't say that she'd been surprised. He'd

been hinting at it from the beginning and everything he said and did backed up his words. Truthfully, she felt the same, but that nagging fear in the back of her mind and heart wouldn't allow her to jump into the deep end.

Her father smiled. "Do your parents live in the area?"

"They live in Granite Bay and are both retired."

Her mom said, "I'm giving nursing another two years, then I'll be joining the club."

Her father lifted his glass. "Retirement is a wonderful thing."

"So my dad says, but I have a few years to go," Jeremy said.

Serita's father had retired earlier in the year after working thirty-five years as a pharmacist.

"Serita, why don't you help me clear the table and bring out dessert," her mother said, rising to her feet.

Jeremy made a move to stand. "I'll help."

"Oh, no. You just relax. We'll be right back."

Serita didn't miss the nonspeaking glance her parents shared. The ploy was designed to give her father time to talk to Jeremy alone. A quick glimpse at Jeremy confirmed that he'd caught on, as well. To his credit, he didn't look bothered by the prospect one bit. She gathered their plates and carried them into the kitchen. "That wasn't too subtle, Mom."

"I wasn't trying to be subtle. It's clear Jeremy is very taken with you and we need to know just how much."

She opened her mouth to tell her mother what Jeremy had said, but changed her mind. Her father would fill his wife in as soon as Serita and Jeremy walked out the door. She helped her mother bring in the peach cobbler and ice cream and caught the tail end of her father's question.

"I can tell you like my daughter, so what exactly are your intentions toward her?"

"Mr. Edwards, I more than like your daughter. I'm in love with Serita and want her to be part of my life. Yes, it may seem like things are moving rather fast, but my feelings for her are very real."

Serita's mother gasped.

"Here, let me take this." Jeremy stood, relieved her of the glass dish and placed it on the table.

Still staring at him, her mother said, "People just don't meet and fall in love that quickly."

He smiled. "Actually, they do. My father, whom I respect and is a great judge of character, met and fell in love with my mother in a week. They've been married for forty years and their love has only grown stronger over the years. I'm not surprised that the same has happened to me, especially with Serita. Your daughter is amazing. How could I not fall in love with her?"

Serita couldn't move. She had never had a man declare his feelings for her so openly and boldly in her entire life. And in front of her parents. It overwhelmed her, and she fought the urge to do what came natural—run to her room, pull the covers over her head and shut down so she could process. Jeremy seemed to sense her plight— she didn't know how he had learned to read her so well in their short time together—and sent her a reassuring smile. With her parents still staring at her in what appeared to be shock, she placed the ice cream, bowls and spoons on the table and retook her seat. "Since you all are just sitting here, I'll start things off." She scooped a portion of the cobbler into her bowl, paused, then added more before placing it in front of Jeremy. She mouthed, *Thank you.* She fixed her own bowl and added some of

the vanilla ice cream. "Dad, I was really hoping you made your homemade ice cream."

"I'll make some the next time you and Jeremy come over."

His smile let her know he approved of the relationship, and it gave her a measure of comfort.

Later, as Jeremy drove her home, Serita sat with her eyes closed.

"You okay?"

"Yep. Just need my bed for a while."

Jeremy placed a hand on her thigh. "The evening was a little overwhelming."

She rolled her head in his direction. Even in the shadows of the car, she could see the concern on his face. "I'll be alright. This is how I handle things. I have to shut down." She figured he should know that about her if they were going to be together.

"We all deal with our emotions differently. I used to disappear from home for about half an hour. Now, I run."

"Ugh. That would stress me out even more."

His laughter filled the car. "Like I said, we're all different." He paused. "Well, I'm about to stress you out a little more."

Serita sat up.

"My parents invited us to dinner tomorrow." He slanted her a quick glance. "The good thing is they've already met you, so I doubt you'll have to endure what I did tonight."

She viewed him skeptically.

"Trust me. My mom just wants to get to know you. If it gets to be too much, know that I'll make sure to find you a quiet place to regroup."

"I love you, Jeremy." The words were out before she could stop them and her heart pounded in response.

"And I promise to protect that love."

She knew he would.

Tuesday evening, Serita sat on the sofa reading with R & B playing in the background. She closed the book when Gabby came in. "You look exhausted. I thought the office closed at five."

"It did. I stopped by my parents' house to help with their home improvement project."

"Oh, yeah. They're redoing the master bedroom and bathroom."

Gabby dropped down in a chair and laid her head back. "The next time they mention fixing up a room, I'm hiring somebody, even if I have to work eighty hours a week. It was supposed to be painting and getting a few new items. Now, they're talking about changing the linoleum on the bathroom floor. My dad started pulling up the flooring and it's a mess. Then they had the nerve to start talking about replacing the tiles in the shower and got upset when I suggested using someone who knows what they're doing, saying it would be a waste of money." She shook her head. "I told them I'd send a list of contractors, packed up and left."

She laughed. "Well, it would save money."

"It won't when they have to hire someone to fix the mess they made and *then* do it right. Anyway, enough about that. I've been waiting to hear all about the family weekend drama and your interview."

Serita set the book on the sofa next to her. Because Jeremy had stayed around both nights after bringing her home and Serita had worked overtime yesterday, she

and Gabby hadn't had a chance to talk. She decided to start with the easier subject. "The interview went well and I should hear something within a week or so."

"I hope you get it."

"So do I. The thirty days at Jeremy's company will be up at the end of next week, so I really need to have something."

Gabby eyed her. "You know as well as I do that man is going to offer you the job. And please miss me with crap about preferential treatment. You're probably the most qualified out of the group. You know it, I know it and *he* knows it."

"I didn't say I wasn't qualified."

"Thank goodness. Now what happened with your parents?"

She shook her head at her friend's ability to change the subject on a dime. "My parents took turns grilling Jeremy, but he didn't seem bothered by it at all. He brought my mother flowers and had her smiling, and my dad invited him back."

"I knew he wouldn't have any problems winning them over."

"Especially after telling them he was in love with me."

Gabby's mouth fell open and she bolted upright. "He did *what*? Oh. My. Goodness. I would've swooned under the table."

"It was impressive." The memory of his impassioned words still made her heart race. She told her what Jeremy had said, including the part about how his parents fell in love after a week and that he wasn't surprised about it happening to him. "You could hear a pin drop when he finished. I had never seen my parents left speechless like that before."

"I know you love him, too."

"Yes, I do," Serita said softly.

She placed her hand over her heart and said dreamily, "This sounds like one of those romance novels."

That's the truth. Only Serita had never been one to believe it could happen in real life. Now she knew better.

"What about his family? I know you were worried about dinner."

"Dinner turned out to be better than I expected. His parents are really nice and treated me like they've known me forever." When they'd arrived, Jeremy's mother had hugged her and gone on and on about how happy she was that Serita and Jeremy were dating and that she was looking forward to her and Serita getting to know each other. While Serita couldn't have been happier about their acceptance, the woman's exuberance eventually started to take a toll on Serita. True to Jeremy's word, he had made sure that she had those quiet few minutes to regroup.

"Where do they live?"

"Granite Bay. Their house is stunning and so big they could host a party for fifty or sixty people and it wouldn't feel crowded." She had told Jeremy the same thing and he said it had happened before, with most of the people being family.

"Maybe the next one will be to celebrate your engagement."

"I think you're getting *way* ahead of yourself."

"No, I'm not. It's about time you found someone who appreciates that cute nerd-girl thing you've got going on."

Serita smiled and picked up her book. "Yeah, you're right."

* * *

"Have you recovered from last weekend's meet-the-parents saga?" Jeremy asked Serita Friday evening as they worked on the console. Elena had been scheduled to work with them, but had to leave early to pick up her sick daughter from school. He had been secretly elated to know they would be alone.

"Barely."

"Just so you know, my family is planning a get-together to celebrate Aniyah's birth. I was specifically instructed to bring you."

Serita eyed him. "Exactly how often does your family have these gatherings?"

A smile played around the corners of Jeremy's mouth. "Do you want the truth?"

"As opposed to?"

"I don't want to scare you," he said with a chuckle. "We do it pretty regularly, but they're not always big gatherings. We have Sunday dinners with my parents about once a month, same with me, Ced, Lorenzo and Alisha. It used to be us four cousins, but now that includes spouses and kids. Then there are the times my LA cousins come up to visit. There are five of them and they're all married."

She held up a hand, bowed her head and closed her eyes. "Okay, okay, I get it."

Jeremy sympathized with her. It would definitely be overwhelming, but they would welcome and love her as much as he did. "It won't be too bad, but I have just the thing to relax you beforehand."

"What's that?"

He carefully removed the part from her hand and laid it on the table. "Come with me." He led her to his

office, closed and locked the door. "I've been fantasizing about making love to you in my office ever since that interlude last week. I promise by the time I'm done, worrying about my family will be the last thing on your mind." He walked over to his desk, opened a drawer and took out a bottle.

Serita brought her hands to her mouth and giggled. "I know that's not the massage oil."

He nodded slowly.

"Jeremy, we cannot do…do…*that* in here."

"Sure we can. I even brought towels."

"I can't believe how scandalous you are."

"You'll believe it soon enough." He placed the bottle on the desk and whipped his shirt over his head.

Serita gasped. Then her expression changed. "Okay." She sauntered toward him and ran her hand over his erection. "Then you might want to hurry up and take these off."

He didn't need to hear anything else. In the blink of an eye, he had them both naked.

She picked up the oil. "You know, I think I want a turn this time." She drizzled it along the length of his shaft and slowly rubbed it in. She lowered her head and blew softly.

Jeremy cursed under his breath. The heat of the oil and the feel of her hands stroking him almost sent him over the edge. And when she took him into her mouth, he swore to let her have a turn. All. Night. Long.

Chapter 16

Monday afternoon, while on her break, Serita took a moment to check her email. She had been stalking it daily, looking for news about the job. Her stomach flipped when she saw it. Her thumb hovered over the link for a second before opening it. Her heart sank. She hadn't been chosen for the position. She placed the phone on her desk and leaned back in the chair. This was the last week of the trial and she knew Jeremy would offer her one of the positions. Serita did enjoy working there, but the rejection made her realize how much she really did want to teach. *Back to the drawing board.*

She went back to the design room where Elena and Shane were working.

"Good, you're back," Shane said. "Jeremy wants me to tag team on the surgical arm for the rest of the af-

ternoon." He finished the part he'd been working on. "Okay, I'm out."

When he left, Elena asked, "Do you like working here?"

"Yes, but it's complicated."

"Not really. I've watched you work, Serita. You're the best person for this job and you won't find a better work environment. It's a great company and the boss ain't too bad, either," she whispered conspiratorially.

Serita agreed with that assessment wholeheartedly. The "boss" was wonderful and amazing. But it still didn't change her disappointment.

"Hey, ladies." Jeremy stuck his head in the door. "Serita, can I talk to you for a minute?"

She searched his face for a clue as to what he wanted, but his face was unreadable. After what had happened in his office Friday night, she had vowed to stay as far away from there as possible. He was too tempting and she didn't seem to have any willpower when it came to his magical kisses. "Sure. I'll be right there."

"Thanks."

Serita shared a look with Elena, who gave her an encouraging smile, then made her way to Jeremy's office.

"Can you close the door?"

She lifted a brow. He must have read her expression because he laughed.

"Relax, this is business. But I have to tell you every time I walk into my office I can't stop thinking about Friday night. It's going to be hard as hell not to seduce you, strip you naked and lay you on that table whenever you cross my path."

That was what worried her. It didn't help that she had been a willing participant in his seduction. She'd

surprised herself the other night with her inhibition. Sex had always been just okay until she met Jeremy. He unleashed some carnal side in her she never knew existed. And she kind of liked it.

"Now that you know you're safe for the time being, you can close the door."

She complied, then sat in one of the chairs opposite his desk. "You said this is business."

"Yes." Jeremy studied her. "Everything alright? You seem a little down."

Serita sighed. "I heard back from Sac State and I didn't get the job."

"Baby, I'm so sorry. I thought for sure you would."

"Me, too."

"Is there anything you need me to do for you?"

"No, but thank you." He looked genuinely concerned. "Really. I'll be fine. What did you want to talk to me about?" she asked, changing the subject. She felt down enough and didn't want to dwell on it.

"Actually, there are two things I'd like to discuss. The first is I don't want to hide our relationship anymore. I love you and we are both consenting adults. It's nobody's business what we're doing and if they find about us, fine."

She understood his point of view and, most likely, everyone already knew. Elena had figured it out the first week and Serita was sure she'd mentioned it to Shane. More than once, she'd caught him smiling at her when he saw her coming from Jeremy's office. And Chris... She didn't even want to think about how he had found out. She had been mortified when he'd walked in and found her sitting on Jeremy's lap. "What exactly does that mean?"

"We won't be having desktop sex during the work-day, if that's what you're concerned about. But if I want

to give you a good-morning kiss—nothing too heavy—then I want to be able to do it. I want to be able to hold your hand and take you out to lunch or eat lunch in here."

The things he'd asked for weren't anything other dating couples wouldn't do. She remembered a few of the professors and other staff members who dated doing some of the same things. They were affectionate, but not overly so. Serita really had no reason to be embarrassed. "Okay, we can do that."

A huge grin spread across his face. "Can we seal the agreement with a kiss?"

She laughed. "You don't ever quit, do you?"

Jeremy shrugged. "I can't help myself. I've never been this out of control with a woman in my life. This is all your fault."

Hearing that she could make him lose control put a smile on her face. She'd happily take the blame. "That makes two of us. I've never done the things we have with any other man, so you're just as at fault."

He placed a hand over his heart. "I will gladly take the blame," he said, echoing her thoughts.

"Didn't you want something else?" He brought out a side of her very few people saw.

"Yes. Hopefully, this will counter your bad news and make you feel a little better." He handed her an envelope.

Serita's brows knit in confusion. She withdrew the sheet of paper and read. "You're offering me the position." She was admittedly excited, but a small part of her still wondered if he had judged fairly.

"And before that beautiful brain of yours starts going places it shouldn't, I decided to hire all three of you."

"Can you afford to do that? I'm sorry, that's none of my business."

"You're fine. Chris and I talked about it and, with a couple of potential contracts in the works, we'll be able to handle it. You and Darryl will have the full-time positions because you have the most experience. Scott will work twenty-five hours to start, with the potential to transition to full-time once those contracts are secured."

She reread the letter. "I'm really glad. I didn't get a chance to work with either of them very often, but I like them."

"Better now?" he asked with amusement.

Smiling, she said, "Much. Do I need to answer now?"

"No. You can just tell me yes on Friday, like the letter says."

Her mouth gaped. "How do you know I'm going to say yes?"

Jeremy stood, came and gently pulled her to her feet. "Because I'm making you an offer you can't refuse."

"Oh, really?"

"Really." He brushed a kiss across her lips. "Would you like to have dinner tonight?"

"Yes, but I'd like to go home and change first."

"That works. We need to drop off your car anyway."

"Or I could just meet you at the restaurant."

He stared at her as if she'd lost her mind. "I'm not even going to reply to that nonsense."

She burst out laughing, having known that would be his response. Smiling, she walked over and opened the door. "Later, darling." Yep. She loved this man.

"You really lucked out with Darryl, Scott and Serita," Chris said to Jeremy as they stood outside the door of Jeremy's office.

"I did. And I'm sure both men will be accepting soon, and alluded to that fact. But Serita is the only one who hasn't given any indication whether she's going to accept." Jeremy had sensed her disappointment at not getting the teaching position and didn't want to add any more stress onto her.

"And her reason would be?"

He shrugged. "I didn't ask her for an immediate answer." He glanced up and down the hallway to make sure no one was coming, then lowered his voice. "She just found out today that she didn't get the job at Sac State and she's a little down. We're going to dinner tonight and, hopefully, I can cheer her up."

Chris grinned. "I bet you can."

"I also told her that we're done hiding our relationship."

"About time. It's not like everybody didn't know anyway, especially with the way you're always looking at her. I'm surprised you haven't set the damn building on fire."

"Hey, what can I say?" Jeremy straightened from the wall when he saw Serita approaching. "You ready, baby?"

"Yep. Are you leaving, Chris?"

"I am. Looking forward to seeing your pretty face around here permanently," he said with a wink.

Serita divided a glance between Chris and Jeremy.

Jeremy waved a hand. "Don't pay any attention to him." As he guided Serita toward the front, he shot Chris a lethal glare over his shoulder. Outside, at her car, he asked, "Any place in particular you want to go for dinner?"

She slid in behind the wheel and angled her head thoughtfully. "No, but I'll think about it on the way home."

"Okay." He placed a soft kiss on her lips, closed the door and got into his own car. As he followed her, he thought about everything he wanted to have with her and decided he needed some advice. He hit the Bluetooth button. "Dial Brandon."

Brandon answered on the second ring. "Hey, cousin. What's up?"

"A few things. I need your help."

He chuckled. "This wouldn't happen to have anything to do with the woman you met six weeks ago, would it?"

"Yes. I'm in love with Serita. I want to marry her and add her name as co-owner of the company." The line went silent so long Jeremy thought he'd been disconnected. "Brandon?"

"What the hell are you talking about? Look, I know you've been spouting that love-at-first-sight crap all your life, but this isn't some fairy tale. It's real life."

"Brandon, don't act like it doesn't happen. You do remember my parents falling in love within a week, right?"

"Yeah, but that—"

"And correct me if I'm wrong, but wasn't it *your* dad who walked up to your mother the day he met her while he was on a two-week military leave and asked for her name and phone number, then married her on the next one?"

"Okay, you've got me on that one."

"I also know that, had you not been acting like such a butthead, you would've acknowledged the fact that you loved Faith far sooner. Need I go on?"

Brandon's heavy sigh came through the line. "Damn, it's like that?"

"It's exactly like that," he said with a chuckle. "So, are you going to help me or not."

"You know I will, and I can't wait to meet this woman."

"I can't wait for you to meet her, too." If Jeremy had his way, it would be soon.

"What do you need to know?"

"As I said, I want to add Serita as co-owner and I want to know how you handle it with Faith." Faith's and Brandon's fathers were best friends and had started Gray Home Safety with a pact that the company would be passed down to their children. Only no one had known about Faith until her father found her after twenty-eight years. Brandon had had no idea that the woman he'd rescued during an accident and begun dating would be his second in command and he hadn't been happy about it. Now they were happily married.

"If you're serious about this, Jeremy, then you need to be able to say that you trust Serita with everything and I do mean *everything*. No second-guessing on decisions, always listening to her suggestions, and when they're better than yours, being man enough to accept them. It means that sometimes you won't be in control."

Jeremy mulled the advice over in his mind. Could he really allow someone else to come in to the company he had built from the ground up and make decisions?

"You're quiet, cuz."

"I'm thinking. Was it hard to give up total control?"

Brandon laughed. "Hell, yeah. And you know me when it comes to business." His cousin ended up with

his foot in his mouth on more occasions than the family could count because of his intense nature. "But I'm learning it's okay. Of course, I still have issues, but Faith keeps me grounded."

"Thanks. That's what I need to know." He drove into the complex behind Serita and parked. "I just pulled up to Serita's, so I'll talk to you later."

"Let me know if you need anything else and I hope everything works out. Later."

He ended the call and got out. That was what he loved about his family—no matter what went on, he could always count on them to give him good advice. Smiling, he caught up with Serita.

Serita stopped and got the mail before going to her unit. She opened the door. "I still have no idea where to go for dinner."

"That makes two of us." Jeremy followed her to the kitchen, where she dropped off her lunch tote.

She flipped through the envelopes. "What would really be good is another one of those five-star meals that you cook," she said, smiling up at him flirtatiously.

"It's a little late for that tonight, but we can do it next time."

"And I can't wait." She opened one of the envelopes and read for a minute. "I don't believe it."

"What is it?" He leaned close and saw it was from a university in Reno.

"The college where I taught in Reno is offering me a position, this time as an assistant professor instead of adjunct." She smiled.

Jeremy's heart started pounding. "I thought you

didn't want to teach full-time, and typically assistant professor positions are just that."

"I know, but this is a great opportunity and would put me on track for tenure."

"I agree. But what about your job here? What about us?"

Serita's smile faded. "I...don't know." She tossed the letter on the counter and paced. "I need to think about this."

His heart pounded harder. "What is there to think about? You said you loved me." He couldn't believe what he was hearing. Was she just going to throw away everything?

"Jeremy, I do love you." She placed a hand on his arm. "I *do*."

He stepped away from her. "Yet you're willing to walk away."

She scrubbed a hand across her forehead. "I didn't say that. All I'm saying is I need time to process all this—two job offers in one day is a lot."

"If the shoe were on the other foot, I wouldn't hesitate because I know what I want. You. If I had a choice between taking a job and staying with the woman I love, you'd win, hands down." Jeremy observed her a long moment. "But, obviously, you don't know what you want," he said softly, his heart breaking.

"I do want you. I want *us*, but this is a big decision."

It came to him that maybe she didn't love him as much as he loved her. "Then I should probably go and give you the time and space you need to figure it out." He pressed a kiss to her forehead, pivoted on his heel and walked out.

Serita rushed out of the kitchen behind him and blocked the front door. "Wait."

"Can you tell me right now that you're not going to walk away from us?" When she didn't reply immediately, he gave her a bittersweet smile. "I didn't think so. I'll see you in the morning." He stepped around her and opened the door. "Be sure to lock up." Kissing her once more, he walked out. *Now what am I supposed to do?*

Chapter 17

Gabriella snatched the covers off Serita. "Okay, that's it. You've been in here for four hours and I've let you wallow in your self-pity long enough. It's time to get up and face the music."

Serita groaned, rolled over onto her side away from Gabby and tried to take the covers back. "I need more time." Ever since Jeremy had walked out the door, she'd been in bed with the covers over her head, trying to shut down so she wouldn't have to deal with the hurt she'd seen in his eyes or the mess she'd made of her life in a matter of minutes.

"No, you don't." She sat on the side of the bed. "You know I love you, right? We've been through pretty much everything together since sixth grade, but as your friend, I have to tell you, you're full of shit."

She flipped over onto her back and glared. "What did you just say?"

"You heard me. You found a great guy who loves you and wants to give you the world, and you're screwing it up. How many times have you cried about one man or another cheating on you or trying to change you?"

Too many times to count. "But I might not get another opportunity to land a tenure-track position. And I'm already established at the school and, if I went somewhere else, I'd have to start from the bottom again."

Gabby stared at her incredulously. "Don't insult my intelligence. You know as well as I do that you'll find another job, and one that will be even more perfect than this one. But you won't ever find another man who adores you the way Jeremy does." She placed a sisterly hand on Serita's shoulder. "Now, do you want to tell me what you're really afraid of, because I know it's more than just about the job."

Serita dragged herself to a sitting position. Why did Gabby have to know her so well? "It is partly the job." She released a deep sigh. "But it's also Jeremy. I love him more than I thought possible, and I'm so afraid everything is going to come crashing down and I'll lose him."

"So...what? You just walk away instead?"

"Every time I think I've found the right guy, something happens. It starts off wonderful, then somewhere down the line things change and the person I am is not the one they want to be with." She thought she had loved her ex, but in hindsight, what she had felt for him didn't hold a candle to the deep emotions that had consumed her with Jeremy.

"Serita, love always carries a risk, but you can't let your fears get the best of you. Remember that tenth-grade girl who built her own robot because the boys

wouldn't let her be part of the team? You need to get her back."

She smiled at the memory. Those boys thought the only thing a girl was good for was writing down the data. When she'd refused, they'd kicked her off the team. She'd buried her head under the covers for two days crying until her mother did exactly what Gabby had just done—snatched the covers off. *So, I guess those boys were right, since you're lying here doing nothing.* She had been so outdone by her mother's words that she'd hopped out of bed and started her own design. She chuckled inwardly, recalling their faces when her project took first place. Serita had been risking it all in her field since that day. Not so much in her personal life, however.

"Sis, don't throw away what could be the best thing in your life because of fear. The worst thing you could do is look back and wonder. You don't want that regret, *trust me*. I know." Gabby fell silent. "I won't do it again," she added softly.

Obviously Serita had missed a few things while living in Reno. She'd get the story some other time, but right now she had more pressing issues.

"What are you going to do?" Gabby asked.

All the moments they had spent together from that first day until now ran through her mind. She would never forget his first words to her: *I don't know what impresses me more, beauty or your brains. It's the brains, I'm thinking.* He'd made her laugh, called her sexy, and he'd never once made her feel that being a nerd was a bad thing. And where would she find another man who would come to her rescue when she felt overwhelmed? Tears misted her eyes. "I messed up. I

can't leave him." Deep down inside, she knew what she wanted, and when Jeremy had asked, she should have swallowed her fears and told him the truth. She wanted him. As much as she wanted to teach—and she did believe she would find another opportunity—she wanted, no, *needed* Jeremy in her life.

She hugged her. "Good girl."

"I need my laptop." Serita jumped off the bed, retrieved it from the desk and brought it back over to the bed. She searched for and found what she needed.

Gabby glanced at the screen. "What are you planning?"

"You told me to get her back, and I'm going to need your help to pull this off." Serita explained her plan.

"If you're going to do it, might as well go all out."

"I don't want to leave anything to chance. The cooking thing might be a little dicey but, hopefully, I can make it work."

She stood. "You're definitely going to need my help then."

Serita laughed. "That's why I love you. You tell me the truth, even when I don't want to hear it."

"You've got that right, my sister. Now I'm going to bed. I need my rest for this."

"Thanks for everything." Gabby was right. Serita loved Jeremy, and she'd be damned if she was going to let another woman take what she already had. His love.

Jeremy woke up Wednesday morning more tired than when he'd gone to bed. He doubted he had slept more than two hours straight all night. He replayed the conversation with Serita over and over, and each time he remembered her not being able to answer his question

broke his heart a little more. He had no idea what to do. He did know that he needed to talk to the one person who had guided him his entire life. Picking up his phone, he sent a text to Chris saying he might be late, then called his father. Even though he had retired two years ago, he still got up early and had probably done two or three things by the time Jeremy showed up at seven.

When Jeremy arrived, his dad greeted him with a hug. "Come on in, son. I could tell by the tone of your voice you've got a lot on your mind."

"I do. Mom still sleep?" he asked, trailing his father to the kitchen.

"She was a half hour ago. Do you want me to get her?" He poured himself a cup of coffee and added sugar.

He shook his head. He met his father's concerned gaze. "I just need to talk to you right now. You can fill Mom in later."

"Then have a seat and tell me what's on your mind."

"Serita. I think I'm going to lose her." All the details of what had happened poured out of him. He told his father about Serita not getting the Sac State job and him offering her one at his company, and then Serita receiving the letter from Reno and saying she didn't know what she was going to do. "You know what hurt the most, Dad? I asked her to tell me she wasn't planning to walk away and she couldn't." Jeremy buried his head in his hands. He had never been this miserable. "What am I supposed to do? I love her."

"Jeremy, you're so much like me it's frightening."

He lifted his head. "What do you mean?"

You've always known what you wanted in every area

of your life and you went after those things with determination and never took no for an answer. Just like
me when I was your age. The problem with love is you
can't control the other person. No matter how much you
love Serita, it will never work unless she loves you with
the same passion."

That was not what he wanted to hear. His misery increased tenfold. "Are you telling me to break it off?"

His father chuckled. "No, unless that's what you
want."

"It's not," he said emphatically. "I want to marry
her."

"Well, the only thing you can do is continue to show
her that you love her. Don't tell her, *show* her. Bring
her flowers, and I don't mean some huge arrangement.
Just something small, so she knows she's on your mind.
What's her favorite beverage or sweet?"

Jeremy straightened in his chair. The flower thing
he had on lock, and he would be stopping at the store to
pick up a bag of Skittles—minus the green ones—and
line them up just as she liked. As far as the drink, he
drew a blank. Then it dawned on him that she'd mentioned not being able to find a good recipe for the café
con leche she'd had in Madrid. He whipped out his
phone and Googled recipes. He tried to recall which
place had the one she liked best and what they'd put in
it. It took him a few minutes, but he found it. "Dad, I
need to use the espresso machine."

"I guess that means you're not giving up on her."

He smiled for the first time since leaving Serita's
place last night. "You guess right."

"Let me get that machine out for you."

He wanted it to be hot, so with a promise to bring it

back later, Jeremy left. He stopped at the store for the ingredients and the candy, then the florist for a red long-stemmed rose. Jeremy planned to leave everything on her desk for her to find when she arrived at eight, and he had less than twenty minutes to get it done. Chris was already there when he arrived. He stuck his head in the office. "Morning."

"I thought you were going to be late."

"It didn't take as long as I anticipated." His father was a man of few words, but he made each one count. Had it been his mother, Jeremy would have been late. He walked to Serita's office, tore the corner off the Skittles and took out the ones she didn't like. He taped the corner closed and attached a small sticky note: *Because they ruin the whole pack.* In the break room, following the directions from the website, he made the café con leche and carried it down to the office. After arranging everything, he stood back and viewed his handiwork. Satisfied, he went to his office. He was going to give her every reason to stay.

Jeremy settled at his desk, powered up his laptop and checked his email. He always wondered how spammers got his address and sent more than a few to that folder. He clicked on one confirming the date to service one of their robots at an outpatient surgery center. He was glad he'd had the foresight to offer maintenance contracts. As he opened a folder to work on the proposal for the manufacturing company, Chris came in.

"Hard night?"

"You can say that."

Chris smiled. "Dinner didn't end the way you had hoped, I take it."

"We never made it to dinner." He got up and closed

the door, then reclaimed his seat. "When we got to her house, she had a letter waiting from the university where she taught in Reno, offering her an assistant professor position."

"Oh, wow. That's a great opportunity for her, but I assume she's going to turn it down and apply for something else here."

"I don't know."

He frowned. "What do you mean you don't know?"

"I don't know. She said she needed time to think about what she wanted to do." Thinking back, Jeremy could have been more patient and not demanded an answer right then. He understood her desire to teach, and she was right about it being a big decision to make. However, the only thing he had been able to focus on was the growing ache in his heart.

"I hate to say this, but you're going to have to let her figure it out on her own. The last thing you want is her having regrets ten years down the line because you pressured her."

"True, but that doesn't mean I can't plead my case in other ways."

"I'm not going to ask. Anyway, I've redone the budget with the added staff, so when you're ready to go over the numbers, let me know."

"We can do it—" A knock sounded. He got up and opened the door. His chest clenched when he saw Serita standing on the other side. "Good morning."

"Good morning. Do you have a few minutes to talk?"

"Chris and I were—"

"I'm leaving," Chris said, standing and crossing the room. "We can talk when you're done." To Serita, he said, "Morning."

"Good morning. You don't have to leave. I apologize for interrupting your meeting."

"You didn't." He exited and closed the door.

For a minute, Jeremy stood there marveling at how much she filled his heart. Even with the uncertainty swirling around their relationship, he couldn't turn off his emotions. "How are you?" She looked as tired as he felt.

"I've been better."

"Join the club. Would you like to sit down?"

"No, thanks. I'm not going to take up too much of your time."

Once again, alarms went off in his head. Had she come to a decision? And would it tear them apart? Remembering what she'd said about his height, he propped a hip on the desk to decrease the difference. She didn't say anything for the longest time, and it made him even more nervous that she had come to end it.

"First, thank you for the rose, the candy and especially the café con leche. It tastes just like the ones I had in Madrid. Maybe you can share the recipe with me."

"I'll text it to you."

"Second, I need you to know that I do love you, more than you know, and I'd like for us to talk."

"Then have a seat."

"Not here. Dinner at my place tomorrow night at seven."

He couldn't take another thirty-six hours of not knowing. Everything inside him wanted to shout, *Just tell me now.* But he didn't. She appeared to be barely holding it together, and he didn't want to overwhelm her any more than he'd already done. Besides, he needed her to be fully locked in when it came to the job. They

couldn't afford any mistakes. "Dinner tomorrow at seven, it is."

"Jeremy…"

"What is it, baby?" He saw the tears forming in her eyes and, unable to stop himself, wrapped his arms around her and held her close. She held on to him as if she didn't want to let go. Neither did he.

At length, Serita backed out of his hold. She swiped at the moisture on her cheeks. "I'd better get started."

He nodded and watched her go. Then he smiled. Jeremy had waited for her all his life and he wasn't giving up that easily.

Chapter 18

Thursday evening, Serita and Gabby moved the kitchen table closer to the lone window. Serita had power shopped online after coming to her senses and tried to transform the kitchen to resemble the Dantxari Restaurant in Madrid where she and Jeremy had dined the first night. She'd found a similar patterned red plaid tablecloth and matching napkins, and white plates at one of the bedding stores, and she had ordered a stained-glass mirror panel and had it shipped overnight.

Gabby placed her hands on her hips and surveyed the area. "It's looking really good in here."

"I agree. I just hope the food is somewhat comparable." She had already warned Jeremy that her cooking didn't hold a candle to his, so she hoped what she had to tell him would make up for that shortcoming.

"The food is going to be fine. You want him to eat as soon as he gets here?"

"Yes."

"Then we'll start around six thirty. The croquettes will be fine warmed and the asparagus will only take a few minutes."

"It's the butter sauce and steak I'm worried about. I'd hate to serve him a steak that's either too rare or as hard as a hockey puck."

"Don't worry. I got you, girl. You're going to be cooking like a pro before it's all said and done. You'll need those skills once you two get married."

"Married? Let me just work on straightening out this part first." She draped the tablecloth over the table and set it according the restaurant's website photos.

Gabby went to gather ingredients from the refrigerator. "One more thing—there's no need for you to keep searching for a place. I have a feeling you and Jeremy are going to be under one roof sooner or later, so it makes no sense for you to go through the hassle of buying or leasing a condo."

Serita paused. "Gabby, I appreciate the offer, but even if we do get back on track, it could be a year or two before we take that step." Admittedly, the thought of being married to Jeremy made her heart skip a beat, but she didn't think that would be on the radar for a while.

"And? Still, it makes no sense. We can talk about that another time. Let's get this food started."

She and Gabby worked side by side and finished the meal at five minutes before seven. She covered the steaks to let them rest and stay warm, and placed the croquettes and asparagus in the oven drawer. They went into the living room and Serita turned on the stereo to a jazz station.

"Okay, I think you're good. I'll see you tomorrow. I decided to spend the night at my parents' house."

"I can't let you do that. This is your house. We agreed on ten o'clock and that's enough time for dinner and conversation."

"Uh-huh. If things go the way I think they will, you're going to need all night." She picked up her bag and hugged Serita. The buzzer rang and she pressed the button to open the gate. "That's my cue. Good luck and you can tell me all about it tomorrow."

Serita nodded. She needed all the luck she could get. Jeremy appeared a minute after Gabby left. When she saw him, it took all her control not to launch herself into his arms. "Hi."

"Hi." Jeremy bent and kissed her, then handed her the red rose. "It smells good in here."

It didn't come close to how good he smelled. She loved the warm, woodsy citrus blend he wore. "It probably won't be quite up to your five-star meal, but I hope it's not too bad." They shared a smile. "We're eating in the kitchen." She gestured with a flourish. "What do you think?"

His surprised gaze met hers. He stared and turned in a slow circle. "The restaurant in Madrid where we had our first date."

"I wanted to recreate the magic we had there because it was where I first knew I was falling for you."

Jeremy whirled around. "Are you saying what I think you are?"

"Although I didn't realize it then, I think I fell in love with you after my first selfie lesson."

A soft smile curved his lips. "I was already a goner by then, myself."

"Have a seat and I'll fix our plates." She went about the task, then brought them to the table.

"You cooked the meal we had, too? This is really special."

"Yep, but you might want to hold off on the praise until you taste it."

He laughed. "I'm not worried." He opened the bottle of wine she had in the bucket on the table and filled their glasses. He held up his. "To recreating the magic."

Serita touched her glass to his. "To recreating the magic forever." Their gazes held while they sipped. She set her glass down and waited for him to take the first bite.

Jeremy cut into the steak and ate a piece. His eyes widened. "This is really good."

Smiling, she started in on her own meal. Both were content to enjoy each other's company without speaking. The sounds of jazz filtered through the room, filling the silence. When he finished, she said, "I have dessert, too."

"The lemon sherbet?"

"Absolutely. Complete with champagne and vodka." As they ate the sweet, tart dessert, she tried to gather her thoughts for the forthcoming conversation. By the time she was done eating, her nerves were a jumbled mess.

He stood and extended his hand. "Let's talk, sweetheart."

She took his hand and let him lead her into the living room, where they made themselves comfortable on the sofa. He didn't say anything as he gave her hand a reassuring squeeze.

"I'm sorry I wasn't able to tell you the whole truth," Serita said.

Jeremy frowned. "I don't understand."

"You said that I didn't know what I wanted and that wasn't the truth. I knew, but I was afraid to hope for it." He opened his mouth to speak and she placed a finger on his lips. "It had nothing to do with you. This one is on me. In my mind, I thought it would be easier to walk away than to risk being hurt again. But not being with you hurt more. I love you, Jeremy, and I *can't* walk away from us. You have been one of the best surprises of my life and I don't want to lose you."

"I love you and I don't want to lose you, either. What can I do to show you that I'm going to be here always?"

Serita straddled his lap and cupped his cheek. "Nothing. From the day I met you, you've shown me what real love looks like. And I love the way you take care of me, not just with material things, but with the stuff that counts. You take care of my well-being, my soul... my heart, and that's all I'll ever need." She covered his mouth in a tender kiss, trying to let him know she was ready to risk it all for them.

"Then let me keep taking care of you."

"I will. There are a couple more things I need to tell you."

He lifted a brow.

"I turned down the position in Reno and I accept the job offer at HJ Robotics."

"I love you." Jeremy crushed his mouth against hers in a hungry kiss. "What time is Gabriella coming back?" he murmured, still placing butterfly kisses along her throat.

"Tomorrow."

His head came up sharply.

She smiled. "I took a drive to Old Sacramento and visited Scentillating Touch. So…"

He jumped to his feet with her in his arms. "Bedroom."

"Down the hall, second door on the right." She loved this man.

Jeremy unloaded the last of the supplies from his class and stacked them in his garage. "Another successful session."

"They were so excited about their robots," Serita said, getting into the car.

He'd been just as excited to have her there with him. Since their reconciliation dinner last week, they'd spent almost every evening together talking and growing closer. When she confessed to still having some fears, but told him that her love was stronger and that would be her focus, his emotions had welled up, and he'd thought his heart might burst from his chest. He got in on his side. "Do you want anything from inside before we get on the road?" He had wanted to take her to his Lake Tahoe home, but with it being mid-November, he didn't want to run the risk of getting snowed in. He hadn't seen it in the forecast, but with temperatures in the twenties, the weather could change in an instant. Instead, they were going in the opposite direction, to spend the weekend in Monterey. Barring traffic—he didn't hold out much hope—the drive would be about three hours. Jeremy had his mind ready for at least four.

"No. I'm good." She turned in her seat to face him. "You know, I just got this job—so I shouldn't be taking off a day already." They wouldn't be returning until Monday afternoon.

"I'll talk to your boss. I'm sure he's okay with it."

She punched him in the arm playfully. "I already agreed that we wouldn't hide anymore, but I don't want everybody to start thinking I can come and go as I please. Don't make me have to look for another job."

"Ha! It's too late. You signed on the dotted line and you're stuck now, baby. Didn't you see that clause about having to agree to stay for five years?"

"What clause?" A few seconds later, she said, "There wasn't any clause requiring five years."

Jeremy laughed. "But you weren't sure for a minute."

She turned away and folded her arms. "I don't know what I'm going to do with you, Jeremy Hunter."

"You will by the end of the weekend." She turned her questioning gaze his way, but he just smiled and kept driving. As he'd predicted, traffic came to a standstill in several places. It took them three hours just to get to San Jose, and it would take another one to reach their destination.

"Traffic has really gotten bad since I left. It never used to take this long to reach the Bay Area."

"I don't come this way often, but Cedric and Lorenzo do and they say it's bad almost all day now." They fell silent for several minutes, but he could hear her humming softly to the music. "Now that it's been over a week, how are you feeling about not going back to Reno?" Jeremy still harbored some concern that she would regret her decision.

"I don't feel as badly as I thought I would. I'm still wondering if I'll ever get another opportunity, but I'm happy with my decision. I have a great job, a pretty cool boss and a man who I am madly in love with, so I consider myself blessed. I'll have to trust that there will be something else down the line. And who knows, I may

change my mind and want to go in a different direction by then. In the meantime, I'll enjoy shaping the minds of the next generation at this great science camp."

"What?" he asked excitedly, turning in her direction. He remembered he was driving and jerked back into his lane. With all the changes she'd been going through, he hadn't brought it up after asking her the first time. "Do you know how happy you've just made me?"

"Yes, but I'd like to be alive when the next session starts, so keep your eyes on the road."

"Yes, ma'am." Jeremy wanted to stop the car and get out and dance. "There's one other thing I'd like your help with. I'm working on a new prosthetic hand that will closely mimic natural function."

"Are you kidding me? I'd love to help you."

Jeremy slanted her a quick glance. "Great. We can talk about it when we get back." By the time they made it to the hotel, neither wanted to go out to eat, so they had dinner in the hotel restaurant and went back up to the room.

"Is it my imagination or did the temps drop by ten degrees while we were downstairs?" Serita asked, rubbing her arms.

"I'll turn up the heat." He adjusted the thermostat and turned on the gas fireplace. "Once it warms up, we can play."

She laughed. "I know you didn't print out more cards for *Jeopardy!*"

"Of course I did. Didn't you enjoy it the last time we played?"

"I'm pleading the Fifth," she said, trying to hide her smile. "We're playing strip *Jeopardy!* again, right?"

"Yes."

She rubbed her hands together. "Good, because I've been studying and this time I'm going to wipe the floor with you, and *I'm* going to see how many ways I can make *you* come."

Jeremy's arousal was instant. He folded his arms. "What happened to shy Serita?"

"She's still here, but I can be me with you, or who I want to be."

"Yeah, you can." He loved this woman so much, and he was glad that the men in her past had never taken time to know her. Their loss was his gain. He pressed a kiss to her lips. He'd meant it to be a short one, but the moment their mouths touched, passion took over.

Serita broke off the kiss. "Hey, no kisses until I'm done whipping you. I will not be distracted this time."

He roared with laughter. "We'll see." They sat on the sofa in front of the fireplace. "We're changing the game a little."

"How?"

"This time, whoever pulls the card will read it and the other person has to answer."

"Okay, I can go with that. Who's first?"

"Ladies first."

"Aw, you're such a gentleman," she said sweetly. "But that doesn't change how fast you're going to be naked."

"Oh, you're just all talk tonight, huh?"

"Oh, no. I'm going to be all action, too."

And he couldn't wait for that.

She pulled the card. "'Abraham Lincoln was shot here in 1865.'"

"What is Ford's Theater?" He smiled smugly and

drew the next one. "'This team was the focus of the 2014 Deflategate scandal.'"

"What is the New England Patriots? Bet you thought I wouldn't know that."

Jeremy shook his head and chuckled. She had indeed studied because, after four more rounds, she still hadn't lost a piece of clothing. He was missing his shirt.

"Ooh, I think I'm going to win tonight. Next question is—'This ends in two hearts being bound together.'"

He made a show of thinking. "I know what it is. Wait, wait."

"Five seconds." She started humming the *Jeopardy!* theme.

He snapped his fingers. "I got it." He slid off the sofa onto one knee at the same time as he opened the small black velvet box. "What is will you marry me?"

Her eyes went wide and she brought her hands to her mouth.

"Serita, I fell in love with you from the moment we met and I promise to keep loving and protecting you. My arms will lift you so you can soar and shelter you when you need a safe haven. You won't ever have to fear being alone because I will *always* be here."

"Oh, my goodness, *yes*!" She jumped into his arms with such force it knocked him backward on the floor. She scrambled up. "Wait, wait. You have to put the ring on," Serita said.

She held out a trembling hand and he slid on the blue diamond solitaire surrounded by brilliant white ones. He'd told her she was a rare jewel and he had wanted to choose something that matched her uniqueness.

"This is the most beautiful ring I have ever seen. And this diamond is blue."

"It's rare and precious, just like you."

"I am so happy I could scream. I love you, Jeremy." She waved her hand around. "Ooh, I have to take a picture to send to Gabby." She dug her phone out of her purse and joined Jeremy on the floor. "I gotta get the angle just right."

Jeremy pulled her onto his lap and smiled at her attempt to do a selfie.

Serita held her hand up, counted to three and hit the button. She checked the photo. "Yes! It's perfect."

"Yes, it is. I do belive you've reached pro status."

A grin covered her face.

"I do have one more thing to show you." He reached for the large envelope he'd placed on the end table and handed it to her.

She opened the flap and withdrew the papers. "What is this?"

"You said you wanted to own a company sometime down the road and I want to make your dream a reality. I'm having the company name changed to HJS Robotics."

She stared up at him, then back down to the papers. "You mean, you're making me co-owner?"

"Yes."

"Jeremy, I don't know what to say. You are… I think I'm going to need to lay down."

Jeremy chuckled. "We have the entire weekend for you to recover."

She leaned up and kissed him. "I'm so glad I accepted that first dinner offer." She went back to the papers, shaking her head as if in disbelief.

"I am, too. So when do you want to get married?"

Serita whipped her head around. "I have no idea. Um…do we have to have something big?"

He chuckled. "No, baby. You can have whatever you want." He knew she didn't like a lot of hoopla, as she'd put it, so something small would work for him, too. Though he didn't know how small it would be once all his family showed up. "What's your favorite holiday?"

"Christmas, why?"

"I have an idea. How about we get married on Christmas Eve? You're the only present I want under my tree this year."

Serita blinked. "As in *this* Christmas Eve…a month from now?"

"You said you don't like a lot of excitement. The sooner we do it, the less time our mothers have to try to turn this into a colossal event."

She gasped. "You're right. But it's too late to try to find a place."

Jeremy wrapped his arm around her. "I have the perfect place. Remember when you said my parents' house was big enough to fit fifty or sixty people? We can get married there. It can just be our families and close friends, and if need be, we can hide out in my old room for a few minutes."

"They do have a lovely house. But will they be okay with it?"

"You met my mother. She's going to be bragging to all my aunts for the next decade. So, is that a yes?"

"It's a yes."

"You know we have to celebrate." He picked her up and carried her over to the bed.

"We absolutely have to celebrate," she said, removing her clothes. "By the way, I won, so we get to play my game now."

He quickly shed his pants and briefs and rolled on a condom. He slid into her warmth and groaned. "Baby, we can play that game all night."

Epilogue

Jeremy stood in the kitchen with Cedric, Lorenzo, Alisha, their five Gray cousins from LA and all their spouses. In ten minutes, he would be a married man and he couldn't wait. Just as he'd thought, his mother had been beside herself with excitement when he had asked about having the wedding there. She had decorated the house in a winter wonderland theme worthy of any amusement park.

Cedric said, "You were the last to fall and the fastest."

Everybody laughed.

"I told y'all, but you didn't want to believe me. I should've made a bet so I could get my two hundred dollars back."

"Too late now, unless you want to bet how fast you'll be parents."

Siobhan, the oldest of the Grays and their generation of cousins, held up a hand. "We are not placing bets

on babies. Jeremy, don't you need to be getting over to the stairway to wait for your bride-to-be? She is such a sweetheart, by the way."

"Yes, she is and, yes, I do."

"Before we go, we need to make a toast," Cedric said. They all picked up their flutes filled with champagne. "To love."

"To love," they choroused.

Minutes later, Jeremy took his place at the base of the staircase with Cedric by his side. Gabriella stood opposite them in a navy blue slim-fitting off-the-shoulder dress. Instead of the traditional wedding song, they had chosen "Setembro" by Quincy Jones. He remembered his parents playing the song when he was growing up, and when his mother suggested it, both he and Serita agreed that it would be perfect. Even more perfect was the woman who would become his wife as she descended the stairs on the arm of her father. The strapless white gown hugged her every curve and had sparkling jewels embroidered all over it. Her hair was up in an elaborate twist with rhinestones woven throughout. His breath stacked up in his throat and his heart raced with excitement. When she reached him, it was all he could do to stand there and not kiss her. "You're so beautiful." Serita smiled up at him, then they turned their attention to the minister. Less than fifteen minutes later, he heard the words he had been waiting for since they'd met.

"I now pronounce you husband and wife. Jeremy, you may kiss your bride."

Jeremy leaned down close to Serita's ear. "Get ready for some hoopla, sweetheart." He kissed her with all the love in his heart and would have kept right on kissing her if Cedric hadn't elbowed him.

Tears shining in her eyes, she said, "Thank you for loving me."

"This was destiny, *our* destiny." He finally had his Mrs. Right and she was designed specifically for him... *by love*.

* * * * *